MW01697876

Immortal Wounds

a novel by

Nicole Grane

IMMORTAL WOUNDS

By: Nicole Grane

Printed in the United States of America
Charleston, South Carolina

ISBN-13 978-0615503417
ISBN-10 0615503411

Learn more about the author at:
http://www.nicolegrane.com

DEDICATION

To my beautiful Phoebe, who lay across my lap sleeping while I created this story. To Ashley and Joey for letting mommy work, more hours than she could count. To my husband Chris for his unwavering support and understanding when I came to bed at three in the morning. And to my parents for their love and constant pushing to get it done! I love you all!

Table of Contents

Prologue

A war had been raging for a thousand years, a war that I was unaware of. Unaware that is until I'd literally stepped into the middle of it.

I don't remember much about the events that took place that night in London that were to change the rest of my life forever. But I can say now, with great certainty, daylight doesn't always mean safety . . .

***

I could feel the cold, rough cement against my face. I forced my eyes to open, blinking repeatedly. I was on the ground . . . had I fallen? My head felt as though it were spinning. I let my eyes fall shut while my mind tried to process what had happened.

"Phoebe . . ." A cool hand brushed against my cheek, lingering for a moment—it wasn't mine. My heart raced at the touch of it, at the sound of that voice. My nose took in a delicious scent that I couldn't quite place. I strained to open my eyes once more. I could barely make out a face. His dark eyes penetrated mine. He was only there for a moment, and then . . . gone.

I jumped, wincing at the pain of it. My fingers sought my shoulder while my eyes wandered, searching . . .

"Who's there?" My words echoed out into the night.

I reached back, my fingertips meeting something moist. My shoulder throbbed at the very touch. Beads of sweat began to form all over my body. I breathed heavily, waiting for someone to answer, praying that they didn't. The sound of the cars passing by, voices in the distance, and the soft trickle of water running down a drainpipe were all that greeted me. The noises seemed amplified. My vision blurred, and then became strangely clear.

I brought a shaky hand to my face and swallowed loudly. It was stained red. "Oh my God." The words were barely a whisper. I spun around, expecting something or someone to be there lurking behind me. I was in the alley way behind the motel near the trash bins. I had been on my way to the car when—

Kim and Leah! I looked around for them. They must still be back at the room waiting for me or maybe looking for me by now? I wasn't sure how much time had passed.

I stood up slowly and reached for my keys that were on the ground a few feet away. My fingers had barely touched them when I heard a deep menacing growl from behind.

I grabbed them up quickly, and watched over my shoulder nervously as I retreated back to my room. Something was watching me—I could feel it.

The TV was on, but there was no sign of the girls. Kim Sanders and Leah Williams were my dearest friends. I'd known them my whole life. We took this 'girls only trip' to England after planning and saving all this last year.

"What a great way to end it!" I grumped as I tossed my keys onto the counter beside the sink. I grabbed a washcloth from the shelf and ran it under the cold tap to wet it. I dug around in my bag searching for the Tylenol. I took two and slunk to the bed when the door to my room flung open.

"Phoebe! Where have you been?" Kim thundered at me as she bounded across the room, not bothering to notice my hand clutched to my heart or the cloth that was draped across my forehead.

"Phoebe, what happened?" Leah was more observant.

I had been asking myself the very same question: What had happened? I told them what I remembered, leaving out the part of my delusional mind seeing things—no doubt the result of serious head trauma!

"Your shoulder's bleeding!" Kim grabbed my shirtsleeve and yanked it back.

"Hey, watch it," I snapped. I turned my body away from her, trying to prevent further injury to my arm.

"Phoebe, that's a bad gash, and there's another one here too," Leah said as she moved closer to examine my arm. "Maybe we should take you to the hospital. I think you need stitches."

"No way!" I hated needles. "I'll take care of it myself."

"That's not such a good idea," Leah argued. "You might need a shot or something."

"Maybe?" I considered, thinking it over. I craned my neck, trying to see the wounds better. I looked at my bloodied shirt. "What I need is a shower!" I pulled myself up and walked to the bathroom.

I could hear Kim and Leah arguing through the closed door. Kim was already offering several possible suggestions as to what might have happened to me, each one as crazy as the next. "Maybe a wild animal escaped from the zoo? Or maybe a crazed psycho from a mental institution is running around slashing people?" I could hear the fear in her voice as she pondered over the possibilities.

I turned the water on muffling out the rest of the conversation. I removed my shirt, tossed it into the waste basket, and examined the gashes behind my shoulder in the mirror. There were two large punctures, like a knife had cut into me—twice. A deep growling reverberated in my mind. I spun around, sweat once again, forming on my forehead.

"There's nothing there." I breathed, trying to calm myself.

I climbed into the warm water. My thoughts returned to the alley way . . . to the stranger I saw for only a moment. Those eyes . . . I'd seen them before. They were dark and intense. That voice . . .

I'm not sure how long I stood there, motionless, in a dream-like trance while the water ran down my body. I was just barely conscious of the thick steam that now hung heavy in the room.

The water started to cool bringing me back to consciousness. I began to adjust the knobs, hoping to get a few more minutes of hot water when a dreadful thought washed over me. Had he been my attacker? Why else would he have left me there? Suddenly, Kim's "crazy ideas" didn't seem so crazy after all.

I quickly turned off the water and stepped out of the shower. I wrapped a towel around me and rushed to the phone. Kim and Leah watched me anxiously.

"Um Phoebe?" Kim started slowly.

"Yes, I would like to change our departure date for tomorrow morning." I spoke urgently to the ticket agent. My ears listened to the loud clicking of her fingernails on her key board as she looked for available flights.

"Phoebe?" Leah was standing next to me, arms crossed and looking extremely worried. I ignored her.

"Yes, the 6:30 flight will be fine. Yes, all three of us. Thank you." I hung up the phone and turned to the confused faces beside me. "Pack!"

"Why?" Kim grumped, "We still have two days left!"

I looked at her in disbelief. "I was just attacked! Someone or something is out there." I pointed to the door.

"I thought you said you didn't know what happened to you," they both asked in unison.

"Yeah well, I don't. But I know we're not safe here. Whatever it was is still out there. He could be right outside that door this very minute . . . waiting!"

"He?" Leah questioned. I could see the fear in her eyes.

They looked at each other briefly, glanced at the door, then began shoving things into their bags, not even bothering to fold their clothes. They'd both seen one too many horror movies not to heed the warning.

I returned to the bathroom to get dressed. The room was still thick with steam. I wiped my hand across the mirror and leaned in closer. A pair of dark eyes reflected back at me from over my shoulder.

I gasped as I spun around, my heart pounding hard from fear. There was no one there.

My eyes darted around the little room, settling on an open window—a window that I had *not* opened. I swallowed loudly. A shiver ran down my spine that had nothing to do with the crisp air that pushed its way into the room. I moved toward the window cautiously, reached out a trembling hand, and slammed it shut. I backed away, never releasing it from my gaze. A new kind of dread took hold of me. He'd been here . . .

Chapter 1: Just a day at the beach

I dreamt all that night and every night for the next month about my mysterious stranger. I couldn't get his face out of my mind, or rather his dark and intense eyes. We were back home now and although I saw Kim and Leah all the time, I still never told them about him.

I lived in the small coastal town of Trinidad California, a small community that survived on tourism and commercial fishing to support its residents: a whopping 311.

It was mid July now, perfect beach weather. Kim and Leah had convinced me to go surfing with them. Apparently, I haven't been the same since our trip abroad. I didn't really feel like going; it had been forever since I'd been surfing. Still, I didn't want to let them down.

I put on my swimsuit and turned to look at myself in the mirror. The deep gashes that once were on the back of my shoulder had healed over leaving tender pink scars as a reminder of my horrific trip abroad. I fluffed my brown hair, wishing it were longer so that it could hide them better.

I continued to look myself over. My face was fairly thin. Everything about me was thin. I was 5'5, and weighed 100 pounds. I looked pretty . . . not as tone as I'd like but still, not bad for 29.

I pulled my shorts over my swimsuit, threw on a tank top, grabbed my bag, and stuffed it with the necessary items: extra change of clothes, towel, munchies, and Band- aids . . . lots of Band-aids. Past experience has taught me that any outing involving Kim usually meant I would need some patching up later.

In the distance, I could hear the loud whining of Kim's car coming up the road. Leah was in the back seat laughing at Kim who was singing "Greased Lightning" . . . again. Her windows were down and the music was blaring. I smiled to myself.

About a minute later, a horn honked outside, and I could still hear Kim singing.

I stopped where I was. How had I been able to hear her from so far away? Even if the music was loud enough, how could I have known Leah was in the back seat?

"Impossible!" I muttered. I stepped out my door where a red Hyundai Scoop was waiting for me. Its contents: our wetsuits, two nuts, and three surfboards.

Kim was waving from the driver's seat with a huge smile on her face. Her thick brown hair hung loosely around her tanned shoulders.

Leah *was* in the back seat, and laughing hard. Her sleek nut-brown hair was smoothed down around her pail freckled face. She was trapped between three surfboards positioned in all different directions, their ends hanging out every window.

I closed my eyes and shook my head. I tried to focus on the obvious question: "Kim. How am I supposed to fit in there?" I asked with mild irritation in my voice.

"Get in Phoebs. There's plenty of room. Hurry, we're gonna miss the sun," she yelled impatiently.

I frowned looking at Leah. She rolled her eyes as we shared the same understanding look.

Clambering in, I ducked under a surfboard. Thank goodness I wasn't very big; a normal sized person wouldn't have fit. We arrived at Moonstone Beach a few minutes later, with the sun shinning brightly overhead.

Kim looked to be in an excellent mood having sung nearly every song off her Grease CD.

Leah however, was trying to straighten out her spine after being pined for so long. "Probably permanent damage," she muttered as she slunk out of the car. "Kim, you really need to get some new music," she began. "And we're not listening to that on the way home!"

I normally loved watching Kim and Leah argue. It was usually about something insignificant, and it never lasted long. But something was different. I began surveying the beach. I could hear voices far off in the distance, dogs barking, and the loud roar of the ocean seemed magnified. There were a few people with surfboards; it looked like they were heading out as well.

Then, my eye's flickered to the rocks out a ways in the water. There was someone standing on them. I was sure of it. I hadn't seen anyone up there before, ever.

"Here Phoebs, the waters going to be cold today." Kim smiled, handing me my wet suit.

"Hey Kim, do you see someone standing on top of that rock out there?" I asked as I pointed to the large rock in the distance.

Kim strained her eyes. "Noooo, wait! No . . . must be a bird or something" she declared a moment later. "No one can see that far anyway!" She walked back over to Leah who was struggling with her own suit.

"Bird," I mumbled under my breath as I continued to stare at the rock. It wasn't a bird.

"Ready," I announced several minutes later. The sound of the Beach Boys "Good Vibrations" booming from a nearby truck, diverted my attention.

The three of us looked over to see a few guys we knew: Jeff Roberts, Brian Hawk, and Sean Hansen.

"Great" I said sarcastically. Brian Hawk, Hawk being the operative word, was a constant nightmare. Waiting like a snake for some poor mouse to happen by so he could strike . . . I unfortunately was the object of his attention as of late.

"Maybe they won't notice us!" Kim spoke to soon.

"Hey girls!" Jeff yelled out waving us over.

We waved halfheartedly back and pointed to our surfboards as if this would excuse us from a conversation with them.

“Phoebe!” Brian was bounding over to me. “Hey girl!” He yelled as he scooped me up into a big bear hug and finished it off with a noogie.

“Ow, Brian!” I rubbed my head vigorously.

“Hey. You look different.” Brian was looking me up and down. "I haven't seen you since you got back from Europe."

What are you talking about?” Leah argued. “She looks exactly the same.”

“No. I can’t figure it out, but there is *definitely* something different about you.” He smirked as he continued leering at me—weird, even for Brian.

I turned my back to him, and did my best to pretend he wasn't undressing me with his eyes.

“So you girls going surfing?” he finally asked.

“No Brian, we’re just carrying around the boards for fun,” Leah said, as she rolled her eyes at him. She really couldn’t stand Brian and had no problem showing it.

Brian being Brian, either chose to ignore her, or he honestly had no idea how much she hated him.

“Hey ladies,” Sean called out as he and Jeff joined us. “You better be careful out there today. The swells are pretty big.”

“Yeah, we’ll be careful” Kim grumbled as she pulled Leah towards the water. I followed along eagerly. We could hear the three idiots laughing loudly as we walked away—why did I let the girls talk me into this?

I noticed a jogger coming up the beach. His dog, a cute German Sheppard looked to be enjoying his run as well. I smiled as they were about to pass, when the dog stopped abruptly and began to bark wildly at me, baring its teeth.

I jumped back, slowly putting some distance between me and the dog as his owner tugged frantically at the leash, trying to pull him away from me; all the while apologizing.

“Gee Phoebe, you really freaked out that dog!” Leah’s voice was as shaky as I felt.

“Yeah, weird . . .”

"What's wrong with your eyes?" Kim's face was inches from mine, examining me closely.

"What do you mean?" I tried to back up a little, desperately needing some personal space.

"They weren't like that yesterday . . . they're wild looking; your pupils are really small."

"She's right!" Leah said, stepping forward. She began examining my eyes as well. "They are different."

"It must be the sun," I suggested sharply as I pushed past them. I was bugged now. If I didn't get some space quickly, I was going to scream. After all, I was just nearly mauled by a dog. Again!

The girls shrugged me off and started paddling out together. I paddled toward the big rock. I needed a little time by myself, and I was also curious about the man who was clearly watching me.

He was squatted down now, one arm on his knee and the other hand holding onto the rock for support. I could feel his gaze on me, drawing me nearer to him.

I pulled myself onto the surfboard, as a gust of wind met my face. And with it, a smell not normally found at the beach. It was sweet and fresh, like a spring rain—I knew that smell! It took only a moment for my brain to connect another subconscious piece of my puzzle.

I looked up abruptly, and although I never should have been able to see from where I was, our eyes locked. My mouth dropped a little in amazement. I knew those eyes in an instant. They were the eyes from my dreams, the eyes of my stranger!

I couldn't look away; they drew me in deeper. My heart began to pump wildly as I saw the corner of his perfect lips curl upward into a smile. He was gorgeous! I tried to imagine Zeus himself looking more handsome. I couldn't. His hair was a deep brown that reflected auburn highlights as the sun bounced off it. His face was just as I remembered it, pale and flawless. I couldn't believe I had remembered such detail, as I only saw him for a few moments.

He continued to smile at me as I watched him. How could this be the face from my dreams? How could we be in the same place again, at the same time, in another country?

His head jerked slightly as his attention was suddenly diverted.

I wouldn't have looked away if I hadn't heard the screams from Kim and Leah. I looked frantically for them and saw that they were on the beach waving their arms wildly and screaming something *to me.*

What were they saying? I strained to hear. "WHAT?" I yelled as loud as I could over the roaring ocean.

I felt a slight nudge on the bottom of my surfboard. I pulled my legs up; something smooth had just brushed against my left leg. I screamed, as it bumped me again, this time rocking me, nearly knocking me off.

I could still hear Kim and Leah yelling at me. Then, the word "Shark!" came across the wind clearly.

A violent bump knocked me clear of my board. I began to swim toward the shore. I hadn't realized how far out I was. I struggled with the waves that crashed down upon me, while the fear of not knowing where the shark was consumed me.

I sucked in a sudden breath of air. Something had rammed me in the stomach. I couldn't breath! I frantically looked toward the rocks. Our eyes met for an instant and I could see a look of sheer horror directed back at me.

Another wave crashed on top of me, this time taking me under. I struggled to find the surface. The waves kept pushing me deeper and deeper. I was going to die.

I tried to see through the murky water. All I could see was red, lots of red surrounding me. My God, was I bleeding?

Something wrapped around my waist and began pulling me. I gasped for air, choking on the water that filled my lungs, as my face broke through the surface.

The sky flashed by overhead. I was conscious of the ocean around me, the waves crashing on my body, and the sounds of birds. But I couldn't see who was pulling me.

The warm sand was comfortable beneath me now. My eyes focused for only a moment. I could see his face lowering to mine. His lips parted and then a cool breeze blew through my lungs inflating my chest with air. He released me as I rolled over to choke out the water. I lied on my side for several minutes, waiting to catch my breath.

I felt something brush across my back.

"Shark!" I jumped, looking around me frantically.

"Shhh" he spoke softly as he held my body still. "The shark is dead, you're safe now," he assured.

I looked over to see his face gazing into mine. It was like an angel's, flawless and smooth. His hair hung down around it. Little drops of water still fell from the tips as he hovered over me, watching me anxiously.

"Are you alright?" he asked. His voice was soft and low. He caressed the side of my face gently with the back of his fingers. The touch of his skin on mine was almost electric, causing my heart to speed up.

"How did you . . .?" I rubbed the water from my eyes. "I saw you on the rocks. You were so far away. How did you know there was a shark?"

He glanced past me. "Perhaps, another time," he suggested, his eyes still gazing down the beach.

I could hear Kim and Leah screaming my name as they ran toward me. I looked in their direction and then back to my savior. He was gone!

"Phoebe! Are you alright?" Leah gasped, trying to catch her breath.

"Yes, I'm fine . . . now." I sat up, looking all around me.

"The shark, how did you get away?" Kim cried as she hugged me tightly.

"What do you mean? Didn't you see that man pull me out?" I asked urgently.

"Nooo," Leah answered, "We didn't see anyone. The waves must have washed you up."

"No, a man saved me! I was drowning, he pulled me out, and then he gave me mouth to mouth. I almost died!"

"What man?" Leah asked as she looked up and down the beach.

"You didn't see him?" My voice was softer now, tired, defeated. Was I the only one who could see him? The only one who could hear him? I put my fingers to my lips. I could still feel the cool kiss he'd left there. I searched the sand around me. The only footprints were from my friends.

They looked at each other and back to me, shaking their heads. They hadn't seen anyone.

"Uh, Phoebe, maybe we should get you home," Kim suggested as she looked to Leah who was nodding her head in agreement.

"Look!" Kim jumped up to get my surfboard that had just washed up. "Not even a bite!" she added cheerfully.

I frowned. Leave it to Kim to be making jokes at a time like this.

Leah helped me to my feet. I took one final look around, hoping to see my stranger. He was gone.

Chapter 2: The Stranger

I couldn't get those eyes out of my mind.

I sat at my kitchen table half-heartedly eating a bowl of granola. I picked up the local paper and began reading the front page: "Local fisherman capsizes boat off coast of Trinidad. Nestled in the heart of the Redwoods and hugged by the Pacific Ocean, a small beach community mourns the loss of one of their own." I sighed, remembering Bert down on the docks selling his daily catch.

"I need a distraction." I plopped the paper down and glanced around the room. The bright yellow walls and powder blue curtains did nothing to brighten my mood.

I'd dreamt about my stranger again last night, only this time, I wasn't afraid of him. This time he'd saved me. I breathed in. I could almost smell him. His scent burned my very soul, leaving my heart fluttering at a rapid speed. I tried to shake away the image. "I need to get out of here."

I put my shoes on, grabbed a sack and my car keys, and headed out the door. I'd been working on a new jewelry collection for work and was running low on supplies.

I stopped suddenly. There he was, dressed in black from head to toe. His pale skin illuminated by the sunlight. His eyes were dark and intense, just as I'd remembered. His lips, a pale shade of pink, were turned up into a warm smile. He was leaning up next to a shiny black motorcycle that alone would look incredible, but next to him it paled significantly.

I was at a loss for words. I just stood there, staring at him like he was an elegant piece of artwork that had just been discovered. He was breathtaking!

I took in a breath, catching his scent on the wind. A hint of a spring rain tickled my nose. I'd smelled that fragrance before . . .

I moved toward him slowly. If he was a mirage—I didn't want him to disappear. He remained still as I approached. I could feel my pulse quicken as our eyes locked. I paused for a moment, still looking into his eyes. I took in a deep breath. My hand reached out until my fingers gently touched his bare arm. It was firm, slightly colder than my own arm, but definitely real.

I closed my eyes and sighed with relief.

He let out a laugh that was intoxicating, and took me completely off guard.

"You didn't think I was real?" He shook his head in disbelief.

"Well, I . . ." I blushed every shade from pink to scarlet I was sure. "It's just that when I think I see you, you disappear. I thought you were . . . in my head," I admitted, reluctantly.

"Phoebe," his voice was soft as he spoke my name. He looked at me strangely, as though I were someone dear to him, as if he'd known me forever.

"What did you call me?"

He stood up straighter now. "That is your name isn't it?"

I looked up into his face. "Yes . . ." I answered hesitantly.

His eyes drifted to my hands that still clutched a canvas sac. "Have I interrupted your day?"

My mouth was open slightly as I marveled at the perfection before me. "Huh? Oh!" I came back to earth. "I was just heading to the beach for supplies. But I can go later," I added quickly. "Would you like to come in?" I motioned to the door. "That is, if you have time . . . I mean, you don't have to . . . only if you want!" I was babbling.

My heart raced every time he smiled at me, as though it were jumping out of my chest. I couldn't think straight for some reason. I was all flustered.

I wiped my forehead with the back of my hand, clearing the sweat that had formed. My body flushed under his lingering gaze. My eyes began to lose their focus, and then fell shut as my legs gave way. I could feel myself falling . . .

***

I opened my eyes slowly and looked around me. I was in my living room, lying on the couch. The stranger was sitting beside me. I jumped!

"No, no, lie down a bit more." His voice was low and calming, almost hypnotic.

My heart rate slowed upon his command. "I'm so sorry," I said as I rubbed my forehead, trying to erase the disoriented feeling I had. "I don't know what happened to me. I've never fainted like that before."

"I guess I'll have to watch the way I look at you from now on." He smiled knowingly.

I frowned a little. "I've never fainted just because someone looked at me." I put my head in my hands. "How embarrassing," I muttered under my breath.

"I doubt anyone has ever looked at you like *that* before," he said with what appeared to be great certainty.

I could feel the heat in my cheeks. I knew he knew exactly why I'd fainted. I was never going to live this down. I shook off the dizziness and forced myself to sit up.

"Are you sure you're alright?" I could hear the concern in his voice.

"Yes, I'm fine." I tried to ignore the uncertainty in mine.

"Perhaps this is a good time to introduce myself. My name is Marcus Ashworth." He said his name slowly as if there was some sort of hidden significance I was supposed to understand.

"Marcus," I repeated quietly to myself. His name fit him perfectly.

I extended my hand to him. "Phoebe Rose." He stared at it for a moment, then took it softly.

"You're cold!" I exclaimed, still holding his hand. "Would you like a blanket?" I moved to get up.

"No!" he said abruptly, releasing my hand. "I'm quite comfortable." His eyebrows furrowed a little. "I wondered . . . how your shoulder was healing?"

"My shoulder? Oh! You mean when that dog attacked me back in London—nightmare," I grumped aloud, rolling my eyes a little. Wait. I looked at him incredulously. How did he know about that? I recoiled a little. My heart reacted to the sudden fear I felt, beating faster by the second.

"What makes you think it was a dog that attacked you?" he asked, ignoring my jolted expression.

"I . . . I don't know for sure." I shifted uneasily. "It all happened so fast." I subconsciously began rubbing my shoulder. "Although, it must have been a giant dog. The tooth marks were huge."

"Tooth marks?" He looked extremely anxious all of a sudden.

"I think they're tooth marks?" I said nervously.

He regarded me carefully for a moment, pondering something over in his mind. "You must be wondering how I found you?"

"Actually, I . . . " I was afraid to ask.

He smiled in understanding. "I'm a tracker, a hunter by trade."

"A hunter?" I had to look as confused as I was.

"I was hunting the night you were . . . *intercepted*." He chose his word carefully. "I was closing in on him when you came around the corner and he literally plunged into you." Marcus gave my shoulder a quick glance. "You're quite lucky I was so close. It didn't have time to kill you," he added darkly.

"Have time to kill me!" I nearly shouted. I was on the edge of the couch now. My eyes were wide with shock. "What do you mean? What exactly were you hunting?"

His face grew serious. His eyes were darker now, and his jaw tightened with sudden tension. "A type of wolf," he said through clenched teeth.

"A wolf! In London?" My brain couldn't register what my ears were hearing. "You must be joking?" I half laughed, remembering Kim's ridiculous 'escaped animal from the zoo' theory. I couldn't bear it if she had been in any way right about that. The thought made me nauseous. I could never tell her. There'd be no living with her after this.

My mind wandered briefly until I felt Marcus's stare. There was no trace of humor in his face.

"What was a wolf doing running through London?" I decided to ask. Hoping not only that I had misunderstood him, but also to break the tension that was now looming over my living room.

"There are unfortunately many wolves that roam the city from time to time," he explained with a hint of venom in his words. "Usually they're killed before they get too close to the city, but there seems to be a rise in the population. We're hard-pressed to stop all of them in time."

"'We're'? There are more of you?"

He nodded.

"Stop them in time for what?" I asked a moment later.

"Before they kill someone, or worse," he added darkly.

My breath caught. "What could be worse than being killed?" I asked, afraid to hear the answer.

He leaned in closer. My head filled with the scent of him. "It could leave you alive after it's mauled you."

I swallowed loudly. "But, I was left alive." My words came out like a whisper.

He shifted his weight. His eyes still showing signs of concern.

"A wolf . . . really? I guess that explains the weird dreams I've been having. Should I have gotten a rabies shot?" I prattled on nervously; trying to ignore the uneasy look he gave me.

"May I see it?" He pointed to my shoulder.

"Um, I guess so," I said hesitantly. "There really isn't much to see."

I could feel his posture stiffen as I turned my back to him. I tossed my hair aside and pulled at the neck of my shirt, exposing my shoulder. I glanced behind me, meeting his stare. "How does it look?"

"Beautiful!" he whispered, his eyes still gazing into mine.

My heart began to race again. I dropped my stare. "I meant the bite marks." I blushed.

He looked a million miles away. His hand paused in mid air as he considered whether or not he should touch me.

"It's ok," I volunteered. "It doesn't hurt. It's just a little pink still, but it seemed to heal pretty fast, really."

His eyes flickered to mine and then back to my shoulder. He inched closer. I could feel his cool breath on my skin as he neared. I shivered involuntary. His fingers gently touched my skin . . .

"OW!"

He literally flew back from the couch and was now standing across the room from me.

My mouth hung open for a moment. "How did you move like that?" I gasped.

"I didn't mean to hurt you!" His face was anxious; his hands were clenched into fists at his side.

"You didn't . . . really. There must be some static in the air," I half smiled as I pulled my shirt back over my shoulder and turned toward him. I could still feel the goosebumps on my skin.

"Marcus, how—" was all I managed to squeak out when a horn honking in front of the house diverted my attention. A new feeling of dread overtook me.

"Oh no!" I said as I hid my face in my hands. I was instantaneously depressed.

"What is it?"

I peeked through my fingers to see Marcus looking from the door back to me awaiting my explanation.

"It's just some annoying guy that won't leave me alone," I said hopelessly. "He's trying to wear me down so I'll go out with him."

I leaned back on the couch and rolled my eyes to the ceiling as he honked again.

"Would you like me to speak with him?" he offered casually. His voice sounded almost devious. I tilted my head over to see a devilish smile on his face. It took me by surprise.

I half laughed as I considered the look on Brian's face if Marcus answered the door.

"No, I'm used to it." I conceded as I got up and walked to the door with my head hung down in defeat.

A thought occurred to me. I stopped abruptly and spun around. "Marcus?"

He smiled knowingly at me. His dark eyes were softer now as he looked into mine.

"Yes Phoebe, I'll be here when you return," he assured. "I'm not going anywhere."

"How did you know? Never mind," I added quickly, hearing the resolve in his voice. I spun around to open the door.

"Phoebee! What's up, girl? You're looking good today!" Brian was right in my face attempting to ooze out charm.

I never disliked hearing my name so much as when Brian said it. I hated it when he accentuated the 'e' at the end.

I pulled the door shut behind me, sparing Marcus from having to endure such a painful conversation. Brian wasn't known for being intellectually stimulating.

"Hey Brian," I offered a small smile. "This isn't a good time. I'm headed out right now."

He looked surprised that I wasn't excited he decided to grace me with his presence today. He looked back at the street and stared at the black motorcycle parked in front.

Shoot, I thought to myself. I'd forgotten about Marcus's motorcycle.

He was looking back at me now. "Whose bike?" He asked suspiciously.

"Uhh . . ." Was all I could say. I bit my lip trying to come up with an answer. He'd never leave me alone if he thought another guy was hanging around, encroaching on his so-called territory. Brian was under the delusion that he and I were an item. Although I'd never gone on a date with him, or said that I ever would, he was . . . hopeful.

"So Phoebs," he went on ignoring the fact that I hadn't answered his question. "I was thinking . . . " I cringed.

"Hey! What's up with your eyes?" He inched closer, his eyes narrowing in on mine. "You get some funky contacts or something?"

"What? No!" I stepped back a little, trying to evade his stare.

"Weird. They're like . . . yellow-looking. Anyway," he continued, unconcerned; "You and I should go out tonight. You know, dinner, movie." He moved closer. Brian's concept of personal space was almost non-existent. "I'll even pay!" he added, like this would seal the deal. " . . . And then we could come back here and . . . " his voice trailed off as his lips curled up into a creepy smile that I'm sure was supposed to be seductive.

He held onto my shoulders, massaging them with as much tenderness as someone kneading bread. He towered over me in such a way that always made me uncomfortable. Brian was easily three times bigger than I was and could effortlessly overpower me if he wanted to. This realization was always in the back of my mind, as I tried to gently turn him away.

" . . . I could stay the whole night if you want," he continued on, not missing a beat. "I'll keep you safe if that wolf comes around here and tries to attack you," he scoffed.

"Wolf?"

"Yeah." he looked surprised. "Right down the road, some guy lost his chickens and a goat, I think. It was in the paper this morning."

"I didn't see that in the paper. How do they know it was a wolf?" I demanded, feeling my heart rate increase again.

"Easy babe, I'll take care of you," he closed in on me.

"Brian. How do they know it was a wolf?"

He frowned. "They found some paw prints, pretty good sized ones, too big to be a coyote," he added offhandedly.

I nodded my head in understanding. My mind was racing. What was a wolf doing in Trinidad? Could this be a coincidence?

Brian must have somehow picked up on my private panic attack. He sounded almost human for a moment. "Hey, don't worry Phoebe. You'll be alright."

I had to regain control quick. “Uh, thanks anyway Brian. I don’t have any animals so I don’t think it’ll come hunting around here.” I tried to sound blasé about the whole thing.

“I could spend the night anyway,” he persisted as his face was drawing nearer every second. I could see his eyes begin to close as his lips moved within inches of mine.

“Brian, I . . . ”

The door flung open. Being that the entire weight of my body was pressed against it, and trying to escape Brian’s clutches, I fell right through the doorway. Marcus caught me before I hit the floor. I breathed heavily as I looked into the eyes of my rescuer with deep relief.

Marcus gave me a little wink as he lifted me back to my feet; placing himself between Brian and me.

With his arm still around my waist, he turned to Brian. “I’m Marcus Ashworth.” His voice was calm yet undoubtedly firm.

Brian looked utterly shocked.

I tried to imagine myself anywhere but here.

“This is Brian Hawk.” I motioned to Brian.

Brian stared at Marcus for a moment then diverted his attention to the motorcycle, and to my surprise, put the pieces together.

“Hi,” he said gruffly, and continued as if Marcus wasn’t there. “So, what do you think?”

“About what?” My head was spinning.

“Dinner, movie,” he paused for a moment. Brian’s eyes were fixed on Marcus's arm that was still around my waist.

“Well Brian, I have to work in the morning, and . . . ”

“Phoebe has already agreed to allow me to take her to dinner this evening,” Marcus announced coolly.

Brian shot me an irritated glare. “You’ve got a date, with him?” he asked in disbelief.

I looked up at Marcus who was enjoying himself a little too much. “Yes?” I answered.

Brian looked beyond irritated. “I guess I’ll check on you later this week then.” He turned and headed back to his car. He gave me one more irritated glance before he turned the music up to blaring and tore off in a rage.

"That went well," Marcus laughed under his breath.

"You didn't have to make him so jealous." I cut him a disapproving look. "You don't know what you've started; he's never going to leave me alone now." I turned toward the door.

Marcus caught my arm gently. "I'm sorry. I was trying to help." He paused for a minute. I could see he was struggling with something.

He released my arm. His eyes were black as coal. The muscles in his jaw were clenched tight.

"I wasn't going to allow him to think he could spend the night with you!" he snapped as he glared in the direction Brian had sped off in. He looked furious. He turned his attention back to me as I slowly retreated backward. "Watch out!"

I tripped backward over the threshold and fell; landing once again with his arms under me, saving me from hitting the floor.

My heart pounded as I looked into his eyes. I was torn by the fear I felt a moment ago, the utter shock of how he managed to catch me so quickly, and the absolute safety I felt in his embrace.

My pulse raced as his eyes looked deeper into mine. I could feel his cool breath on my lips. The sweet smell of his body encircled me as his arms held me close to him.

"You don't ever need to fear me: I would never hurt you." His voice was soft, velvety. His eyes were golden brown and tender as they gazed into mine. They'd changed somehow . . .

"Marcus, I . . . " I didn't know what to say. I'd never had anyone react to or treat me this way before. "Thank you." It didn't feel like the right words. But they were all I knew.

"I'm sorry I frightened you," his words came across like a whisper. I felt my head nodding in understanding.

"I don't trust your friend, and I can't bear the thought of him being so intimate with you." His voice was calm but his words were sharp.

"He's not my friend," I breathed.

He held me a second more before he set me back on my feet.

A thought came to me, and I unfortunately laughed out loud.

"What's so funny?" his face was full of wonder.

"No, it's nothing," I said, waving him off.

"Please."

"Well, it's just that . . . " my laugh became a nervous one. " . . . I was thinking to myself . . . that Brian's not the first guy who tried to sleep over. He's just a bit more pushy that's all. I mean, you'd have to be glued to my hip if you expect to ward off all the tacky guys I come in contact with." I cringed a little as I thought back.

Marcus's face fell.

"Please ignore that. I don't know why I said that out loud." I was horrified with my big mouth. Of course he wouldn't think that was funny. "I don't think sometimes before I speak; it just sort of . . . falls out," I added quickly.

"Other men try to . . .?" He broke off mid sentence. He had a look of shock across his face.

"I can imagine how far-fetched it must seem but yes. Other men have tried to stay over as well," I grumped, feeling insulted now.

Marcus looked at me disapprovingly. "I believe other men find you attractive; it's just unthinkable they'd be so forward about it. It's not very gentlemanly."

My mouth gaped a little. I was truly amazed. Who was this guy? More importantly, why hadn't I met him sooner?

"Let's try not to worry about the past." I wanted to change the subject—quick!

There was, however, one question I wanted to ask desperately. But I would wait for later. Now was not the time for another heavy conversation.

"Would you like to go with me to the beach?" I asked. "I was heading there when you came. I need some shells for my new jewelry design."

I could see that he saw through my diversion. But, being the gentleman he obviously was, he dropped the subject. "I'll drive."

Before I could blink, he was on his bike smiling, waving me over.

I stared at him in disbelief.

“One sec!” I dashed into the house, grabbed my things and met him at the street.

He shook his head as he watched my hesitant expression. He gave my hand a quick yank and I was instantly on back, straddling the seat behind him.

He laughed at the bewildered look on my face.

“Where to?” he asked, still snickering.

“Up the coast a little, I know a spot that’s pretty good.”

“Hold on!” he yelled back to me.

Chapter 3: My Hero

I instinctively grabbed hold of his waist and held on tight.

My gosh he smelled good. I felt instantly comforted by the light fragrance of a spring rain—I inhaled deeply.

I found myself resting my cheek against his back. His body tensed suddenly. I debated whether I should lift my head when I felt a gentle caress across the top of my hands that were locked around him. He seemed just as content as I was. It was strange, the automatic connection I felt with him . . . he must feel it too.

We zipped through traffic at crazy speeds. I was sure I was going to fly off at any moment if I didn't hold on for dear life. I frowned as we pulled into the parking lot area at the beach. I wasn't ready to let go.

It was a beautiful day, fairly warm and only a few clouds in the sky. I'd been here dozens of times, but never before had I been able to hear the ocean from here.

I shook my head in confusion. I realized I was still sitting on the back of the motorcycle with my arms tightly locked around Marcus.

He cleared his throat softly. "We could stay here like this if you want but it seems a shame not to at least collect a few shells," he said with a laugh.

I released him from my death-grip. I couldn't explain the feeling I had. It was as if I'd known Marcus all along. His very essence was so familiar to me. Maybe it was because he'd saved me? He was my own personal hero. Or maybe it was something more? Another piece to the puzzle I was desperately trying to figure out.

We started down the long path that led to the beach. I watched as he took everything in. His hair shined in the sun. He lowered his face suddenly, reached into his jacket pocket and took out a pair of sunglasses. His movements were quick. Had I not been paying such close attention, I wouldn't have noticed him reach for the glasses in the first place—they would have simply appeared on his face. How did he move so fast? One thing was certain. There was much more to Marcus than he was allowing me to know. He glanced my way, smiling out the corner of his mouth. He'd caught me staring.

I blushed.

"Marcus?" I asked smiling shyly. "Do you feel like we . . .? "

"We what?"

I took a deep breath. "Like we know each other?"

I could see his expression perk up a little. He looked almost delighted. And then, as quickly as his smile came, it was gone. He now looked worried.

"I'm not sure I know what you mean," he said casually.

So, it was going to be like that was it? He was going to make me spell out everything—leave me exposed for embarrassment and possible rejection. I had to play this carefully.

"I mean, that when you look at me," I bit my lip, "it's like you've known me all my life." I hesitated for a moment. "I feel like a memory of you is buried somewhere deep in my mind, I can't see it clearly, but I know it's there. Does that make sense?" I asked sounding confused myself.

He walked along side me quietly. His lips were pursed together. He looked like he was deliberating with his answer.

"I'm not sure how to answer you, Phoebe," he finally spoke. "I think we should discuss this another time," he said with a hint of finality in his voice.

I stopped walking. "Another time? Either you know me, or you don't!" I blurted out.

"But how could you?" I whispered quietly under my breath.

"That's not such an easy question," he continued, not bothering to notice that I wasn't beside him. His tone was a little harder now. "Sometimes the mind has a difficult time processing certain . . . situations." He spoke cautiously.

That was it! No one was going to tell me that my brain couldn't handle "certain situations."

"I think I am capable of grasping whatever it is you won't tell me," I said, catching up to him again.

I waited for him to speak. Nothing!

"Since we're being so open," I added sarcastically, "I'd also like to know why you just left me on the ground, bleeding, after I was apparently attacked by some wild wolf!"

I could tell by the look on his face he did not expect my sudden hostile mood change. He was obviously not used to women!

He stopped walking and turned toward me. "I never left you," he growled.

There was anguish in his words, as well as another meaning that I couldn't decipher. Something told me not to press him about it. Clearly he was upset about something he wanted me to know but didn't feel comfortable talking to me about.

We continued walking, neither of us in the mood for shell hunting; that much my little brain could figure out on its own.

I was fuming. I was so busy glaring at him that I didn't notice the narrow walk on the trail ahead.

I screamed as my foot lost ground on the soft shoulder. I slid off the trail, down the side of the cliff. My hands tried to grab onto anything as the rocks crumbled below my feet.

Marcus grabbed my wrist before I was lost. He yanked it sharply and pulled me back up with such force, I landed on top of him, knocking him to the ground.

I stared at him wide eyed. I could feel him breathing heavily below me. I started to cry. By the panicked expression on his face, he hadn't expected that.

He held the side of my face to his chest. "Shh, I've got you." He put his arms around me, holding me close to him.

"I'd have thought you'd have outgrown your clumsiness by now," he half laughed. "My silly girl," he added affectionately. He was stroking the side of my face with his hand as his body rocked me back and forth.

Being cradled so closely to him seemed to ease my mind, but not the pain I was now fully aware of. I reluctantly slid off his body to look myself over.

The palms of my hands were scraped badly, and stung. My shirt was torn a little. Small red patches of blood had already bled through. My legs faired the worst. My jeans hadn't been able to stop the sharp rocks from scraping my knees.

"You really should be more careful," he said through clenched teeth.

He was mad at me! How could he be so nice one minute, and so disgusted the next? Yes, he was disgusted with me; there was no other explanation for the expression on his face.

I started to cry again, harder this time. "I would have been watching if I didn't have to glare at you for keeping secrets from me! My whole body hurts, I nearly just plummeted to my death, and you're yelling at me!" I sobbed.

"You're . . . bleeding." He had trouble saying the word.

He turned his head to the side and took a deep breath as the ocean breeze reached us. His eyes were closed. His face looked paler than normal. He staggered back a little.

"Are you alright?" I sniffled.

"The blood . . ."

"You're afraid of blood!" I was completely shocked.

He turned his head so I couldn't see his face. The muscles in his arms tightened as he took in every breath.

"Your leg . . . the cut is deep." His voice was gruff.

"How can you tell?" I could feel he was right, but how could he possibly know that?

He paced a little in front of me, rubbing his forehead with his hands. He took a few more deep breaths before he walked back to me.

Without a word, he put one arm around my back and the other under my legs. He scooped me up effortlessly into his arms and started back up the hill. I could just barely see his eyes through the corner of his sunglasses. They looked . . . amber? His jaw was still clenched. He seemed to be holding his breath.

"I'm sorry if I'm heavy for you," I said awkwardly, not knowing what really to say.

"Humph." His lips curled up into a smile.

I couldn’t be more than a hundred pounds, but having to carry me up this hill I’m sure wasn’t easy. He had a look of pure concentration on his face.

I could feel my leg pulsating as the pain increased. I started to feel light-headed. The ringing in my ears was getting louder now. I didn’t do pain well, and I didn’t weigh enough to lose blood . . . at least not this much anyway.

I looked at my pants; there was a fair amount of blood that had soaked through already.

“If I pass out . . .” I started to say when my mind went blank.

I could feel a gentle shake to my body.

“Phoebe! Can you hear me?” Marcus's voice was anxious.

“Where are we?” My eyes were still closed.

“We’re in the parking lot. You fainted,” he answered, his voice still strained.

I opened my eyes slowly and looked around to see that we were once again beside his motorcycle.

He looked at the bike and my crumpled body in his arms.

“Oh, I can ride,” I said trying to look alert.

He looked at me skeptically; his eyebrows were raised in disbelief.

“Really, I’ll be fine.”

“We’ll go quickly,” he promised.

He placed me on the back of the bike, gave me another uneasy look, and got on.

I held on halfheartedly. My arms and hands were so sore; they felt like they were on fire. As for my leg, I’d have to get these jeans off to see the extent of the damage.

I don’t remember the ride home. It may have been that I was in so much pain that I’d passed out, yet managed to hold on. Or it may have been that we traveled at such a speed that would have made the crew of the Starship Enterprise jealous.

I was in front of my house and back in his arms in minutes. He carried me inside and placed me on the couch.

“Let’s have a look, shall we?” He wrinkled his nose.

"You don't have to," I insisted. "I can do it." I gently tried to push him away.

I put on my game face quick. There was no way I was going to have him clean me up.

I saw how sick he looked; there was no need to gross him out any further.

This was just my luck. I finally meet an incredibly handsome man that seems to truly care for me—though I can't figure out why—and what do I do? I fall off a cliff in a pout and mangle my body. It was classic Phoebe at her worst.

I started to get up. My mind was lifting me off the couch but my legs wouldn't cooperate. My top half fell over, and my bloodied hands came out to block my face from hitting the floor.

"Ow, ow." I pulled myself up and slumped back on the couch. I was blowing on my hands, trying to relieve the burning sensation.

Reluctantly, my eyes met his. He turned his head so that I couldn't see him smile.

I glowered at him, annoyed that he found this funny.

He cleared his throat and composed his face as he turned back toward me. "Are you ready to let me help you?" he asked. He turned his head quickly, trying to hide a smile.

"Bathroom, top shelf!" I pointed to the bathroom.

He came back with my first aid kit still smiling. "I think we'd better wrap your hands first…you may need them if you try to get off the couch again."

"Very funny," I frowned.

He took my hands carefully, wrinkling his nose as he examined them. His eyes grew darker as he stared at the drying blood.

I gently slipped my hands out of his. "I can do it," I said quietly.

"No. I can help you."

"They're really not that bad," I said as I started squeezing on the Neosporin tube.

He unwrapped a Band-aid for me and softly placed it on the palm of my hand, being careful not to touch any of the blood.

"You see, I can do this," he said proudly.

He was trying so hard to help me that he was willing to endure what clearly made him sick. Who was this guy? I smiled to myself.

My hands were the easy part. My elbows hurt worse than they looked. There was a large scrape across my stomach that was still bleeding lightly. He cringed away when I lifted my shirt. He closed his eyes, got up and walked to the other side of the room.

He was looking out my window, his hands in fists on either side of the frame, holding on for support.

"Are you ok?" I asked after a few minutes.

"Blood…has a different effect on me than most." His voice sounded different, not his own.

"Is your throat alright; your voice sounds funny, almost raspy. You're not getting sick are you?" I worried.

"No! Are you ready to look at your leg?" he asked impatiently.

"No I'm not," I answered quickly.

He turned to me; his face was strained, but it was softening as he could see that I was done bandaging my stomach.

"Why don't you want to take care of your leg?" He looked perplexed.

I shifted uneasily.

He lowered his head to mine, folded his arms across his chest, and waited.

"I can't get my pants off, without them rubbing across my knees"

He frowned at me, interrupting my train of thought.

"It'll hurt!" I insisted.

He looked at me with disbelief. There was no question he thought I was a wimp; I was sure of it. He should talk. I wasn't the one freaking out over a little blood.

"Well, if your leg was ripped open, you wouldn't want to scrape denim across it either!" I said defensively.

"And reason number two?" he asked, looking not very hopeful after hearing reason number one.

I looked away. I didn't want to see his face. "I'll just wait until you've gone. I don't want to gross you out any more than I have," I said in almost a whisper.

I felt his fingers lightly take my chin. I hadn't even heard him move. He turned my head so that I had to look up into his glorious face.

"You don't 'gross' me out." He smiled softly as he repeated my phraseology. He knelt down beside me.

"Maybe not me personally, but I know all this . . . " I pointed to my arms and held up my hands for him to see the many Band-aids that now covered me, ". . . makes you sick."

I could feel the tears starting to build up in my eyes. I held them back. I felt so bad for him, trying to help me when it clearly made him ill . . . and me being such a wimp about being hurt. I wanted to curl up in a ball and hide. This had to be the most painful fall I'd ever taken. Why did it have to happen in front of Marcus?

He cracked a smile. "I think I can get your pants off without hurting you," he said confidently.

I rolled my eyes. "Like I haven't heard that before," I muttered sarcastically.

He shot me a disapproving look. "Hmm . . ." He reached out and began to unbutton my pants.

I put my hands on top of his to stop him. Embarrassment coated my cheeks, while worry filled my eyes.

"I promise," he spoke tenderly. "It will not hurt."

My grip loosened, I didn't understand why I trusted him so much. I knew they had to come off, but my tolerance for pain was extremely low. I closed my eyes tight.

I felt a quick pull at my zipper, and then a loud *rip*!

My eyes popped open as I looked at my naked and badly bloodied leg. Marcus turned his head, averting his eyes. I hastily pulled the denim back over my lower half, covering my underwear.

"How did you do that?" I gasped.

"I'm really strong," he shrugged, looking back at me.

My chance to marvel at his super human strength was short lived. My legs were worse than I'd thought. They were scraped from my knees down both shins. The more severe cut on my right thigh was bleeding heavily now that the pants were no longer there to clot it.

Marcus's eyes fixed on this particular area. He instantly flinched away from me. His nose wrinkled as his lips started to curl up over his teeth. A dull hiss escaped from within him. He turned abruptly so I couldn't see his face.

I instinctively pulled my legs back, ignoring the pain as I tried to move myself into the couch as much as possible. Every instinct told me to run, but I was frozen. My mind raced as I tried to understand what was happening.

"I can't help you," he hissed.

"It's . . . ok," I said shakily. "Y—you don't have to stay, I'll take care of it."

"I don't want to leave you without explaining." I could hear the pain in his voice.

"I'll be back when you're finished." He moved so fast through my door that if my eyes had been relaxed enough to blink, I'd have missed it.

I sat on the couch motionless, completely in shock. My eyes darted around me, my heart beating wildly. What was going on? Marcus acted like some kind of feral animal. Hissing? That was not normal.

I took a deep breath and sighed with relief, he was gone.

I accidentally bumped my leg with my elbow. "Damn it!" I yelled.

I pulled the rest of my pants off and launched them across the room with as much force as I could muster.

I tried to put pressure around the cut to see just how badly it was bleeding. Stitches? I thought to myself. Probably, but there was no way I was going to get stitches. I growled mentally.

I began cleaning and bandaging my leg as best I could. My knees received a few little Band-aids but mostly they were covered in raspberries like my shins.

I leaned back on a pillow, closed my eyes, and wondered if I would see Marcus again. Did I really want to see him again? On one hand, I felt drawn to him for some unexplainable reason; I wanted him close to me. I needed him. On the other hand, I was afraid of him. All sense I had told me he was dangerous, that I should run . . .

Chapter 4: Wild Animals

I heard a quiet knock at the door. I stared at the doorknob for a minute before it opened slowly.

Marcus peeked his head through. "May I come in?" His face looked as calm and as beautiful as it did when I first saw him this morning leaning against his bike. I watched him closely for a second to see if any part of him resembled the Marcus that scared me—the Marcus that left me no more than half an hour ago—this was not that Marcus.

I nodded yes.

He walked in slowly, as if approaching me with caution. His hands extended like he was stopping traffic. My body tensed up as he drew nearer.

"I'm so sorry Phoebe. I want to explain so many things, but I don't think you could handle it all at once." His face looked torn.

I couldn't speak. I wanted to say I wasn't afraid of him, but I couldn't. I had seen something in his eyes. And, although the eyes that were looking at me now were soft and kind, the ones I couldn't get out of my mind were deadly. There was a dark, unnatural side to Marcus, that much was certain, and it scared me.

He was only a few feet into the living room, his hands still extended out to me. "Phoebe, I won't hurt you . . . I swear it."

I could hear the hurt in his voice as he said this. He seemed to truly care for me, to want to protect me, even from himself.

I shifted uneasily on the couch. "I'm all cleaned up," I said, offering him a small smile.

He lowered his hands and smiled gratefully. Still moving slowly, he walked around to the front of the couch and stopped dead in his tracks. His eyes were fixed on me. He looked stunned.

I became instantly aware and horrified all at once. I had been so distracted by Marcus's reaction and bandaging myself up that when he knocked on the door, I had forgotten that I wasn't dressed yet.

There I was on the couch with nothing on but a tank top and underwear—covered here and there in Band-aids and gauze.

I saw his jolted expression at how exposed I was—it was nothing compared to mine.

"I, uh," I stammered. "I didn't have time to get dressed! Don't look!" I jumped up—rolling completely off the couch, landing on my face.

I lay there motionless, bottoms up, wishing I were dead. "There is *no* dignified way out of this. None!" I mumbled into the carpet.

Marcus scooped me up and put me back on the couch without so much as a smirk. His eyes wandered the room for a moment before settling on an open door.

"Wait here." He dashed to my bedroom and returned with a quilted blanket from my bed.

He'd draped it over my legs and was tucking it around my waist when I put my hand on his bicep. He stopped abruptly, not looking at me. I tilted my head to the side. His eyes reluctantly met mine. They were a deep chocolaty brown now. No hint of anger tainting them.

My eyes dropped to his lips. I could feel his cool breath escaping them, kissing mine. My pulse quickened.

"Thank you," I breathed.

I wanted to kiss him . . . I was certain he wanted to kiss me too. I sat there, frozen. The only movement from my body was my breathing in and out. He stayed there leaning over me . . . so close but never touching. I watched his lips hovering over mine.

"Your welcome," they whispered back.

He pulled away abruptly and took a seat beside the couch.

I placed my hand subtly over my heart, trying to slow it. What was wrong with me?

"So, is it safe to assume you won't be working tomorrow?" He pointed to my legs.

I laughed a little. "I guess not." I was glad that the conversation had taken a lighter tone.

"Although," I continued, "I'd rather not be home in case that wolf comes back." I shuddered as I remembered Brian's offer of protection.

Marcus's expression was unreadable. "What wolf?" he asked flatly.

"Oh," I waved him off. "When Brian was here earlier, he said a wolf killed some chickens and a goat up the road last night." I paused for a second as I watched his face; he looked worried now.

"I just got a little scared when you were talking about the wolf problem in London, and when I heard a wolf was near my house, I just . . ." I hated to admit it out loud. "I just thought maybe it was the same wolf that bit me, and it's followed me here." I shook my head at such an absurd thought. "I know it's crazy," I added, dismissing it.

"Marcus?" His eyes were jet black. Not the soft brown as before. "You're scaring me." I felt myself scooting into the couch cushions.

He quickly gained control of himself, clearly forcing a smile.

"Phoebe, I've only been here a little while. Do you know when the last full moon was?" he asked as if this was a normal question.

"What? I don't know . . . I don't keep track of lunar activity," I said taken aback by the question. "Why?"

He didn't answer. He sat there, looking thoughtful.

"I have a calendar in the kitchen, it might say—"

He was up and in the kitchen before I'd finished my sentence.

I sat open mouthed. "What is going on?" I said under my breath.

The wind picked up outside. I'd heard earlier on the news a storm was coming, and heavy rain was in the forecast. I looked over to my living room window. The rain tapped against it lightly. I watched the water drops running down the windowpane. And that's when I noticed a pair of yellow eyes peering in at me.

Marcus came running into the living room at the same moment that I began screaming. He was beside me instantly, hovering over me protectively.

"The window!" I screamed.

It was still at the window—growling ferociously at the sight of Marcus.

"Wait here!"

"MARCUS!" I screamed after him. He was gone.

I pulled the blanket around me tightly. My mind was racing. I jumped at every sound. Several dark windows in the room stared back at me. Too scared to get up and close the curtains, I pulled the blanket up higher over my head, blocking them from my view.

How could Marcus just run out there like that? What was he planning to do anyway? He could be hurt or killed! I was going crazy with worry.

My door flung open suddenly. The wind and the rain rushed into my living room, as I screamed from under the blanket.

"Phoebe it's me!"

I peeked out as Marcus hurried over to me. His hair was soaked, and his clothes were dripping wet.

"Marcus!" Without thinking, I jumped up, threw my arms around his shoulders, and hugged him tightly, ignoring the water that was dripping all over me.

"I can't believe you went out there; you could have been killed!" I scolded, as I held him tighter to me.

I could feel his arms around my waist, holding me gently. "I'm fine," he assured, though his voice cracked slightly.

"What was that?" I asked, still not loosening my grip around him.

"A wolf."

My mouth hung open as I pulled my face back to look at him. I held onto his shoulders tighter now, my legs were beginning to wobble. He caught me as I started to slip through his arms.

"You'd better sit down. Your legs are still quite weak."

"I'm fine," I said flatly, my eyes were fixed on his. I needed to hold him close to me. I didn't understand why but I couldn't bear to think I wouldn't see him again, I couldn't lose him . . . not now.

"That couldn't have been a wolf. It was gigantic! Where is it now?" I asked in a panic, looking toward the window.

"Phoebe, really it's fine. I tracked it a few miles away from here. It's still running north."

I closed my eyes and took a deep calming breath. I could feel his body stiffen suddenly. I opened my eyes. A look of surprise swept across his face.

"What is it?" I whispered. Fear was creeping up on me again. I looked at the window and then back at Marcus. Had he seen or heard something I didn't?

His fingers began moving slowly down the side of my hips. I could feel goose bumps as his cold fingertips touched my skin. My pulse began to race as I sunk deeper into his stare.

"Forgive me, I didn't mean to touch you like that." He looked away, releasing my eyes.

Embarrassment swept over me. In my absolute elation when he walked back through the door, I jumped up to embrace him, still half dressed. Neither one of us had noticed my blanket had fallen.

"Marcus," my cheeks flushed scarlet. "Excuse me. I was just so happy you were alright, I didn't think . . . "

I tried to back away from him, to grab my blanket, but he held my body tight.

"Marcus?" My voice was shaky.

He looked longingly into my eyes. "I never thought I would ever get the chance to hold you this way again." His thoughts were far away, like he was talking about some distant memory.

His hands were moving to the small of my back now, the cool touch of his fingers, working their way slowly up my spine, pausing in the middle. My breathing grew shorter. He lowered his head closer to mine. My pulse quickened as he pulled my body against his.

"I can feel your heart beat," he mused.

He brought his forehead to mine. The touch was electric. I could feel my legs burning now—they wouldn't hold me much longer.

His eyes were growing darker. Specks of crimson now swirled among the black, as he looked deeper into my eyes, holding me in a dream-like trance. I couldn't move even if I wanted to.

He gently pressed his lips to my forehead, causing my heart to skip. I could feel him smiling as he moved his face along mine, lightly tracing my skin with his nose. He breathed in deeply. My body shivered as I felt his cool breath on my face. It smelt delicious . . .

My instincts were telling me this was dangerous, that I should run for my life. My heart was telling me not to ever let go.

I struggled for the words I needed to say, my mind raced along with my heart. I wanted to kiss him more than anything.

"Phoebe?" he whispered into my ear. His voice was like velvet, soft and smooth.

I swallowed and tried to remember how to answer. "Yes," I said quietly.

"You don't know what I was going to ask you," he said with a smile.

I couldn't speak. I was putting all my strength into standing, and not passing out, I couldn't concentrate. My mind wouldn't do simple conversation.

His face was buried in my hair now. He moved his lips along my ear, kissing it softly.

My legs trembled beneath me. My world began to spin.

"Phoebe…" his voice was hypnotic.

I jerked my face toward his, the side of our lips touched. I could feel Marcus's lips tremble next to mine. His breathing, heavy like my own. His hands were wrapped around my waist, holding it firmly. I was afraid to move. Never had I wanted to kiss someone so badly in all my life.

He slowly backed away from me, his hands reluctantly releasing their hold. I sunk back onto the couch in disbelief, my heart still pounding . . .

"I want to kiss you Phoebe; you can't imagine how badly. It's just that I . . ." his words broke off in anguish.

I suddenly felt self-conscious. "You don't have to explain," I said shyly. "I guess I misunderstood." I shrugged, pretending to be busy adjusting my blanket. A tear escaped from the corner of my eye. I wiped it away quickly, hoping he wouldn't notice.

He walked back to me and knelt down beside me. His hands were on the sides of my face cupping it gently so that my eyes couldn't escape his.

"You didn't misunderstand. I do want to kiss you," he said as he smoothed his thumb across my lips. "I just can't be with you that way, not without hurting you. I could never forgive myself if I hurt you." His voice sounded as tortured as he looked.

"I don't understand? Did I do something wrong? Do you have a girlfriend?" I asked reluctantly.

"No!" I could see the frustration building in his face.

"Marcus, you can tell me anything," I encouraged. My eyes looked hopefully into his.

"It's so hard for me to be this close to you and not hold you the way I want to. To not kiss your lips the way I used to . . ." I could see the uneasiness in his eyes. He had said more than he'd planned to. He backed away from me again, turning toward the window so I couldn't see his face.

"The way you used to?" I repeated. "Marcus, I think I'd remember if I'd kissed you before."

He said nothing but continued to stare out into the rain.

"I don't understand. Are you trying to tell me that we've had some sort of relationship before that I don't remember?"

I stared at the back of his head, waiting for an answer. He finally turned around. His face looked more troubled than I'd ever seen it.

"Phoebe," he began. His voice sounding tired now. "Have you had any strange dreams since you were attacked that night?"

My face wrinkled in confusion. I thought back on the many dreams I'd had since that night—too many. Some so vivid that I'd wake in a sweat, screaming at times.

I nodded. "They're more like nightmares," I said with a shudder. "Why would you ask me that?"

"Would you tell me about them?" he asked, ignoring my question.

"I'd rather not." I shifted uncomfortably.

"Please." I could see the resolve on his face. He wasn't going to let this go for some reason. I gave him a defeated look.

"It's the same dream over and over really," I began. "I'm running, at least I think it's me? The girl, in my dreams, she looks just like me," I said defensively, as if he'd argued the point.

"Something is chasing me. I can feel it getting closer and closer . . ."

I subconsciously pulled my legs to my body. Marcus's face was paler than normal.

He didn't look entirely surprised at what he was hearing—like this was a nightmare he was all too familiar with. I stared at him curiously. He said nothing, waiting for me to continue.

"I'm screaming something . . . someone's name I think. I don't know whose. I can't ever hear it." I closed my eyes for a moment, trying to recall the memory.

My eyes went wide. "The growling," I breathed. "It was just like . . ." I put my hand over my mouth and looked back toward the window, and then to Marcus.

He looked uneasily at me.

"I wasn't fast enough," my voice cracked. "He had me by the throat. I can actually remember feeling the cold," I admitted as I put my arms around my shoulders, holding myself.

I closed my eyes and took a deep breath. *It was just a dream* I kept reminding myself—a very vivid dream of my horrific death, but still just a dream. A dream I never spoke of out loud to anyone, not even myself.

Marcus walked over to me and wrapped his arms around me. "Phoebe, I'm so sorry for making you relive that." His hands held my face now. He looked devastated. "I'm sorry I wasn't there in time to save you. I would have given my life for yours if I could have."

"Don't be silly. It's just a dream," I said wiping the tears off my cheeks. I smiled flatly. I didn't want to think about it any longer.

The sound of the clock chiming in the other room startled me. "Holy cow, it's 8:30?" As if on cue, my stomach growled. I suddenly realized how hungry I was and forgot all about the odd mood Marcus was in. "You must be starving! I can fix us something to eat."

"No, I'm fine. I ate when I stepped out a while ago," he added, still staring at me uneasily.

"You did? Oh, well, if you don't mind I'll just be a minute." I moved to get up.

"Would you like me to help you?" he asked.

"No!" I shouted, motioning for him to stay where he was. "I mean, no thank you," I repeated softly. There was no way I was going to relive the last "close encounter" again so soon. It was too hard having Marcus holding me so closely. The effortless attraction I felt toward him unnerved me a little.

He smiled understandingly and stepped out of the way.

I very carefully pulled myself up, keeping the blanket wrapped around my waist. I held it tightly with one hand, and with my free hand, I reached out and grabbed each piece of furniture along the way with great effort. I was hunched over like an old woman, moving slowly but deliberately. I glanced at Marcus. He was trying not to watch me—I think he was trying not to laugh, actually. I did my best to ignore him. I couldn't afford any distractions.

I was almost to my bedroom door. I smiled confidently. I stretched my arm out as far as I could. My fingertips were almost touching the wall. I lunged . . . and missed!

Boom! I was face down and in total agony. I moaned.

Marcus rushed over to save me from myself as he'd done so many times today.

"Just leave me here," I protested his help. "I'll crawl to the bedroom." I buried my face once again in the carpet.

He lifted me into his arms and carried me to my room, gently setting me on the end of my bed. He was smiling as though he were amused by something.

"Something funny?" I asked.

He shook his head, but the smirk on his face gave him away. "It comforts me to know that you are just as you've always been." He laughed out loud now. It was only the second time I could recall him laughing so heartily . . . under any other circumstance it would have been welcomed.

"I'm not always incapacitated!" I thundered. "I did fall off a cliff today, or did you forget?" I was angry now. How could he make fun of me like that?

"And your temper hasn't changed much either," he said still laughing.

"What are you talking about?" I yelled as I chucked a pillow at his head. "I don't have a temper!"

He dodged it effortlessly. "No." He laughed harder now. "You never did!"

I knew there was a double meaning here. But I was too angry to bother trying to figure it out.

"If you don't mind," I pointed sharply at my bedroom door. "Would you please get my robe from the back of the door?"

He grabbed my robe and held it out to me. His face held a crooked smile. He was clearly trying to suppress his laughter.

I snatched the robe abruptly from his hands and put it on.

"Now you don't have to be grossed out looking at my mangled body!" I snapped under my breath. Him brushing me off in the living room still smarted. "I'm sorry to have embarrassed you!"

I tied the robe securely around my waist before I looked up into his face. He looked as though he'd just been slapped.

I suddenly felt self-conscious.

"Maybe that was a little rude of me. Sorry," I apologized through gritted teeth. I evaded his stare. How is that fair? He laughs at me, and I'm the one apologizing?

"Phoebe, you misunderstand me completely." All sign of humor was gone. "Nothing about you embarrasses me. You're absolutely beautiful—scrapes, bruises, covered in Band-aids . . ." he looked at me lovingly. "I don't care what you look like. I'm just so happy you're alive!"

I frowned.

"As for my assumed embarrassment . . ." he moved closer to me, his hand gently caressing my cheek. I could feel my heart begin to race again at the touch of his skin on mine.

"I was taken by surprise seeing you so . . . exposed again. Feeling your skin so close to mine . . ." I closed my eyes as his fingertips trickled down my neck. His touch was strangely familiar, and I found myself leaning into it.

"It's been so long since I've seen you . . . held you . . ." his fingers brushed my lips, causing a breath of air that I hadn't known I was holding to escape. My heart felt like it could burst at any moment.

"I have to be so careful with you now." He spoke tenderly as his eyes looked deeper and deeper into mine.

"There is so much I want to tell you, so much I need to explain . . ." he spoke softer still. His voice was hypnotic. He could have asked me to jump off a cliff, and I wouldn't have argued.

"For now . . . you need to eat." He broke his stare and I snapped out of my drunken state.

Chapter 5: Breaking Down

My legs wobbled as I tried to get up. I couldn't quite shake the disoriented feeling I had.

As if sensing my confusion, Marcus offered to help me into the kitchen. "We don't want you to fall on your face again," he teased as he put his arm around my waist.

I let him help me. We did not want to fall on our face again. I thought to myself.

"Now, what may I get for you this evening?" he asked like he was a waiter at a fine restaurant.

I couldn't help but laugh at him. I found it hard to stay mad at Marcus when he was being so incredibly charming.

"I'll have the left over chow mein in the fridge," I said still grinning.

He picked up the Chinese carryout carton, printed with dragons and pagodas, and looked back at me questioningly.

"The forks are in the top drawer by the sink," I added.

He nodded as he went to the drawer.

"I'll just eat it out of the carton; unless you want some?" I offered.

"No, really, I'm fine." He wrinkled his nose as he handed it to me.

"I got it yesterday. It's not old!" I said defensively as I sniffed the chow mein to make sure it didn't stink.

"No, it's not that," he insisted.

"Then what?"

"I just don't like Chinese food much," he shrugged as he turned his face away from me.

I watched Marcus curiously as he fidgeted in his chair.

"Phoebe? Have you noticed anything . . . different about me?" he asked casually his eyes still evading mine.

"Yeah, You don't like Chinese food," I said in disbelief. I took a small bite of my vegetable chow mein—I loved it cold.

Marcus frowned at me from across the table.

"Ok," I conceded. "There are lots of things different about you."

He watched me in silence, as he seemed to be considering something. "Yes, well, I'm speaking about anything *extraordinarily* different," he clarified.

I took another bite. I didn't realize just how hungry I had been. I chewed while I deliberated over my response.

"Would you like something to drink?" he asked as I took another bite.

"Yes, please. There's soda in the fridge," I said as I continued to chew. Not very polite, but I was starving. And apparently *unattractive!* So why worry now about the rest of my appearance? Clearly I wasn't getting kissed anytime soon!

He had my soda in front of me before I could finish rationalizing my bad table manners.

"Thank you," I said as I opened the bottle and took a drink.

"Would you like one?" I offered.

"No, I'm fine. Thank you." He sat down again and waited for me to continue.

"You look at me like I'm some long lost love," I blurted out, catching him off guard. He opened his mouth to say something, and then shut it.

"I've only been with you for a day, but you make me feel like we've spent a lifetime together, a lifetime I don't remember;" I added softly, dropping my eyes. "But you do remember it, don't you?" My voice was barely a whisper.

Marcus opened his mouth to speak but said nothing.

I nodded my head.

"You are unlike any man I've ever known. Any human for that matter," I added offhandedly. "Aside from the fact, that you're a gentleman."

He raised his eyebrows a little.

"A rare quality these days," I explained, a hint of sarcasm coated my words.

I watched Marcus for a moment as he stirred uneasily in his chair. It was odd to see him looking so uncomfortable. He always appeared to be so sure of himself.

"I've never seen anyone with reflexes as fast as yours." I continued. "I still don't know how you saved me from falling down the cliff," I added, further validating my point.

"You can fly, I think?" I paused. He kept his face even, his eyes carefully watching me. His reaction was completely unreadable.

"Your eyes change colors with your moods. You run off into the night to chase down wild animals. You growl, hiss, become physically ill around blood," I half laughed to myself. How could anyone so strong have a reaction like that to blood?

"Yes, I *have* noticed something different about you," I mused as I took another bite.

He could see that I was debating something. His expression became guarded.

"Marcus . . .?" I quickly shook the thought away.

"What?" he urged, forcing a smile on his face; he looked just as nervous as I was.

"Forget it. It's too embarrassing. I can't believe I'd actually considered it." I took another bite.

"Tell me," he urged again. His face still held a faint smile.

I bit my lip, considering how stupid I was about to sound. "It's only one of the theories," I admitted with rose-colored cheeks. "Could you . . . I don't know . . . " I looked around the room, finally settling my eyes on the table before me. "Could you lift this table up . . . with one hand?" I continued to bite at my lip nervously.

"Can I what?" He looked stunned. He stared at me blankly as if he'd misheard me.

"You know, lift heavy objects? Punch a hole through a brick wall? Fly through the air?" I frowned, irritated by his vacant expression. Clearly he was going to make me spell it out.

"Fight the forces of evil, and all that good stuff," I explained.

"You think I'm a super hero?" he asked, his face full of wonder.

"Yes . . . maybe?" My voice didn't sound as confident as before. "It's better than the alternative." I shivered.

"I'm afraid to ask now," he frowned again.

"Oh come on, it can't be that farfetched?" I argued. "You dove over the side of a cliff, rescued me from a fatal fall, and carried my battered body back home. All in a matter of minutes! That's super hero stuff!"

He stared at me—expressionless.

"I've seen you fly across the room!" I insisted. "Well, sort of," I admitted softly, noting the disapproving stare that now hung on his face.

"The other conclusion?" He asked dryly, as he pinched the bridge of his nose, as if this conversation had suddenly become painful.

I huffed, deliberating whether or not I should continue.

He leaned back in his chair and folded his arms across his chest.

"Alright, but don't get mad." I took a deep breath. "I thought maybe you might be . . . a wolf?" I whispered the last part, hoping that by not saying it aloud would prevent him from thinking I was a lunatic.

"WOLF?" His eyes popped open.

"I don't mean a regular wolf," I interjected quickly, "I mean a . . ." I couldn't believe I was saying it out loud. "I mean you are human too, at least . . . I think so? So you must be . . . a *werewolf*?" I winced as I uttered the name. My shoulders rose above my ears cringing as I waited for the fallout. I didn't have to wait long.

"WEREWOLF! You think I'm a WEREWOLF!" he yelled the name each time he said it. He looked livid. Clearly, he had not expected this assumption over all others. I couldn't really blame him—it was completely absurd.

"Okay, okay, so you're not a werewolf. Superman! Are you like Superman? He could fly! You don't have to be *exactly*

Superman but similar, right?" I was babbling, and grasping for anything to pull me out of the hole I was now in. "Please don't tell me you're like the Hulk. You just don't strike me as the green type, although . . . that would explain the growling," I teased nervously.

"You think I'm the wretched beast I hunt?" he yelled out, still dwelling on the unintentional slam on his character.

My mouth popped open. For the first time in my life, I was without speech.

He couldn't avoid it now; he knew what was coming, and by the look on his face I knew he was bracing for it.

"I WAS BIT BY A WEREWOLF?" I yelled out in disbelief.

He sat there across from me, his eyes closed now. His hand was pinching the bridge of his nose again. He shook his head back and forth. He wasn't saying I was wrong.

"Marcus!" I yelled for his attention. "Was I bit by a . . . a werewolf?" I had trouble saying it out loud.

Nothing.

"Am I a werewolf?" I gasped. "Is that why you don't want to . . ." I put my hands over my mouth. I couldn't even finish the sentence. I was overwhelmed. It all made sense now, sort of. I stood up from my chair, and then sat back down. I didn't know what to do.

"NO!" he yelled out.

I jumped in my seat. His face was fierce.

"No," he repeated softer. "You are not . . . completely," he gritted his teeth. I could see anger building in his eyes. "And I do want to!" he snapped at me as if that remark would distract me from the other.

"What do you mean 'completely'?" I asked, making little quotes with my fingers in the air.

"It's complicated."

I pushed myself up from the table. "Now you listen to me Marcus Ashworth, you un-complicate it fast. You don't just show up out of nowhere, spend the day with me, and finish it off with announcing that I'm not 'completely' a werewolf!"

"Oh my God!" I slapped my hand over my mouth again. "Did I kill those chickens up the road . . . and that poor goat?" I squeaked. "Is that why you wanted to know when the last full moon was?" I was beside myself. I sat down again, my hand still covering my mouth, trying to hold back the impulse to be sick.

Marcus was pulling me up into his arms. "You did not kill those animals," he said as he yet again wiped away my tears. "You are not like the others—"

"Not like the others?" I interrupted. "This can't be happening . . . This isn't real! There. Are. No. Werewolves!" I shouted.

I was in the middle of a full breakdown; I could feel it. I ignored all sense of pain. I was numb all over. I pushed away from Marcus and ran clumsily out the front door into the night.

"Phoebe!"

The wind and rain just added to my misery. I couldn't tell the tears from the rain. My life as I knew it was over. I was a monster . . . not even human anymore. Marcus was a hunter and he was here to kill me. How long did I have before I would turn into some vile beast from hell? My friends, and family, I could never see them again. No one would ever be safe around me . . . not even Marcus. A deep void suddenly took hold of me. I could never be with him the way I wanted to. I was a fool to think he was in love me. Why would he be when he knew I was going to turn into a monster?

I ran until my legs couldn't carry my weight anymore. I fell to my knees, defeated. The rain, taking no mercy on me, fell harder.

I would never get married or have children, I thought as the storm beat down on me. "Who'd want to be married to a rabid dog?" I shouted angrily into the darkness. "Who would ever want to love me now?" I cried. I could feel my heart breaking into a million pieces as I curled into a ball, and lay lifeless on the road, hoping a car would come along and run me over.

The rain continued to fall, but it didn't bother me any longer. My tears had stopped. I stared off into the blackness; there was nothing left for me but death, and I waited impatiently for it.

I felt arms around me, pulling me up. Marcus was holding me. I didn't want to run from him again. I rested my head on his chest. I needed someone to hold me, if only for a little while.

"You are not a rabid dog," he said lovingly as his arms held me closer to him, shielding me from the rain. He started walking back toward the house.

"As for someone loving you, and wanting to marry you . . . " his voice cracked.

"I know," I interrupted. "I understand now why you didn't kiss me before . . . I don't blame you. And I won't be surprised when you have to kill me. It wouldn't be safe to leave me alive," I said hopelessly, accepting my fate.

"You should not have come out into the night alone." His words were harsher than his tone. "It's not safe."

But by now we were walking through my living room and I was a wet dog, literally. He brought me into my bedroom and sat me on the bed. His eyes, meeting mine. "Stay here."

Where was I going to go? My legs were limp noodles, and my will to live was gone.

He came back with some towels from the bathroom. He wrapped one around my shoulders, and with the other, began gently wiping my face dry. I sat there staring off into nothingness.

"Phoebe." He shook me slightly.

I looked at him through blurred eyes.

"Phoebe, I'm not going to kill you," he began. His eyes were soft, tender like his words.

"I could never kill you. Even if you were a . . . " he didn't finish. "You're not a werewolf!" His words were absolute.

"But you said I was bit." I grabbed onto his shoulders with both hands. I looked frantically into his eyes. He shifted uneasily at the sudden closeness of our faces.

"Yes, but from what I can tell, the bite wasn't deep enough," he sighed as a blank expression took hold of me. "The venom couldn't have had time to enter your bloodstream, at least not much of it anyway."

"Phoebe!" He shook me to attention again, my mind desperately trying to make sense of his words. "Think! Has anything changed about you since you were bit?"

I tried to think. I thought about hearing the ocean earlier from the parking lot when we'd taken a ride to the beach.

"I can hear things far off in the distance . . . things that I hadn't been able to hear yesterday," I admitted.

"The full moon . . ." Marcus murmured. "Is that all?" he asked.

"I could smell you earlier, when I stepped out my door," I admitted bashfully.

"You could smell me?"

"You smell like," I took in a deep breath. "The air after it rains." I couldn't look at him, it sounded so corny.

"You can smell my scent." It wasn't a question. He was awestruck.

"Then there are the nightmares." I continued. It's almost as if they're through the eyes of—"

"The wolf that bit you. It passed on its memories to you." Marcus spoke knowingly.

He'd finished my thought. I stared at him incredulously. How could he possibly know that?

"Anything else?" he continued excitedly, ignoring my shaken expression.

"Isn't that enough?"

"Phoebe, your sight, hearing, and sense of smell have changed, but that's all. Apart from the memories you're recalling," he added as an afterthought.

"I'm not a . . ." I couldn't believe I was saying it, "a werewolf?" I asked leaning closer, not wanting to chance anyone else hearing.

"No, you're not."

"I won't turn into a dog and howl at the moon?"

"No," he cracked a smile.

"Marcus, are you sure?" I could hear the desperation in my own voice.

"Yes. If you were going to turn into a werewolf, you'd have done it by now." He spoke with great assurance.

Without hesitation, I threw my arms around his wet body. I was elated; I wasn't going to die! I wasn't going to turn into a monster from hell! I could hear the hallelujah chorus playing loudly in my head; until I felt the instant tension that seemed to move through him. Remembering myself, I loosened my grip, shrugging as I tried to pull away but his hold around me became tighter.

"Phoebe . . . " Marcus's cool breath blew across my ear, sending a shiver down my spine. "I still can't do this . . ." His words were firm, but soft.

I let my hands drop into my lap. I felt his breathing become more erratic as I untied my soaking wet robe and let it fall from my shoulders. His eyes, a luscious shade of chocolate, wandered over my naked shoulders before they met mine again—a small glint of red now swirled through them.

I ignored the little voice in my head that told me to back away . . . I felt myself being pulled deeper into his stare. My hands moved involuntarily up his shirt. I could feel the tight ropes of muscle that made up his stomach and chest beneath my fingertips. He was a perfect masterpiece. God-like.

He moaned softly. His hand felt its way slowly down my side, resting itself on my thigh. He squeezed it gently, giving me a sensation of excitement and unexplainable fear, all at the same time. Still, I couldn't pry myself from his arms, or ask him to let go. I was right where I wanted to be. His fingers had twined their way into my hair. I could feel him gently pulling my head back. I breathed heavily, while his lips glided along my throat, barely touching. He pressed his nose against my skin, inhaling deeply. I gasped, surprised by his sudden action. His hands were behind my back now, holding me to him, leaving very little air between us.

My eyes fell shut as I took in the sweet smell of his breath, the cool touch of his hands, and the soft uneven rhythm of his breathing . . .

"Phoebe," he could barely speak my name. His voice sounded distant, like a dream. I didn't open my eyes. I leaned into his kiss; my neck longed for his lips to touch it again.

He released me abruptly, pushing me off him.

I stared at him, dazed, as if I were drunk. I tried to collect my thoughts, but his eyes still held mine, drawing me in again.

"We have to stop." His words were sharp.

"What? Why?" I reached out to him, resting my hands on his chest. The very feel of his skin against my hands was electric. "You really don't want me to stop, do you?" I asked playfully, still not breaking my stare.

He whirled me around so fast I landed on my back in the middle of the bed, his body on top of mine. He held his head down tight against my shoulder. I gasped, trying to catch my breath.

The sudden movement of my body under his as his fingers trickled down my side was more than he could stand. He moaned, the sound of it drawing me deeper under his spell.

My heart beat faster now with anticipation. I couldn't explain the wild attraction I felt for him. The raw need I had, to be possessed by him, physically. But also, a feeling of going home. I'd loved Marcus before; I could feel it.

"I can't," he shook his head. "I won't hurt you." His voice sounded frustrated, almost tortured.

"I'm sure I'll be fine," I panted under the weight of his body. He lifted up slightly as he realized my struggle. I moved my hands over his shoulders and down his arms.

"This can't be happening . . ." He whispered. "This isn't real. You *can't* be real"

I found his hand resting on my hip. I rubbed my fingers across the top of it and gave it a gentle squeeze. He tensed as I drew it up to my chest and placed it on my heart. "This *is* real!" I whispered a kiss across his ear. I knew he could feel every beat of my heart.

"You shouldn't have done that." His tone was firm. "You're making it impossible for me."

"That *was* the idea," I admitted bashfully. "I feel so comfortable, so safe with you."

"Don't!"

The harshness of his tone should have frightened me, but it didn't. "I feel like I've known you forever," I said, ignoring his warning. "I feel like we've been here before . . . close, like this." I lightly pressed my face against his cheek and inhaled . . . filling every part of my soul with him. I felt deliciously dizzy. I let go of his hand and with great effort, lifted his head away from my neck.

"Marcus, open your eyes . . . please."

"I can't." His voice was shaky. "I'll scare you."

I stared at his unprotected lips and decided to take a chance. I pressed my lips against his. It was like a surge of electricity had run through us. My mouth touching his seemed to jump-start his heart. My hands held his face as he kissed me intensely, almost wildly. It was as if he'd been waiting all his life for this moment, our lips were finally touching and he couldn't deny himself any longer.

His mouth fit mine perfectly. Our lips seemed to know each other. They moved together, anticipating every touch. His hand was moving down my waist and around my thigh now. Instinctively I wrapped my leg around his hip and gave him a gentle squeeze, my battered body long forgotten.

That seemed to be all the encouragement he needed. He put his arm under my back sharply and pulled my body tighter to his. His kissing was much more aggressive; I knew I'd won him over.

I held onto him, meeting every kiss eagerly. My heart pounded erratically, I had never expected our first kiss to be so powerful. I didn't want it to end.

His lips drifted from my mouth, leaving me gasping for air as they traveled over every inch of my neck, searching for the perfect spot to rest, but they never did. He worked his way down the base of my throat, pausing momentarily to watch my chest rise up and down with each breath I longed for. He glanced at me with dark amber eyes. My mouth popped open; a feeling of fear washed over me once again. He didn't let it linger. He quickly pulled me back to him. His lips claiming mine with such ferocity, I melted into his embrace. I wanted him desperately; the way I felt he wanted me.

I couldn't breathe . . . I put my hands up to his shoulders, my fingers digging into his skin. I tried to push him away. He misunderstood my heart's sudden reaction; his kisses became more passionate as he pulled me closer still.

My legs loosened their hold around him. The ringing in my ears was the only sound I could hear . . .

"Phoebe! Phoebe, can you hear me?" I could feel my body being shaken softly as

Marcus anxiously called out my name. "PHOEBE!" he shouted out again, slightly louder now.

My eyes flickered slowly, trying to regain focus. I could just barely make out his silhouette hovering over me. I could see his troubled face now as he moved my head from side to side examining my neck, searching for something. He looked at my shoulders, the top of my chest, frantically searching.

His eyes darted back to mine—they were full of fear. "Are you alright?" he asked urgently.

"I think so." I still felt disoriented.

"You scared me. I thought I . . . " his voice trailed off as he looked my body over once again.

"What are you looking for?" I asked a little annoyed.

He put his hands around my face, cupping it gently. "Never scare me like that again!" he commanded.

"I'm sorry," a tear leaked out the corner of my eye.

"No, no. It's alright," he assured quickly. "I didn't hurt you."

"Didn't hurt me?" I was so embarrassed. "What are you talking about? I ruined everything," I said through sobs. His face looked completely shocked. "I couldn't breathe right. My heart was pounding so fast, I . . ."

He drew me up into his arms and gently rocked me like a child. "I'm sorry I took your breath away," he mused.

I shook my head. "I didn't do that right," I cried. "I've never been with anyone like that before. I wanted you to be my first . . ." I cried into his chest, overcome with embarrassment.

He stopped rocking me.

I looked up into his face. He had a blank expression. His eyes drifted down to meet mine.

"You've never . . . been with anyone . . . intimately?" He spoke each word slowly so that I couldn't misunderstand the question.

"No," I squeaked. I was mortified. Marcus had to think I was an emotional wreck. I expected him to run out the door any minute.

He stared at me, his eyes soft and full of wonder. "Please don't misunderstand me, but why ever not?"

I was sniffling now, surprised by his line of questioning. I looked up into his face.

"I never found anyone I was *comfortable* with," I admitted.

His eyes widened. "You're . . . 'comfortable' with me?" His face held mixed emotions.

"Yes."

A strange expression crossed his face. He hadn't liked what I'd said. He stared at me apprehensively.

"I've had boyfriends. It's not that they didn't try, that I haven't been close before," I said defensively. I didn't want him to think I was completely naive. "I've just been waiting for someone my soul connected with."

"Your soul connected with *mine*?" His voice was barely a whisper.

My eyes were as low as they could go. I couldn't look him in the face now. All my cards were on the table. I was exposed and completely open for heartbreak. This was a disaster of epic proportion. I'd been too honest. This was too intense for a first date. This whole day had been too intense for a first date. I've never jumped into bed with anyone I'd just met. But I didn't feel that way with Marcus. My soul was telling me I knew him. Somehow I knew him, and that I was his. With everything that had happened, my time with Marcus had to be ticking away. I fully expected him to run screaming from my house at any moment.

"You've . . . never?" He was truly in shock.

I took a deep breath. "Never," I breathed out.

Marcus remained speechless.

"You must think I'm completely weird," I said, rolling my eyes slightly.

He shook his head. His eyes were full of excitement. He looked overjoyed as he pulled my face to his and kissed my lips softer, but just as eagerly as he had before.

I was taken aback. It took me a few moments to realize that I was back in his arms. My lips remembered what to do.

He gently pulled back. A look of peace hung on his face. "I can't believe you've waited for me all this time? That you've never loved another!" He was elated.

"I didn't know when I'd find you," I admitted shyly.

He smiled. "Are you truly alright?" he asked, sounding worried again.

"Yes, I'm fine . . . just embarrassed." I blushed, dropping my stare once again. "I keep passing out on you."

His finger caught my chin, lifting it to meet his stare. He smiled kindly. "You don't need to be embarrassed. Not with me . . . never with me."

He wrapped his arms around me, and cradled me against his chest. His hand soothingly stroked my hair. I closed my eyes and smiled, as I felt the love and safety of his embrace.

Chapter 6: Confession Time

I put my hand over my mouth as I yawned unexpectedly.

"It's late. You've had an unusually long day," he said as he rose from the bed.

"NO!" I grabbed his arm, pulling him back beside me. I felt suddenly flushed. I didn't want to tell him, but I knew that my reaction to him leaving would not be swept under the rug.

"I'm afraid to sleep," I admitted. "I don't want to dream anymore, and I don't want to be asleep if that monster comes back." I felt myself nearing hysterics.

Marcus reached out, placing his hands at the base of my neck. His fingers gently rubbed, as if trying to sooth me—it didn't work.

"I mean, what am I supposed to do? How would I fight it? Do I need a gun—are we talking silver bullets? Marcus, I'm not that good with a gun, and if it comes to sword fighting like in my dream . . . "

He put his hand over my mouth, silencing me. His face grew serious, his eyes flashing black with anger. "He'll never touch you."

I found myself inching slowly away from him. His words made me cringe, and although they were not meant for me, they terrified me, almost as much as the look on his face.

"Phoebe I'm sorry," he reached out quickly, taking my hand in his, and pulling me back to him. "I don't want you to fear me." His eyes were a soft brown again. Tender, like his words. I didn't doubt that he meant them. But still . . . there was something strange and familiar about his eyes. About the way he looked at me.

"What is it?" he asked.

My thoughts darted around my mind, back to my kitchen when he asked if I had noticed anything different about him. I gasped, as I began to fit the pieces together. "Your eyes," I breathed. "They change colors with your mood."

His face paled. He watched me anxiously, not making a move.

"You're incredibly fast," I whispered under my breath, as I remember how Marcus had grabbed me as I fell off the trail on the cliff. "You can fly!" He stood there, frozen while I ticked away the evidence, one item at a time.

"Your skin—" My eyes dropped to his hands, the cool hands that had just held mine. "It's always cold . . ." I shook my head in disbelief.

"Phoebe." Marcus reached for me, and then paused, as if changing his mind.

"You growl and hiss like some sort of animal when it's cornered," I insisted. "Your body tenses up every time my heart beats faster . . . my pulse gets stronger, and you . . . " My eyes locked with his as I put the last piece in place. I stared at him knowingly. "You're not afraid of blood, are you?" My question was completely rhetorical. He didn't answer. He didn't need to. "You're attracted to it!"

Marcus's face fell.

"No! It's not possible." I shook my head again, this time in disbelief. Hoping he would tell me I was wrong. "You can't be . . ."

Marcus said nothing and watched as shock engulfed me once again. There was nothing he could do.

My hands gripped my neck—the neck his mouth had been all over minutes ago.

"They're not real!" I told him, as if we'd been having a two-way conversation. As soon as I said it, I knew that couldn't necessarily be true. We'd just been discussing what percent werewolf I can add to my pedigree.

"Marcus . . . " My words broke off. This was crazy; there was no way I was going to say what I was thinking out loud. After the werewolf insult . . . no way! "No!" I shook my head and rose from the bed.

"Phoebe, we have to talk about this." He spoke firmly as he saw my sudden change of thought.

"No we don't. This is ridiculous . . . I don't even care!" I laughed nervously, trying to push the revelation from my mind.

"Phoebe," he warned.

"No!" I spun around facing him squarely. "I know it seems as if we just met, but somehow I don't believe that . . . and neither do you!" I pointed out quickly before he could object. "I'm falling in love with you, again." My eyes shifted uneasily. "It doesn't matter what we are. You're Marcus—just Marcus!"

I moved past him and opened my dresser with more force than necessary. I randomly grabbed some pajamas from the drawer and turned toward the bathroom. He was blocking my way.

"You're falling in love with me?" he asked, sounding surprised.

"Of course I am. How could I not?" I motioned to his perfection.

He sighed. "This isn't going to go away Phoebe. We *need* to talk about this." He sounded so rational, so calm, that I hated having to disappoint him.

"There's nothing to talk about . . ." I held the palm of my hand against his cheek. "I'm fine!" I assured, trying to ignore the cold against my skin. It wasn't freezing, but it was noticeably cooler. I forced a smile for him. He's *just Marcus* I told myself.

He reached up, took my hand, and held it gently between his before he pressed a kiss across the top of it.

"Stay with me tonight. Please. Whatever you are, you don't scare me." I wasn't sure whom I was trying to convince. All I knew was that I didn't want to be separated from Marcus again. My need to have him near me was stronger than ever.

"Phoebe . . . " he spoke slowly now. His words meaning to sooth, not infuriate me, but that's exactly what they did. "You can't help but be afraid of me; it's instinctive. Maybe in time . . . we're just not ready." He sighed. "It's best if I don't stay with you. I won't be far, should you need me."

He won't be far? Should I need him? Of course I *needed* him! Hadn't I just told him that I was afraid to be alone? And now he was telling me that he was leaving me, that we weren't ready to be together? Something inside me snapped.

"Fine. Go." I pulled my hand from his and walked toward the bathroom. "I'm going to take a shower. You can let yourself out," I said bravely over my shoulder. I wasn't going to stand here any longer and listen to Marcus telling me how much he loved me but couldn't be with me speech. If he thought I was one of those silly girls that could be lead on, he was sorely mistaken.

He caught my arm firmly. "Don't be angry." His voice was weary. "There is still so much you don't know."

I wouldn't look at him.

"Phoebe, you don't know how long I've loved and protected you," he began. His hands moved up and down my arms gently, the friction warming my skin. I could feel my heart start to beat faster. I was sure he could too. Why was he doing this to me?

"You don't know the life we had. The life I remember that you can't possibly and most likely never will." There was so much pain in his voice; it tugged at my heart.

"You don't know what it did to me when I lost you. You can't even let yourself imagine what I am."

"Then tell me," I breathed. I still wouldn't look at him. I wouldn't chance a glance at those eyes, those beautiful eyes . . . if he loved me like he said, he'd prove it. He'd be honest with me. He'd stop toying with me, bringing my heart to the point of explosion, and then stomping out the flames. If he loved me, he wouldn't leave me to the wolves . . . again.

"I won't make you fear me anymore than I have," he finally said, his voice a little tighter.

I pursed my lips. That was not the admission I'd hoped for. "I know more than you realize," I admitted reluctantly. "I know that it was your name I was calling for the night I died. Wasn't it?"

For a moment, I thought Marcus had stopped breathing. I looked back over my shoulder and met his bewildered stare.

"How could you know that?" His words were barely a whisper.

I bit my lip, deliberating my answer. "When I was lying on the road tonight, praying for death, it was just like in my dream, only then you never came for me."

His eyes glossed over. "I was too late." I could hear the devastation in his words.

I stared at him for a moment. "I had another life, didn't I? A life with you."

He looked uneasily at me, as if debating whether or not to answer.

I nodded my head in understanding. He didn't really have to say it. I knew by the look in his eyes that I'd guessed correctly. Somehow, I'd already known. Marcus and I had had another life together. And by some miracle, we'd found each other again.

I turned toward him and cupped his face with my hand, claiming his attention. His skin was soft, smooth, like the wings of a butterfly. I marveled at the feel of it. "I promise Marcus, I'm not afraid of you. Whatever you are, you're not dangerous to me. You'd never hurt me." My heart betrayed me. The very touch of his skin jump-started it. I debated for half a second before drawing my arms up around him. I kissed him desperately.

He hesitated then pulled me closer, eagerly meeting each kiss. His hands were around my neck, holding my face to his.

"We need each other," I breathed out, my lips claiming his again and again. I could feel it in my very bones. This felt right. I did need him, like he needed me.

"I do need you." He kissed me harder. "I need you alive!" With what looked to be all his strength, he pulled away from me. I staggered back a little, my body crying out in protest.

"I'm more dangerous than you can imagine," he shook his head. There was no play in his words.

"What does it matter who or what we are as long as we love each other?" I demanded. My resolve was strong. "I know you love me; I can feel it!"

"I do love you!" he snapped.

His admission should have brought a smile to my face. But it didn't. He was pushing me away still, and I didn't understand why. I could feel my blood start to boil again.

"I'm not staying with you until you know what I am. Not until you know the risk you're taking being this close to me. You're not ready yet. I saw that tonight," he added with regret in his voice.

Not ready? "I think I'm capable of deciding whether or not I'm ready to love someone."

"Not this time," he mused.

"I don't understand you," I scoffed. "You say you love me. You've all but admitted that we've had another life together . . . and here I am, willing to love you again, and you're pushing me away? I'm just asking you to stay with me—that's all!"

He cut me a look that suggested he wasn't going to dignify my challenge with an answer.

I threw my hands into the air. "Fine. You don't want to stay with me—don't. I can take care of myself." I turned and walked away from him, madder than ever. "I'll bet Brian wouldn't leave me to the wolves," I mumbled angrily under my breath.

Marcus appeared in front of me, stopping me short, his face tight with anger. He leaned in, close. The anger radiating off his body surprised me. "I'd kill him before he reached the door." His eyes were as black as ebony, deadly—like his threat.

I swallowed the sudden lump in my throat. My heart was pounding wildly from within as I studied his expression. He still hadn't backed away from me. The closeness of his body and the sweet smell of his breath called to me again. I tried to ignore it.

"I'm sorry," I whispered softly. I was still shaken by his reaction. My words came out broken, weak.

"Phoebe you don't understand," he growled, his eyes still fixed on me. "I could kill you!" His words were harsh and absolute.

"How?" I beseeched. "We've made love before, I never died from that."

His hard expression faltered. "I won't lose you again." His hand came up, cupping my cheek.

"Lose me? You won't lose—"

"No!" He held my shoulders tight, his fingers pressing into skin. "This conversation is over." His walls were back up. Marcus's resolve was stronger than ever. He released me, turned his back, and started to leave.

"Fine!" I yelled after him, all sense of rationale leaving me. I was beyond mad. It wasn't so much that he kept tugging at my heartstrings, only to keep me at bay, Marcus was hiding things from me. Things I desperately needed to know.

He kept walking.

"You shouldn't have let me think you wanted me," I continued. "Maybe we were together in another life, maybe you *did* love me, but obviously not enough. You let them hunt me down and slaughter me!" I was shouting, spitting the words with such venom, I didn't know where they'd come from. "I screamed for you! You left me to *die*, and now it's happening all over again!

I watched as the muscles in his back tensed with each tongue-lashing I gave—I wasn't finished. "Just save yourself the trouble of pretending to care and let them kill me. Or better yet, why don't you just do it yourself! Since I'm part werewolf anyway, you have an excuse!"

Marcus stopped at my bedroom door.

I put my hand over my mouth. I'd crossed the line, and I knew it. I was so angry I didn't think how cutting my words might be. I hadn't cared. I was terrified of him leaving—I'd surely driven him away now.

I could feel his tension. One hand was on the doorknob—squeezing it so tight I thought it would break off. The other was balled in a fist at his side. I could see his whole body seething with rage.

I moved away from him in case he turned around. I decided I didn't want to be that close to him after all.

He turned around to face me. His eyes were filled with anger. His lips were pressed together in a hard line. He was terrifying, more than my nightmare had been.

"Well, you get my point," I stuttered nervously. "I'll just see you later . . . maybe." I held my hands out at arm's length, motioning him to stay where he was and retreated backward slowly toward the bathroom.

"You think I left you to DIE?" he thundered.

I jumped, dropping my pajamas from my hands.

The gap between us was getting smaller. He was closing in on me slowly. I had backed myself against a wall. There was nowhere to go.

He was extremely close now, holding my arms firmly again; it didn't hurt, but I wasn't going anywhere.

"You don't know how many of those beasts I had to fight through, only to find your dead body. All because you wouldn't stay where you were told!" he hissed. "You can't imagine what that did to me!" His face was full of pain.

I couldn't speak. I was frozen with fear and a newfound guilt. Was that Phoebe responsible for her own death?

"*Maybe* I loved you? You don't think I love you now? I've never loved anyone but you!" His words were harsh as he spit them at me. Yet they were also full of a sadness I could never fathom.

"I'm leaving because *I- love- you!* Because I can't bear the thought of hurting you! I could never live with myself if I . . ." He shook his head back and forth, as if trying to shake away the thought.

"You have no idea how badly I want you. How long I've waited to hold you again. And here you are . . . so close . . . so willing to love me back, and I can't give you that. It takes all my strength to fight my instincts." He looked longingly at me. "Your heart beating next to me . . . your pulse racing when I touch you . . . you think I can't feel that?" he growled in frustration. "I'm denying my very existence by turning away from you now." He was nowhere near finished yelling at me. And I deserved it. To a point.

"Your control seems just fine." The words didn't come out as strong as I'd intended. "You have no problem pushing me away after you draw me in." My voice came back as I pushed his hands off me. "I shouldn't have been so open. I shouldn't have trusted you with my heart like that. I can't imagine what I was thinking?"

His eyes flashed blacker as a low growl came from his throat. He was truly frightening. I tried to step away from him, but he grabbed my waist and lifted me so fast my back slammed into the wall behind me. "You think I don't want you?" His body pushed up against mine, pinning me there. He had one hand on my waist and the other on my thigh, his fingers gripping me tightly.

I trembled against him. My heart pounded faster as his cool breath licked at my neck. "I can taste your skin without even touching you," he said breathlessly. His face moved along my throat, his nose, inhaling deeply. "I can smell your fear even now." he pressed his lips against my skin.

I gasped at the abruptness of it.

"I can feel your heart beating from across the room." His voice was strained. His eyes were fierce, animal like. I felt as if I could be eaten alive at any moment. I tried to look away, but his amber colored eyes drew me in deeper, the anger in them being replaced by desire.

"Do you honestly think I don't want to kiss your lips?" His mouth took mine forcefully, the very taste of it, intoxicating. I couldn't resist kissing him back. I didn't want to.

"I can feel your blood moving through your veins," he whispered in my ear. "It calls to me . . ." His eyes, still smoldering, watched my shaken reaction. "I've never loved anyone but you . . ." His voice cracked. His tone had changed. It was softer now, like swirling honey. I closed my eyes and let myself drown in it.

"I told you I'd never hurt you . . . that doesn't mean I couldn't." He growled with frustration. "If I lost control with you, I could easily kill you. I don't know if I'm strong enough . . . if I have it in me to not . . . I'd never had to worry about your humanity before. You and I were the same."

I stared at him open mouthed. Bits and pieces of my dream were fitting together before my eyes. No. I wouldn't let them. I pushed the thoughts away. He was Marcus I kept telling myself. Just Marcus!

"Being with you . . . close like this . . . makes me lose all sense of myself." His mouth glided across my neck again.

I swallowed loudly. I could feel the walls closing in around me. "I trust you."

My words came out shaky. I didn't believe them myself.

"You're not, understanding me."

My heart pounded with a need I'd never felt before. He opened his mouth to speak, and that's when I kissed him, hard and needy.

He pulled his face back abruptly, his mouth, gasping for air. "If I bite you, you'll die!"

The harshness of his words cut deep. I took in so much air that I started to hyperventilate. My eyes were large with panic. "I . . . can't . . ." my words broke off. Hearing him say it out loud sent me over the edge.

He released me instantly and sat me on the floor. His amber eyes were softer now as he watched me anxiously. He pushed my head between my legs. "Breathe."

It wasn't working. I was having a full-blown panic attack. I knew what he was telling me. I didn't want to believe it. He couldn't be. This wasn't happening! I was shaking my hands in front of me, trying to distract myself. "I . . . was . . . right?" I said each word between gasps of air.

"You've got to calm down Phoebe, breathe!" He urged again.

"You're . . . a . . . vampire?" I gasped again, struggling for each breath.

This was absurd: werewolves outside, vampires inside. Is Frankenstein going to knock on my door next? No, no, no! He didn't say that, I misunderstood. He'd said we were the same once?

Marcus was furious with himself. "Phoebe, can you ever forgive me? I didn't mean to scare you like that. You got me so *frustrated*." He was gritting his teeth a little. "I wanted you to understand. It's not your fault. I shouldn't punish you because you can't remember." There was anguish in his words. "I'll never hurt you like that again," he said as he put his hands around my face, trying to hold me still.

I grasped his wrists with my hands and looked at him with pleading eyes. "You're . . . a . . .*vampire*?" The word came out a little clearer this time.

"Yes," he said flatly. His eyes stared into mine.

"I was a . . ." I couldn't say it. "NO! You . . . can't be . . ." I shook my head.

"Phoebe, you need to calm down, you're not in any danger, I swear, I won't hurt you."

I trusted him. I couldn't explain why, but I trusted him without question. I just couldn't catch my breath.

"It's . . . okay . . . I'm fine . . . really."

"You are not fine. Now quit trying to talk and breathe slowly," he scolded. His eyes were a lighter shade of brown now. All signs of anger were gone.

I sat there on the floor with my head between my knees for some time before I felt like I could speak without passing out.

When I looked up, I found Marcus watching me anxiously.

"How are you feeling?" he asked. His voice was calmer now, yet still guarded.

"Fine."

He studied me for a few moments longer. "Phoebe, I'm so sorry I scared you." He reached out to take my hand. I flinched, pulling it close to me.

He paused and nodded his head in understanding. A look of sadness hung in his eyes.

I couldn't bear that. I forced a smile. "I guess I should take that shower now." I moved to my feet. A sudden wave of dizziness hit me. I held my head in my hands. Marcus caught me as I fell back.

"You're in shock." He looked really worried now.

"Shock?" I laughed. "That's silly, why would I be in shock?"

"I think that shower should wait," he suggested firmly.

"I'm fine, I just felt dizzy. I must have gotten up too quickly, that's all." I stood up slower this time, holding my head until I felt oriented. "See? I'm perfectly fine." I smiled at him as I wobbled into the bathroom and shut the door. He hadn't looked convinced.

"Phoebe, would you like me to leave?" he called through the door.

"Leave? Why would I want you to leave?" I laughed again. "I'll just be a few minutes. There's food in the fridge if you're hungry!" I shouted out as I turned on the shower water and got in.

The hot water eventually dulled my senses. The sharp sting that had hit my wounds had all but vanished. I let the water run down my face and body . . . I was beyond tired.

"Shock?" I mumbled to myself. Why would he think I'm in shock? That's ridiculous!

My thoughts drifted deeper and deeper as my eyes fell shut. It felt good to close them. I was so exhausted; I just wanted to sleep. I leaned my head on the side of the shower wall, letting the hot water sooth me as I drifted off . . .

Chapter 7: Sweet Dreams

I could feel the warm sunlight on my face. My eyes protested. They weren't ready to open. The blankets felt unusually soft around my body. I snuggled into their warmth. I was still so very tired.

I'd been dreaming all night, and my mind was having a hard time trying to decipher between dream and reality. All the visions from my sleep came rushing at me in an instant.

It was more like a slide show than a solid dream. Marcus had been there. I saw the two of us in a beautifully lit room filled with flowers, red roses to be exact. He was holding me—the way I wanted him to. He was kissing me passionately, our bodies together, like we were made for one another.

Then chaos: people in dark clothing rushing around, some wearing armor and carrying swords. I was looking out a window watching Marcus mount a horse. He was dressed all in black with a gleaming sword hanging from his side. Our eyes met as he gave me one last fleeting look before he rode off . . .

I saw myself running down a dark road. The moon overhead was my only light. I caught my reflection in a puddle as I ran past. My clothing resembled Marcus's. I was dressed like a warrior, with a sword in my hand.

I could see the shapes of bodies all around me in the darkness. Some were people I knew, friends I think. The rest were the mongrels that had invaded our land, the traitors that betrayed us. I could hear the snarls and screams from the battle up ahead. I ran as fast as I could through the bodies toward the fight. I needed to help Marcus. By the bodies on the ground, I knew that our numbers were dropping. I could hear myself clearly this time. I was screaming out his name, looking for him, hoping I wouldn't find him in the carnage.

The sound of paws coming along behind me was getting closer and closer. I'd killed so many already . . . I had to find Marcus. I had to tell him before it was too late.

I picked up my pace, running faster toward the meadow. I could see Marcus fighting not far from me. I moved toward him when I heard a deep growl from behind me. I spun around, drawing my sword high . . .

I recognized him immediately. Damen! His teeth in the light resembled a sinister smile. He wasn't looking for me this time—he was looking for Marcus.

"You won't touch him," I hissed as I asserted myself between them.

He growled, warning me to step aside. I held my stomach for a moment. I knew I was saying goodbye. Damen's eyes narrowed. He watched as I raised my sword up into the moonlight. A loud growl greeted me as I ran toward him, taking on my final fight.

Startled, I sat straight up, gripping my stomach as I had in my dream. I looked around the room frantically.

Marcus was in a chair beside the bed and was instantly at my side.

"Where is he?" I yelled out, still not focusing on any one thing in the room.

"Who?"

"Damen!" I shouted. "He was just here!"

Marcus leaned slowly back from me, his eyes wide.

"Who?" I could hear the uneasiness in his voice.

I was trying to see out my bedroom window from the bed—I didn't see anything but the tree outside. I frowned.

I looked at Marcus and saw his shaken expression. "How do you know that name?" he hissed.

"He's the one that killed me!" I said excitedly, as if I'd just cracked the biggest mystery ever.

"How did you know that?" he spat.

"You did?"

"Of course. He was seen fleeing after he . . . but you couldn't have known that."

"I was dreaming about it, just now." I paused thoughtfully, a blush coating my cheeks. "I saw so many things . . . You and I in this beautiful room filled with flowers." I snuck a glance his way. His mouth opened to speak, then closed. He looked . . . awestruck.

"I saw you leading troops to battle the werewolves, and me rushing to help, hoping to find you so I could tell you I was . . ." I stopped suddenly. I debated quickly and decided to skip this memory for now. I bit my lip nervously. "I even saw my fight with Damen."

I reached out to touch Marcus's face, noticing my bare arm for the first time. I followed it back to my body, looking down—I was completely naked.

"MARCUS!"

He immediately knew what I was thinking. His expression went from murderous to shockingly embarrassed in a fraction of a second.

"You fell in the shower and hit your head!" he said defensively. "I didn't look, honestly. I wrapped you in your towel and put you right into bed. I've been sitting right over there ever since, watching you, making sure you were alright." He pointed to the chair in the corner.

I looked down and lifted the covers back. I was wrapped in my bath towel. I reached behind my head, rubbing the small knot that was throbbing as we spoke.

"I told you that you were in shock," he scolded, trying to divert the attention off him. "You could have drowned!"

I smiled at him through flushed cheeks. "It appears you have me at a disadvantage Mr. Ashworth."

His face looked puzzled.

My eyes dropped as I smoothed the covers over me. "It would seem that there is nothing left for the imagination where I'm concerned," I teased.

Marcus blushed in his own way. But I could see there was something else weighing on his mind. He sat on the edge of the bed; his eyes reluctantly meeting mine.

"Marcus?" I was starting to feel uneasy.

"Phoebe, I have to ask. Do you really believe that I let you die? That I didn't . . . love you enough?" His voice cracked as he spoke.

I hung my head in shame. "No, I don't believe that. I think you loved me more than I can imagine. I don't know why I said those things to you last night." I buried my face in my hands.

Marcus scooted over, pulling me against him. I rested my head on his chest and breathed in deeply. It seemed like forever ago that I took in his sweet scent. "I was afraid for you to leave me," I admitted. " Marcus. I don't want to die."

"You won't!" he said with a hint of finality in his voice. "As for Damen . . . " His tone had turned venomous.

I shook my head. "I don't want to talk about Damen." I wiped my face. "Why bring up things that will only hurt you?"

"Hurt me?" he asked curiously, pulling back to see my face. "What do you know that would hurt me?"

My face gave me away.

"Phoebe," he warned.

"It was just a dream," I shrugged. "By some miracle, I was able to see bits and pieces from our past. Some good. Some bad. And some I don't understand yet . . . " I puzzled momentarily. "Besides, it doesn't matter anyway," I added cheerfully. "He's dead. And good riddance!"

I secured the towel around my body and went to my dresser for some clothes.

He caught my hand just as I reached for the handle.

"What makes you think Damen is dead?" he asked.

"Uhh, he would have to be, that dream I had would have been . . . " I paused to consider the era. " . . . at least five-hundred years ago. We've all been long since dead." I looked at him like I'd just stated the obvious.

He leaned in close to me. "Not all of us!" he whispered with a crooked smile.

My mind wrapped around that thought for a half a second. My eyes popped open as I realized what Marcus was saying.

"He's still alive!" I gasped. "But how could that be? How would you know that unless you're . . .? "

"Still living too," he finished my thought.

Every bit of last night came crashing down on me. Werewolves, rejection, panic attacks, vampires . . .

Marcus was a vampire, a *real* vampire! I looked at him out the corner of my eye. I smiled nervously.

"How old are you?" I asked.

"Hmm" he thought briefly. "I'd say . . . seven hundred and forty-nine this November."

"Seven hundred and forty-nine?" The words stuck in my throat.

He could see my wheels turning, slowly.

"You're . . ."

"Immortal? Yes," he admitted flatly.

He watched me closely, probably expecting me to crack up again—he wouldn't be disappointed. I put my hand on my forehead, trying to steady myself. My mind was on overload. I hadn't considered he was immortal.

"Perhaps you should lie down again," he suggested, eyeing me carefully.

"You're a . . . v . . . vampire?" I stuttered. I looked into his deep brown eyes. Saying it out loud didn't make it any easier to accept.

"And I'm . . . was . . . "

He reached out to hold me . . . but hesitated.

I stared at his arms that were half extended to me. Even though the thought of Marcus being an actual vampire scared me, I couldn't stand not being in them. I closed the gap between us and sunk into the love of his embrace.

He brushed his lips across my forehead. They eventually made their way down to mine. He pulled me into a kiss that sent a jolt of electricity through my body. Everything but my lips went numb.

I smiled into his glorious face. He was truly beautiful, and he loved me as much as I loved him. We'd always been meant for each other. Lifetime after lifetime, and now we were together again, with nothing to separate us.

Marcus watched the smile slip off my face. "What is it?" He looked alarmed.

"Was that . . . " I knew the answer before I asked the question. I'd seen those eyes in the window before. They were the very eyes that stared into mine before they killed me. I could feel my pulse begin to quicken. "Marcus, was Damen here last night?" The sudden look of rage that claimed him, answered my question. "Damen bit me?"

"Yes," he hissed.

Several things occurred to me at once. First, Damen was alive! He would remember the past. If he were to somehow tell Marcus the secret I'm hiding from him, Marcus would surely try to kill him. Marcus could die. I could lose him. But was it really my secret to keep?

Second, Damen had killed me. The look in his eyes last night was no different than in my dream: Murderous!

Third, and most disturbing of all, was that Damen had bitten me. I shared some of his memories. Damen would now be after me, now to turn me into a werewolf like him. Somehow, I knew this. He could have me like he wanted so long ago. I didn't want to share that information with Marcus either.

"Oh my gosh, is that the time?" I said in a panic. I stared at the clock wide-eyed. It was 10:45 am. "I gotta hurry! I forgot I'm supposed to meet Kim and Leah for lunch at noon." I abandoned my original choice of attire and rushed to my closet for a dressier outfit.

"Who?" Marcus asked.

"My co-workers. We're supposed to meet a new client." I shouted over my shoulder as I dug deeper through my wardrobe. "Do you have anything planned for today?"

"A little hunting trip," he said darkly. I could almost hear him smiling.

I spun around and looked at him with panic in my eyes. "You're not going after Damen are you?"

"You don't need to concern yourself Phoebe. I'll take care of this." He spoke as if he were going to drop off dry cleaning.

"No! Marcus, you can't. Just let him go."

"I like the black one. You always looked good in black," he mused, his head tilting slightly to the right, as if imagining me in it.

My attention was briefly diverted to the two dresses in my hands. I frowned. He was trying to distract me.

"Marcus, don't go alone. If you have to go, let me come with you, I'm sure . . ."

"NO!"

I nearly fell backward into my closet

"You're not to be anywhere near him. Do you understand?" His words were harsh and direct.

"I only thought that maybe if there were two of us, you'd have a better chance."

He flew at me, holding me tightly in front of him so that he had my full attention.

"I don't want to be in any way unclear about this," he growled. "You are not to get involved. You can't fight him. You'll lose!"

"I could distract him or maybe if you showed me . . . "

"NO!" he hissed. "I never liked you fighting before, and you're less equipped to do it now."

I suddenly felt insulted. "What do you mean, less equipped? I know I'm not the most athletic girl, but I'm sure I could fight off a . . . " I couldn't even believe I was having this conversation. I put my hands on the side of my face, trying to keep my head from exploding. " . . . werewolf, if my life or yours depended on it." Besides, I owe him. I thought. He took more than one life that night!

"You wouldn't last a fraction of a second before he rips your throat out again," he said harshly.

My hands were instinctively shielding my throat. He was right, and deep down I knew it. Still, I couldn't let him go. I felt just as protective of Marcus as he did for me. I lifted my chin high.

"I fought them before. With training, I could do it again," I said firmly. I didn't like being told I couldn't do something, even if it was for my own good.

"You had over a century of training; you're not coming with me, and that's final!" he thundered.

The clock chimed eleven.

"You'd better get ready; you only have an hour," he announced smugly.

I growled mentally. I threw the red dress back in the closet, not even bothering to hang it up, and stomped to the bathroom. I turned around to see Marcus beaming like the Cheshire cat. Foolishly, he thought he'd won.

"This conversation is *not* over," I said with authority as I slammed the bathroom door shut.

Chapter 8: New Opportunities

Kim and Leah were going to have a field day when they saw me. Kim would take full advantage of any opportunity to point out that she didn't cause my injuries this time.

Assessing the damage, I peeled away one of the Band-aids from my knee. "Unbelievable!" I removed a few more, squealing mentally as each one came off.

I opened the bathroom door to find Marcus right where I left him. He still looked irritated.

His expression dissolved almost instantaneously as I stepped out. I was wearing a slender black tank dress that hugged every curve of my body. I looked amazing, and I knew it. I used this to my advantage.

"Your healed!" he exclaimed.

"Well, all but the gash on my thigh." I tilted my body as I lifted my dress up my leg.

"It was a bit deeper, but by tomorrow, I think it will be gone too!" I smiled as I looked from my leg to his face.

He was staring at the pink scratch on my thigh.

"It's amazing isn't it?" I said excitedly, rubbing my finger over the new skin. "Maybe I have super healing powers! That's going to come in handy. This werewolf thing might not be so bad after all," I joked.

A soft moan came from his throat as he pulled me to him. His hands gently moved up my back, while his mouth claimed mine. His kiss was so passionate, so heady. It took my breath away—literally.

"Phoebe! Phoebe! Phoebe can you hear me?"

I could faintly hear Marcus's strained voice. I was still in his arms.

"Phoebe!" he called again.

A smile came over my face. I slowly opened my eyes to see relief in his.

"If kisses could kill," I mused.

"Not funny," he growled disapprovingly. "They can!"

"I didn't do it on purpose!" I smiled sheepishly. "I forget to breathe when you're kissing me. But," I sighed, "it's a price I'm willing to pay." I pretended to look put out.

I stood up straighter now, still keeping my arms around him. "Would you like to join us for lunch?" I asked sweetly as I played with the collar of his shirt. "You can meet my friends . . . we're having Italian . . ." I drug out each sentence with a sing-song note, trying to make it sound more inviting.

"I don't think your friends would like to watch me eat," he joked. "As for me joining *them* for lunch . . . " he broke off in laughter.

"Marcus!" I was horrified. "You can't eat my friends! Promise me you won't eat my friends!" I gripped his shoulders tightly, the thought of it made me instantly sick.

He howled with laughter. "Phoebe, I promise I won't eat your friends."

I sighed with relief. Marcus's diet hadn't occurred to me. Truth be told, I was avoiding that part of reality.

"What exactly do you eat?" I winced as I asked the obvious out loud.

"It's more drinking then eating," he clarified with a smile.

"How often do you . . . drink?" I closed my eyes, cringing as I awaited his answer.

"I can go a week without drinking if I need to," he said, sounding pleased with himself. "But any longer than that, I start to get weak. In my line of work, being weak isn't an option."

"Last night, you said you weren't hungry because you just ate," I prompted.

He knew what I wanted to know, but he let me squirm a little.

"Marcus!" I asked impatiently. "Did you . . . kill . . . " I whispered the word, " . . . someone last night." My body suddenly felt flushed. Perhaps ignorance was bliss.

"Phoebe, I am a vampire after all."

He watched the stunned look on my face then decided to let me off the hook. “Phoebe, I don’t have to hunt people for food.”

“You don’t!” I blurted excitedly.

“No.” His lips curled up into a smile. “That was the vampire of old. There are still some who prefer the old ways, but most are able to drink without killing humans now.”

He had my full attention.

“We own most of the blood banks around the world; we don’t need to take it when they give it so willingly.”

“You went to a blood bank last night?”

“No. I keep a small supply with me at all times just in case.”

“So you don’t have to . . . ever?” I was speaking in code now, hoping he would figure out the words I was trying *not* to say.

He grinned. “I haven’t had to kill a human for many decades now. But if I had to in order to survive . . . ” he paused, “if I were to get too close physically and lose control, or be tempted by a gushing wound, for example,” his eyebrows raised. “You were extremely lucky yesterday.” I could tell by the look in his eyes. He was serious. I couldn’t help but shudder.

“I’d better get going. We’re supposed to meet some guy from abroad that is interested in promoting my designs overseas.” I clapped my hands in excitement.

“You’d better not be late then.”

“How do I look?” I spun myself around—my dress twirling around me.

He caught my hand and held me out at a distance, as he looked me over. His lips were curled up into that infectious smile that made my heart skip.

“Hmm . . . you make it nearly impossible for me to resist you.”

I snorted. “Yeah right. You resist just fine.”

I stared at him for a moment, the smile on my face slowly slipping away as I wondered if I’d ever see him again. I wondered if maybe this had all been a dream, and as soon as I stepped outside, he’d disappear.

His fingers gently brushed my cheek, causing millions of goose bumps to run down my arms. I shivered. He was real all right.

As if reading my thoughts, Marcus smiled knowingly at me. "I'll see you soon. I'll try and pick up Damen's trail as quickly as possible."

"Marcus?"

"Phoebe, relax. I've been doing this for hundreds of years," he said casually, trying to dismiss my fears. "I'll be back as soon as I can; tonight, maybe tomorrow at the latest. It just depends where he leads me." He stepped closer. His hand reached around the back of my head and gently rubbed the knot that still smarted. I will destroy him this time," he added darkly. I couldn't help but shiver.

His eyes lightened a little as he took my arm and escorted me out the door.

It was a beautiful day outside. The sun had chased all the clouds away, not one was in sight.

I reached in my purse for my sunglasses.

Marcus was a step ahead of me. He already had his on.

"Hey, aren't you supposed to hide inside when the sun's out?" I asked casually as he opened my car door. "Don't you catch fire or something when the light hits you?"

"Don't believe all the legends, my love," his lips were on my neck before I had time to blink; he kissed it softly. "Daylight doesn't always mean safety," he grinned as he watched my shaken expression.

"Great!" I smiled flatly, thinking of all the ghouls and monsters that might come running down my street at any moment. "I'll see you later then?"

"You'll see me later." He smiled as he shut the car door for me.

I started the engine, waved, and zoomed off. I took one last look in my rear view mirror—he was gone.

***

I arrived at the restaurant with a few minutes to spare. Kim and Leah were already inside waiting for me.

The three of us had been in business together for six years. I designed, Kim helped create the packaging and displays, and Leah took care of all the marketing. We worked well together, a true testament of our friendship.

“Hey Phoebe!” Kim called out when she saw me. I waved and made my way over to our table.

“You look cute,” I complimented. Kim’s wild brown hair was pulled up into a lose ponytail. She wore a bright red sundress that had a bold flower print on it. It hugged her figure, flattering her subtle curves.

“Is he here yet?” I asked as my eyes searched the restaurant.

“No, but he should be here any minute,” Leah said glancing down at her diamond faced watch. Leah was decked out in the usual high-end designer suit. Today she wore a stylish, gray, pin stripped suit. It was flared at the waist, giving it an elegant cut that accentuated her narrow hips.

“He sounds very charming with that accent on the phone!” she gushed.

“What’s his name again?” I asked.

“D. Balfour,” she showed me a note with his name scrawled on it. The writing was very stylish.

“Balfour? What kind of name is that?” Kim asked.

“Scottish, I think . . . ,” Leah said as she stared at the signature again. “He sounded Scottish on the phone.” I could hear that dreamy tone in her voice. Leah was a sucker for a guy with an accent.

“What’s the D stand for?” I wondered aloud.

“I didn’t ask,” she admitted.

“I think he’s here,” Kim whispered as her eyes flickered from Leah to the door.

We both shared her reaction. It was like Apollo himself had walked in. A shockingly attractive man, with brilliant blue eyes that would shame the ocean, was staring back at the three of us.

My eyes couldn't help but take in the scenery. His skin was lightly tanned. His hair: shoulder length, golden brown, and neatly combed. It looked softer and healthier than any woman's I'd ever seen.

I couldn't help but note the muscled chest through his white button up shirt. His sleeves were rolled up partly, almost to the elbow. As for the khaki pants—they were tailored with him in mind. He was immaculate, down to his Italian leather shoes.

I took in a deep breath—I could smell a pleasant musky fragrance about him.

Where were these gorgeous men coming from? Were the gods falling from the skies?

His body moved fluidly as he walked over to us.

"Wow," Leah muttered under her breath.

"Would you be the lovely ladies I have the pleasure of joining for lunch?" he asked with a bow.

Leah stood up quickly and extended her hand. He took it as he bent over to kiss it softly.

"Mr. Balfour?" Leah's cheeks were all aglow.

He nodded.

"We spoke on the phone yesterday, I'm Leah Williams, this is Kim Sanders, and our designer—Phoebe Rose." She now motioned to me.

He kissed Kim's hand and turned slowly to me. His eyes were piercing. I stared at them, momentarily lost.

"Mr. Balfour," I found myself blushing.

He paused for a moment as he took my hand. His lips trembled against it. "Interesting fragrance you're wearing my dear," he said as his nose wrinkled a little.

"I'm not wearing any perfume," I admitted awkwardly.

Did I stink? I suddenly felt self-conscious.

Kim leaned over and took a subtle whiff. "You do smell good Phoebe."

Leah shot her a disapproving look.

"I'm sorry if it bothers you. Perhaps you'd be more comfortable sitting across the table?" I suggested as I motioned to an empty chair between Kim and Leah.

"I think I can endure," he smiled, leaning in closer. "You're really quite alluring, especially the color on your cheeks."

I blushed a rare shade of scarlet to be sure.

I was glad the waiter came over to take our drink order; it diverted everyone's attention.

"We really do appreciate you taking the time to meet with us Mr. Balfour," Leah began.

"Not at all Miss Williams, the pleasure is all mine."

We got acquainted over lunch. Kim told all about our recent trip to England—leaving nothing out.

"You should have seen her," Kim said as she shoved in another bite.

He glanced casually my way. "How is your arm now?" he asked. His eyes not connecting completely with mine.

"It's fine—" I blurted out quickly, "It really wasn't such a big deal after all."

"Not a big deal!" Kim continued. "You should have seen the blood."

I shot Kim a quick look of death. She ignored it. She was too captivated by our guest.

"Did you get a look at the man?"

"Oh it wasn't a man. It was some kind of dog," Kim blurted out.

"A dog?" his attention seemed piqued.

"Kim, I'm sure Mr. Balfour doesn't want to hear about what a bad time we had in his country," Leah scolded while still maintaining a pleasant smile.

Kim blushed as she took another bite.

"Well, it's not really my country," he interjected. "I just base a great deal of business out of London."

"Would anyone like any dessert?" The waiter appeared suddenly. The question was for everyone, but his eyes were on me. A large grin spread across his face. He was almost leering at me.

"No thank you," I spoke up. I wanted to get out of there quick. Something felt very wrong . . . and creepy.

Mr. Balfour cleared his throat, snapping the waiter out of his fixated stare.

"None for us either," Leah answered as she shook her head no to Kim.

Kim frowned and placed her napkin on the table. "No, nothing for me. Thank you."

"Just the check then," Mr. Balfour instructed.

"So, when would you like to see one of our displays?" Leah was taking charge of the conversation again—thank goodness.

"Perhaps tomorrow afternoon?" he suggested.

She nodded her head.

"If there won't be anything else," the waiter began.

Mr. Balfour had his wallet out before the waiter handed him the check. He placed some cash in the booklet. "That should take care of it, my good man."

"Oh, please, let us treat you," Leah said as she extended her hand to the waiter, reaching for the ticked book.

"Absolutely not. The pleasure has been all mine," he said as he rose from the table.

I stood along with him. "I have to be going as well. Thank you again, Mr. Balfour." I extended my hand.

He took it and brought it to his lips once more. I could hear his heart beating rapidly now, his blue eyes looking right through mine.

I shifted uneasily. I couldn't help but think I was having a moment of déjà vu. I couldn't figure out why I was so uncomfortable around him. I felt like he knew things about me that I didn't.

"Until tomorrow . . . perhaps we could discuss that trip abroad." He moved in closer, his hand still holding mine. "I can assure you: your travels will be safer with me." There was something sinister about the way he said that.

"Ladies . . ." he smiled brightly as he tipped his head and walked away.

"Now, that's a man!" Kim nearly shouted when he was out of earshot.

"Kim, I've never been so embarrassed," Leah thundered. "Why did you have to tell him about Phoebe getting attacked? She doesn't want to talk about that, and do you really think he wants to hear that she was bit by some rabid dog, or worse—some psycho while visiting his country?"

"I've got to go," I said abruptly, grabbing my purse.

"Phoebe I'm sorry, I didn't mean to embarrass you."

I looked into Kim's big brown eyes. She was always so kind, I could never really be mad at her. "It's alright. Don't worry about it," I smiled at the both of them now. "I really have to go, I'll call you both later, ok?"

I didn't give them time to answer. I rushed out the door. Something was wrong—I could feel it.

I drove home, constantly looking over my shoulder. I felt like I was being followed; although, I didn't see any actual evidence of it. I couldn't figure out where I'd heard that name before?

"Balfour . . . Balfour . . ." I repeated it over and over in my head.

Tap, tap, tap.

I jumped in my seat. I stared out my car window with a confused look on my face. I'd driven home and was parked in my driveway without even remembering getting there. I turned my car off and opened the door.

"May I?" Mr. Balfour extended his hand to help me out.

I hesitated for a moment. Not wanting to be rude, I took his hand.

"I must confess: I followed you," he admitted with a forged look of guilt on his face. "I hope you don't mind?"

I opened my mouth to speak but nothing came out.

"You forgot this." He handed me my wrap.

"Oh! Thank you. I didn't realize I'd left it."

"Perhaps in your haste to leave?" he suggested with a smile.

I suddenly felt self-conscious. I could feel myself blushing again.

"Miss. Williams suggested that since I was returning your wrap to you, I might take a moment to look at your latest collection."

"I wish she'd called me. I don't have anything to show at the moment. I gave Kim all my completed pieces last week for packaging. I can give you some snap shots, I suppose. I keep them for reference," I explained. "Or if you'd prefer, I can make up a few pieces; I'll just need a few days."

"The photos will be fine," he assured.

"I'll just be a minute." I ran inside to my desk, pulled out an envelope with the latest photos, and turned back toward the door.

"Huh!" I jumped. I brought my hand to my heart, trying to steady it.

"I didn't mean to frighten you," his voice was low.

"No, I just didn't expect you to be behind me," I laughed nervously. "Here you are." I handed him the envelope.

His thumb caressed the top of my hand as he took it slowly.

"I make you uncomfortable, don't I?" he said knowingly, the corners of his mouth curled up a little.

"It's just the way you're looking at me," I confessed, trying to avoid his stare.

"I'm sorry. I don't wish to make you feel uncomfortable . . . it's just that you remind me of someone, someone I knew a very long time ago . . . someone very dear to me."

I nodded my head in understanding.

"Well, I'll leave you to your evening," he leaned in and kissed me softly on the cheek, his lips lingering longer than necessary. "Until tomorrow," he bowed his head and slipped out the door.

I stood there for a while with my hand on my cheek. I could still feel his kiss. His scent lingered heavily in the air . . .

"Where have I heard that name before?" I thought aloud.

I looked over to see Marcus standing in my doorway—I hadn't even heard him open the door.

"Marcus!" I rushed over, throwing my arms around him. "You're back!"

He pulled back abruptly.

"What's wrong?" I found myself stepping away from him.

His eyes darted around the room.

"What is it?" My voice cracked.

"I can smell him; he was in the house," he growled.

"What?"

I inhaled deeply . . . I could smell the ocean, I could smell the sweet smell of Marcus, and . . . My eyes widened. "I had a visitor."

"You let a werewolf in your house?" he hissed.

"A werewolf! No, it was that man I met for lunch, the one who wants to promote my jewelry line."

Marcus moved in closer. "I can smell him on you." I could actually see his anger rising as he looked me over.

"He wasn't a werewolf." I protested.

"I know his scent," he snapped. "I've been tracking it ever since I left you. I was just past the Washington boarder when I realized he doubled back here."

I looked at him in disbelief. "Washington? How did you get there and back so quickly?"

"I'm fast."

I didn't have a chance to marvel. "Marcus, I promise you . . . there was no one else here. I'd have seen a werewolf in my living room, I'm not blind!"

"Phoebe, he wouldn't necessarily be a wolf now. There's no full moon." Marcus turned his head slightly, looking at me through the corner of his black eyes.

"What do you mean he wouldn't be a werewolf?"

"I mean that he would look like a normal human."

My mind couldn't comprehend what he was saying.

"You're safe." He sighed contently, looking momentarily relieved that I was all right. His black eyes sparkled like ebony as they looked into mine. I could feel my pulse begin to race as his cool fingertips ran along my jaw line and down the side of my neck. I closed my eyes as he pulled my face toward his. I waited for the moment his soft lips would touch mine. The moment he held my body close to his as he embraced me tightly . . . this would not be that moment.

I opened my eyes to see his face dangerously close to mine. He was frozen. His eyes stared past me. They were black with fury, his jaw clenched tight. I could feel the tension running through the fingers that still held my face.

"Marcus?" I breathed. "You're scaring me."

His eyes flickered sharply to mine. I instinctively tried to back away—he held me tight.

"That beast was close enough to kiss you, and you didn't tell me!" His voice echoed with rage.

"What are you talking about?" I asked desperately, trying to pull away.

"He kissed you!" he hissed through gritted teeth. He held my arms tightly—I wasn't going anywhere.

"It was just a polite kiss on the cheek!" I said defensively as I tried to pry his fingers away.

His eyes narrowed. His fingers released their hold on me.

"Did he hurt you?" His voice was anxious.

"What?"

"Did he hurt you?" he asked again, more impatiently this time.

"No! No more then you just did," I snapped, rubbing the circulation back into my arms. "At least Mr. Balfour didn't man handle me."

"Balfour?" His expression became lethal.

"Yes. The man that was here—he wants to promote my jewelry line overseas," I said crisply. Annoyed that I had to keep repeating myself.

Marcus closed his eyes and pinched the bridge of his nose again. A look of frustration overtook him.

"I didn't mean to hurt you," he began. "It's just that when I smelled his scent on your skin—" he wrinkled his nose in disgust. "Phoebe, he could have easily killed you."

"I smell?" I couldn't help but feel insulted.

"Phoebe," he paused for a moment; he looked as if he was trying to collect himself. "I know that name . . . Balfour. Damen Balfour."

"Damen? No. That can't be." I shook my head.

I stared at Marcus, hoping I'd heard him wrong. My mind drifted back to Mr. Balfour's deep and intense eyes—how they looked at me so longingly, so knowingly. I couldn't understand why I felt uncomfortable around him, why I couldn't get away from him fast enough. Even his smell seemed so familiar . . .

A flash from my dream came at me. His eyes, staring down at me . . . his yellow eyes . . .

"D. Balfour . . ." I repeated his name under my breath, still in a trance like state.

"Marcus!" My eyes were full of fear—I knew he spoke the truth.

"He won't touch you again Phoebe, I swear it!"

I shook my head in disbelief. "I thought he wanted to kill me? Why would he kiss me? It doesn't make any sense?" I felt myself holding my cheek again.

By the look on Marcus's face, I knew he had the answers to my questions.

He sighed. He retreated to the couch to sit before he reluctantly met my stare—I couldn't help but marvel at his beauty.

"This was so long ago, and I'm not sure me telling you now will help?" He looked worried, as if something bad were going to happen.

I walked over and sat down beside him. I wasn't afraid of Marcus. I didn't hesitate for a moment to put my arms around him and hold him close to me. There was no safer place for me. I rested my head against his shoulder.

His arms wrapped around me and my heart reacted as it always did when he was so close—erratic. I looked up into his glorious face and took advantage of his unprotected lips. I kissed him feverishly. I wanted him to know that he didn't have to worry, that I loved him, and nothing would change that. Not some pushy werewolf, and especially not something that happened five hundred years ago.

"Careful . . . " he whispered.

I pulled my head back to examine him closer. "You don't have fangs."

"Not always," he grinned.

At that, my mouth dropped open.

"You would only have to rub against them a certain way . . ." he didn't need to finish; the look of shock on my face told him I understood. He grinned.

He took my hands and brought them to his chest, holding them there. His eyes looked tenderly into mine. "I love you. I've always loved you. From the moment I saw you so very long ago . . . I've never been able to let go of you."

"I know," I nodded. And I did.

"All right . . ." he conceded.

Chapter 9: Vampires and Werewolves

"I can't possibly tell you everything now, but I will try to tell you everything I can." He spoke slowly so that I could take it all in.

"The feud between the vampires and werewolves has gone on for nearly one-thousand years. Before the war, werewolves were our protectors during the daylight hours, but over the centuries we've evolved and found that we could also go out into the sunlight. With this new freedom, vampires became aware that our daytime protectors had been forming a secret army to annihilate our species." He paused briefly then continued. "They resented the vampires for keeping them as slave-like creatures. They wanted their own freedom to roam as they pleased, without restrictions."

"I guess you couldn't fault them for that; everyone wants to be free," I said.

"No!" Marcus hissed. "Werewolves cannot be allowed to roam as they please. They wreak havoc everywhere they go. They *have* no control. They kill all in their path or infect entire populations and create more werewolves."

"Oh, I didn't know . . ." I looked downward as I thought of me being partially werewolf now. Was I going to infect others? Would I kill as well?

Marcus somehow read my mind. "You are not like these werewolves Phoebe; you are not truly a werewolf. You can't turn others." His face looked worried now. "I don't understand how, but somehow Damen managed to bite you without infecting you, completely."

"Why does that bother you, aren't you glad I'm not a werewolf?"

"Of course, it's just . . . how did he maintain that control? I've never seen anything like it. He's changing again. I don't know what his limits are. That makes me very worried."

I tried to understand the magnitude of what Marcus was saying, but couldn't.

"Now, during the initial uprising," he continued. "Damen, who was a relatively young werewolf at the time, joined Aidric—the leader, and the oldest of the werewolves. Aidric gave Damen his own army of werewolves to lead against the vampires. There were nearly fifteen hundred by the time we became aware of the population growth. They outnumbered us greatly, nearly five to one."

I stared at him. I was completely engrossed in his words.

"Vampires have always tried to keep a secret identity. It has secured our existence for many thousands of years. If the werewolves' numbers were to grow too large, the knowledge of their existence, as well as our own, would be at stake." I could hear the desperation in his voice.

"Are there that many of you still?"

He nodded his head. "There are central covens on each of the main continents, to maintain the population growth and to ensure our secret way of life. We are free to come and go as we like, so long as we honor the rules of the ancient one."

I was on the edge of my seat. "I had no idea . . ." I was truly amazed. It was like an ancient civilization had been discovered, and I was the only one in the world who knew about them. They had their own rules, government, and lifestyle. It was amazing, and frightening, how long they've lived among us—undetected.

"I was born in England in the year 1260," he continued thoughtfully. "The war had been going on for nearly three-hundred years when it passed through my family's lands. I was twenty-six at the time. I had arrived home to the brutally murdered bodies of my father, mother, and two younger sisters." His face looked devastated, as if speaking of the carnage brought fresh sorrow to his heart. "The werewolves killed everyone. The servants, the livestock; I had nothing but stone walls left."

I reached out and gently squeezed his hand. "I'm so sorry, I can't imagine." My heart ached for him.

He smiled flatly. “It was at that time that an elder named Luther came through the ruins of my family’s estate, with a small army at his side.”

I opened my mouth to speak but said nothing.

Marcus's eyes locked with mine. “I knew what they were the moment I saw them,” he said. “There’d been whispers of such men . . . legends . . . I remember how scared I was of them.”

My thoughts were spinning wildly in my mind. Never had I imagined that I’d be sitting in my living room, talking to a vampire, about an ancient war with the werewolves.

“The werewolves had taken everything from me.” He spoke desperately. As if that was to justify what he was about to say next. His expression hardened. “Luther took pity on me. He gave me the choice of immortality to avenge my family. To rid our land of the vile beasts that plagued them.” He spat the words with such hatred . . . I found myself cringing at them.

“So that’s how you became a vampire?” He had finally answered the question I had been nervous to ask.

He shook his head. “That’s how I *decided* to become a vampire. Not how I was turned. But that is another story,” he added quickly as he saw the question pop into my head.

“After I was turned, Luther organized an elite group of vampires known as Moon Hunters to track down and destroy all werewolves—with the exception of a few. There are only twenty-six of us.”

“Twenty-six?” I couldn’t help but notice the similarity. Marcus had been twenty-six when he’d been turned, he’d said.

“I thought it was a good number—symbolic.” he smiled slightly.

“We’d managed to wipe out most of the pack, or so we thought. Damen had always kept his strongest wolves with him. He retreated for a time and came back with stronger werewolves—much stronger than we could have imagined.”

Marcus got up and started pacing the room. His hand began rubbing the back of his head.

I knew that reaction. “What is it?”

"The wolves have an unusual ability . . . they can turn whenever they want." His eyes met mine.

"WHAT?" I jumped to my feet. "You said he could only turn when there was a full moon!" I protested.

"I didn't say that!" His voice raised in defense. "I said he wouldn't necessarily be a werewolf; he could be in a human form."

I couldn't believe what he was saying. Damen could turn from a human to a werewolf at will . . . he could bite me, or kill me, anytime he wished?

"The full moon means nothing?" I asked, trying to remember all the stories I'd ever heard.

"The werewolves have also evolved. But they are still slaves to the moonlight."

"He could have killed me earlier . . . " My eyes wandered the room, not focusing on any one object.

I hadn't even seen Marcus move toward me. He was holding me close now. I leaned into his chest, using his body for support—I felt as though my legs could give out at any moment.

I listened for his heart—still no beat. How can someone so real, so physically alive, have no heartbeat? I gripped him tighter.

"He kissed me," my words came out softer than a whisper. I could feel Marcus's arms tensing up as they held me. "Why?"

"I can only guess, I'm not certain . . ." his voice trailed off. His thoughts sounded far away. I didn't press him. It really didn't matter.

"He knows you're with me, doesn't he?" Somehow I knew the answer. He nodded.

"Of course. He could smell you on me at the restaurant. His nose was all wrinkled up like I stunk." I huffed.

"He thinks *I* stink?" Marcus said in disbelief.

"He knows things about me . . . the old me . . . doesn't he? I could tell by the way he looked at me."

Marcus's eyes were darkening again. "He knows that you've changed," he growled. "He knows exactly how *much* you've changed."

I stepped back a little, giving him space. I was trying my best not to be frightened by his expression. "Marcus . . ."

I jumped when the phone rang. I had forgotten all about the outside world. I reached for the phone, took a breath, and said rather weakly, "Hello."

"Hey Kim, what's going on?" I looked at Marcus. His condition hadn't improved. In fact, it had gotten worse. I could see the muscles in his jaw tightening.

"No, I can't make it over right now . . . I'm packing, I have to head up to Oregon in the morning, remember?"

Marcus looked at me sharply. He was hanging on every word I said. His face showing he was more anxious by the second.

"I'll be gone a few days. I may have to head up to Seattle," I continued with my conversation—my eyes never leaving Marcus's.

"If I have to go all the way up to Seattle, I won't be back for another week," I explained. "They still need me to okay their set up. I'm just waiting on their call."

"I will. I'll talk to you soon. Bye."

I hadn't even hung up the receiver when Marcus began grilling me. "You didn't tell me you were planning on leaving tomorrow."

"I have to," I began. "I have customers who are expecting me. I was supposed to leave today, remember, but I didn't think I'd be able to after the fall I took?" I smiled sheepishly, still embarrassed that the reason I'd fallen off the side of a cliff was because I was pouting.

You're not going anywhere without me. It's not safe."

"Why don't you come with me," I suggested, shrugging my shoulders a little.

"I should get you out of here . . . Damen will have a harder time finding you," he thought aloud to himself.

"Do you have family here in town?" Marcus asked suddenly.

"Um, my mom used to live here. She died a few years ago," I explained. "I don't have any siblings."

"Your father?" he prompted.

"He passed away some time ago . . . I was very young." I got up and walked into the kitchen for a glass of water, and drank slowly. I didn't like to talk about my dad to anyone. It was too painful.

"I'm sorry," Marcus said from behind me as he rubbed my arms gently.

I turned to face him with a forced smile.

"So, you'll come with me?" I asked again, desperate to change the subject.

"I'll come with you," he said as he lowered his lips to mine. His kiss was soft and sweet.

He pulled his head back a little. I could feel his eyes watching me—my eyes hadn't opened yet. I was imagining myself in this moment forever.

Reluctantly, I opened my eyes to find his face curiously watching mine. "What are you thinking?"

"I was thinking about the first time I saw you, " he laughed lightly. His eyes were far off as he recalled what seemed to be a fond memory—he smiled to himself. "You were in the garden practicing with Raymose," He grinned.

"Raymose?" Why did I feel like I knew that name?

"Your mentor, and friend," Marcus explained.

"You were so swift with a sword—graceful; it was like watching a beautiful dance," he continued, his eyes, still having that far off look about them.

"Raymose was enamored of you, like many others." He winked. "You could have run him through and he wouldn't have complained."

"Was I very good?" I asked. The thought excited me.

"You were good in controlled settings," he admitted. "Raymose would never have taken the upper hand."

"He let me win?" I asked in disbelief.

"Well, you were only practicing. Your father wouldn't have allowed you to fight, at least not any formal battles. You were . . . protected." He smiled and bowed his head.

"That's funny, Damen did that earlier." I foiled my eyebrows, recalling the memory.

Marcus's smile was gone. "Did what?" Marcus hissed.

I jumped a little. I still wasn't used to Marcus's hissing.

"He bowed when he met me. I thought it was . . . unusually polite," I shrugged my shoulders as I took a banana from the counter and began peeling it.

Marcus's eyes were black again. His lips were pressed in a fine line. I could see his face hardening. "He *bowed* to you?" he nearly spit the word.

"Yes," I squeaked, taking an unusually large bite.

"He has the nerve to *bow* to you, to *kiss* you?" he thundered.

"Marcus, I don't understand." I mumbled, trying to swallow the obstruction in my mouth. "Why would him bowing offend you?"

"Damen was your personal protector!" He said angrily.

"My what?"

"Your father wanted you protected at all times. Damen was the strongest werewolf he'd seen . . . aside from Aidric. He knew that if Damen were in charge of your safety, you'd never be in danger. He didn't count on the beast falling in love with you."

The thought clearly repulsed him.

"He was in love with me?" I gasped. It was like a light clicked on in my head.

Marcus looked at me with alarm.

My eyes darted around as my brain worked fast to recall the memories of my dreams.

They flashed from the beautiful room where Marcus and I were holding each other—to the room where I was looking out a window, watching Marcus ride off to battle the werewolves, to the street where I was running toward the battle. Then to me, standing before Damen, before he attacked. I looked . . . frightened.

I gasped. "The images . . . they not mine!" I nearly shouted. "They're Damen's!"

"What do you mean?" his voice was shaky.

"Not all of them, anyway . . . I thought they were my visions last night . . . but they're not.

Marcus was trying to understand what I was saying.

"In my dreams," I explained. "He's watching us. He saw us in our room!" I felt strangely embarrassed. "He saw me naked!" I cringed as I covered my chest with my arms. My face felt instantly flushed. I felt violated at the very idea.

Marcus looked murderous. "How could he have been so close without my knowing it?" he snapped.

"You were . . . otherwise . . .distracted?" I suggested, blushing a rare shade of crimson.

Marcus couldn't help but grin. "Perhaps," he conceded.

"He watched me as I watched you ride away," I continued slowly. "He watched me run down the street calling for you . . ." I stopped talking as I considered what I was about to say. My mind worked silently as I debated.

"You're not telling me something." Marcus's tone was accusing, sharp.

I backed away from him, allowing a good three feet between us.

"I'd rather not say." I put my hands out, motioning him to stay where he was.

He closed the gap between us before I could blink.

"Phoebe!" he demanded.

"I'm sorry. I can't. I don't trust these memories. I don't understand them." I insisted.

He reached out and touched my face softly. "Let me help you," his eyes were softer now, but still dangerously insistent. He was trying to work his magic of persuasion.

"I don't want to hurt you." I hid my face in my hands, breaking his stare.

"Is it that bad?" his voice was growing rougher.

"I think it is," I ducked away from him and walked out into the living room.

"Phoebe. You don't have to hide anything from me." His voice was assuring, but not enough.

“Please Marcus, let this go . . . It was so long ago.” My hands were clasped together. I was begging him.

His eyes narrowed as he deliberated. I could see that I wasn’t going to win.

I sighed. “I promise, as soon as I figure this out, I’ll tell you . . . good or bad.”

He looked to the window. It was dusk. He sighed as his resolve broke.

“How do you feel about flying?” he asked with a smirk, still gazing out the window.

“Flying?” I was surprised by the question. “I don’t mind it . . .why?”

“Maybe you should change your clothes; you may want a coat.” he suggested.

I looked at him skeptically. I watched him as I walked into my bedroom. I could hear him chuckle from the living room.

I quickly changed into jeans and a long shirt. I grabbed a jacket from the closet, put my shoes on, and returned to Marcus feeling anxious.

“So, you have an airplane or something?”

“Or something.” He grinned as he extended his hand to me. I took it cautiously.

Chapter 10: Flying

I could feel a cool breeze kiss my face as we stepped out into the night. I snuggled into Marcus's side as he wrapped his arms around me.

"Ready?" he grinned.

"Ready for what?"

I felt a sudden pull at my waist—Marcus's arm was around it, holding me tight. My feet weren't touching the ground any longer. We were flying!

"Ahahh!" I cried out. I grabbed onto his body and tried to bury my face in his chest as he shot like a rocket through the air. He was shaking with laughter.

"Phoebe," he laughed heartedly. "It's alright." He pulled me up so that I was standing. I tapped my toes around . . . I couldn't feel the earth below me. I peeked out from the safety of his shirt to see that we were well above the redwood trees—suspended in air!

I screamed as I scrambled to twine my legs around his body as if I were climbing a tree.

"You're still a scaredy cat!"

"How are you doing this?" My voice was muffled through his shirt.

"I can fly, as you so calmly pointed out last night," he teased. A hint of sarcasm coated his words.

"Yeah, but I didn't mean fly, fly!" I took a quick peek and buried my face once again. "Are you magic?"

"Magic?" he half-laughed. "I'm a vampire."

"But you're flying!"

"I can also swim without breathing; jump from any height and land as softly as a feather; climb any object effortlessly; and move at such speeds that if I didn't want you to see me, you wouldn't. It's part of my immortal make up." I could hear him grinning.

"Phoebe, I won't let you fall. I promise."

My death-like grip became tighter. I could feel his cool hands on my cheeks. His fingers gently lifted my chin up, exposing the petrified expression that was on my face. I could feel his stare, though my eyes were glued tight.

His lips surprised me as they moved over mine. I forgot myself for a moment and opened my eyes. His skin gave off its own illumination in the moonlight.

"Watch," he said, as he pointed to the mountaintop beyond. The moon was just beginning to peek over. It looked so big, so bright, so close . . . I found myself reaching out as if I could touch it.

"Shall I catch it for you?" he whispered across my ear.

I smiled. "I believe you could."

Without thinking, I rested my chin on his shoulder, watching the moonrise. He didn't seem to mind that I was still twined around him.

"This is amazing. How long can you do this?" I asked, wondering if we might fall out of the sky at any moment.

"As long as you like."

I sighed contently.

The night air smelled clean and fresh; we were surrounded by millions of stars, speckling the sky like diamonds. He wrapped his arms around me tighter, trying to shield me as a cold wind embraced us.

"What are you thinking?" He spoke quietly.

"That you're amazing—I told you you're a super hero."

"Ahh, if only that were true," he mused.

"It's a good thing I am immortal; your grip would squeeze the life out of anyone!" he joked.

"Sorry, but I'm not letting go for anything!"

"I'm counting on that." There was an odd tone to his words. Was he counting on my fear of heights to bind me closer to him at this moment, or was there something more? Was Marcus afraid that I might one day let *him* go? Impossible!

"You never could fly well," he teased, interrupting my reverie.

“I could fly?” I looked at him in disbelief.

“You wouldn’t go higher than a barn,” he laughed. “Even for a vampire, you were always fairly cautious.”

“I never had to worry, except when you felt the need to join the hunt.” I could hear the annoyance in his voice.

“I was a hunter too?” I sounded way too excited for Marcus's liking.

“Yes,” he said flatly.

“Was I any good?” I wasted no time. To hear that my former life was fraught with excitement, although this one hadn’t been exactly dull lately, was thrilling.

“You were fair when it came to one on one; you were light and fast on your feet.” he admitted.

“So, did we fight together?” I was beamed at the thought.

“A few times . . . ” he said hesitantly. He had a look of disapproval on his face. “I couldn’t stand to see you in danger. I begged your father to reconsider allowing you to be a hunter,” his jaw tightened.

“What did he say?” I nearly demanded; my tone became defensive.

“He said his daughter’s place was fighting for the good of the coven. He wouldn’t deny you that just because he was worried about your safety.”

“Well, he was right.” I said firmly. “I wouldn’t want to be told what I could or couldn’t do . . . especially as an adult.” I grumped. “That should have been my decision anyway.”

“Phoebe, it’s a different life. You do as you’re told. You would have obeyed your father or you would have been punished. Your actions affect the entire safety of the coven.” he spoke seriously.

I tried to let the words sink in. It was still so unimaginable, even here, suspended in mid-air high above the trees. I still couldn’t envision a world with such creatures.

“I thought you said my father wouldn’t allow me to fight?”

“At first he didn’t. Not hunts anyway. Something happened. You were so determined to fight. You had a personal hate for the werewolves that I never understood. Your father had no choice. You were sneaking out on your own, slaying as many of them as you could." I could hear the concern in his voice. Even now, after hundreds of years, I knew Marcus hadn't wanted Phoebe to fight.

"Your father agreed to allow you to be a hunter under the condition you never went alone. Come," he said suddenly as he wrapped his arm tight around my waist.

We glided through the air once again. If it weren't for my fearful periodic squeals I made when I decided to sneak a peek, we would have been virtually silent. He moved stealth like through the night. I tried to imagine how many vampires had flown over my house unknown over the years. The thought was chilling. We landed in my back yard, minutes later.

"You can open your eyes now," he teased.

I held onto his body tightly as I tapped my foot around on the earth below me.

"Oh come now, it was a little fun wasn't it?" he asked playfully as he tried to unlock my arms.

"A little," I admitted, trying to suppress a smile.

"It's getting late. Why don't I take you to dinner?"

"Mexican sounds good," I admitted. "But I'm paying. It's not like you'll be eating."

"Oh no. Ladies do not pay." He looked like I'd just insulted him.

I grabbed my purse. "Fine, but I'll provide the transportation this time!" I held up my car keys, jingling them in the air.

The corners of his mouth were turned up. "Agreed."

I reached for the doorknob and paused. "Marcus?" I turned slightly, whispering as if someone might hear. "Do you have money?"

He laughed hard. "I think I have enough."

I pursed my lips. "Well, how would I know?" I shouted over his laughter.

"Just get in the car!"

He climbed in, still chuckling.

"So, how do you earn a living?" I asked as I started the car. "You can't possibly get paid for hunting werewolves."

"My family was extremely well off." he said as his laughter subsided.

"But that was over seven hundred years ago. You can't have any money left?" I tried to focus on the road, but the wheels in my brain were spinning at extreme speeds.

"We had a lot of money, and I do get paid for hunting werewolves." He cut me a sideways glance. "I also make a few financial investments here and there." He shrugged.

We arrived at the restaurant before I knew it. Time always seemed to slip by when I was with Marcus.

"Maybe we can just get it to go," I suggested as we walked hand in hand toward the front door. I could smell the food from outside.

"What's the matter darling . . . afraid to be seen with a vampire?" He joked.

"No." I rolled my eyes at him. "It's just not the most private place to talk."

"Ah . . . to go, it is." He opened the door, and the tantalizing aroma of sizzling fajitas greeted us.

"Why humans like to eat this is beyond me," he wrinkled his nose in disgust.

I huffed. "Not all of us are on a liquid diet."

"You shouldn't knock it," he grinned, his eyes flashing crimson for a moment.

"Stop doing that," I whispered then looked around me, afraid someone might have noticed him. I caught myself as I subconsciously reached up and held my throat. I gave him an exasperated look.

"Stop doing what? Reminding you that I'm a vampire?" Marcus laughed again. He was clearly enjoying this.

I placed my order and sat at the bar with Marcus, while he pretended to snack on chips and salsa while we waited.

"So, how old was I when we met?" I asked when the hostess was out of earshot.

"Hmmm, you were one-hundred and ten. I remember it well. It was your birthday."

"My birthday?" I took a bite of a chip and leaned in closer.

"You had been gone that first year I was turned. I hadn't met you until your father arranged a party in honor of your return." His eyes looked far away as he remembered the memory.

"I do believe you're blushing," I teased.

"Impossible, I can't blush;" he tried to evade my eyes.

"But if you could, you would be!" I smugly pointed out. "You look just like you did when I discovered I was completely naked this morning." I smiled triumphantly as I watched how sweetly embarrassed he was.

The hostess returned with my to-go bag. Marcus pulled out some cash, instructing her to keep the change.

"That was very generous of you," I commented as we walked back to the car.

Marcus shrugged.

"So, where had I been all year?" I asked, once we were back in the car.

"You were tracking the wolves."

"Tracking . . . by myself?" I couldn't even get the key in the ignition. I was horrified to think I would be doing something so dangerous.

"No. Raymose was with you, as well as a few others. As I said, your father had limits to his tolerance of your duties." he spoke carefully, bowing his head slightly.

"Duties?"

There was so much I wanted to ask. I didn't want to waste time with mundane necessities such as eating, but I was starved. I started the car and headed toward the house.

"You were tracking Damen specifically."

My mouth popped open again. The look on Marcus' face told me this was not a pleasant topic of conversation—I reluctantly dropped the subject.

The rest of the ride home was quiet. I wasn't much of a night driver, and with the rain starting to drizzle; it made a terrible glare on the road.

"Would you like me to drive?"

"No, we're almost there . . ." I was leaned as close to the windshield as I could straining to see through the pounding rain.

I was glad when I pulled up in front of the house. I turned the car off and sat there for a minute with my hands on the wheel.

"Marcus, was my father some sort of leader?" I asked off handedly.

"He is the leader." I could hear the respect in his voice.

"Luther!"

He nodded his head.

"He's still alive then?" I asked excitedly.

"Yes . . ." Marcus was watching me apprehensively now.

"Was I very close to him, I mean back then?"

He knew where I was going. "Phoebe, I don't think this is a good idea," he warned.

"I'm just curious Marcus. It's not like I'm asking to meet him. He's not my dad—he probably wouldn't even recognize me. I mean, it's not like he wants a half human, half werewolf daughter anyway," I mumbled under my breath.

I felt Marcus's hand on mine, squeezing it gently. "He wouldn't be able to tell the difference. The resemblance is . . . amazing!"

It was then that I understood the look of awe Marcus had when he looked at me. I gave him a hopeful smile.

"Phoebe, I'm so sorry about your father's passing. I'm sure he was a wonderful man. I would have been honored to meet him."

I nodded, giving him a half-smile.

"But you must understand, that if I brought you to Luther . . . you wouldn't be safe."

"Do you think he'd kill me?" I gasped. I hadn't thought of him as a vampire. I thought of him as my father from another time. I missed my dad so badly. Maybe if I could spend time with . . . I shook the idea away.

"You're right. It's a crazy idea." I got out of the car and ran to the front door, shaking the rain off my jacket. Marcus beat me there.

"You're fast!" I exclaimed. I took the bag of food from him and fumbled with the keys, eventually finding the right one and opening the door.

"It's really coming down, isn't it?" I set the bag on the coffee table. Small talk was not my forte.

Marcus cornered me against the couch. His hands cupped my face, claiming my attention.

"Phoebe, I'm sure Luther would have been thrilled to have you back. He would have given all that he has to have you again, but there are other considerations now."

"What considerations?" I asked desperately, my hands seeking his. I hadn't realized how important this was to me.

Marcus's soft brown eyes were staring sadly back at mine. "I can't bring you into my world; I have to protect you from it. I can't let them find out about you—ever."

"Why? Have you changed your mind about me?" my voice cracked.

"No!"

"Then why?" I begged.

"You're part wolf—they'd kill you on sight." His eyes were filled with a devastating sadness. My heart was breaking all over again. All hope I'd had, just crumbled before me.

"Oh, I see." I felt so foolish. "Of course," I walked over to the couch, picked up a pillow, and held it tightly to my chest as I sat down, sinking into the depths of despair.

"He might have wanted me if Damen hadn't bitten me," I resided. "We can never be together—not really. I've lost you all over again, haven't I?"

Marcus appeared beside me. I sank into his open arms and cried.

"You don't need to cry." He held me to him, smoothing my hair softly. "I'll find a way, I swear it!"

I pulled my head back and studied his face. There was such passion in his eyes. He meant what he'd said. Although, I knew he was making a promise he couldn't possibly keep. I shook my head.

"I won't let you go. Do you understand me? Not ever!" His lips collided with mine, as if the force of this kiss would convince me that he could fix anything. I almost believed that he could. Hot tears continued to stream down my face. I would have to burn this moment into my mind forever, for as I feared, my time with Marcus was fleeting.

I put my whole body into that kiss. I rose to my knees, my lips never leaving his. I could feel him gently trying to pull back. I wouldn't let him. I ran my fingers through his hair, holding his head firmly to mine. His body responded. His hands pulled me closer. I climbed onto his lap. I wouldn't let him go without showing him how much I wanted him, how much I needed him. We should be together—it could work—I just had to help him find a way.

"Phoebe, stop!" His words were sharp as he jerked away from me. He panted, his breathing just as labored as mine.

"You know I can't make love to you," he growled in frustration.

"You said when I knew who you were . . . I know who you are! I don't care!" I yelled, trying to inch closer.

"Phoebe, we're not ready," he rubbed his forehead like he was in pain. "You don't understand the danger you'd be putting yourself in."

"I don't care anymore. I don't care about any of it. You're going to leave me anyway! I'd rather die trying than not have had the chance to love you again."

"I'm not going to leave you," he said incredulously. "Why would you think that?"

"You said if you took me with you, I'd be killed. You can't escape your world, and I don't know how you could hide me from it. What choice do you have?"

"I told you I'd find a way, and I will!" His resolve was strong.

I shook my head and turned away from him.

"I have to be so careful with you. If another vampire comes across your scent, and I'm not there . . ." he didn't have to finish, I could hear the dread in his voice.

"What about Damen? Are you going to hide me from him as well?" I said hopelessly.

"I will do whatever I have to do to keep you safe," he said sharply. "He could have killed you twice now . . . but why hasn't he?" Although he said this aloud, the thought was clearly meant for him to consider privately. He looked far away now as his mind mulled the question over and over.

Chapter 11: Painful Memories

"Tell me about Damen . . . and me?"

Marcus's face grew hard. His eyes narrowed as he considered my question.

"Why?"

"Our relationship wasn't very friendly, was it?"

"Why would you say that?"

"If he was my protector, I'd assume we were close, friends at the very least. Something tells me that wasn't the case, at least, not in the end."

Marcus shifted uneasily. "I only know bits and pieces. It isn't much."

I looked at him with hopeful eyes.

"All of this was before my time," he began. "From what I understand, Damen was assigned to you by your father when you were ten years old. He was to protect you during the daylight hours, when your father couldn't be with you. Damen was never to leave your side.

"Ten? Where was my mother?"

"I believe she died of a fever. I know nothing more than that," Marcus added quickly.

I clutched my heart. How tragic. Had I always been so cursed to lose a parent so young?

"By night," Marcus continued, "He was to keep a close distance. He wasn't to interfere with your meals once you became immortal."

"Once I became immortal? I wasn't always?" This was new. If I'd been a vampire, I hadn't considered that I'd been human in any way.

"You became immortal when you were thirty-five," he explained. "That's when you drank blood for the first time."

I closed my eyes, cringing at that very thought.

"Phoebe, they didn't have blood banks back then. Vampires fed directly from humans—some still do," he added disapprovingly.

I nodded my head in understanding. It still didn't make it any easier to accept.

"Now, I told you the war had been going on for nearly a thousand years, but at its birth, not all the werewolves felt the same. Some were content serving the vampires; Damen was content serving you. He didn't want to leave you—ever!"

I listened with hungry ears. This was what I'd been waiting for, another piece to my puzzle.

"Your father watched him relentlessly, constantly testing his loyalty to him and the coven. Luther feared Damen's devotion to you was much more than him just being loyal to the coven. Even then, Luther knew Damen's feelings would betray you one day;" He spoke with venom in his words.

"You had been with Damen for so long. You didn't realize his feelings for you had turned into a deep love—a forbidden love. He was insanely jealous of anyone who got close to you."

"So I didn't have any . . . relationships?" I asked casually. I could feel my cheeks burning from embarrassment. I tried to avoid Marcus's eyes.

"You had a few interests," he shrugged. "You and Raymose were involved at one time."

"We were?"

"Many years before we met, I believe Damen had a role in the downfall of that relationship, although he'd never admit to it," Marcus scoffed. "Years later, Raymose naturally tried to win your affection back, but I'm told, you were much too busy slaying werewolves." His laugh touched his eyes. "That was my good fortune to be sure," he bowed his head.

"I'm sure it was my good fortune as well," I said, meeting his stare.

His eyes grew slowly darker. "There was a time, the year before your birthday, the one in which we first met . . . something happened to you. You never spoke about it."

“I looked at him curiously, trying to search my mind for any pieces Damen may have left me.

“You left the safety of the coven,” he prompted.

I gasped. “I remember! Or rather, I remember Damen’s memories,” I clarified. “Some of them anyway.” I sank back into the couch, my mind wandering through bits and pieces of the past.

Marcus watched me for a moment. “*What* do you remember?” He asked apprehensively.

“We were walking through a forest, Damen and I. It was dark. I remember there was a full moon . . . I was dancing under its light. We were laughing,” I smiled at the image in my head. “I misplaced my foot and fell—”

“Naturally,” Marcus commented.

I gave him a dry look. “Damen lifted me off the ground. It wasn’t the first time he’d picked me up.” I recalled. “But it was the first time he’d ever really held me, close I mean.” My thoughts slipped into a chasm deep within my mind.

“What is it?” Marcus interrupted my reverie.

I shook my head. “Damen, he . . .” I couldn’t say it. My heart started to pound. The reality of it was too awful. No one should have to carry the burden of these images.

“He what?” Marcus urged me to continue. “You never told me about this,” He moved closer to me. “You never told anyone but Raymose,” I could hear a hint of jealously in his voice.

“There’s a good reason you were never told.” I could envision how Marcus would have reacted to the mental slide show going on in my head—I shuddered at the thought.

“Phoebe, you’re scaring me.”

“Marcus, I—I don’t know what to say. I feel like a deer in headlights. I can’t. That Phoebe didn’t want anyone to know what had happened. I shouldn’t have these memories. I don’t *want* these memories! They’re not mine. They’re his!” I nearly shouted.

I held my head tightly. The images were so clear, as if they'd just happened—as if they'd just happened to *me*. The blood; the screaming . . . I couldn't escape them . . .

"I'm sorry," I breathed. I covered my face with my hands, trying to clear my mind. I could feel Marcus standing over me now. I looked up into his face.

"Tell me."

I shook my head no. "It's too dreadful."

His hands gripped my shoulders tightly, his fingers digging into my arms as he lifted me off the couch, shaking me slightly. "Tell me!" he commanded.

"He mauled her!" I cried. The words fell out of my mouth faster than I could think to catch them. I watched Marcus's face fall as I uttered the words. His mouth opened, but nothing came out. He released me as he staggered back a little.

I fell back onto the couch. I sat there, quivering. I stared at him in disbelief, tears pooling in my eyes. "How could he?" I asked. "He said he loved her. He told her that he was in love with her!" I cried freely as I witnessed the attack once again in my head.

I clutched my head in my hands as I rocked myself back and forth. I would never be able to wipe these images away. Never.

"Phoebe . . ."

"She laughed at him," I said through tears. Cutting off anything Marcus might have said. "She called him a romantic fool," I scoffed. "She told him that she could never love a werewolf and that he needed to spend time with his own kind."

I shook my head in disgust. "I hurt him. She hurt him!" I said defensively. "No wonder he wants to kill me, she was so hateful—how could he have loved her? How could you have?" I demanded.

I pushed myself off the couch and walked aimlessly around the room.

"Phoebe, look at me. Look. At. Me." Marcus's voice was sharp.

I reluctantly met his stare. "She . . . you couldn't have known he'd react that way." Marcus's voice was surprisingly low. "You were an amazing woman. You were kind to everyone, and I mean everyone! You wouldn't have said those things if you didn't have cause."

I shook my head. "Then why do I feel a sense of guilt for what she'd said to him," I clarified. "A sense of anger even for what he did to her." I looked at Marcus for understanding.

"What . . . did he do . . . exactly?" he spoke each word slowly through gritted teeth.

I felt chilled all of a sudden. I rubbed my hands up and down my arms, trying to warm them. I couldn't think of this woman in the memory as me. I had to separate us. *That* Phoebe, no matter how much we looked alike, no matter the reason for me owning her memories, was not I.

"He threw her on the ground." My eyes drifted back to Marcus's. He looked murderous—anticipating the worst—he wouldn't be disappointed.

"He's stronger than any man she'd ever fought or any werewolf for that matter," I admitted. My tone was matter-of-fact. I had to keep us separated, although the panic I felt was very personal. It began to consume me.

"He was wild, uncontrollable!" I continued, cringing at the memory. I held my hands, trying to stop them from shaking. "The weight of his body was crushing me." I sucked in a breath of air. I couldn't separate us any longer. The Phoebe getting mauled in my head and the Phoebe standing before Marcus were one in the same.

I stared at Marcus in disbelief. "I couldn't push Damen off me!" I cried. "He began to change. I thrashed and hissed . . . I couldn't break free!"

Marcus looked as though he were coming completely unstuck. He reached out to hold me. I put my hands out, not wanting to be touched; I cringed away from him.

"If these are Damen's memories . . . I wouldn't have this perspective," I argued. "If these were Phoebe's . . . they couldn't be in my head."

Marcus's face looked pained. By the look in his eyes, I could tell there was so much he wanted to say, but he remained silent. Perhaps he couldn't find the words? It didn't matter right then. My words would be the ones to change everything:

"They're mine," I gasped. A single tear ran down my face. I felt it slide down my cheek and linger for a moment before it fell; and with it, part of my sanity slipped away too. I closed my eyes and took a deep breath. Marcus wrapped his arms around me, pulling me into the safety of his love. "They're my memories." I cried.

"Darling I'm sorry. It was selfish of me to make you relive that," he said in shame.

I let him rock me slowly, the rhythm calming me slightly. I forced a smile as I looked up at him. "I must seem an emotional wreck to you?"

"No." His eyes were so gentle as they looked upon me. "Why did you not tell me?" I could hear the pain in his voice. He pulled me back to him. This was a burden he'd have gladly carried for me . . . for her . . .

I smiled to myself. Even Marcus had accepted that she and I were one in the same.

"Raymose told me later that my father was furious with Damen for returning without me," I explained. "Raymose was the one sent to find me. He brought me back to my father."

"Did you ever tell your father what had happened; what Damen had done to you?"

I shook my head. "He suspected, although he never knew the full truth. I could never tell him. It was . . . shameful." I tried to rub away the headache that was pounding across my forehead.

"Luther ordered Damen's death immediately after my return, yet Damen had already fled," I added.

Marcus nodded his head in understanding. I guessed that he knew this part of the story. He didn't ask any more questions.

"No wonder Raymose was so protective of you." Marcus spoke as if I'd just uncovered a small mystery that had been haunting him.

"Marcus. I can't fight him," I admitted without thinking. "He's too strong." I could hear the panic in my voice as I watched the attack once again in my mind.

"You won't have to," he promised as he rocked me gently in his arms. "You won't have to."

"I remember my father's face."

Marcus stopped rocking me. He swallowed loudly then pulled back to look at me. "Phoebe, you have to give me time to figure this out. I can't just show up at your father's house with you, like this. Please understand."

"I do. It's just . . . I just look like her. I have her memories." I said in frustration. "I know. I'm not her. I can't be her." It was a lie, and I knew it.

"You are my Phoebe! The same Phoebe I loved more than life itself! You will remember." I could see the certainty in his eyes. "I don't know how but you've come back to me."

I tried to look away but his eyes held mine.

"I *will* find a way. I swear it. I won't live without you again!" His lips collided with mine. I could feel the desire in them to kiss me harder. He wanted me, but held back. My heart pounded wildly as my pulse raced. I wrapped my arms around his neck while his hands moved up and down my back fluidly, pausing at my waist. He surprised me by lifting me up off my feet and spinning me around. I laughed—carefree like a child.

Marcus was smiling too; he truly looked happy.

"Stay with me tonight, please?" I held his hands close to my heart so he could feel its erratic beat.

He sighed. I could feel the instant tension in his body as he felt the blood pumping through my heart.

"Phoebe . . ." he breathed. He was trying to maintain control; he was trying to be rational.

I reached out and held his cheek. His eyes closed.

"Marcus." My voice was soft and low. "I just want you to hold me . . ."

He opened his crimson eyes reluctantly. I took a brave breath and stepped closer. He couldn't help but smile. "You had me at hold you." He brushed my lips gently with a kiss. "I never could deny you anything."

I smiled victoriously. "I'll remember that."

"But don't trust me completely Phoebe. You're not entirely safe with me. I don't trust myself."

I dismissed his warning, waving him off. How could I be in any danger with Marcus?

Chapter 12: A Bad Idea

"I'll be right back."

"Wait! Where are you going?" I grabbed onto his arm as he turned for the door.

"To scout out the area." He spoke as if this was obvious.

"But it's dark out there!"

"I think you'd be hard pressed to find anything more dangerous than me outside," he half laughed as he reached for the doorknob.

"But what if Damen's—"

"I'll be right back," he interrupted, not paying any attention to my fears as he ducked out the door.

I decided to get ready for bed. I brushed my teeth, put on my pajamas, and crawled into the soft covers.

I kept checking the clock. Marcus had only been gone ten minutes, but it felt like hours had passed by. I skimmed through an old copy of *People Magazine* when Marcus appeared in my doorway.

"Geez!" I jumped. "Do you have to sneak up on me like that?" I held my hand over my heart, trying to slow it.

He frowned. "You left the front door unlocked?"

"Who'd be stupid enough to break in with a vampire outside my house?" I asked.

"You're too trusting," he mumbled under his breath.

I held the covers open and patted his side of the bed. "You aren't going to wear your clothes to bed, are you?"

He looked at me apprehensively.

"Oh come on, don't you trust me?" I made my question sound as though I were deeply insulted.

"I suppose I could remove my shirt . . ."

"And your shoes, I hope?" I tried to suppress a smile. The look on Marcus's face told me I was pressing my luck.

"And my shoes." He gave me a dry look.

"Try not to act to put out," I taunted him playfully.

He climbed into bed and pulled the covers over him. I watched his eyes wander the room as he pulled the sheets up tightly to his chin.

"You act like you've never slept in a bed before." I studied him curiously.

"Not for a few hundred years anyway," he admitted, still looking around the room. "And then, it wasn't by choice."

"Oh my God. Don't tell me you sleep in a coffin." The very idea was enough to send me into near hysterics. I hated confined spaces. There was no way I could imagine myself snuggling with Marcus in a coffin.

He gave me an exasperated look. "No Phoebe. I don't sleep in a coffin.

I sighed in relief. "Then . . . how do you sleep?"

"I don't. Not the way you do anyway." He fidgeted a little under the sheets.

"Care to elaborate?" I asked as I got out of the bed and walked over to the light switch to turn it off.

Marcus didn't answer.

I turned around to ask him again when I noticed a vacant expression on his face.

"You're wearing that . . . to sleep in?" His voice sounded hoarse.

I looked at my pajamas—a red silk nightdress—and then back to Marcus. "Yeah, they're pajamas. You know, clothes you wear to sleep in." True, it was a little dressier than my flannels but not entirely uncommon for me. I turned out the light and ran to the bed with a jump.

Marcus leapt up as well when I hit the bed. "What is it?" He was looking around the room frantically—his arm out stretched in front of me protectively.

I laughed so hard I cried.

"What?" he sounded annoyed now.

"I always jump into bed," I said between laughs. "Just in case something is under it waiting to grab my feet." I laughed harder now. "I never expected I'd jump into bed with a vampire!"

Marcus couldn't help but laugh too. It was pretty funny, considering the nothing under my bed couldn't kill me.

"What time do you want to leave in the morning?" his laughter subsiding a little.

"We just need to leave by noon. It takes about four hours to get to Portland. Why?"

"I need to eat."

"Oh! Um, I . . ." I was pulling the covers up around me as subtlety as I could.

"I'm not talking about you!" He laughed heartily as he touched my arm—I jumped.

"I could have taken you hundreds of times by now if I wanted," he mused.

I didn't find it as amusing. The thought of Marcus truly being a vampire was still scary. I knew we'd been kissing . . . a lot. But still, part of me liked pretending he was just . . . Marcus. It made dealing with my own werewolf quirk more bearable.

"I'll leave town early, before we go," he continued. "I'll just be a few hours."

"You're leaving me alone?" I shrieked. "You can't! What if Damen comes back?"

"Phoebe, you'll be fine. I'll scout the area again. If there's any scent of him, I'll take care of it." His tone left little room for doubt.

"Right. I'll be fine," I repeated thoughtfully. I tried to come up with the words to make him stay, to make him realize that I wouldn't be fine. That I wouldn't be fine ever again without him, but I also didn't want him to suffer because of me. Ever.

I growled mentally. "I don't want you to go hungry because I'm being a wimp," I admitted reluctantly. I could hear the shame in my voice.

"Hardly," he put his arm around me and pulled me to him. I rested my head contentedly on his chest, taking in the sweet smell of his skin.

"I don't blame you for being scared." He gave me a gentle squeeze. "Damen can be quite ruthless." He ran his fingers down my bare arm, making me shiver. "You're just . . . needier than you used to be. Not that I mind," he interjected, "it's just going to take some getting used to."

"Great, 'needier' sounds *real* attractive," I grumped. "I'd much rather be stronger, tougher. More like the other Phoebe."

"It's very attractive." He kissed the top of my head. "I'd much rather look after you than have you pushing the limits, taking on the whole werewolf population single handed again."

I craned my neck and looked up into his glorious face. He smiled. His cool breath blew across me. I breathed in, feeling a little disoriented. This effect probably made it easier for them to distract their prey—the dangers of being with a vampire I'd deduced.

Considering how I'd reacted when Marcus mentioned he was hungry a few minutes ago, I couldn't believe what I was about to suggest; although, it was easier to deal with than the alternative—him leaving me alone.

"You don't need a lot of blood, do you?" My voice cracked on every word.

Marcus froze. His fingers stopped mid way up my arm. He'd still been caressing it.

"You're not . . . suggesting . . . what I think you're suggesting?" he asked cautiously, his eyes staring long into mine.

I swallowed loudly. I sunk my head back into his chest, shielding my eyes from his. "Maybe? I mean, if you need a . . . a little?" I could feel my hands start to sweat. "So you don't have to leave me," I quickly explained.

Marcus had pulled his arm out from under me and was now looking me squarely in the face. "You want me to take . . ." he swallowed, " . . . your blood?"

I cringed at the thought. "Will it hurt?"

Marcus's mouth popped open. "Will it hurt?" he asked incredulously. "You're not going to find out!" He threw the covers off him and rose from the bed.

"Marcus!" I jumped up, throwing my arms around his neck and pulled him back down. He sat with his back to me.

"I'm sorry. I didn't mean to offend you. I don't know what I was thinking," I stammered. "I just . . . I just don't want you to suffer because of me. If you have to leave, go. I'll be fine. I'm sure Damen isn't going to waste his time on me." I had to convince myself of this, or I'd go crazy every time Marcus left me alone.

Marcus turned slowly, his face was tight with tension, yet his eyes smoldered with desire. "Never . . . offer yourself to me again," he warned. "Never."

I nodded. The warning had been sharp and absolute. Yet . . . he still wore a look of desire on his face, like perhaps my suggestion wasn't so offensive after all.

"Will you still stay with me?" I whispered, after a few moments. I could feel the tears welling up in my eyes.

"It's not a good idea, us being this close, like this." His mouth said one thing, yet his eyes said another. "I should go."

"No!" I leapt at him so quickly I landed right on top of him, the both of us colliding to the floor in a loud thump. A defensive hiss came from his throat. My chest was beating loudly against his. I had taken him completely by surprise—he wasn't the only one.

"Sorry," I cried out. I'd never moved that fast before. My whole body trembled against his.

"Werewolf thing?" I squeaked. I flinched as his hand moved across my back, rubbing the soft silk I wore.

"That's dangerous." His body was as tense as mine. His eyes were on my lips. He wanted to kiss me. There was no mistake about it.

"I'm sorry," I breathed. "I didn't mean to tackle you like that."

"Not that." His tongue moistened his lips. "The way your body moved over mine just now," he clarified in a sultry tone.

His hands moved up my sides, as I lay frozen on his naked chest. I could feel how muscular, how perfectly defined his body was. The only thing separating my body from his was the thin piece of silk I wore. I bit my lip, trying not to think about his body beneath me.

"It's been so long since I've been this close to a human and not . . . drunk." He had trouble saying the word. My eyes were still focused on his perfect lips.

"I've never . . . been this close to a human, like this." His hands squeezed my hips tightly. I let out a gasp for air.

His hands moved up and down my back again. The rhythmic movement wasn't calming at all. My heart raced faster. The desire I felt was overwhelming.

"I'm sorry," I apologized again. "I didn't mean to make you upset," I said, remembering his reaction to being lunged at.

"The old Phoebe would have growled back," he teased, rolling me over so that he was now on top of me. His stare was piercing.

"I'm not the old Phoebe," I panted. "I'm not strong like her," I said this like it was a bad thing.

"There's no question; you're much more *sensitive* . . .." He made the word sound seductive.

My eyes drifted to his. He wanted me. Badly.

I moved my hands up his chest and rested them on his shoulders. His skin was cool next to mine. I reached around his neck, pulling his face to mine. Our lips were nearly touching . . .

"I wouldn't be a very good vampire, would I?" I breathed across his lips.

His face pulled back a little. His eyes adjusted as they studied mine. "I wasn't under the impression you were considering that."

"I'm not!" I exclaimed. "But, I have wondered." I could feel my cheeks burning bright now. "I mean, I used to be a vampire, right? Maybe—"

"No!" Marcus rolled away from me. "Do you think I'm going to let another vampire close enough to smell that you're not only human, but part werewolf as well?" He looked at me like I was insane. "They'd kill you without question."

My mouth popped open at the harshness of his words. "I guess I can accept that, but what about you?" My voice got smaller. "Why can't you do it? I mean, how else would you feel comfortable being with me . . . physically."

He reached over and gently pulled me to him. His strong arms wrapped around me as he cradled me against his body. I stared back into his eyes, watching the crimson swirl amongst the chocolate brown I'd grown to love.

"You can see me, clearly, in the dark, can't you?" He had a look of wonderment.

"Yes . . ."

He shook his head. "Your body is going through so many changes. I'm not sure where it will stop. I can't take the chance of turning you . . . I don't know how you'd react to being bit now that you've been infected by a werewolf. Our bite can be extremely lethal to them."

I realized then that Marcus *had* considered turning me. He had to want to be with me as much as I wanted to be with him. There had to be a way . . .

"If I were immortal, we could stay together, right?"

He nodded hesitantly. His eyes searching mine for where I was going with this.

"What if I were . . . " I had to be insane. I took a deep breath and braced for the explosion. "What if I were bit again . . . by a werewolf?

His face fell. "What?" He pushed away from me and rose from the floor, his body suddenly on the other side of the room. His eyes were once again black and intense.

"I said—"

"I heard you! I just can't believe you'd suggest it!" He spat the words at me.

"You don't have to get so mad. It was just an idea, I thought—"

"You didn't think!" he snapped. I could feel the moisture building in my eyes.

"I don't want you anywhere near a werewolf. They'll be looking for you as it is. Let's not make it any easier for them."

"What do you mean they'll be looking for me?" I jumped to my feet, clutching my hands to my chest.

"They'll be wanting to turn you . . . if you've survived."

"If I've survived?"

"Not everyone survives a bite from a werewolf, Phoebe. Most die either from shock or the venom. I'm surprised, with your intolerance for pain you lived at all. I can only guess it's because he didn't infect you completely," he added as an afterthought.

"I was just trying to think of a way to stay with you," I said in a small voice.

Marcus face softened. "They're drawn to their own kind. I don't know if anything like this has happened before. I can't imagine Damen will want you to remain half human. He wants you. Now after all this time, he's taken the upper hand and turned the tables . . . without even planning it," he mused darkly. "It has to be why he's followed you here."

I stared at him in disbelief. A hundred different questions popped up in my head at once.

"You're not a vampire anymore. He must think if he turns you completely, he'll have a chance with the heart he couldn't have so long ago."

"But that's crazy!"

Marcus said nothing.

"So that's it then," I said in defeat. "He'll keep chasing me until he bites me again. I'll have to live in fear forever? Maybe I should just let him and get it over with."

"He won't get the opportunity," Marcus growled.

I smiled flatly at him. "He already did," I pointed out, remembering Damen in my living room, brushing my cheek with a kiss.

Even in my dark bedroom, the look of fury that settled on Marcus's face was frightening

"And if he succeeds?" I shrugged, "Could you still love me?"

Marcus moved toward me. His hard expression had all but vanished. He pressed his lips to my forehead.

I closed my eyes, feeling his kiss move along the side of my face and down my jaw line to the hollow of my neck where he paused. His lips trembled as my head, so heavy now, fell back a little—exposing my throat to him. A low moan came from within him. I could hear my heart beating louder and louder as his mouth hovered over my neck. He held me close, supporting the weight of my body effortlessly.

"I can hear the blood flowing through your veins," his voice sounded gruff.

And as if he commanded the rhythm of my heart, it beat faster still. I could feel him watching my chest rise with every breath I took. I couldn't move. I was in the arms of my one true love. The only love my existence has ever known. A predator who could kill me instantly, yet . . . I wasn't afraid.

Marcus lowered me onto the bed. His body in sync with mine, he lay on top, careful not to burden me with his entire weight. He stared long into my eyes.

"I'd love you no matter what you were," he finally said. His words like music to my ears. I smiled. "Phoebe . . ."

The smile on my face slipped away. Marcus's eyes were a frightening shade of amber.

"I can't let you go." He sounded scared now. He'd been pushed too far, and he knew it.

My earlier *offer* to give Marcus a little of my blood was now a terrifying memory that paled in comparison to the danger that gazed upon me.

"Marcus. You don't have to stay with me. I'll be fine." I trembled in his arms. He tilted his head, better angling it with my neck. He licked his lips.

"I can't leave you alone . . . and I can't let you go," he hissed through his teeth. He looked like he was in physical pain. He wanted my blood—bad.

"Marcus, I'm going to back away slowly . . ." I spoke like there was a bomb that could be detonated at any moment. "I'm just going to scoot through your arms . . ."

I got as far as my waist, putting my heart right about eye level. I froze. I knew he could hear it beating—louder and louder—it was almost deafening. His eyes met mine.

I jerked quickly through his arms but found myself flat on my back again, the weight of his body holding me down. He held my wrists to either side of my head. His eyes were wild, animal-like. His teeth gleamed white.

"Marcus. You don't want me like this." I breathed heavily. There was no denying it. At this moment, he was a vampire—and I was afraid.

"I do want you . . . I need you . . . "

I yelped, as his lips touched the hollow of my throat abruptly.

"Marcus." I breathed heavily beneath him. I had to distract him, to shake him. It was the only way he'd be strong enough to let me go. The only way he'd fight the urge he was so afraid of—the urge to bite me.

I seized my moment. My mouth claimed his as he lifted his head up to look at me. He responded as I hoped he would. He released my wrists and kissed me eagerly, wantonly.

I grabbed his pants waist and jerked his body to mine. His breath caught. He pulled his head back and stared wide-eyed at me.

"We're ready." I twined my fingers through the back of his hair and pulled him into a kiss that would stop any man's heart. He didn't protest.

My right leg freed itself from under him and wrapped around his waist, squeezing him against me. I kissed him feverishly, tasting the delicious flavor of his mouth. I couldn't get enough. I brought his hand from my thigh up over my hips, across my stomach and continued upward when the last straw broke.

"No!" He pushed away from me, my body instantly mourning the loss of his touch. "I can't do this."

I felt an incredible pull to Marcus, each taste made me want another. His very smell was drawing me closer . . . I'd forgotten what I'd been trying to do. I couldn't think clearly. All I knew was that I wanted him, desperately. Now. And I was willing to overlook all danger to have him.

I reached for his face, taking it gently in my hands. I tried to pull him back to me. I needed to taste his lips again.

"No Phoebe. I won't risk it. Especially when I'm hungry," he growled in frustration. I could hear how tortured his voice sounded. "I was afraid for this to happen. Afraid I'd want you this way." His eyes dropped to my neck. "Afraid I'd need you this way."

I didn't know what had come over me. I found myself tilting my neck, offering him what I knew he wanted. "I survived a werewolf bite. I'm sure I could handle a little nip from you."

"You're not going to find out," he hissed, snapping me out of whatever trance I'd been in.

I stared wide-eyed at him. His face was hard. A muscle ticked under his right eye.

"You offered yourself to me again."

I opened my mouth to speak, and nothing—I didn't know what to say.

"Your humanity cannot resist me. It's how we lure our victims." His voice cracked. He wasn't apologizing, but the look on his face was one of disgust. He didn't like the thought of that . . . at least with me being the potential victim.

My eyes widened in understanding. That was why I was willing to do anything to have him. Even offer my blood. I reached up and touched my neck. His eyes followed. He still wanted it. He still wanted me. But he was in control now. He wouldn't take me. Not like this.

I took a deep breath and sighed.

"You seem relieved," he noted.

"It took a lot of effort to help you resist me. I don't think I have the strength to do it again.

"You?" Marcus laughed, taking me completely by surprise. "You're dangerously clever . . . that may not have worked in your favor though."

A thought I was now aware of. "It was a risk I was willing to take," I admitted shyly.

Marcus shot me a disapproving look that faded into a smile. He leaned over and brushed his lips against mine. "You need your sleep."

"Do you still need to go?" I asked.

"I'll stay as long as I can." He promised. "I'll be back before you need to leave."

I climbed into the covers beside him, settling my head in the crook of his neck.

"Marcus?" I yawned.

"Yes my dear?" his voice was low, like a whisper.

I smiled to myself as I repeated "my dear" over in my head. I liked the way it sounded. Especially when he said it. "Do you remember making love—when I was the other Phoebe?"

He stiffened. "Yes. A memory I hold dear," he added softly.

I thought about that for a moment, my heart racing at the very idea. "Marcus?" I hesitated for a moment, hating to ask the next question.

"Yes my love?"

"Is it safe for me to fall asleep?"

"Nothing will harm you." He answered without hesitation. "I give you my word."

With one arm under my neck and the other around my waist, I felt quite safe and comfortable with him. I smiled as I drifted off to sleep almost instantly.

Chapter 13: Danger

I had been so tired that I didn't even wake when Marcus got out of the bed. I didn't even know what time he'd left. The early morning sun shining through my bedroom window gave promises for a beautiful day. I didn't want to dwell too much on last night. Today was going to be great! Marcus and I were off to Portland. We'd have several days away to relax and hopefully get closer. I had to believe that we could find a way to be together . . . safely.

I looked out the window as I finished my bowl of cereal. It was one of those days I couldn't wait to be outside. The air was warm, the sun—bright, and birds were singing. I was in love. Everything was rose colored.

I glanced at the clock 9:00 a.m. This was the usual time I took my morning run. I could be back in an hour if I hurried. "I'd probably beat Marcus back," I thought aloud.

I looked out the window once again. That scared feeling I had last night when I didn't want Marcus to leave me, was creeping back. Damen was out there somewhere, maybe looking for me, and I knew it.

"But he wouldn't think to look for me at the park, would he?" I shook away the thought. I couldn't let myself be afraid like this. I couldn't shut myself away in my house forever. If I didn't leave now, I'd never go out alone. I'd always be afraid. I looked back to the window. The sun was out and I really had no reason to think Damen would be looking for me today. For all I knew, he'd left town!

I was already packed, and aside from needing a quick shower, I was ready to go.

It was silly to just sit here and wait. I changed into my running clothes, put my hair in a pony, and wrote Marcus a quick note—just in case he did return before I did.

Dear Marcus,

I'm all packed to go. I had a little time to kill so I went for a quick jog through

Redwood Park. (South East of here) I should be back around 10:00.

Xoxo (kisses and hugs)

Phoebe

I left the note on the table, hoping Marcus would check the back door and find it find unlocked for him, then headed for the park.

If I run for half an hour, that would give me plenty of time to get back by 10:00, I thought as I got out of the car and checked my watch.

There didn't seem to be anyone else around. Weird, on a day like today, I thought this place would be crawling with joggers—or at least running with them. I couldn't help but laugh at my bad joke.

I started up one of my favorite paths, thickly shaded by Redwood trees. I loved to look at the moss that grew up the trunks and over the fallen trees that lay on the forest floor. I ran by giant ferns that grew taller than I was, and occasionally, I might get to see one of the many forest animals hurrying along with their busy day. My favorite part of this place was when I paused to look up at the treetops. The trees seemed to reach up into the heavens. Bits of sunlight peeked through here and there, warming my skin and casting an orange glow on the needled path.

My feet moved lightly over the thick needles that covered the path. I couldn't get over how quiet everything was today. I couldn't hear a sound. Not even a bird . . .

I started to run faster; I sensed something was very wrong. This was a mistake. I shouldn't have come alone. I could feel eyes watching me. I tried to listen as I ran, but my feet seemed noisier as fear took hold of me. I caught a distinct smell across the wind. It wasn't Damen . . . but it did smell familiar . . .

There was a fallen tree up ahead blocking the path. The tree had to be a good two feet around. I could jump it—I would try. I couldn't slow down. I needed to get out of here. Now.

Beads of sweat dripped from my forehead. My heart was pounding its way out of my chest. I looked around. My eyes darted in every direction, looking for anything that might be a threat.

I was fast approaching the tree. One, two, three—I was in mid air hurdling the log when I was tackled from the side and knocked clear from the path. I flew fast through the air, landing hard on my back, my bones cracking on impact. I gasped for air—

My eyes wouldn't focus, but I was painfully aware that something was on top of me. "Brian?" My eyes narrowed, trying to make out his face. "What are you doing?" I was somewhat relieved it was Brian and not Damen.

"I didn't mean to tackle you so hard," he said flatly.

"What the heck is wrong with you? You could have killed me!" I choked on the words, each breath more painful than the next. "Get . . . off . . . me!"

"No!"

"No?" I gasped.

"Why was that guy at your house all night?" he asked angrily.

"Were you spying on me?" disgust coating my words. "Who the hell stalks someone all night?"

"I wasn't spying. I was coming to ask you out to dinner when I saw the two of you leaving together."

"So how do you know he stayed the night?" I asked sarcastically as I struggled painfully beneath him. Futilely trying to push him off.

"Because I saw you come home with him," he growled through his teeth. "And he didn't leave until early this morning."

"You stayed outside my house all night?" I gaped in disbelief.

"What kind of guy sneaks off in the night?" His tone was accusing.

I huffed. "What kind of guy *stalks* someone, all night?" I threw his words back at him.

Brian narrowed his eyes. His stare was lethal.

"He needed to leave early . . . and it's none of your business anyway! Now get off me! I think you broke my ribs . . . " I moaned.

"I don't get it?" he continued, ignoring my efforts to free myself. "I'm a good looking guy, I have money. We've been friends since high school. I've been more than patient with you. And you let this guy that shows up out of nowhere sleep with you right off." He glared at me, possibly considering his next move.

"Sleep!" I snapped. "That's all we did was sleep Brian, and again. It's none of your business. We're not dating!" I hit his shoulder with my fist. My temper was rising to an all time high.

Brian grinned.

"I mean it Brian, get off me. I don't like being held down like this." An image of Damen on top of Phoebe ran through my mind. Although I knew Brian wouldn't be turning into a werewolf, I was still starting to feel a panic attack coming on. The situations were too similar.

"You're not going anywhere until you explain why you won't go out with me. What's this guy have that I don't—except for that snobby British accent," he scoffed.

"Manners!" I shouted.

"You don't know what you're missing," he said with smug confidence.

"What I'm missing?"

His face closed in on mine. "There is something different about you . . . I noticed it before. I can't get you out of my head. You're driving me crazy—even your smell—" he stared at me with a dream like gaze.

"It's called soap Brian, now get off me!"

He leaned in and pressed his nose against my neck. I cringed away from his touch.

"It's you . . . it's your skin . . ." he took another deep breath.

"Quit smelling me!" Somehow I'd managed to slap his face.

He jerked his head back and glowered. In the next instant, his mouth came crashing down on mine. He pushed hard against my lips, crushing them with his. I kept my mouth closed. His lips, sloppy and wet, moved over mine eagerly, ignoring my protests.

The pain in my ribs was excruciating. I could hardly breathe under the weight of his body. Tears leaked out the corners of my eyes.

"Get off me!" I choked—my mouth finally breaking free.

Suddenly a look of surprise flooded his eyes. A hand appeared on his shoulder and ripped him off me with such force—his body went flying backward into a tree a good fifteen feet away. The only sound was the air escaping his lungs upon impact.

I laid there in shock, staring at my rescuer.

"Phoebe!"

I was too scared to speak.

Damen turned to Brian who was shaking his head in disbelief.

"You really shouldn't force a lady against her will—no matter how appealing she is," he growled.

"You're going to regret that," Brian snapped, jumping to his feet. His temper was boiling. This wasn't the Brian I knew . . . or thought I knew. This man was crazed.

"I think you'd better leave if you ever care to use those lips again," Damen threatened. There was no play in his words.

I could see the fear in Brian's face. He looked at me still frozen on the ground, covered in dirt and redwood needles. "This isn't over," he promised.

"I wouldn't advise you attempting that again," Damen warned. "You won't leave walking next time."

I stared open mouthed at Damen. He was letting Brian go?

Brian backed away slowly, maintaining constant eye contact before he turned and ran down the path.

I had one eye on Brian fleeing and the other on Damen as he now turned to me. His face was full of worry.

He walked slowly toward me, his hands outstretched. I held my aching ribs firmly and scooted backward, backing myself right into a tree—I was trapped!

"I'm not going to hurt you!" he said calmly, as he approached.

My eyes narrowed, I didn't trust him.

"Are you alright?" I could hear the worry in his voice. All I could do was stare. I knew what he was, and more importantly, I knew what he was capable of. I'd seen him kill a thousand times . . . in my dreams anyway.

He stared at my clothes that were all askew—he suddenly looked angry. "I got to you before he . . ." His words broke off. He closed his eyes, took in a deep breath and opened them again—

His yellow eyes now stared back at me, I swallowed hard. I knew those eyes . . .

"You're alright now." I didn't know if he said it for my benefit or his.

I heard a twig snap off in the distance. I gasped as I jumped and clung onto the tree behind me for safety. No one was going to separate me from this tree. I looked wildly around . . . searching for any trace of Brian. Praying he wouldn't come back.

"He's not coming back. Phoebe. I swear on my life; he will *never* touch you again!" His words were full of malice . . . I knew he meant them. There was something familiar about the fierceness in which he was protecting me.

"Do you want me to take you home?" he asked.

I jerked away from his reach.

"Phoebe. I can't leave you here like this. Do you understand me?" He spoke slowly, like my mind might not be able to comprehend what he was saying.

I nodded sharply.

"I'm just going to lift you up," he said slowly as he moved toward me again.

"NO!" I yelled. It didn't even sound like my voice.

His hands came out again, motioning for me to calm down. He knelt on the ground a few feet away, his eyes, still yellow, were reflecting concern.

I felt as though I were falling apart. I held onto the tree tightly. My teeth chattered inside my head as my body shook with fear. What was happening to me? I leaned my head against the tree, trying to steady myself.

"I should have killed him for touching you like that," he said with regret as he looked down the path Brian had taken. He looked back to me. I could see him deliberating whether or not he should go after him. I gripped the tree tighter, hoping my body would somehow merge with the tree so I could escape.

"I should have been watching you closer . . ." he growled. "I knew the risk."

I looked at him with confusion.

"He couldn't help himself you know, he was obviously attracted to you before, and with the change, you're more appealing to him than ever." He spoke casually like there was nothing unusual about our conversation. "He's drawn to you, like an animal in heat. It's part of your allure now. It's what makes them easy prey for us." I watched him closely, taking in as much of what he was saying as I could. My mind was reeling . . .

"You're probably wondering how I found you?" he asked lightly. "I went to see you. I found the note you left on your table and followed you here. A good thing to wouldn't you say?"

I shifted a little. The pain in my ribs was becoming unbearable. I held my arm against it, trying to hold it as best I could. I had to admit, a small part of me was glad he'd come.

His eyes softened. "My heart sunk when I heard you scream for help. Phoebe . . . "

I flinched away from his touch.

"I got here as fast as I could. I'm sorry it wasn't fast enough," he added with remorse, as he looked me over once again. "No one will touch you like that again," he promised darkly.

I pulled my legs up closer to my body, trying to get as much distance from him as I could.

"I understand you don't trust me, but you need to let me help you."

"NO!" I shook my head. "Don't touch me! I don't want anyone to touch me!"

With considerable effort, I got to my feet and started backing slowly away. My hand shook as I extended it out between us. "I won't let you hurt me again."

"Again?" He looked confused. "Phoebe, I've never hurt you."

"I saw what you did to that other Phoebe in the woods!" I shouted, tears falling from my eyes. I held onto my forehead, trying to steady myself. I could feel the world spinning around me.

"No! You couldn't know that. You misunderstood. I never meant to harm you—her. I. Loved. Her!" I could hear the desperation in his words. He'd somehow managed to take hold of my arms without me seeing him move.

"I've never stopped loving you. It's *always* been you." He pulled me to him, his eyes piercing mine.

I shook my head, clearing away the fog. "This is madness, I'm not that Phoebe!"

I tried to pull away. He held me firm. "I have your memories," I blurted out. "I saw what you did to her body. I saw you kill her—and her baby." I looked at him with such loathing. "How could you?" I added in disgust.

"You were supposed to protect her!" I cried. "You were her friend!"

He looked as if I'd just stabbed him unexpectedly. "No," he breathed. "Phoebe." He gripped me tighter, causing me to cry out in pain.

Damen released me. His eyes searching—they settled on my arm protectively holding my side.

"You're hurt," he growled. His eyes showed no sign of mercy now. He looked back toward the direction Brian had fled.

I turned and ran aimlessly through the forest. I didn't know where I was going. I didn't care. I needed to get away from Damen. I kept looking over my shoulder to see if he was following me—he wasn't.

I turned my head back toward the direction I was running when I ran right into Marcus's open arms and collapsed.

Chapter 14: Home Sweet Home

I lay there frozen while my eyes looked around my bedroom—I was alone. I was lying in bed, wrapped snuggly in a blanket.

It was a dream, I thought thankfully. I was just about to sit up when Marcus walked through the door. I jumped—a painful mistake. I clutched my side in agony. It wasn't a dream.

"What's wrong?" I could hear the dread in his voice.

"Nothing," I lied. The pain had subsided some. I breathed out slowly, trying to calm myself.

"Phoebe."

"Really, I'm fine. You just scared me; that's all." I forced a small smile.

He studied me for a moment. "I'm sorry I wasn't here when you woke up," he said with regret. "I brought your car back for you."

"Thanks. I just opened my eyes actually."

He sat down beside me. His face looked strained. I knew he had questions for me . . . questions I did not want to answer.

I could feel the tears building up and spilling over. "I should have stayed home," I cried, the very act causing my body unprecedented pain. "I shouldn't have gone out alone."

"No, no." He shook his head as he lifted me gingerly onto his lap and rocked me. I winced mentally. There was no way I could tell Marcus I'd been injured.

"I've always been safe there," I sobbed. "He's never acted like that before. I couldn't get him off me. He was crushing me . . . pulling at my clothes . . . I couldn't breathe." I cried hard now that I was safe in Marcus's arms. I held on to him, ignoring the shooting pains in my side.

His grip on me tightened. "Who?" He asked flatly.

"Brian," I sniffled. "It was Brian."

Marcus's breath caught. "He hurt you."

I looked up into Marcus's face. I could see the fear in his eyes as he waited for my answer. I turned away from him.

"Phoebe?" his voice was shaky.

A long moment passed before I had the courage to look at him. He looked furious. His eyes dropped to the tattered shirt where my fingers where nervously fiddling.

"Brian did that to you?" It wasn't really a question I needed to answer. He knew.

"Marcus . . ."

"I'll take care of it." His face showed no sign of mercy. His eyes, black as ebony, looked sadly into mine as he sat me back down on the bed. "Don't think on it any longer my love." He kissed my forehead and stood up to leave.

"Wait! Where are you going?" I grabbed onto his arm desperately.

"To track a different kind of monster," he said. His words were laced with venom. "I'm not going to allow him to live after what he did to you."

My heart stopped, and for a moment, time itself stood still. Marcus was going to kill Brian? He couldn't. I couldn't let him have Brian's death on his hands because of me . . . and part of me didn't think Brian deserved such a horrific death either.

"Don't leave me alone!" I cried.

"Phoebe, you're safe now." He touched my cheek with the back of his hand. His eyes were growing deadlier by the moment. "You don't have to worry about Brian touching you again."

"Marcus please don't leave me alone . . . I'm begging you, please!" I cried, pulling him back to me.

He stared at me, probably thinking my tears were based solely on fear, if he only knew.

"Very well my love, I won't leave, just yet," he added subtly as he sat down and wrapped his arms around me once more. "I'll stay with you as long as you need me."

I sighed with relief. I was safe with Marcus. He'd never let any of them touch me. I snuggled in to his body, allowing him to hold me tighter still.

"Phoebe," I could feel the tension in his arms. "I must ask, did he . . .?"

"No." I knew what he was implying. "He didn't get the chance," I added thankfully. "Although, I don't think he would have stopped if Damen hadn't torn him off me." I shivered as I recalled the attack.

"Damen was there?" he hissed.

"Yes," I squeaked. "He pulled him off me when he was . . ." I stopped, and shuddered. I didn't want to remember Brian's hands on my body. I folded my arms across my chest protectively.

"I didn't mean to frighten you." He rubbed his hands up and down my arms, trying to warm them. "Damen *helped* you?"

I nodded. "He threw Brian into a tree!"

"He didn't kill him?" Marcus mocked.

"No . . . he didn't," I said incredulously, still amazed myself that Damen had let Brian go. "Brian was so jealous you stayed the night with me . . . I've never seen him so crazed. He's never forced himself on me before."

I shivered, recalling the hateful look in Brian's eyes. "He'll be back. He said this wasn't over."

"He's right, it isn't over," Marcus threatened. "He won't come near you again."

"Damen tried to persuade me into letting him take me home," I added reluctantly, avoiding Marcus's stare. "I wouldn't let him. I know he helped me, and I am grateful . . . but I can't trust him." I prattled on nervously. "I won't listen to his lies. I saw his memories. I *know* the truth." I was ranting now. The events of today had finally cracked me.

"He kept saying I misunderstood things, but I didn't. I saw him in the woods with Phoebe; I saw him kill her and the baby. What kind of monster—"

Marcus grabbed hold of me, bringing me to attention. He held my face, his eyes wide with wonder.

"What baby?"

My mouth hung open. I was speechless.

His face was shrouded in shock as he realized what I'd said, what had been kept from him, all this time.

"You were with child?" His eyes looked down at my stomach as he was trying to comprehend his own question. He looked back at me with a wild, uncontrollable rage in his eyes.

"She," I clarified.

Marcus looked at me as though I were splitting hairs. "*She* was with child?" He rephrased the question, through gritted teeth. "How do you know this?"

"My dreams," I admitted. "The night she was killed, she wanted to tell you desperately, but Damen challenged her when she wouldn't step out of his way. He was going after you!" I exclaimed.

Marcus's eyes wandered the room, as if looking for answers elsewhere.

"She loved you more than anything," I continued, trying to defend her actions. "She knew she was going to die. She sacrificed herself to save you," I pointed out, like her sacrifice had been for a good cause.

"For me? She died . . . to save . . . me. She sacrificed *our child*, to save me?" he growled angrily.

I bit my lip.

"I had no idea," he sounded far away as he thought.

I reached out to touch his arm. He slammed his fist down on my bed, causing me to recoil.

"I would never have allowed her to hunt if I'd known!" he thundered.

"Marcus." My heart ached for him. "I don't know how long she knew," I stammered. "Remember, these are Damen's memories I have—"

"Not all of them," he hissed, silencing me. "How would he have known?"

"I'm not sure," I admitted softly. "He was chasing Phoebe. I think he was hoping she'd lead him to you. I . . . I don't think he would have killed her if it weren't for . . ." I paused. "If it weren't for her strong intent in defending you."

I watched Marcus as he became consumed with anger and loss, all over again. I reached out to him. He fell into my lap, hugging my waist. I ignored the pain in my ribs. It was my turn to comfort him.

I played with his hair, smoothing it back while he rested his head on my leg.

"I didn't mean to blurt it out like that. I'm sorry." I felt so ashamed. Why did my mouth have to be the size of a cavern?

"I'm glad you did. I needed to know." His eyes were full of sorrow. "I feel like I've lost her all over again, if I didn't have you now . . ." He held me tighter, and I closed my eyes, wincing at the pain.

"You'd never have known," I breathed. "And you wouldn't have to be looking after me now. You'd be off somewhere happily killing werewolves."

"I am happy," he smiled up at me. "We've been given another chance, you and I. I couldn't ask for more." His eyes met mine. There was so much love looking back at me.

"Marcus forgive me but . . . I just assumed that being immortal you couldn't have children like normal humans could."

"We can't . . . unless the woman is part human to begin with," he explained. "Your mother was human. That made you half human, half vampire. You were immortal but you could have children."

I listened intently. Trying to comprehend what he was saying.

"If you had had a daughter . . ." his voice cracked. "She wouldn't have been able to conceive. Her human gene wouldn't have been strong enough."

We sat quietly, deep in our own thoughts, letting the silence pass.

"Marcus?"

"Yes, my love?" He absentmindedly ran his fingers up and down my calf.

"Could we have a baby?"

His mouth dropped open.

"I don't mean now!" I interjected quickly. "I meant someday . . . if we wanted to."

There was a long pause. The silence was making me feel self-conscious.

"I honestly don't know Phoebe. I'm not sure how much of your make-up has changed. Until we know more about you . . ."

"Why are you looking at me like that?" I could feel the blush on my cheeks. Marcus was looking at me like I was a delicate figurine on a shelf.

"I'm sorry. It's just that I have to worry about you so much as it is. The thought of you having a child frightens me. I couldn't stand it if anything were to happen to you. You'd be more vulnerable than ever. More than before."

I opened my mouth to speak.

"Had I only known," he growled in frustration. "I'd have made sure she was protected. She would never have been left alone."

I looked at his tortured expression. My heart broke. I tried to offer words of comfort. "I'm sure she just didn't want to worry you. Your mind needed to be elsewhere."

"Do you honestly believe that?" he asked.

I shook my head. "She didn't want you to keep her from helping you."

He nodded. He'd already guessed as much.

I wasn't sure how I felt about that. It meant that the old Phoebe was reckless, and in the end, chose her husband over their child . . . Would I make the same decision if I were in her shoes . . . again?

"I don't want to think on this any longer. You are my concern now. How are you feeling?"

"My arms a little sore," I admitted, lifting my shirtsleeve to reveal one of the fingerprint bruises on my arm.

"Funny. I didn't think he'd squeezed me so hard." My voice cracked. I nervously began rubbing my arms as if the action might rub the marks away.

My ribs still throbbed. I looked down my shirt to see similar marks on my chest. I looked up quickly and met Marcus's enraged stare.

"It's not as bad as the ones on my arms." I lied. It was worse. I figured I could hide them from him until they healed.

"He had no right to touch you like that," he snapped. "It drives me crazy to think what might have happened if Damen hadn't stopped him. You realize Damen could have easily decided to kill you instead of help you," he added darkly.

I shuddered. I knew he spoke the truth.

"As it is, I despise the thought of owing Damen my gratitude," he said with disgust.

I looked at the clock, 11:15.

"You're not going anywhere without me," he growled, guessing my thoughts.

I looked down at my clothes. "I think I'll wash up a little. Promise you won't leave me!" I hated how needy I sounded. "I'll just be a minute."

"I'll be right here, waiting for you." He leaned over and kissed my cheek.

I walked with great care toward the bathroom. I stopped suddenly and turned around. "When you came back just now, you said you'd just picked up my car . . ."

"Yes?"

"How did you get me home from the park?"

"I flew. It was the fastest way. A bit tricky not being seen, though," he added with a smirk.

"Humph, good thing I was passed out," I muttered under my breath. The corner of his mouth twitched as he suppressed a smile.

I cleaned up as quickly as I could. My body was screaming in pain. I couldn't believe it: My arms already had large bruises where Brian had squeezed them.

I could feel the tears welling up in my eyes again. My chest and along the right side of my body had similar bruises. The worst had to be my lower right ribs—they felt broken. I'd have to somehow hide it from Marcus.

"Crap!" I realized I'd forgotten to grab clothes when I came into the bathroom.

"Ok, don't panic . . ." I thought aloud. I took a towel from the shelf and wrapped it around me. "I'll run to my dresser, grab the first thing I see and run back before Marcus has a chance to notice."

I held onto the door handle, counted to three, and flung the door open. I didn't exactly run because my wounded body wouldn't allow that—so I made my way slowly to my dresser. I yanked open drawers, grabbed a random outfit, and turned toward the bathroom—busted!

"What are you doing?" Marcus was surveying the clothes I'd somehow managed to toss onto the floor.

"Looking for something to wear," I gave him a sheepish smile. "I'll just be a minute." I maneuvered around him and headed back toward the bathroom.

"One moment please," he said firmly. It wasn't so much a request as it was a command. I stopped in my tracks.

His cool hand moved lightly over the bruises on my arm—it felt good. "I'm sorry I wasn't there," he sighed.

"They look worse than they feel." I held back the impulse to cry. I was going to be strong. And I might have gotten away with it if he hadn't put his arms around my waist. I winced loudly, flinching and moving away from him. Another mistake. I blew out a painful breath of air.

He dropped his arms. I couldn't hide the tears that leaked out the corners of my eyes.

"Show me."

"No! It's nothing" I shied away from him. I tried to laugh—mistake. I was now holding my side, trying to breathe.

"Phoebe!" He moved to grab hold of me but paused when I put my hand out to stop him.

"It's fine. I'll be ready in a few minutes." I was slightly hunched over, clutching my side as I made my way to the bathroom door.

"Wait! How bad is it?"

"I don't know," I said in defeat. "I think my ribs might be broke."

"He hit you?" Marcus hissed. His tone had gone from mad to lethal in a fraction of a second. I was afraid to look at him. I was in too much pain. This accelerated healing made symptoms come on too quickly; I only hoped they'd leave just as quickly. It was nearly unbearable.

"He tackled me from the side and knocked me off the path," I recalled the painful memory.

"He what?" Marcus snapped, making me flinch.

"Ow!" I whined. "He tackled me!"

"Phoebe you have to show me. If they're broken, they'll need to be wrapped."

"I can't," my eyes were downcast. "I don't want anyone else touching me," I admitted reluctantly. "I'm sorry."

"I would never take advantage of you; you know that." I could see the hurt in his eyes."Phoebe, I can't take you to the hospital—they'll notice a change in your blood. You can't suffer like this."

I rubbed my hands over my face. I knew he was right. "Be careful," I pleaded.

"I promise to be as gentle as I can, as well as discreet."

I nodded. "I'll just . . . be a minute."

I went into the bathroom and dropped the towel. It took longer to put my pants on than I'd thought. Bending over was nearly impossible. There was no way I was going to get a bra on. I couldn't lift my arms high enough to get through the straps. As for hooking it . . . that would be hopeless.

I dug around in my cupboard and found some gauze I purchased last Halloween. Kim wanted to make a mummy for one of our displays. Funny, I never thought I'd need it to wrap myself in.

"Phoebe, are you alright?" Marcus called through the door several minutes later.

I took the deepest breath I could. He was going to freak out when he saw the bruising . . . there was no hiding it now. I wrapped the towel around me and opened the door.

"Will this work?" I asked as I held out some extra large gauze wrap.

Marcus looked at it curiously. "I'm sure it will be fine." He held out his hand and led me to the edge of the bed and sat me down.

"There's a little more bruising than I admitted . . . I just didn't want you to worry," I added quickly, seeing his darkened expression. He said nothing.

I watched as Marcus unrolled a little of the gauze. He looked at me nervously.

"This will be uncomfortable," he warned.

I nodded my head.

He moved the towel aside just enough to see my ribs. I closed my eyes; I didn't want to see his face.

He gasped. "He's a dead man!"

I turned my head so Marcus couldn't see the tears escape my tightly closed eyes. I wanted to kill Brian myself.

I felt Marcus pressing lightly on my back where he started to wrap. A low growl escaped him, each time I winced.

I tried to comfort myself with thoughts of running Brian over with my car or letting werewolves rip him to shreds. Part of me didn't even care if Marcus *did* kill him. I wanted Brian to feel pain like he'd caused me. Why on Earth would he do this? We were supposed to be friends. Phoebe and Damen were supposed to be friends too, but his assault on her wasn't so very different than Brian's was on me.

"Phoebe, you need to lift the towel a bit more; this needs to go a little higher." Marcus's tone was soft but all business. He was doing his best to detach himself from what he was doing—my guess, he was trying not to run out the door and kill Brian.

I lifted the towel so that it was just covering my chest. You could have heard a pin drop. The silence was deafening.

"I swear to you . . . I *will* kill him."

"No!" I grabbed onto his arm as he moved to stand up, wincing at the pain of it. "You promised you wouldn't leave me alone," I cried.

He looked torn. I knew he wanted nothing more than to rip Brian apart—literally.

"Please Marcus!" I took in a shallow breath. "It looks worse than it feels," I lied, trying to lighten the mood.

He sat down reluctantly and continued without another word. His eyes, deep red and swimming with anger flickered to mine.

"How bad is it?" I asked after a few minutes, groaning as he pulled the gauze tighter.

"I'm fairly certain your ribs are cracked." His eyes met mine for only an instant. This was almost as painful for him as it was for me. "I hardly doubt he was strong enough to break them."

"Thank you for helping me." I gave him a small smile. "I know I'm awful to look at."

"What's awful is that I wasn't there to prevent this from happening in the first place," he growled. "I shouldn't have left you!"

"Marcus. This *isn't* your fault. You can't always be there. You need to take care of yourself too."

"I need to take care of you first."

I reached out and cupped his face, giving him a small smile. "God only knows what else can happen to me. Since I was bitten, I've had nothing but extremely bad luck. If I get struck by lightning tomorrow as I step outside . . . well, let's just say you might not want to walk so close to me."

"I hope it hasn't been all bad?"

His hands reached up, cupping my face. I couldn't help but grin. "No. It hasn't been all bad."

With help, I stood up and walked over to my closet and found a shirt.

"How are you going to sit in a car for four hours?" he asked from behind me.

"Tylenol—lots of Tylenol. I'm not staying here. If Damen, or worse Brian, decides to show up looking for me . . ." I shuddered.

"They wouldn't reach the door step," he promised darkly.

I couldn't help but shiver again.

"New plan," he announced.

"What?"

"You're coming with me to England. Tonight. Right now."

"What?" I realized I'd just repeated my question, but somehow I felt I was missing something—like an entire conversation!

"You'll be safer there. Just until I can deal with Damen," he explained. "Besides, it will be much more comfortable for you to travel by plane . . . you can lie down across the seats if you need to."

"But my customers—"

"Will understand that you are unable to personally deliver the jewelry," he concluded. "We'll have the jewelry mailed."

"I guess I could . . ." I thought aloud, debating whether or not I should.

"Pack. I'll have the plane fueled and ready within the hour."

"Plane?" My mind was spinning. "You have your own plane?"

"You didn't think I flew here? Over the ocean?" He watched my confused expression with mild amusement. "Pack, and I'll explain along the way.

Chapter 15: New Plan

"Let me help you." Marcus opened the car door and helped me in. He went around to the driver's side and squeezed himself into the seat. He looked funny sitting behind the wheel of my little red car. I tried to suppress the laugh.

"Owww!" I held on to my sides.

"What's wrong?" he looked as if he was trying to find a safe place to touch me without causing more pain.

"You look so funny driving my girlie car." I laughed and cried at the same time—the pain was almost worth it.

Marcus glowered at me. "You shouldn't be laughing; you'll hurt yourself further," he snapped.

I turned my head and looked out the window. It was safer not to look at him. The temptation to laugh was too great.

"Hey, what about your motorcycle?" I asked. Thinking back, I hadn't seen it outside the house.

"I parked it in your garage. I hope that's alright?" He glanced over at me.

"Yes, of course." I forced a smile. My ribs felt like they were on fire. Even conversation hurt.

"Luckily, the airport is only a few minutes away," he said. "It's rather quaint really."

"Quaint?" I groaned, trying to get comfortable in my seat.

"Yes. Old fashioned, charming."

"I know what quaint means," I nearly snapped. "I don't need a dictionary definition." I tried to recline back in the seat. I couldn't get comfortable for a five-minute ride . . . how the hell was I going to last on a ten-hour flight?

"You must be in pain, you're crabby."

My mouth popped open. "Yes, I'm in pain. How can you sit there and joke about it?"

"Because if I don't, I'll jump out of this car right now, track Brian down, and literally rip him apart, piece by piece!"

I closed my gaping mouth and looked forward for the remainder of the drive.

He pulled into the long-term parking, put the ticket in the window, and got out of the car. He came around to the passenger side, opened my door, and extended his hand. I looked at it with apprehension. With one swift movement, he scooped me out of the car painlessly.

"Would you like me to carry you?"

"No, I can walk . . . just not fast," I added quickly.

He set me down on my feet and took up my luggage. We walked through the little airport, with his arm around me for support. We moved though the security gates, and continued down a small hall that led to the private planes. There, standing apart from the others, was a beautiful Lear jet.

"Is that yours?" I gasped.

"I've impressed you, at last!" he laughed lightly as he bounded up the stairs and into the plane. He returned for me a few moments later, still smiling.

Without warning, he gingerly lifted me up into his arms. "We don't have all day for you to decide whether or not you can climb stairs, or wait for you to do so," he said with a wink. Actually, I think he enjoyed any opportunity to hold me—something he'd been missing for centuries.

I leaned my head against his chest and inhaled as deeply as I could without causing physical pain. I closed my eyes, savoring the moment . . . I suddenly felt very sleepy, as I always did when I'd taken in too much of him.

"You rest here until we take off," he instructed as he sat me down on a luxurious leather seat and clasped my seatbelt for me.

"Where will you be?" I grabbed onto his hand in a panic.

"Right next to you silly." He reached out and cupped my cheek in his hand. "Relax. You'll be fine."

I nodded and, with some reluctance, released his hand. "Wait! Then, who's going to fly the plane?"

"I have a pilot."

"Is he a . . ." I looked around to see if anyone else was there, " . . . vampire too?" "No." Marcus was quick to answer.

"Does he know that you are?" I whispered.

"Yes. I hired him many years ago. He's very discreet, and very trustworthy. I needed to find you without any of the others around . . . I couldn't risk anyone else finding out what I was doing here."

Just then, a slender man with dark black hair and green eyes walked through the door.

"Good afternoon Sir . . . Miss," he bowed his head and I nodded in return. "Sir, I have several messages for you from Mr. Raymose, and one from a Mr. Balfour." He handed Marcus the slips of paper.

I turned to Marcus in a panic. He ignored me.

Marcus took the papers. "Was Damen here personally?"

"Yes Sir. Not more than half an hour ago."

Marcus held a hand out in my direction. "Richard, this is Miss Phoebe. She does not wish to see Mr. Balfour under any circumstances." He looked at Richard in an odd way—like the two of them shared some sort of code I wasn't privy to.

"Very good Sir. Will there be anything else?"

"Yes. Here is our flight plan. I'd like to take off immediately. We've already shown the officials our passports."

"Yes Sir." He took the itinerary from Marcus and headed into the cockpit.

"He's a polite one! Why does he keep bowing and calling you Sir?"

"I told you I was a nobleman—a lord actually. I'm part of the royal family," he said casually.

My mouth popped open.

"My family line is different than the one that holds the throne today. We had to arrange it that way. I don't want to call attention to myself. People would notice that I'm not aging," he explained.

"Well, you're certainly full of surprises." I shook my head in disbelief.

Marcus took the seat opposite me and began looking through his messages.

"Marcus, Damen was here?" I spoke in a low voice, just in case Richard could hear.

"Yes, he left this letter addressed to you." He started to hand me the letter, but I shunned away from it, wincing as I did so.

"Very well," Marcus sighed. He opened the letter and began relaying the message

"He says he knows you're with me and that he doesn't want to hurt you. He needs to see you, he has to explain . . ."

"Explain what?" I snapped. "There's nothing to explain!"

"Don't shoot the messenger Phoebe." Marcus gave me a disapproving look.

I rolled my eyes. "Sorry . . . Just . . . read the letter," I said impatiently, ignoring Marcus's frown.

Dearest Phoebe, (Marcus choked on the salutation.)

Please allow me to apologize to you for having to write this letter. I know that Marcus is looking after you right now and would never allow me to speak to you in person. I must first tell you that you are in no danger from me. I wouldn't hurt you anymore than I'd hurt myself.

This must all seem so confusing to you. I understand that you have acquired many of my memories, but I must tell you that you only have bits and pieces of the past. That being said, you must allow me to explain that I didn't intentionally harm Phoebe. I only wanted to make love to her. I never meant to ravage her the way that I did.

Marcus stopped reading and looked up at me, a look of betrayal hung heavy in his eyes. As if he thought I'd been keeping something else from him.

My breath caught. My hands were clasped over my mouth—I was absolutely speechless. "Marcus, I . . ." I shook my head back and forth. "I don't remember that," I said honestly.

The muscle under his eye ticked as he looked back at the letter and continued to read:

As for the baby you spoke about, I am truly sorry you have the burden of carrying that memory with you. But, Phoebe gave me no choice. She asserted herself between Marcus and I; she wouldn't let me pass without a fight—she was unfailingly loyal that way. I've regretted her death deeply and have carried the loss of her life with me these many centuries.

You and I are connected now in a way that cannot be broken. You have always been the love of my life, and now you belong to my world! Your father cannot deny me you any longer. I can finally end this war once and for all. The werewolves will have the freedom they've so deserved, and I shall have you. We will be together very soon!

With all my love,

Damen

Marcus put the paper down and began looking at the other notes.

I was on the edge of my seat. "That's it?" I gasped. "You're not going to say anything?" I snatched up the letter and read it to myself.

Marcus stared at me incredulously. "There is nothing more to discuss. If he wishes a fight, then he shall have it."

"You're going to fight over me?"

"I will *die* before I let him have you. You. Are. Mine!" he growled. His eyes had all but turned black.

"I'm not a prize," I snapped, turning my attention to the window. I was flattered, and infuriated at the same time. That Marcus would actually *fight* over me . . . he could get himself killed.

"Phoebe. You are my life. You always have been. I've been without you for far too long. I won't allow him to take you from me. Not again!" His resolve was undeniable.

I pursed my lips. I tried to take a deep breath—my ribs burned like they were on fire—I gasped for air.

"Darling, please. Don't worry yourself about this; I'll take care of it. Just rest." He smiled warmly at me and resumed his reading.

"Rest? Are you crazy? There is a psychotic lovesick werewolf who has concocted an insane plan to win my heart! Like that will somehow put an end to a war that's been going on for a thousand years?" I shouted. "Let's not forgot about delusional Brian who thinks that he can excuse his behavior by saying my scent was so alluring he couldn't help himself—he *had* to have me." I rolled my eyes and continued my rant. "Then there's the vampire . . ." I motioned to Marcus who was watching me, as he no doubt thought I was cracking up. " . . . Who thinks I'm such a treasure he'd risk his life to keep me. I don't know which one of you is craziest?" I huffed.

"This has to be a dream," I thought out loud as I scrubbed my hand over my face. "No. Not even my imagination would hurt this much," I grumped as I held my ribs again. "Stupid Brian!"

I became aware of Marcus's stare. I had to look away.

"You *are* a treasure," he spoke softly. "I knew the moment I saw you in the garden, I'd love you the rest of my existence."

I turned back toward him. My anger, melting away . . .

"I've loved you for so long . . . even in death . . . there is no other way for me to exist. Now that I have you back . . . I can't lose you again. I won't!"

"But to risk your life for me . . . I'm not the same Phoebe you loved so long ago." I felt sad as I said this. I so wanted to be that Phoebe for him.

Marcus leaned forward and took my hand. "You are my Phoebe. I knew it the moment I saw you back in London. You fill the hole where my heart should be . . . I would *die* for you!"

"Marcus . . . " I sighed. "I hope I don't let you down. I hope I'm truly the Phoebe you want to love."

He leaned in and kissed my cheek softly. "You are," he whispered across my ear.

The plane started to move, and I looked out the window as we taxied toward the runway.

"Lord Ashworth, we're cleared for takeoff Sir," Richard's voice came over the intercom.

"You weren't joking . . . Lord Ashworth." I grinned.

Marcus moved back to his seat and fastened his seatbelt. The plane made a smooth upward climb, and we were airborne in minutes.

I watched Marcus as he studied one of the notes Richard had given him.

"Is anything wrong?" I asked.

"It's from Raymose. Luther needs me back immediately. The werewolves have been growing in numbers far faster then we'd expected . . ."

"What does that mean?"

"It means that Damen has been very busy. He not only has time to torment you, but he's also managed to form an army and create more werewolves." He crinkled the note in his hand and threw it across the floor. He then pulled a ringing phone from his pocket and flipped it open.

"Raymose! I'm sorry; I just received your messages."

I stayed perfectly silent. There was something frightening about knowing Marcus was talking to another vampire—a real vampire, Raymose at that. This still seemed like a strange fanciful dream to me. My recollection of Raymose was sketchy at best.

"Please give my apologies to Luther. I've been otherwise engaged." He shot me a quick glance.

"Of course it's important. Do you think I'd have left if it wasn't important?" Marcus's tone became sharp. I found myself recoiling painfully in my chair.

"No, I didn't want to pull anyone else away . . . It was a snap decision. I wasn't certain where Damen was heading . . . It's just a hunch, but I believe he's on his way back to England as we speak."

I looked at Marcus incredulously. How could he know that?

"I'm in the air right now. I should be there in about thirteen hours," he said as he glanced at his watch.

Thirteen hours? I whined mentally. How was I going to last that long? I slumped in my chair.

"I'll see you then." He snapped his phone shut and returned to his messages.

We had been in the air for nearly half an hour. Marcus stared blankly out the window. He had been so quiet since his phone call with Raymose; I didn't quite know what to make of it. I decided to break the silence since *he* obviously wasn't.

"Marcus, are you upset with me?"

"Why would you ask that?" He looked genuinely surprised by the question.

"You haven't spoken a word to me since we took off. You've acted strangely since . . ." I almost hated to mention it. "Damen's note." I could feel the tension return almost instantaneously.

"I don't seem to be able to keep him from finding you," he sighed.

"He said that he and I are connected now . . . that he can track my scent." I tried to casually sniff under my arm to see if I smelled.

"It's not that kind of smell," Marcus laughed.

I was turning red again; I could feel the heat of the blush on my cheeks.

"You are connected, but only because he bit you."

My eyebrows furrowed.

"A werewolf never forgets the scent of the ones they change," he explained. "They can usually smell each other within a mile. But not you . . . Damen has a stronger connection to you. He can track you from much further away. Not only that, but he knew you'd be on this plane with me." Marcus growled in frustration. "I don't know how he's doing it."

We sat in quiet for some time, watching the clouds out the window. The sun was shining through the heavens, and it was breathtaking. But all its beauty couldn't lift the tension that was undoubtedly looming over us.

"Marcus?"

"Yes my love?"

I kept my eyes to the window. I wasn't sure I wanted to see his reaction to my next question.

"I'd just wondered if you've reconsidered . . . turning me?" My voice was softer than I'd intended.

"No. I told you. I don't know what that would do to you. There's never been—" he shook his head. "Not if there's another way. I won't chance it."

"But what if there isn't another way? What if Damen finds me and—"

"He won't!"

"Marcus, I've thought about this. I don't want to be like him. I'd rather be like you."

"Phoebe . . ."

"What if I were dying and biting me was the only way to keep us together . . . would you do it then?"

He reached out and took my hands. His eyes gazed into mine, drawing me deeper and deeper into his stare. I could feel my heart begin to flutter as I watched the crooked smile on his face move closer to mine. I could feel his cool breath on my lips as he took them eagerly—I didn't protest.

"There is always another way . . ." he whispered across my lips.

Ignoring the pain, I threw my arms around him. I didn't want to let go. I didn't share his view. There wasn't always a way, and I couldn't help but feel that my time with Marcus was ticking away. There was something in Damen's note that left me believing my mortality was nearing an end. I could sense it.

"Darling, what is it?" He pulled gently away from me, staring at my torn expression.

"Marcus please—"

"Phoebe, this is ridiculous," he growled in frustration. "You're not dying!" He removed my arms and sank back into his chair. "Don't ask me to do this . . . I can't turn you. If I didn't stop drinking . . . I'd be the cause of your death." He shook his head wearily. I knew he didn't like to deny me, but in his mind, my request was beyond reason.

"I haven't bit a human in so long; I've avoided the temptation. If I were to revert . . ." He looked like he was going to be sick. "Don't ask me to damn your soul!"

"Damen already did that, didn't he?" The words flew angrily from my lips.

Marcus's head dropped with a sigh.

"You'd let me die then . . . again." It wasn't a question.

His head snapped up. I could see the anger building in his eyes.

"If I'm going to die anyway, wouldn't you want to take a chance on saving me?

"Unless of course you don't want to spend the rest of eternity with me." Oh God, I hadn't thought of that.

"You know I want to spend the rest of time with you," he growled. "But you wouldn't be just a vampire. You're asking me to turn you into the unknown."

I turned away from him. Tears were threatening to spill over any moment.

"Phoebe, you must understand—"

"I'm sorry I put you in this position. I know it's not in your nature to love someone like me."

Marcus caught my chin and turned my face back to his, his thumb gently wiping away a tear. I could see his resolve break.

"Alright," he sighed in defeat. He went down on one knee and bowed his head. "I promise. I will move heaven, or hell for that matter, to keep you with me. Even if that means turning you."

I threw my arms around him.

"But only if there is no other way," he reiterated. "You have to literally be dying—"

I held onto him tighter still. The rest of his words lost. Nothing else mattered. I knew that if the worst were to happen to me, I'd always have Marcus. He'd find a way to save me—he'd never let me die.

Chapter 16: Demands

With each passing hour, I felt more and more anxious about returning to England.

"Are you alright?" Marcus asked as he reached over and held my hand.

"I was just thinking about the last time I traveled here . . . so much has happened since then."

"I promise: no werewolf will bite you this time."

"I'm not exactly worrying about the werewolves," I said under my breath.

Marcus's forehead creased. "You're worried about vampires."

"Obviously."

"You needn't worry. My home is very secluded; I don't have many visitors."

"I thought you belonged to a coven?"

"I do, but I don't reside with the coven. I still live in my family home. It's more private for when the Moon Hunters meet," he explained.

"So other vampires *will* be there?"

"On occasion," Marcus hesitated with his answer.

"You're not worried they'll . . ." I leaned in closer, " . . . smell me?" My voice was almost a whisper.

"Mmm. You do smell good," he mused as he slowly moved his nose along the side of my neck, inhaling deeply. I involuntarily shivered.

"You really could take me anytime you wanted . . . couldn't you?"

"Mm hum," he breathed into my hair.

His lips moved across my throat slowly. I could feel my heart beating faster and faster. I sat, nearly frozen in my chair. He had a certain power of rendering me helpless whenever he wished—a vampire thing no doubt—which Marcus used playfully to his advantage.

"Marcus," I breathed, gripping his shoulders for support. "Aren't you worried they'll discover that I'm there?"

He paused momentarily. "There is no doubt in my mind they'd know you were there . . . if I let them get close enough." I could hear the smile in his words. He kissed my neck softly.

I forced my mind to focus. "And the werewolves? Will they be close as well?"

"No." His lips were on my ear now. "They do not trespass on my land."

I sighed in relief.

"Do you honestly think I'm going to let any of them near you?" His eyes, a luscious shade of red, were staring into mine. "I wouldn't put you in danger like that."

I nodded in understanding.

He held my face in his hands. "You see darling, nothing to worry about. I've already instructed Richard that if for some reason I do not return, he's to bring you back to your home." He kissed my lips briskly.

My heart stopped. "What? Where are you going?"

I could see the resolve in his eyes, and he could see the determination in mine. He began to look nervous.

"You will not put yourself in danger for me . . . never again," he warned.

"There's going to be a battle," I gasped. "That's what your note said—the one from Raymose, didn't it?"

"There's no need for you to concern yourself. You'll be protected. No harm will come to you." He rose from his seat and made his way toward the cockpit door.

"But what about you?" I called after him. "Marcus, I just got you back. I don't want to lose you. If you'd only let me—"

"No, no, no! It's completely unthinkable! You're human!" he thundered.

I knew he spoke the truth, but there was something pulling me. I couldn't let him risk his life to keep Damen from me. No. If it came to that, I'd leave. I would go to Damen if that meant sparing Marcus. I could live in misery, but I couldn't live if

Marcus was killed because of me. Damen knew this. He knew that I would put Marcus before myself. He was counting on it. That's what he meant in his letter: "We'll be together very soon". I became aware of the hole Marcus's eyes were boring through me. I smiled meekly at him.

"NO! Whatever you've reasoned out in your head is out of the question!" His eyes were black as coal. He gripped my arms tightly—there was no escape.

"You will not *defy* me!" he hissed through his teeth. "Is this in any way unclear?"

I couldn't look away; I was too scared. Never in my life had anyone spoken to me like this—I'd never have allowed it! But deep down I knew, Marcus had said this to frighten me into obeying him. He was trying to protect me—and I loved him for it. I would truly do what he asked, without question, as long as it didn't mean sacrificing his life for mine. I knew that he would not let this go unless I gave him the answer he wanted . . . so I bent it just a little . . . in my favor . . . naturally.

"You are very clear Marcus, I understand."

He released my shoulders.

I stepped back slowly to my seat, rubbing the circulation back into my arms. I took up the blanket that was waiting for me and sat down in my chair.

Marcus watched me for a moment. His eyes, dark and untrusting, followed every movement I made. Without another word, he disappeared into the cockpit to relieve Richard.

Richard came out of the cockpit looking tired. He smiled warmly as he approached.

"May I get you something from the kitchen, Miss?"

"No thank you, Richard, I ate a little while ago."

I watched as he walked to the back of the plane to fix his dinner. He wasn't gone long before my eyes closed and I drifted off to sleep.

I began dreaming of a lightly wooded countryside. The sky was dark and the air was moist. I ran as quickly as I could through the unfamiliar landscape. The moon, my only light, was peeking out from behind the clouds. A loud howling broke the silence . . .

I bounced in my seat—the plane was experiencing a little turbulence. I opened my eyes and saw Richard sleeping on a nearby chair. He opened his eyes as the plane continued to bounce around.

"I hope you don't mind me sleeping here Miss?" he asked when he saw me staring at him.

I blushed, having been caught watching him. "No, please, Richard go back to sleep."

He looked at his watch and started to get up slowly.

"I better get back and relieve Lord Ashworth." He covered his mouth quickly to conceal a yawn.

"But you haven't had any sleep," I protested.

"Oh, I've had a good seven hours Miss, I'll be just fine."

"Was I asleep for that long?"

"Yes Miss," His eyes glanced toward the cockpit. "You were . . . whimpering in your sleep."

"Whimpering? People don't whimper Richard, dogs do." My mouth gaped open as I realized what I'd said. I looked at Richard out the corner of my eye—he pretended not to notice.

"If you don't mind me asking, are you alright, Miss?" I could hear the genuine concern in his voice.

"I'm fine. I've just had some trouble sleeping lately. I'm sorry if I disturbed you."

"Forgive me Miss. It was out of line to ask you such a personal question." He rose and made his way to the cockpit. "But if you should need anything . . ." he added before he reached the door, "anything at all . . . please don't hesitate to ask." He bowed his head and ducked into the cockpit.

I was trying to decode Richard's cryptic message when Marcus came into the room.

"Richard said you were awake." He hesitated for a moment, testing the air before he sat down beside me. He slowly reached his hand out, gently pushing my hair off my shoulder. "Did you sleep well?"

"I must have. I didn't realize how long I'd slept."

"Are you alright? Richard mentioned you had a restless sleep."

"I'm fine. Really. You don't need to worry." I forced smile. "I think I'll go fix myself up a bit."

I got up and went to an overhead compartment. I tried to reach for the handle but stopped mid way.

"What is it?"

"Nothing," I said in a strained voice. "I tried to reach out once again—instant pain; so much for quick healing.

"Why didn't you just ask for my help?" Marcus reached over my head, opened the compartment, and took down my overnight bag from home.

"I could have done that myself." I snatched the bag out of his hands.

"I'll just leave you to it then." He put his hands out and backed away. "There. You can pick out what you'd like—*all* by yourself," he mocked.

"That's not what I meant," I huffed.

"I know what you meant," he chuckled. "As much as I regret it, you're still in pain."

I folded my arms in a pout. I was still fuming at his closed minded opinion about me helping him.

"You can be such a child at times . . . it's really quite amusing!" he laughed heartedly.

"I'm glad I amuse you. You'll see; I'll be better in no time. I won't always be so helpless," I growled, huffing past him.

Marcus grabbed my arm, halting me in my tracks. "Just what exactly do you mean by that?" He studied my face. "What is going on in that head of yours?" his eyes were growing dark.

"What are you talking about?" I decided to play dumb.

"You know exactly what I'm talking about. You do remember what you promised before I left you to sleep don't you?"

"Of course I do." I looked him right in the eyes.

He watched me carefully for a moment then released my arm.

"I'll be back in a bit," I said quickly as I dashed for the bathroom to wash.

It felt good to get cleaned up. My bandages were starting to come loose. I knew it would have to be redone, and I knew I couldn't do it myself.

"Damn. I hate being so dependent," I grumped out loud.

I finished my hair and makeup, brushed my teeth, and put on my jeans before I took a deep breath and opened the bathroom door. Marcus was sitting on a chair, reading the newspaper from yesterday.

He looked up to see me standing in the doorway with one hand holding a hand towel across my chest, and a roll of gauze in the other. The expression on his face caused me to instantly blush.

"I was wondering if you could help me with this?"

"You're asking for my help, Miss Independent?" he smirked.

I stared at him, pursing my lips as I tried to think of a real zinger—I had nothing.

He got up and walked over to me. His cool fingers brushed my hand as he took the gauze. His eyes met mine. There was a look of devotion; unlike I'd ever seen reflecting back at me. As if he was saying, I didn't even need to ask. I smiled back at him.

"This looks better," he said encouragingly as he tilted his head, examining my arms.

"Yes . . . sort of."

"What's wrong?" He looked taken aback.

"Could we just get this over with please?"

Marcus followed me over to a chair and knelt down beside me.

"Are you sure you're comfortable doing this?" I asked, once I'd sat down.

"I helped you yesterday. Why would it bother me anymore today?" he looked confused by the question.

I took the deepest breath I could before I shifted my towel. I knew he was going to freak out. There was no way around it.

"How is this possible?" he hissed.

"Marcus, please. Don't look at it, just wrap it!" I said through closed eyes.

My torso was covered in painful deep purple bruises. What wasn't visible before certainly was now. There was no sign of it healing.

"If we weren't over the ocean right now . . ."

"What, you'd jump out of the plane?" I mocked. Having my ribs unwrapped made my injuries feel worse. I was a bit cranky.

Marcus shot me a menacing look.

"You'd jump out of the plane!" I nearly shouted in disbelief.

"Phoebe, have you looked at yourself?"

"Of course I have," I replied sharply.

"I'll find him."

"Marcus please . . . just let it go . . . I'm sure Brian won't bother me again." I winced, as he pulled tighter on the wrap.

"I will not let this go. Do you think I would ever let you go home, knowing that that pathetic excuse for a human is walking the streets?"

I squinted my eyes while Marcus made his final pass across my ribs. I let out a breath of air. "Thank you. I couldn't have done that myself," I admitted quietly.

He placed his hands on my shoulders. His thumb lightly moved along the base of my throat. I could feel my heart pounding harder and harder. His eyes were turning a beautiful shade of amber—a color that would have frightened anyone—but not me. They drew me in deeper and deeper.

"I *will* protect you," his lips promised with a kiss.

It seemed like forever since he'd kissed me like this. I could feel myself melting in his arms. He held my body to his. My fingers ran through his hair, pulling him closer with each kiss. His lips glided softly down my neck as I gasped for air. It was as if he commanded my blood to flow faster. I opened my eyes and watched the room spin around me. His lips, now moving down my shoulder, made me keenly aware that I was still underdressed. I was no longer holding the towel.

I slammed my body into his.

"Phoebe, what are you—"

"My towel's gone!" I shrieked. I held him to me, concealing my chest as I tried to maneuver around, searching for the towel.

Marcus laughed. "Really, you're choosing to be modest now?"

"They're your rules," I griped. "You've got me so flustered! I don't have to cover up. You're the one who wants to keep things tame, not me!"

"No, no," he warned playfully. He felt around and found the towel in question. He palmed it for a moment, as if considering whether or not to give it to me. He let out a frustrated groan and reluctantly handed it over.

I secured the towel over my chest and clambered to my feet. The blood rushed to my head. I steadied myself before I stepped past him to retrieve a shirt.

He looked as flustered as I felt. I knew it took all his strength to deny himself the one thing he desperately wanted—me.

The fasten seatbelt sign came on again.

"Lord Ashworth, we've been cleared for landing. The car is already waiting at the gate," Richard's voice came over the intercom.

"My home is just outside of Durham . . . about a five hour drive," Marcus remarked as I took my seat. "Nice shirt."

My eyes met his. A slight grin hung on his face. "Thanks," I replied dryly.

I looked out the plane window as we touched down. It was just about dusk when the plane came to a stop. I stared out at the unfamiliar scenery. My eyes fixed on a man leaning against a shiny black car off in the distance.

"Phoebe?"

I pressed my face up against the plane window, straining my eyes to see through the darkening sky.

I jumped back, nearly toppling over the seat behind me. I cried out in pain, uttering obscenities under my breath. I'd forgotten about my wounded body.

"Phoebe!" Marcus leapt over a seat to get to me. I pulled him down close to me and whispered, as if the man outside could hear.

"Raymose is outside!" I breathed.

"What?"

"Raymose. He's outside." I pointed to the window above my head. "There, by the car!"

Marcus looked out the window for a moment and then turned back to me. He looked uneasy.

"Do you think he saw you?"

"I don't think so." I was still whispering.

"How did you know it was him?"

"I just . . . recognized his face."

"Stay here." Marcus shot me a stern look before he opened the hatch and stepped out into the night.

I stayed on the floor quietly for several minutes before I decided to sneak a peek. I couldn't stand not knowing what was going on. I prayed he hadn't seen me.

Raymose was talking to Marcus by the car, his back to me. Marcus must have positioned the conversation that way so there wouldn't be a chance of Raymose seeing me if I decided to look through the window—he knew me well.

I ducked my head. Marcus had started to walk back toward the plane. It didn't look like Raymose planned to leave anytime soon.

Marcus walked through the door just as Richard came out from the cockpit.

"Are you quite alright Miss?" he asked as he noticed me sitting on the floor.

"Yes Richard, I'm fine. I just wanted to make sure I hadn't dropped anything before I left." It sounded like a good excuse to be on the floor.

"Richard, I need you to drive Miss Rose directly home. It is extremely important that she doesn't leave the plane for at least ten minutes."

"Yes of course, Sir. I'd be happy to see Miss Rose home. I'll just be a moment up front."

Marcus knelt down in front of me. "Phoebe, I don't have much time. Raymose is here to take me to Luther. The werewolves have been ravaging the countryside, killing most but turning as many as they can."

I stared at him with wide eyes.

"Richard will take care of you—"

"But what if Damen comes? How can Richard take care of me?" I begged.

Marcus's brow furrowed. "Phoebe, I haven't been completely forthcoming with you regarding Richard." He stared me squarely in the face. "I didn't want to frighten you, but now I find that I have no choice. Richard is a werewolf."

"What!" I gasped. "You want me to ride for five hours in a car with a werewolf?"

"Phoebe, I trust Richard with my life . . . and with yours," he added firmly.

"But what if there's a full moon? What if he turns into a werewolf?" I was on my feet now heading for my bags.

"What are you doing?" He sounded tired. "Phoebe, I really must go."

"Then go! I'm going to catch a commercial flight home."

He grabbed my arm and spun me around.

"Ouch," I winced. "Marcus . . ."

"You are not going home without me!" he warned. "It's not safe!"

"And riding in a car with a werewolf is?" I snapped back. "I'll take my chances with Brian thank you."

Marcus's expression softened. "Phoebe, please. Trust me. I have to leave you with Richard now . . . he will take care of you. I promise. You like Richard don't you?" He played on my good will.

"Yes . . . but now that I know he's a werewolf . . ."

"And I am a vampire," he interrupted. "Do you think any less of me?"

"That's not fair, and completely not the same thing!" I protested.

"Phoebe!" he pleaded. His hands were cupping my face, his eyes demanding my full attention. I looked long into them.

"Oh, alright." I resolved. "I'll go with him, but if he tries anything wolfish, I'm out of that car," I threatened. "I'll *walk* back to the airport!"

"You will not travel alone. Damen is back now—you're not safe," he stressed, his hands gripping my face firmer now. "None of us are." He took my hands, pulling me to him. "We'll be together soon, I promise."

I nodded. Fighting back the tears that threatened to fall.

"My home is your home," he lifted my hands to his lips, kissing the tops of them, one at a time. "It used to be your home too, once upon a time." He smiled warmly.

A tear fell. "Marcus, please be careful."

His mouth crushed into mine, taking me completely by surprise. The intensity of his kiss frightened me. As if he was asking me to hold onto him and never let go.

He pulled back—as breathless as I was—and was out the door before I could whisper good-bye.

Chapter 17: Richard

"Are you ready to leave now, Miss?" A voice from behind me called out.

"Richard!" I clutched my hand to my chest, trying to still my heart. "Yes. I'm ready."

"Very good Miss. Let me help you with these." He picked up my bags and carried them off the plane. He looked around before he gave me the all clear.

After a few minutes discussion, Richard agreed to let me sit in the front beside him. If he was going to do anything wolfish I wanted to make sure I didn't miss it. We started down the highway and had been driving for about twenty minutes before Richard broke the silence. "Are you excited to be visiting England Miss?"

"I suppose. I didn't have such a good trip last time . . . that's not true, most of it was wonderful," I prattled on nervously. I looked out the window trying to see something, anything. All I could see was endless black. I couldn't tell if it was the countryside or sky—it all blended together. I sighed, slumping back into my seat.

"Are you alright Miss?" Richard asked as he continued to drive into the darkness.

"I'm sorry Richard; I don't mean to be impolite. I'm just worried about Marcus."

"I'm sure he's fine Miss. He's very capable of taking care of himself. I wouldn't worry too much if I were you." He smiled—I could see his white teeth gleaming in the dark. I shied away from him. I had a vision of me as Little Red Riding Hood sitting beside the Big, Bad Wolf.

We drove on in silence. I kept trying to close my eyes and sleep but my mind kept wandering to the werewolf that was sitting beside me—I couldn't relax. I looked at the clock, an hour had passed and neither one of us had spoken a word. I decided it was my turn to break the awkward silence.

"Richard, how old are you?"

"Well now, I'm..." he paused for a moment. "Thirty-six Miss."

"I mean how old are you *really*?" My question was implying.

"Miss?"

"Marcus told me you're a . . . werewolf." I added the last bit quickly.

We drove in silence for a mile, then two, three . . .

"Say something Richard, please!"

"I see."

"That's it. You see?"

"What would you like me to say, Miss?"

"I don't know, I just thought we should be honest with each other," I shrugged.

"Very well Miss. What would you like to know?" His tone was pleasant. Like we were old friends talking about ordinary things.

"For starters, how old are you?" I asked again, a little impatiently this time.

I could see Richard smirk a little. "I'm six-hundred and thirty years old."

My mouth dropped open. I had to consciously make myself shut it. I still wasn't used to hearing how old my new acquaintances truly were. Even Marcus admitting he was seven hundred and forty-nine still didn't seem possible.

"Why are you working for Marcus?" I continued.

"I've been working for Lord Ashworth for nearly ninety years now," he explained. He's honest, and treats me with respect. There aren't many places a gentleman like myself can live and work." Richard chuckled, making me feel more at ease.

"But why would you stay with him? I thought there was some sort of war going on between the vampires and werewolves?" I wasted no time continuing this line of questioning.

"I'm not a traitor, Miss, if that's what you mean."

"No, of course not." The thought hadn't even crossed my mind.

"The werewolf that created me was bit directly by Damen. I don't share the same views as the majority of the werewolf population. I don't wish to annihilate the vampire species. I think we can co-exist as we have for thousands of years. That's not to say I believe in the slavery of werewolves either," he pointed out quickly. "But I am hardly a slave. I belong to no one." There was so much pride in Richard's voice. I didn't doubt him. He stayed with Marcus because he believed in him.

I thought about his words. My eyes darted back and forth as I realized what he'd just said to me.

"Richard. Were Damen's memories passed down to you as well?" I knew the answer.

"Yes Miss."

"Then you know about Phoebe? I mean the other Phoebe," I spoke excitedly.

"You look just like her, Miss." He smiled, glancing my way.

I smiled to myself. Not only did I have the other Phoebe's memories, but I looked like her too . . . I was beyond pleased.

"Now you, Miss." Richard seemed to be feeling comfortable now. "Would you like to tell me why you're still part human?"

My breath caught.

"Why haven't you changed?" I could hear the uneasiness in his voice.

"Marcus didn't tell you?" I asked, honestly surprised he hadn't.

"Lord Ashworth doesn't explain everything to me, Miss. My job isn't to question what he does, but to assist him."

I sat quietly for a moment before I told Richard the whole story: from my attack in London only a month and a half ago, to the attack this morning in the park. I found Richard surprisingly easy to talk to. He listened well and didn't ask pointless questions.

We had been driving for three hours when I had brought him up to date on my life thus far.

"Richard, there's one memory in particular that I need to figure out. There was a time when Damen and Phoebe were in the woods, and—"

"I won't discuss that, Miss."

"Why not?" I protested, taken aback by the firmness of his voice.

"There are certain things that need to be left in the past. Besides, you were bit directly by Damen. Your memories are stronger than mine would be," he conveniently added.

I crossed my arms over my chest. Richard was apparently going to be a dead end.

"So how did you find Marcus?" I asked, looking back toward the window.

"My memories from Damen helped me to learn who would share my views on the war. I came to Lord Ashworth's estate ninety years ago and have been with him ever since."

"Are we almost there?" I sounded like an impatient child.

The corner of Richard's mouth twitched. "Yes, Miss, we're almost there."

"So, what do you do when you turn into a werewolf?"

"Do, Miss?"

"Yes. What happens when you change?" I rephrased the question.

"For starters, I know when a full moon is coming. I usually keep to the castle—away from everyone, just in case I lose control."

"How do you keep control? I thought werewolves run wild and kill everyone."

"It's taken nearly a century to master it Miss. One must have a strong mind, and the will to not want to kill everything in sight!"

I looked at him out the corner of my eye.

"Don't worry Miss. There isn't a full moon tonight." He nudged my arm playfully.

I nudged him back. I was completely at ease with Richard. I understood now why Marcus trusted him with me.

"Wait. Did you say castle?"

"Yes Miss, just there."

I looked off in the direction Richard had pointed. It was hard to see but I could barely make out a giant stone castle off in the distance. The moon had provided just enough light for an adequate silhouette.

"Home," Richard announced.

"Marcus didn't say he lived in a castle!" I pressed my face up against the windshield, hoping for a better look.

"Lord Ashworth is a bit modest," Richard said as he pulled into a long driveway that appeared to be lined with trees. A cloud cover had passed over the moon, making fine detail impossible.

The entryway ahead was lit with giant lamps, illuminating a magnificent set of double doors that had to be two stories tall. My mouth popped open in awe. A lady wearing a plain black dress waited to greet us at the door.

"Sarah!" Richard called out.

Sarah was beautiful. Her bright green eyes and peaches and cream complexion complimented the curly red hair that was braided loosely down her back. She couldn't have been much older than I was.

She was beaming at the sight of Richard. Her eyes quickly turned to me, and her smile faded as she shot Richard a betrayed look.

"Sarah, this is Miss Rose; Lord Ashworth's guest."

A welcoming smile appeared instantaneously on Sarah's face.

"Oh, it's a pleasure to meet you, Miss." She bowed her head, and motioned us into the house.

I smiled back. "Thank you Sarah. It's nice to meet you too."

The entry hall was as big as my little house. Beautiful tapestries adorned the room. A large chandelier hung in the center and lit the way to a spectacular stairway.

"You must be hungry," Sarah said as she took my coat.

I was hungry. "Very."

"Richard! Shame on you for not thinking of stopping along the way and getting her something to eat." Sarah scolded as she took my arm and led me down the hall into a brightly lit kitchen.

The room was filled with many smells: fresh bread right out of the oven, bubbling soup on the stove, and a fresh pot of tea on the table.

A very round woman with short black hair and a jolly smile placed the warm bread on the table.

"Ah, Richard, it's about time you've decided to come home," she said brightly. "Who is this bonny lass?"

"Charlotte, this is Miss Rose, Lord Ashworth's guest."

"And where is Mr. Marcus this evening?" She asked as she sat me into a chair.

"He had a meeting with Mr. Raymose." Richard said as he took a chair opposite me.

"Ah, so we may not see him for a few days then?" Sarah replied as she helped Charlotte pass out the bowls of soup.

"Nonsense! He wouldn't leave this lovely girl here all by herself now would he?" Charlotte said giving me a wink. "No, no, he'll be back soon."

"May I help you?" I offered to cut the bread.

"Never you mind dear, rest yourself," Charlotte insisted as she took up the knife and began to slice the bread.

The four of us ate around the little kitchen table. Richard and Sarah exchanged subtle glances—it was obvious they were in love. And that's when I wondered. Was Sarah a werewolf too? Was Charlotte? Oh God, were they . . . No. They couldn't be vampires. They were eating.

"Are you alright dear? You look a little pale," Charlotte remarked.

"I'm fine," I answered quickly. "Just a little tired." It was true.

Charlotte was delighted to have a houseguest. "There has never been a woman, other than the ones that have worked here, in this house," she said disapprovingly.

"I don't understand it," she continued. "He's handsome, wealthy beyond reason. Why hasn't he settled down?"

"Charlotte! It isn't your place to speak about Mr. Marcus like that." Sarah's eyes flickered to me.

"Don't mind me," I raised up one hand.

"Thank you dear but Sarah's right; I shouldn't speak ill of Mr. Marcus, especially in front of a guest. He's really a lovely man. Frustrating as can be," she thundered. "Hardly an appetite that one. Can't get him to take a single bite of meat! But a lovely man."

I tried to hide the smirk on my face. Charlotte had no idea what Marcus was.

"Well now, you've outdone yourself again, Charlotte," Richard complemented as he rose from his chair. "I'll just show Miss Rose to her room now."

"Thank you for dinner." I smiled.

"We'll see you in the morning dear," Charlotte called after me.

"They seem like lovely ladies," I remarked to Richard as we climbed the giant stairway in the entry hall.

"The very best, Miss."

"So, you and Sarah . . ." I teased, nudging his elbow playfully.

"You noticed?" His face went pale. "Oh, Miss, please don't say anything to Lord Ashworth. I know it isn't proper." Richard had stopped walking and was standing in front of me with large pleading eyes.

"Richard, what's wrong with it?"

"Sarah and I are employed by Lord Ashworth. It wouldn't be proper for the two of us to be carrying on while in his home."

"Surely Marcus wouldn't care if the two of you are in love."

"No, he wouldn't. But, that's just not how one conducts themselves . . . especially when one is a werewolf and the other isn't."

"Does Sarah know you're a werewolf?" I whispered the question, guessing the answer.

"No! I'd rather protect her from that as long as I can. I don't want to frighten her."

If Sarah didn't know Richard was a werewolf, than I doubted she knew Marcus was a vampire. How were they keeping that from the staff?

"Well, she won't hear it from me. But Richard, you should tell her."

"Not everyone is as accepting as you, Miss. I'd rather not send Sarah screaming from her home."

We continued up the stairs and down a magnificent hall decorated with priceless paintings and medieval armor—things that should be in a museum.

"Richard! Is that an original Monet?" I knew it had to be I was ecstatic.

"You're familiar with his work, Miss?"

"Yes, he's who inspired me to start oil painting in the first place." I admitted, not taking my eyes off the painting. "Although I haven't painted for some time. My work keeps me busy."

"Then you should enjoy exploring tomorrow, Miss. The castle halls are filled with such paintings." He motioned to a Renoir across the hall.

My mouth gaped open as I walked over to the painting. I stared at it for a moment longer before I reluctantly tore myself away and followed Richard.

"I could have Sarah relocate the painting to your room, Miss, if you'd like. I'm sure we can find something else to decorate the hall with. I heard Mr. Marcus mention that he'd just acquired a rare Matisse the other day.

"I'd love that!" I exclaimed, as I followed Richard through a door. "I know this room," I whispered to myself as I stepped inside.

The room alone seemed larger than my little house, but not quite as large as the entry below. The large four-poster bed that stood in the center of the room was adorned with ornate detail. A trail of old vine roses was carved into the headboard. The quilt that was spread across the top of the bed was white, and embroidered with little pink and red roses. It had to have been hand stitched. I'd never seen such intricate work before, or had I? The bedding looked so soft and billowy; I'd be sleeping on a cloud tonight. I was beyond tired and longed to jump into that bed and sleep for days.

Richard set my bags down by an elegant armoire that took up a quarter of the wall to the right of the doorway. "I hope you'll be comfortable here. Mr. Marcus has kept it just as you'd liked it."

That was it. The rest of my heart officially broke. I hadn't heard of anything more sad or romantic in my life.

"It's perfect Richard," I spoke softly. I didn't want to wake myself if this was indeed a dream. I wandered the room, touching the familiar objects, smiling as I remembered . . .

"I'm not sure when Mr. Marcus will join us again. I think it best that you keep close to the castle until his return." I nodded while Richard spoke, my thoughts too far away to speak.

"There are horse stables to the east, and the kitchen is open whenever you need it."

"Thank you Richard, I'm sure I'll be fine." Something shiny caught the corner of my eye. Above the fireplace, hung on the wall was a brilliantly polished long sword.

"Oh Richard, it's lovely!" I went over to the fireplace to admire the sword closer.

"Do you know how to use it, Miss?" he asked hesitantly.

"I used to . . . " I muttered under my breath. I couldn't take my eyes off it. I was mesmerized.

"If there won't be anything else, I'll take my leave now, Miss."

"Thank you, Richard. I'll be fine." I gave him a small smile and resumed staring at the sword. I heard the door close a moment later.

Eventually, I pried myself away from the gleaming weapon and went to my bag, looking for pajamas. I found a nightdress, black satin. I hoped Marcus would like it. Oh well, there'll be other nights, I thought to myself.

I turned out the light and climbed into bed. I lay there in the dark for several minutes deliberating.

I'm just going to hold it, I thought as I clicked the light back on. I walked over to the fireplace and took the sword from the wall. An instant flood of memories came rushing to me. I glided my fingers over the filigree handle, remembering the delicate design. I recalled its swiftness as I swung it around. The swooshing sound as it sliced through the air. I smiled at the memory of my father giving it to me when I turned thirty-five—it was a gift, marking my immortality. I sighed. I remembered practicing with Raymose for countless hours as he trained me. This *was* my sword.

I hung it back on the wall. With one hand on the handle and the other stupidly holding the tip, the blade sliced my hand across the palm as easily as if it were cutting through butter. It was as sharp as ever.

The sword slipped from my grasp, landing at my feet with a loud clatter. I stared at the blood that was gushing from my hand and fell to the floor. My eyes could barely focus. The ringing in my ears was deafening. I brought my hand up to my face—the blood flowed steadily out the wound.

I could hear footsteps approaching from down the hall. The soft clunking of boots as they moved over the stone floor.

"Help!" I breathed.

The door flung open almost instantaneously.

"Phoebe!"

My head rolled to the side, looking toward the door. "Marcus, stay away!" My voice was weak; I could feel my eyes rolling back in my head as Marcus's cool fingers gently held my face.

"What have you done to yourself?" he hissed.

"I'm sorry. Please, leave me . . ."

"Never," he spoke through gritted teeth. "RICHARD!"

More footsteps came quickly up the hall. "Miss Phoebe! What happened?" Richard asked as he entered the room, forgetting all formality. “I just left her not moments ago,” he added frantically.

“It seems that she was playing with the sword and has sliced her hand open,” Marcus explained angrily. His eyes met mine. They were as red as I’d ever seen them. The blood had to be driving him crazy.

“I’ll have her fixed in no time, Sir.” I heard Richard promise.

“Richard, I can’t . . . ” Marcus's voice was strange, almost pained.

I didn’t understand what they were talking about. The room was spinning. I had to close my eyes to stop the whirling.

“Of course Sir, I understand. Forgive me Miss . . .”

Arms moved under my neck and legs. I felt myself being lifted off the floor. I opened my eyes. Bright yellow eyes stared back at me. I screamed, thrashing to get away, then felt myself suddenly back on the floor.

“Forgive me, Miss. I didn’t mean to frighten you.”

“It’s alright Phoebe, I’ve got you.” I felt Marcus's arms around me now, lifting me up off the floor. I closed my eyes and took in a deep breath, taking in his sweet smell. I sighed.

“Richard was only trying to help you,” Marcus spoke softly in my ear.

“Richard? I’m sorry Richard. I didn’t realize—I thought it was—”

“It’s alright, Miss,” he interrupted.

I tried to bring my arm up around Marcus's neck, but couldn’t.

“Let me help you with that hand, Miss.” Richard held my wrist firmly while Marcus carried me to the bed and laid me down.

“She’s pale as a ghost Richard. Do you think she’s lost too much blood?” Marcus spoke through gritted teeth. His cool hand smoothed my hair off my forehead.

“Perhaps you should leave, Sir, I’ll take care of her.”

“I won’t leave her like this . . . I have to learn to ignore the smell of her blood. It’s the only way.”

"She'll be fine, Sir. We heal rather quickly."

"She's not like you," Marcus snapped. A muscle ticked in his jaw.

"Of course not, Sir . . . but they're traces in her blood none the less." Richard spoke carefully.

"I'll need to go get my bag . . . you'll have to put pressure on her hand for me . . . you'll have to hold it like this." I felt a sharp pain in the palm of my hand, squeezing my skin back together. I cried out.

"It's alright darling, I've got you," Marcus said in a strained voice. He looked beside himself. As if my pain was physically hurting him as well.

"Will you be alright Sir?" Richard asked.

"Yes Richard . . . please hurry."

Richard stepped out of the room.

"Marcus, I'm sorry. I was just looking at it; I didn't think it would be so sharp."

"It's alright darling. Richard will stitch you up. Please. Try to stay awake."

"It was Phoebe's sword, wasn't it?" I asked, trying to keep my mind moving.

"How did you know that?" he asked incredulously.

"I recognized it the moment I saw it. I remembered its feel as I swung it around," I admitted reluctantly. Marcus shot me a disapproving look but said nothing.

Richard came back through the door with a black doctor style bag in his hand.

"Do you know what you're doing?" I asked nervously.

"Yes Miss."

"Richard is somewhat of a medic. He has to be able to take care of himself when he needs repairing," Marcus interjected as he held my arm down.

I felt a small prick as a needle punctured my hand. "Ow!" I cried.

Marcus pressed his lips hard against my forehead, as if the very act would take away the pain.

"That's just a pain killer Miss. We'll just wait a few minutes and then I'll stitch you up." Richard spoke like this was routine surgery.

I tried not to look as Richard worked diligently on my hand. He had it stitched and wrapped before I had time to pass out, which would have made things a whole lot easier for all—I was a terrible patient.

"There Miss. In a couple of days you won't even be able to tell. Now, if there won't be anything more, I'll take my leave . . . again." He gave me a subtle wink before he gathered up his things and left the room.

"Marcus, I'm sorry—"

He held up his hand, stopping me.

"I didn't think you'd be back tonight," I spoke softly. I knew I was in trouble.

"So you decided to play with a sword?"

"I was not playing . . . I was trying it out," I explained.

"It's a good thing I did come back. You'd have bled to death on the floor," he pointed out firmly, but I could see the relief in his eyes.

"Thank you for helping me . . . again." I gave him a small smile. "I keep getting into trouble, don't I?" It wasn't really a question. It was a fact.

"Shall I leave you to sleep now, or will you be playing with swords again?"

"I will not be playing with swords!" I grumped as I watched him slowly make his way to the door.

"Marcus, please don't go," my voice cracked. He turned around, his eyes on mine.

"I don't want to be alone. I get nervous sleeping in strange places," I admitted.

"Although, it's not so strange, is it?"

He walked back to me and removed his shirt. It had splotches of blood all over it. How he'd managed to keep it on him this long, I didn't know. He threw it into the fireplace.

"I'm sorry I ruined your shirt." My eyes were downcast.

"It's just a shirt Phoebe. I have many more."

My eyes wandered to his chest. He had muscles that went on for days. Never had I seen anyone more stunning than Marcus. I couldn't help but marvel at his beauty.

"Does this mean you'll stay?" I asked, the corners of my mouth curling up a little.

He nodded, kicked off his boots, and lay down beside me.

His arm slipped under me. I snuggled into him, resting my head on his shoulder, before he leaned across and turned out the light.

"I wouldn't want to be anywhere else . . . " He kissed the top of my head.

I smiled contently as I closed my eyes and drifted off to sleep happily in our bed.

Chapter 18: Roses and Thorns

I woke up to a brilliantly lit room. The sunlight that poured through the window stretched across the bed. I could feel its warmth through the blankets.

My eyes protested as I tried to open them. I stretched my arms out and felt something soft and velvety all around me. I sat up to find the bed covered in rose petals. The room had been filled with them! There were hundreds of roses, beautifully arranged in elegant vases throughout the room. It was absolutely breathtaking.

I got up and wandered my own private garden. Breathing deeply, I took in the fragrance of the room and smiled.

As I leaned forward to smell one of the bouquets, I felt familiar arms wrap around my waist. "Good Afternoon my love." Marcus pushed my hair aside and kissed the back of my neck. I couldn't help but shiver. I turned around and stared into his glorious face.

"Afternoon?"

"It's nearly twelve thirty . . . you must have jet lag," he suggested with a smile.

"What is all this?" I motioned to the flowers around me.

"I just wanted to show you how much I love you." He tilted his head and kissed my lips briskly.

I gasped, a realization taking hold of me: "The room with flowers! From my dream!" I could feel my eyes begin to water. "You did this for me?"

"It was our wedding night—you loved roses—red of course." He smiled coyly.

I was speechless. I looked around the room once again, overwhelmed by the fragrance, beauty, and love that filled it.

"I can't possibly show you how much I love you . . . but I will keep trying . . . until the end of time," he whispered from behind. I felt something cold touch the front of my chest. I looked down to find a heart shaped stone hanging from my neck.

I looked back at Marcus, wide-eyed. "Is this a real—"

"Ruby? Yes." He smiled as he adjusted it.

"Marcus, this is too much," I protested. The stone had to be the size of a quarter.

"It most definitely is not too much," he said playfully, brushing his finger across the tip of my nose.

"Marcus, this wasn't—"

"No. It was my mother's." He had a fond look in his eye as he stared at the necklace he'd just placed around my neck.

"You never gave this to Phoebe?" I had to admit that I liked the thought that he'd never given it to another soul—not even mine—all those centuries ago.

"She didn't really wear jewelry," he half-laughed. "Funny that you make it now. She used to say it wasn't practical. I never even bothered to show it to her," he added with a shrug.

I tilted it between my fingers, letting the sunlight dance through it.

"It's beautiful on you," he said admiringly. I could feel my face blush the shade of the stone.

"Would it have mattered if it had been Phoebe's?" he asked as he wrapped his arms around me, resting his chin on my shoulder.

"Marcus, I know you say I'm the same Phoebe you once loved. But you must know . . . we're really different people. Even if that were possible . . . and most of me believes that it is," I added quickly, seeing the protest in his face. "I'm just not the same woman I once was. Do you understand that?"

"Of course I do." He brushed a kiss across my lips. "I know you're not exactly the same woman I loved so long ago. But no one could deny that you look the same. You share so many memories from that life . . . you even have the same knack for getting into trouble." He gave me that crooked smile that I'd grown to love.

"I love you, Marcus."

And just like that, his lips took mine. His hands were on my hips now, his fingers digging in—it didn't hurt—it made my heart race all the faster. My arms wrapped around his neck, pulling him harder against me. My leg had somehow moved up his, hooking around his hip. His hand was on my thigh, squeezing it, holding it to him.

"I want you—" he gasped between kisses. "My Phoebe Rose—"

He lifted me up. My other leg wrapping around his waist as well as he carried me to the bed.

"I want to love you. You!" He looked me squarely in the face as he declared his complete and utter love for me.

I glanced around the room; taking in the love he'd showered me with. The ruby, still on my neck was warm against my skin. "I want to love you too," I said eagerly, reaching for his face and pulling him back to me.

His hand, still on my hip, traveled down my leg and back up, bringing my nightdress up. He continued to my waist and past my panties. His fingers gently glided up my stomach while his mouth took my neck, his lips, eagerly moving over every inch of it.

My breath caught. My knees clamped hard against his hips. He let out a frustrated moan. His eyes were on mine, a luscious shade of amber reflected back at me. I smiled. I wasn't afraid this time. I held his face with my hands.

He held my wrist tight in his hand before I even realized he'd moved. He was holding it close to my face, and I could see that small splotches of blood had seeped through the gauze. I'd torn the stitching and didn't even realize it—but Marcus had.

"It's not so bad this morning" I lied. Truthfully . . . it was killing me. "Marcus?"

"I forget how fragile you are . . . how easily you could be hurt." His grip around my wrist was firm. "I'm sorry. I don't know what I was thinking. I want to love you, in every way." There was anguish in his eyes where passion used to be.

My mind raced for a moment, trying to comprehend what was happening—and then I understood. Marcus was still afraid he'd hurt me.

"Marcus, I love you!" My lips caught his by surprise, my teeth nearly smashing into his. He responded eagerly, just as I hoped. My heart pounded harder and harder against his chest as he deepened our kiss. I yanked his shirt up and over his head, trying to ignore the burning sensation in my hand—I'd pay for that later.

My fingers trembled as I moved them up his bare chest, feeling every muscle, memorizing them as I glided my fingers back down to his waist. I paused. He'd stopped me before . . . would he do it again?

My good hand managed to undo his pant button and zipper. I felt a sudden change in his lips. I opened my eyes to see him looking at me. His eyes were darkening to an almost blood red—my heart raced faster. "You want me too," I said in a sultry tone. "I can feel it." I debated for a moment. Self-preservation or physical satisfaction . . .

I looked away from his eyes, kissing his neck and shoulders. My lips moved knowingly over his chest, tasting the fragrance that intoxicated me. His skin was smooth and soft . . . it was like touching silk.

My hands had worked their way down his side and over his hips, pushing his pants down a little, when Marcus gave me a sideways glance. His mouth held a devious smile.

"Don't even think about it."

"Marcus," I protested.

"No way. Not until you get that hand re-stitched." He rose from the bed, replacing his shirt in record time.

I sat there, staring at him incredulously. "You're kidding, right?" I could still feel the heat where my body had smoldered against his.

"You and I together physically is dangerous enough without having prior injuries to be careful of." He shook his head. "I can't be so reckless with you." He looked ashamed.

"Will you stop acting like a yoyo?" I thundered, slamming my fists into the mattress. "Look." I unwrapped my hand dramatically, tossing the gauze across the floor. "It's just a little blood! Hardly any reason—"

Marcus flew at me, the weight of his body slamming into mine. He had my wrists in his hands, pinning them over my head in less than a second. I gasped, choking on the air I'd sucked in.

His jaw was clenched tight, his eyes fierce. I could see the conflict that rose within them—I was tearing him apart.

"It's ok Marcus," I swallowed loudly. "I didn't mean to push you. I know you're just worried about me."

I was aware of his chest heaving in and out against mine. His eyes, red with lust stared hungrily at me.

"Alright my love . . . I won't deny you any longer . . . or myself."

I could feel a small pool of blood in the palm of my hand now. It had seeped past the stitching and was dripping down my wrist—a detail Marcus hadn't missed.

"Marcus?" My voice cracked.

His eyes were on me, heavy with desire, but for what?

I panicked. "Marcus, get off me! Get off me! I thrashed below him, screaming for him to back away.

He jumped off me so fast the rose petals that covered the bed flew up into the air, raining down on my body. Their beauty distracted me for a moment as I watched them cascading down through the sunlight.

I backed myself into the headboard, clutching my wrist to my chest. Small beads of blood ran down my arm.

Marcus stared at my bloodied hand. His tongue grazed his lips.

"Marcus . . ."

It took him a moment to pull his stare away from my hand. His eyes met mine for a brief moment, the desire in them—unmistakable. He fled from the room without a word, leaving me alone . . . and bleeding.

I rose from the bed and retrieved the gauze I'd so carelessly removed. My heart pounding stilled with the sound of a knock at the door.

"Miss Rose." Richard's voice reverberated through the thick wood.

I ran to the door and flung it open. Tears fell from my eyes. "Richard . . ." I ran at him, throwing my arms around him as I cried into his shirt.

"Are you terribly hurt Miss?" he asked as he carefully brought me back into my room.

"Oh Richard. I really made a mess of things." I lifted my hand for him to see.

"There, there Miss. It's just a little tear." He opened his bag and pulled out some tweezers.

"How did you . . .?" I stopped. "Marcus sent you?"

"Yes Miss. Try not to worry. He just needs some time. He's extremely worried about you." I let Richard fix my stitching and rewrap my hand. It wasn't as bad as I'd thought. All the blood had made it look much worse.

"There, now. Good as new. Well, nearly anyway," Richard teased, trying to make light of the situation.

"I pushed him Richard. I thought he was ready. I thought he could handle . . . being with me. Like that." I hung my head, feeling embarrassed I'd burdened Richard with my love life, or lack-there-of.

Richard's hand came out, lifting my chin up. "He loves you Miss. Never doubt that. It's just going to take some time. Some things cannot be rushed. Do you understand?"

I nodded. "Thank you, Richard. For everything." I held up my bandaged hand, giving him a small smile.

"Perhaps next time you wish to use a sword, Miss, you'll allow me to assist you." His eyebrows rose slightly.

I frowned at what I assumed was a poor joke.

"Lord Ashworth has put you in my charge when he's away on business," he announced with pride.

"Your charge? You mean, you're supposed to baby-sit me?" I asked playfully, thinking this was another one of Richard's dry jokes.

"Actually, Miss, my duties are more . . . of a protector. With Mr. Marcus having to leave the castle to meet with the *others*," he emphasized the word, "he is unable to watch over you as closely as he'd like."

"You're supposed to protect me from Damen, aren't you?" The look on Richard's face gave him away. "Well, I won't let you. It's bad enough Marcus puts himself in danger for me, I don't want to have to worry about you too."

"It isn't your choice, Miss. Lord Ashworth has asked me to protect you in his absence, and I've gladly accepted." Richard was just like Marcus. Stubborn. No wonder they got along so well.

"Look. If Damen shows up . . . I'll just leave. You won't have to worry about me."

Richard leaned in closer to me, his eyes, locking with mine. "You are no longer safe, Miss. Anywhere!"

I leaned back, swallowing hard.

"Damen's fixation on you will make you harder to hide. It's only a matter of time before the werewolves discover that you're here. You *need* my help, Miss."

I stared blankly at him. My options didn't look so good.

"I tell you what, Miss. You want to look after yourself, I'll teach you to use that." He pointed to the sword above the fireplace.

"Richard," I half laughed. "Marcus would kill me if I so much as *think* of touching that again. If he knew you were *helping* me . . ." I shivered as I thought of Marcus's reaction.

"When Mr. Marcus leaves for his meetings, Miss, you'll need something to pass the time away. He didn't exactly say you couldn't touch it now, did he?" Richard looked almost . . . devious.

"No . . . he didn't," I answered.

"Although, it might be a subject you may want to avoid bringing up." He raised his eyebrow again.

I shook my head in understanding. I stared at Richard. My head was spinning in a million directions.

"Well, now that that's settled . . ." Richard rose from his chair. "Oh, I almost forgot. Charlotte asked me to let you know that she's prepared a warm lunch for you when you're ready."

"Thanks, Richard. Tell her I'll be down in a bit."

He nodded and left me to my thoughts.

Chapter 19: Ashworth Castle

With some difficulty, I managed to remove the wrappings around my torso. I was ecstatic to see that the bruising had gone from purple to yellow. I was also able to twist my body . . . gingerly of course, without too much pain. “Bye-bye bandages!” I said happily. “At least something’s going right today.”

I looked outside the window and sighed. The sky was overcast. I could see a slight breeze blowing through the many oaks that surrounded the castle like a miniature army. I put my hand on the windowpane . . . the glass was cold. “Warm clothes it is.”

I showered, dressed, and headed downstairs as quickly as I could—I was hungry—my stomach growled in agreement.

“How are you today, dear?’ Charlotte hugged me as I entered the kitchen. Marcus was sitting at the little table . . . sipping a cup of tea?

“I’m fine Charlotte.” I smiled, taking a seat beside Marcus. I shot him a questioning look.

“Wonderful, I have a nice quiche that’s just come out of the oven!”

“Mmm. It smells good.” I smiled.

Charlotte stood at the table with her hands in fists, resting on her hips. “Are you going to tell me that you’ve already eaten today!” she looked at Marcus with scolding eyes.

“Of course not, Charlotte, I’d love a slice.” Marcus flashed a brilliant smile Charlotte’s way.

“Uh huh…” she frowned skeptically at him.

I laughed under my breath.

Charlotte set our plates down in front of us, along with two glasses of juice.

“Oh, I almost forgot!” She rushed over to a closet and took out a hand basket. “I’ve forgotten to get the potatoes out of the garden. We’ll be having Irish Stew tonight,” she mused.

"Help yourselves to more if you'd like, dears," she shouted over her shoulder as she rushed out the kitchen door.

"Marcus, how are you going to eat that?" I asked, as he broke a piece off with his fork.

"Just like you of course." He took a bite . . . then made an awful face before he broke into laughter. "I can eat food if I have to . . . let's just say it doesn't stay down for long." he winked.

I cringed a little.

"Marcus—"

"Phoebe, stop." He held up his hand to silence me. "I'm the one who needs to apologize."

"No Marcus, it's my—"

"It's not your fault," he interrupted again, his voice raising slightly. "You shouldn't have to be afraid that your lover is going to kill you simply because you've sliced your hand open." His gaze dropped to my newly bandaged hand.

"It's fine. Richard took care of it," I offered. "Thank you for sending him."

He nodded. "I should have been there to help you." There was anguish in his eyes. "I'm sorry I frightened you. I'm sorry I . . . left you in need."

Understanding washed over me. Marcus wasn't just upset about how he reacted to my hand; he was upset because he left me in a state of passion. A state of passion he'd intended to fulfill. I blushed. "Perhaps another time?"

He took my bandaged hand and brought it to his lips, kissing the palm of it. He inhaled deeply. His eyes flashed with small specks of crimson. "Indeed. Another time."

I ate my lunch quickly, while Marcus carefully hid his portion in the trash bin. He was eager to take me on a tour of the castle.

There were fifteen bedrooms, each with their own bathrooms—a modern renovation; a grand dining room, several sitting rooms, and a magnificent library. There was also a music room that was adjoined to a well-lit ballroom. Marcus took this opportunity to twirl me around the highly polished floor a few times—I unfortunately tripped over my own feet.

"We'll have to practice . . . if you'd like?" he said, spinning me around once again.

"I'd love to! I've always wanted to dance at a ball. You know, like a princess." I blushed at the childish thought.

"Then a ball we shall have." He smiled, as he whirled me around the floor once more. "You are my princess," he said affectionately, brushing my cheek with a kiss. I actually giggled. I felt as though Prince Charming himself was dancing with me.

We continued through the halls looking at artwork and items that gave new meaning to the word antique.

Richard was relocating the Monet at that very moment to my bedroom. Marcus was overjoyed that I'd taken such a liking to it and told me if there were any others I'd like to have, I only needed to ask. I mentioned the Renoir was a personal favorite as well, but I didn't expect him to relocate all the paintings. The Renoir had a new home an hour later: beside the Monet.

It was late afternoon by the time we headed outside. The grounds were breathtaking, with rolling hills of green as far as the eye could see. There were flower gardens the likes I'd only seen while watching Victory Garden PBS back home. Everything was immaculately kept. Not a leaf out of place or a withered flower in sight. Soft sounds of water trickling from nearby fountains added to the beauty of this wondrous place.

We ended up at the horse stables hours later. Marcus had at least twenty horses. All were unique in color, and all exquisite! I'd never seen such sleek, muscular horses in all my life; definitely show quality.

"Marcus, they're beautiful."

"Yes, I make sure they're well taken care of. We use them on hunts." He walked over to a caramel colored horse and stroked it gently on the nose.

I reached out to pet a stunning black stallion.

"He's one of my favorites . . . extremely fast, fearless, and surprisingly gently," Marcus said as he came over and said hello to his friend.

"What's his name?" I asked, standing on my tiptoes to nuzzle the horse on the nose.

"Rain."

"Why Rain?"

"Because he likes the rain. I've never seen a horse that loves to run through the rain like this one. He almost dances in it."

Rain snorted loudly, blowing air on the back of Marcus's neck.

"I don't think he likes you talking about him," I laughed.

"He can also be very ornery at times as well," Marcus rubbed Rain on the head, messing his mane. They looked like old friends mucking around.

"You may have him if you'd like." Marcus glanced my way, grinning.

I gasped. "Really? No—really?" I was nearly jumping up and down.

He laughed. "Of course. I have many others. Besides, Rain is far too grand to be used on a hunt. I'd rather think of him taking you on quiet rides through the countryside."

"Oh Marcus, I love him!" I reached over and nuzzled Rain again on the nose and got a very wet kiss back. I laughed excitedly.

I turned back to Marcus and threw my arms around him. "He's wonderful. Almost as lovely as this . . ." I held up the ruby necklace he'd given me earlier.

"I'm happy you like it."

"You don't mind if I wear it, casually I mean? I couldn't bear to take it off."

"Wear it whenever you like." He leaned over and kissed my lips softly.

I turned back to Rain and patted him on the neck. "I'll see you tomorrow, boy."

We walked back toward the castle. Marcus's arm was around my waist, holding me close. I was especially glad, for the air had gotten cooler and the sky carried dark, foreboding clouds. No way would I have wanted to walk across the 'yard' alone.

We'd been having such a wonderful time; I hadn't even noticed the sun had gone down. The stars were twinkling. There had to be thousands of them, dancing in the sky like little diamonds, trying to punch their way through the cloudbank that threatened them.

"Aren't you worried about werewolves?" I asked, looking up at the moon. It hung directly overhead, as full as I'd ever seen it.

"No darling. I told you. They do not trespass on my land. You're safe here."

I nodded, but molded my body a little closer to him still.

A loud howl echoed off in the distance . . . although, it was not so distant.

Marcus stopped. He held me tight as he whirled around wildly looking for the source.

"Marcus, was that a . . ." I couldn't say it, I was too afraid. I could feel my heart in my throat.

The howling was getting closer, and the pitch was changing. There were several howls now, all getting closer by the minute.

"There's more than one!" I said in a panic.

"Phoebe, you need to do exactly as I say. I want you to run back to the horse stables . . . go back to Rain and stay with him; he can protect you!" Marcus held my face in his hands. His eyes were full of fear. "Do you understand me?"

"I can't leave you . . . there are too many of them . . . you'll be killed!" I cried.

"Don't worry about me," he kissed my lips quickly. "Now run."

"Marcus . . ."

"Phoebe, run!" He shouted as he pushed me toward the stables.

I ran as fast as I could. I flung the stable door open, slammed it shut behind me, and locked it with a wooden bar. Just as the bar dropped in place, I peered through a crack in the door. Several shadows emerged from the trees, while something was approaching Marcus from behind.

I gripped the handle of the door tightly. Marcus didn't see the one behind him. He was going to be killed! I couldn't just stand here and watch. My heart pounded. Why wasn't he turning around? Couldn't he smell him? I was going out of my mind!

"Marcus behind you!" I screamed through a crack in the door.

Marcus jerked his head in my direction—so did one of the wolves. I backed away from the door, stumbling over my feet. I fell in front of Rain's stall. He was bucking wildly, all the horses were. His nostrils were flaring, in and out—hot breath escaping him.

I screamed, covering my ears—something had smashed into the stable door. The wood was splitting like a giant tree being cut down, one blow at a time. I scooted back across the floor, trying to put as much distance between the door and me. My heart pounded loud enough to drown out all noise from the horses, but not the sound of the stable door being attacked again. I screamed louder, tears already streaming from my eyes.

"Marcus!" I screamed, as the door was struck again. This time, a fragment of wood broke in. Large snapping teeth protruded through the small opening. I scooted back further, screaming frantically. My pounding heart amplified the loud growls and barking, amongst the horses hooves on the wood floor.

Rain bucked his hind legs against his stall door. The hinge broke free. *He can protect you*! Marcus's words rang in my ears. I looked into Rain's eyes, a brilliant shade of . . . red? He pushed his way out and ran up beside me, nudging me to get up.

I jumped to my feet. Using a crate on the floor, I climbed onto his back without hesitation.

The stable door came crashing in just as Rain took off at a full run. I clamped my knees tight against his body while grabbing a hunk of mane—I was holding on for dear life. He charged the wolf, jumping up and over its head, narrowly missing its snapping teeth.

Rain bolted across the lawn as if his tail were on fire. I held my head down tight to his neck, praying I wouldn't fall off. Our speed quickened. We flew across the grounds, reaching the trees in a matter of seconds. I wrapped my arms around his neck tighter. I could feel his breathing, rough and shallow as he pushed himself harder.

He took us through the forest. I could hardly see the trees as we past them at insane speeds. I looked behind me. A pair of wolves still chased us. They were falling behind now, unable to keep up with Rain.

"We're losing them boy!" I exclaimed.

Rain ignored my excitement and continued to run. He never slowed; he never seemed to tire.

The moonlight revealed a large ravine up ahead. Rain had a sudden burst of energy as his speed quickened. I closed my eyes and buried my face in his mane. I could feel him leap up, and then there was nothing but air below us—

Time seemed to stop as we drifted . . . I couldn't look until we were safely on the ground again . . . trotting as we came to a stop. I sat there, hunched over, hugging his neck, waiting for my heart to slow. He was breathing just as heavily.

The wolves howled in the distance.

I knew we were safe. He saved me. Just like Marcus said he would.

"Marcus . . .?" My heart sunk.

I don't know how long I sat there on Rain's back, crying into his fur. Never once did he act impatient with me by trying to lie down, or wiggle me off.

"I love you boy," I cried. "Promise you won't ever leave me!"

He craned his head around and nudged my leg gently. His nose snorted loudly, breathing hot air against my leg.

"You understand me, don't you?" I could see his red eyes sparkling like rubies in the moon's light.

He neighed.

The cold damp air surrounded us quickly. I tried to snuggle in closer to his body, searching for any warmth I could find. The sky rumbled above, and little raindrops began to fall all around us. Time was passing by as if nothing unusual had happened.

Rain began trotting around in a circle, bouncing me on his back as he went. “No dancing, Rain.” I patted his neck softly.

He walked over to a large tree and stood near the trunk, sheltering us from the falling water. I closed my eyes and tried to let sleep take me. My clothes were soaked through to my skin. I shivered violently while my mind drifted in and out of consciousness.

I moaned. I’d toppled off Rain’s back onto the hard ground. I sucked in air, and my lungs protested. My nearly healed ribs screamed out in pain. I looked around me . . . the night wasn’t so dark any more . . . it had to be early morning.

My head felt heavy. I couldn’t lift it off the ground. Trying to hold in what body heat I had left, I curled up into a ball. Soft horsy hairs tickled my face. Rain snorted loudly, blowing his hot breath at me.

“I’m ok boy, j-just a little c-cold,” I stammered.

Rain nudged my body again, trying to get me to rise. I couldn’t. Not this time. Something was wrong me—very wrong.

“I’m sorry boy. I can’t.” My eyes wouldn’t open any longer. He kept his face close to me, his hot breath, my only heat. He neighed loudly, continually snorting in my face.

“What is it boy?” I croaked.

“Phoebe . . .” Someone was calling out my name. Marcus . . . it was Marcus.

Rain neighed again. Louder this time—as if to answer for me.

“Phoebe!”

My eyes opened, just barely as Marcus dove to the ground beside me. I watched him lifelessly.

“Darling are you hurt?” He held my face, looking me over anxiously.

"Marcus . . . you're alive." I didn't even recognize my own voice.

His cool hand on my forehead startled me. "You're on fire!" he said with alarm.

"No, I'm c-cold." My body convulsed. I could feel his arms lifting me off the ground. I snuggled into the warmth of him.

"Rain!" he shouted.

Cold air began instantly whipping past my face. My eyes flicked open to see that we were on Rain's back and moving quickly through the forest. We'd managed to jump over the ravine just as effortlessly as before. He was faster than anything I'd ever seen in my life. Even with the both of us on his back, I couldn't imagine Marcus could have flown any faster. I could just make out the castle in the distance. Our speed quickened as we broke through the trees and flew across the lawn.

"Phoebe, stay awake—we're almost there!" Marcus shouted as he leapt off Rain's back onto the castle steps. I looked over his shoulder to see Rain standing at the bottom of the steps, neighing loudly after me.

Sarah screamed as Marcus kicked through the front doors, blasting cold rain and wind in with us.

"Sir, you found her!" Richard shouted as he ran into the room—no doubt reacting to Sarah's shrieks for help.

"Yes Richard, but she's very ill. She has a very high fever," Marcus reported as he ran up the stairs with me still in his arms.

"Let me help you with her clothing Sir," Sarah shouted after us.

I kept drifting in and out of consciousness, like I was in a thick fog. I felt my wet clothing being pulled off me moments later. I could hear the voices around me but I couldn't quite make out their faces. I was soon dressed and tucked into the soft bedding. Hot water bottles were stuffed around me, heating the sheets to a toasty warm. Marcus's cool hand rested gently on my forehead. Despite my protests of being cold, he insisted that I was burning hot.

"Oh my, is she alright?" Charlotte fretted about the room.

"A few more hot water bottles Charlotte, and some warm soup as quickly as you can," Richard instructed as he poured something into my mouth.

"Of course, the poor dear," Charlotte muttered as she rushed out of the room.

My eyes fell shut. I felt like I could finally sleep. The warmth of the blankets, the crackling of wood in the fireplace, and most importantly knowing Marcus was there safely beside me was all I needed.

Chapter 20: Promises

I could feel my body going from hot to cold as I tossed and turned. My mind moved through dream after dream, pulling me deeper into a sleep from which I could not awake. A brilliant light moved slowly toward me . . . I held my arm over my eyes, shielding them, as it got closer.

Soft hands gently held me around the neck. I looked up into Damen's face. His eyes, an endless sea of blue stared longingly back into mine.

"Damen?"

His mouth took mine, crushing it forcibly. I broke free, slapping him across the face. A deep menacing growl escaped him.

"You can't do that! I never said I loved you!" I yelled defensively.

"How can you deny it?" he snarled.

I could feel myself stepping away. His body shook with anger. His eyes, bright yellow now, glowered back at me—watching as I slowly retreated.

"I won't ever love you," I breathed. Even as I said them, I knew they weren't true.

He flew at me—his sharp claws swiping across my body, spilling my blood all over the ground. He had ripped my clothes and skin to shreds. I thrashed wildly under him, trying to break free. Screaming for him to stop.

"Phoebe! Can you hear me?"

Marcus! I couldn't call out to him. Now Brian was on top of me—crushing my body with his. His mouth moved over mine, denying me the air I so desperately struggled for.

"No!" I cried, gasping, as my mouth broke free from his. "Get off me," I begged.

"Phoebe!" I could hear Marcus's voice, faintly calling out my name, but I couldn't see him. I couldn't find him anywhere! His voice sounded so far away.

"Phoebe, come back to me." I could hear the pain in his voice. "I beg you . . . don't leave me again."

"Marcus . . . " my voice was weak.

"I'm right beside you. Can you feel my hand?" He sounded desperate. "Phoebe,

I've got your hand; I'm squeezing it now. Can you feel me?"

I could feel something . . .

"Marcus, hurry! Before they come back!"

"No one's going to hurt you, love. I won't let them." Marcus's voice sounded urgent, louder now. He had to be close. But where was he? I still couldn't see him . . .

"They already did," I cried in defeat.

"No! Phoebe, you're safe. You're in bed. You're dreaming. Open your eyes."

"They are open," I cried out. "I can't see you . . ." Hot tears streamed down my face.

"Please darling, open your eyes." I could hear the pain in his voice. I didn't want him to be in pain. Ever. "Darling please . . ."

I put all the strength I had into trying to open my eyes like he'd asked. It was as if I were trying to lift bricks with my eyelids. There was a small strip of light at first. It was extremely bright. I wanted to look away.

"That's it darling, open your eyes, I'm right here beside you." I could feel his hand, still squeezing mine.

Little by little, my eyes opened. Everything was blurry at first. I could just barely make out Marcus's anxious face looking back at me. I don't know where I found my strength. I reached up and pulled him to me, my lips taking his by surprise.

"I'll give you some privacy Sir." I heard Richard say as a door closed.

I didn't even look his way. I had Marcus, my beautiful Marcus. "You're alive!" I continued with the barrage of kisses across his face.

"Phoebe," he tried to speak past my lips.

"I was so scared. When you didn't come for me, I thought—" I couldn't say it. It didn't matter anyway. He was alive, and I wanted him desperately.

"You scared us," Marcus spoke past my lips. "Richard had to revive you, you stopped breathing!" Careful not to put his entire weight on me, he let his body fall on top of mine.

"Marcus, I need you . . ." My lips took his again and again. He was just as eager now. His hands held my face, pulling me deeper into his kiss.

"I'm right here darling. Tell me what you need and it's yours," he said without hesitation—and without understand my meaning.

"I don't want to wait any longer, Marcus. I want you to make love to me—now."

I ran my fingers through his hair, pulling his face closer to mine, as if that were possible. The sudden tenseness in his posture told me he'd finally understood my meaning.

"I won't waste another day. You could be taken away from me at any moment." I ran my hands down his hips and back up his shirt, lingering at his chest. It was hard and muscular . . . I shivered. "Love me . . . like you used to . . ."

He pulled his head back, his eyes staring into mine incredulously.

"I need you!" I unbuttoned his shirt slowly, one button at a time.

His eyes burned with desire. He wanted me. Oh how he wanted me. I peeled away his shirt, revealing his magnificently sculpted chest. I ran a finger slowly down the center, pausing at his naval. His breath caught.

"You're beautiful," he said. A soft smile settled on his face.

"How would you know? You won't let me take a stitch of clothing off," I pretended to pout.

"You forget my love: I rescued you from drowning in the shower."

"Oh!" I don't know why but a feeling of surprise washed over me. I felt myself blushing. "I thought you said you didn't look!"

He grinned. He'd seen me . . . *all* of me.

"That makes you blush! You're trying to seduce me, but the fact that I saw you naked in the shower while saving your life—yet again I may add—makes you blush?" He laughed in disbelief.

I lifted my nightshirt off, throwing it to the floor. His laughter had stopped instantaneously. The cool air on my fevered skin felt good. Small beads of sweat on my arms and chest glistened in the soft glow of the room's light.

I could see Marcus's chest rising up and down rapidly as he gazed upon my naked body. I watched his eyes turn from chocolate brown to amber in almost an instant.

"Phoebe?" He let out a soft moan. He straddled me, his hands now resting on my hips. "The entire household would kill me if I made love to you now; you nearly died! They'd think I was a selfish cad—especially Richard. He worked tirelessly to bring you back to me."

"I'll thank Richard later." I grasped his shirt and pulled him to me.

He could have easily resisted. He was much stronger than I was. But he fell on me, his chest pressing into mine, while his mouth took my breath away, swallowing the soft moan that escaped me. His kiss was heady. He reached his arm around me and hefted me up, allowing him to push away the blankets that separated us. I could feel my body getting warmer still. I didn't know if it was from desire or my fever returning. His touch alone was enough to heat my blood to boiling. His hand moved down my thigh and back up, hooking my leg around him.

"Phoebe . . ." his voice was soft in my ear. "You'll have to let me know if I'm hurting you . . . I might not be able to tell."

His eyes met mine—they were red, like the ruby that still hung around my neck.

"I'm not afraid," I whispered, unbuttoning his pants and pushing them down with my feet. He allowed the action this time.

I couldn't feel any clothing between us any longer. The soft bedding beneath me was nothing compared to the way Marcus's skin felt against mine. I wrapped my legs around his hips, causing another moan to escape him. My body reacted, trembling at the touch of his fingers moving over my skin.

I held the back of his neck, pulling him to me. I kissed him fiercely. Never had the need been so great. I needed him as if he were my last breath of air.

"Careful darling," Marcus warned as he tried to pull back a little. I wouldn't let him. I felt desperate. Like we could be separated at any moment.

An image of Marcus and I, making love—in this very bed, surfaced from deep within my mind. The room was darker then; the flames from the fire were our only light. I remembered how their shadows flickered and danced across his face . . . I remembered how he moved in me . . .

The urgency of my kiss struck him. He fisted my hair, pulling me harder against him. His mouth took mine with no hesitation.

"Are you sure?" he breathed. While his lips moved down my neck and over my shoulder.

"I've never been more sure of anything." I closed my eyes, savoring the cool touch of his skin. His mouth was on my stomach; soft kisses had cascaded down my body, electrifying it. I'd never felt so alive . . .

"Phoebe, will you marry me?"

My eyes popped open. "What?" It was an all stop.

"Will you marry me and be my wife until the end of time?" he asked again, a little more fancifully this time. His lips made their way across my ear.

"Now?" I gasped.

I could feel my cheeks flush. They were getting hotter by the minute. I don't know why his question took me by such surprise, perhaps because we've only been reacquainted again for such a short time, although our life together was not to be compared with the normal course of an ordinary relationship. Marcus and I seemed to be old souls, forever intertwined. I guess I felt like Marcus and I were already married. Clearly we weren't—that was the old Phoebe—lost over seven hundred years ago. Or maybe the old Phoebe wasn't so *lost* after all? Maybe she was right here with him now. Maybe she's always been here. Maybe the reason I never committed to anyone else was because there was no one else—no one but Marcus, that is.

"Phoebe." Marcus claimed my attention, drawing me from my reverie. "I never made love to you before we were married. I won't dishonor you that way now."

"Marcus . . . "

He smoothed the hair from my forehead, pinning me with a penetrating stare. "I will promise you now, and before God, that I will marry only you and love only you. I will care for you and protect you, putting your life and happiness before mine, always! Until the day I perish from this earth, all that I have is yours."

My mouth gaped open. I stared at him—speechless.

"You only have to say yes . . ." His eyes, a soft amber, stared hopefully into mine. He held my bandaged hand, kissing the palm of it—proof that I was safe with him.

Never could another love me as much as Marcus did. He would die for me in an instant if it meant sparing my life. He loved me with every fiber of his being. He would always love me. And *I* would always love him.

My eyes filled with tears. I tried to think of something wonderful to say. Something that would be as poetic, and although all I could manage to say was a simple "yes," the look of joy that filled his face told me it was enough.

He lips collided with mine. I could feel the excitement in his kiss as he held me close to him, rolling over so that I was now on top. I lifted my head back to look at him.

"Did I hurt you?" he looked momentarily panicked.

"No!" I smoothed his face with my hands. "I just wanted to know if we're officially engaged now? Or was that a private wedding we just had?"

"I guess you could call it both," he said with a smile.

"There was a time when a man and woman could declare themselves to each other . . . and they'd be married. It's what *we* did centuries ago," he added. His eyes sparkled as they stared lovingly back at me. "Do you remember?"

I searched every corner of my mind. My breath caught. "On the bluff, when we first kissed!"

"Yes." The smile had spread across his face, touching his eyes.

The day Marcus first kissed me was the day he'd married me. I smiled at the memory. He'd said, at that moment, he knew he wanted to spend all of eternity with me.

"So we're sort of . . . married now?" I bit my lip, suppressing a squeal.

"I can have the official paperwork here before the end of the day if you'd like." He lifted his head, his mouth moved along my shoulder, nibbling gently, but never breaking skin. He laid his head back, his eyes searching mine. A look of worry now filled them. "What is it? Have you changed your mind?"

"Are you sure you want to pledge your love to a . . ." I closed my eyes, trying to swallow the lump in my throat. " . . . Half werewolf . . . disaster zone?" I asked, lifting my hand for him to see. He took it gently, kissing it once again.

"As you have proven, you *heal* rather quickly." His fingers now traced over my ribs. They were still a little tender, but nowhere near as distressed as before.

"And you are not a werewolf!" he added firmly. A smile hung on his face

I nodded my head, still not trusting in those words. "But you're still afraid to make love to me . . . aren't you?" I wiped my forehead with the back of my hand. This conversation was making me sweat. My whole body felt clammy now.

"Yes," he admitted flatly, his eyes looking squarely into mine. "I am afraid to make love to you."

"I understand." I gave him a small smile as I moved to get up.

"Oh no you don't," he teased, flipping me onto my back. My breath caught as I hit the mattress. "I believe we were in the middle of something when I'd asked you to marry me?"

"But, I thought you were afraid?" I protested.

"I'd be a fool not to be." His voice was husky now. "I don't ever want to hurt you." His lips kissed mine gently before they moved over my neck. My heart jumped into motion, pumping faster for him.

"I'm doing it again aren't I?" I could hear him grinning. "Making your heart call to me . . ." His mouth was on my throat, his teeth just barely grazing my skin. I shivered.

"I never said I didn't want to make love to you," he mused. "Or that I wasn't going to try now, did I?" He looked at me with a somewhat devious expression on his face. "You didn't think I could say no forever did you?"

"I hoped not," I said in a sultry tone. I hooked my leg around him, squeezing his body to mine again. He let out another frustrated groan.

His hands were on my hips, his fingers digging in slightly. He moved them up my torso careful, so careful, not to press too hard on my ribs. His fingers had memorized every inch of my body, while his mouth paid special attention to mine. He left me breathless once again, roaming down my neck and shoulder, eagerly tasting my skin—it tickled.

I giggled, flinching away from him. A moment later, I was sweating profusely. My ears began to ring as I watched the room spin around me. My eyes were going in and out of focus.

"Marcus." I gripped his shoulders tightly, trying to center myself. "Something's wrong with me."

His face came back to mine, his features were still out of focus. His hand rested on my cheek, and then my forehead . . .

I moaned, the coolness of his touch, relieving the fog momentarily.

"You're burning up!" he exclaimed. His eyes wandered over me, pausing at my shoulder—I didn't think it was possible for him to turn so pale.

"Marcus?" my voice sounded far away, muffled even.

"Phoebe? Can you hear me?"

I read his lips. I shook my head no. I couldn't hear a thing over the loud ringing in my head. My eyes, so heavy, started to close.

"No! Phoebe, don't go to sleep. Stay awake." He shook me lightly.

My head swayed from side to side—my eyes wouldn't focus again.

He jumped up and began putting his pants back on.

"Where are you going?" I asked sleepily. "Did I do something wrong?"

"No, I did!" he growled.

"Marcus." I rolled over, as I tried to sit up. "Ow!" My hand clutched onto my throbbing arm.

Marcus rushed back to me. "Phoebe I'm sorry! I don't know how—my tooth must have—I was being so careful!" he hid his face in his hands.

"You bit me?" I gasped. I released my shoulder and stared at my fingers, small traces of blood now stained them. "I'm bleeding!"

I jumped up, but the room whirled around me. I didn't want to leave an open wound, no matter how small it was for Marcus to see. I pulled the sheets around me and started toward the bathroom. I staggered about seven steps when I crumpled to the floor like a house of cards.

"PHOEBE…!"

Chapter 21: A Close Call

I could hear a soft buzzing around the room. The whispers were getting louder as it turned into bickering. I left my eyes closed for the time being, hoping to avoid any disapproving stares.

"Well, what were you doing to cause her to overheat like that?" Charlotte snapped. I could picture her right now. Her hands balled into fists atop her large hips.

"I can assure you Charlotte, I wasn't the instigator," Marcus tried to defend himself.

"No one blames you, Sir," Richard spoke—always the peacemaker. "I'm sure it was bound to happen. She isn't quite over this yet," he added sympathetically. "Any exertion whatsoever would have caused her to relapse and overheat."

"All the more reason to mind your manners! Honestly, the things you men say to justify . . ." Charlotte's voice trailed off as she walked out of the room.

"Can I get you anything, Sir?" Sarah's small voice asked kindly.

"No thank you Sarah. All I need is for Phoebe to come back to me . . . and forgive me," he added under his breath.

Forgive him? For what, I thought.

"I'll go and see if Charlotte needs any help," Sarah offered.

My eyes fluttered, slowly opening to see Marcus sitting beside the bed with his hands over his eyes. "Marcus."

"Phoebe. Thank God." He took my bandaged hand in his, kissing it gently. His forehead had long creases from worry. I'd have thought he'd been crying if I didn't know any better.

"Marcus, what's wrong? Are you alright?" I looked him over quickly. My mind instantly jumped to all sorts of horrible conclusions.

"Darling, I'm fine. It's you," his voice cracked. "I was so worried about you."

"Me? What's wrong with me?" I could hear the panic in my voice.

"How are you feeling Miss?" Richard joined us, his tall body looming over Marcus's. His thoughtful eyes fixed on me.

"Just tell me Richard: how bad is it?" Marcus asked impatiently, not bothering to wait for my answer.

"How bad is what?" I looked back and forth between them. I began to prepare—anticipating the worst.

"I was being so careful," he growled. His eyes glanced at my shoulder. I followed. A small bandage covered it. I looked back at Marcus with a look of confusion.

"It's only like a scratch," Richard offered quickly.

I couldn't help but laugh.

"Phoebe, I don't find this funny at all," Marcus scolded.

"I'm sorry," I tried to compose myself. "I thought something serious had happened."

The two of them stared at me blankly as Charlotte burst into the room with a big bowl of chicken soup. The smell of it, reached me before she did—my stomach growled.

"Oh you're feeling better," she beamed. "Now you just finish this up and rest . . . quietly!" Charlotte glowered at Marcus before she left the room.

I roared with laughter, almost tipping my soup. "She does think you're a cad!"

"Just . . . eat your soup!" Marcus growled. "If you can?" He watched me nervously. I ate the soup, every bit of it, under watchful eyes.

"I'm not a vampire!" I laughed. "Besides, wouldn't I have some sort of vampirish smell that you could detect if I were? Is that even a word . . . 'vampirish'?" I mused thoughtfully.

Marcus shot me a disapproving stare. "No. It is not a word," he answered sharply.

"Let's just call that a love nip," I suggested, grinning playfully.

"You really must be more careful, Sir," Richard spoke. "Had that been any deeper—"

Marcus lifted his hand up, stopping Richard in mid-sentence. "It won't happen again, I can assure you."

I dropped my spoon in my bowl with a loud clatter. "What? Exactly what won't happen again?" All humor was gone. "The love nip, or . . ."

"I think I'll let the two of you finish this conversation in private." Richard hurried from the room—a wise man.

"Marcus?" I pushed the bowl aside and sat up. I held my forehead in my hands, trying to keep the room from spinning. I'd moved too fast.

"Lay back down," Marcus sighed. "You're not well."

"Not until you tell me what you meant by that." I lifted my chin in determination.

Marcus narrowed his eyes. "I'm not going to allow myself the opportunity to hurt you again. Richard's right, had that been any deeper . . . I simply won't chance it." He turned and walked toward the door. This was a pattern for Marcus. When something he deemed as reckless happened, he'd try and put as much distance between us as he could. Not this time.

My first thought: be tough. Fight him with logic. My second thought . . . was a bit more . . . emotional. I went for the latter. I felt weak anyway. I started to cry. He rushed back to me in a panic, trying to comfort me—as I hoped he would.

"I thought you loved me," I sobbed. "You said you wanted to marry me!"

"I do love you. I do want to marry you. I *did* marry you! Phoebe, I don't understand?" He looked bewildered.

"If you loved me, if you want to be my husband, you won't push me away," I sobbed into my hands. Real tears. I couldn't stand being pushed away any longer.

"I'm not pushing you away—"

"You are!" I cried. My tear streaked face, meeting his. "You can't tell me that you won't ever hold me like that again. That I won't get the chance to ever really love you." I toppled over onto the bed in defeat, burring my face in the blankets. "Just let me die," I moaned.

"You are *not* dying." Marcus growled in frustration.

"I will if you say you'll never hold me like that again," I promised. "If you won't make love to me because you're always afraid . . . there's no point in you staying with me." My voice was flat, lifeless. "I may as well leave."

"Phoebe, I said I'd protect you, not hurt you! And you aren't going anywhere without me."

"Well you are hurting me." The tears continued to flow. Why couldn't he see that?

He was yelling now. "Phoebe, don't you realize that by accident, I could have ended your life today?"

"Marcus, it's just a scratch. You'd never really bite me. I know it!"

He sat quietly, deliberating his position. I didn't dare look at him. His hand settled on my lower back, lightly rubbing it. My blood started to heat again.

"Perhaps when you are well . . ." His voice cracked.

I smiled into the blankets.

"I'll leave you to rest now," he said, sounding a little tired himself now.

"Marcus!" I reached out, grabbing his hand before he'd risen. I rose to my knees and gingerly put my arms around him. "I love you."

"You will be the death of me," he smiled crookedly as he playfully tussled my hair.

"Oh no, not me . . . you won't ever die because of me." My demeanor had changed.

"Why does that make me nervous?" His guard was up again. He observed me carefully. I shrugged my shoulders, trying to look as meek as possible.

"I promised to protect you, and I will—no matter the cost to myself. You will not put yourself in danger to spare me."

He'd somehow figured me out. "Marcus be reasonable—"

"Absolutely not!" he thundered as he rose from the bed. "Didn't last night scare you?"

"Yes it did. It terrified me. I couldn't stand not knowing if you were dead or not. If I had only stayed with you—"

"NO!" He faced me squarely. "I can't worry about your safety when I'm trying to stay alive myself. I can't protect you if you're taking unnecessary risks!"

I got up slowly. It felt strange to stand, like I hadn't been on my feet in days. I fought the dizziness. I held my head in my hands as I made my way over to him.

"You shouldn't be out of bed." His voice was softer now.

"I'm alright," I lied.

"You are not alright." His hands gripped my arms, steadying me, I was glad for the support.

"Marcus. Please understand. I just want to help you. I'd do anything to keep you safe with me."

He brushed a lock of hair from my face. His fingers lingered as they grazed my cheek. "I understand better than you know. But darling, you wouldn't have lost me. Richard was there."

"Richard was there?"

"Yes. The one that was running up behind me!" he prompted.

"That was Richard?" I gasped, trying to remember. My face had to be a brilliant shade of red. "Sorry." I winced in embarrassment.

"I know you were trying to protect me, and I love you for it." He lowered his knees, looking me squarely in the face.

"You do know that had Rain not been with you, you'd have never gotten away. Neither of us could have got to you in time."

"I'll be more careful next time," I promised.

"Let's hope there isn't a next time. At least one that involves you." He took my face in his hands. "I was never more terrified than the moment I saw you racing away with those wolves literally at your tail. And me, powerless to help you."

I looked up into his loving eyes. I understood how he must see me now. I was weak, fragile, and human—someone he would always have to look out for.

He was strong, virtually indestructible, and immortal. I'd be worried about me too if I were in his position. How pathetic I must have seemed.

I could feel my legs beginning to burn. They wobbled under the weight of my body. I couldn't fall. I wouldn't. I had to be stronger, for Marcus's sake as well as my own. I didn't want him to have to worry about me so much.

Marcus had me in his arms before my legs could collapse. He'd clearly sensed my weakness—wonderful.

"Rest today. You really were very ill. Your fever was so high, I thought—" his voice caught, unable to say the words.

"I'm sorry to be so much trouble," I said as he tucked me back into the bed.

"I'm thankful I have you to look after." The look in his eyes told me he'd meant it. "I hope you still want to get married tonight? I mean . . . officially . . ." I grinned. "Wouldn't you rather wait? We could have it outside in the garden? With you standing on your own feet instead of lying in a bed," he teased. "I could have Kim and Leah flown in if you'd like?"

"No. I don't want to waste another minute. Either one of us could have been killed last night. I want to start our life together . . . again." I winked.

He leaned down and kissed my lips.

"I do have a surprise for you." He baited the hook, smiling coyly. "Charlotte's bringing dinner up here tonight."

"Oh. That . . . sounds nice." I admitted softly.

"I'll have Sarah look in on you after a while." He kissed me briskly and started for the door.

"Where are you going?"

"I'll be back," he winked, shutting the door behind him.

I lay there, thinking of how close Marcus and I had been to making love. How once again I'd managed to screw it up. I thought about his beautiful proposal and about how much he loved me. He'd do anything to protect me, but he wouldn't hear of me protecting him. Marcus was a bit old fashioned; understandably, he was seven hundred and forty-nine, after all.

I sighed. Marcus was immortal. How could I hope to stay with him forever? I wasn't like him—understatement of the year, I thought. I rubbed my forehead vigorously. I could feel a headache coming on.

"The important thing is that I love Marcus and he loves me. The rest will fall into place," I decided aloud.

There was a quiet knock at the door.

"Come in."

"It's just me Miss." Sarah peeked her head in. "I just wanted to know if you needed anything?"

"No I'm fine, Sarah, thank you."

"Very good, Miss." She closed the door—with her still in the room.

"Was there something else, Sarah?" Her hands had gathered the front of her apron, wringing it. She looked nervous.

"Yes Miss. I don't wish to pry, but I wanted to ask if you and Mr. Marcus were still . . ." she blushed. "Forgive me, Miss. It really isn't my place. I just wondered . . . you see, Mr. Richard has been taking a special interest in you as well, and I wondered if you and he . . . "

It took me a few moments to understand what Sarah was trying so gently to ask. When I did, I almost swallowed my tongue. Were Richard and I an item too—as in, addition to Marcus?

"No!" I blurted, choking on the word. "Sarah, Richard and I are only friends. He's offered to look after me when Mr. Marcus is away. You know, keep me occupied, or rather out of trouble," I added under my breath.

She looked relieved. Me too. The thought of her thinking Richard and I were involved, while I'm clearly involved with Marcus, was beyond embarrassing.

"Well then, you and Mr. Marcus have a lovely evening tonight. Let me know if there is anything I can get you Miss." She smiled brightly as she practically danced out of the room.

Chapter 22: A Misunderstanding

I managed to shower and get changed into my sweats and a t-shirt without killing, or otherwise harming myself. With my luck as of late, this was no easy task. Marcus seemed to bring out my completely helpless and disastrous side—something he didn't seem to mind at all. I, however, was having a hard time with being such a menace.

Someone had been in my bedroom and lit a fire in the fireplace. The room was toasty by the time I'd gotten out of the shower. A table had been set for two with candles in the center. A new vase filled with freshly cut roses had been placed on a table by the bed.

I looked down at what I was wearing and back to the table that was dressed better than I was. A wave of panic hit me all of a sudden. This was supposed to be a romantic dinner, and I was dressed like I was going to a ball game.

I rushed back to my closet and rummaged quickly to find something more appropriate. I'd just grabbed a sleek red dress when I heard a knock at the door.

"Just a minute!" I called out. I tried to take my sweat pants off so fast that my foot got caught in the leg—I toppled over into the closet with a loud thud.

The door flung open.

"Are you alright?" Marcus asked as he ran over to the closet, his eyes wide with panic.

I stared up at him. He was dressed in a tuxedo of all things.

"You might have mentioned it was a black tie affair!"

He looked down at my leg, still caught in my pants, understanding reaching him. He chuckled as he reached out for me. "Let me help you."

"No *thank* you." I grouched. "I can change right here."

"Darling you don't have to change. Considering the circumstances, I think you're dressed quite appropriately—you nearly died after all." Marcus extended his hand once more—and still clearly amused by what he saw, he couldn't stop grinning.

"I can't eat dinner in sweats when you're in a tuxedo!" I said incredulously. My god, was he that clueless? I pulled my legs into the armoire and shut the door, grumbling under my breath.

After several minutes of fancy maneuvering and loud clunking, I pushed open the closet door dressed for the occasion.

Marcus was waiting patiently. He stared down at me for a moment, biting his lip. It was obvious he was trying hard not to laugh—I was still sitting on the closet floor.

"May I help you now?" His smile reached his eyes—it took my breath away how handsome he was. I reached out and took his hand.

"That was well worth waiting for . . . you're stunning." All humor aside, Marcus stared at me like I was the reason for his next breath.

"Thank you." I blushed.

"Shall we sit down?" he motioned to the little table. He walked me slowly over to it and sat me in a chair.

"Marcus, everything is beautiful. You didn't have to go through all this trouble." He gave me a sheepish look. "I had a little help," he admitted.

"Still, it wasn't necessary."

"You're my wife. Well, nearly. I will always do such things for you. I only want your happiness." He took my hand and kissed the top of it softly. Then he began turning it this way and that way, as if examining it.

"Anything wrong?" I asked, confused by his behavior.

"I just wanted to make sure I didn't scratch you again," he said, looking it over once more.

"Well, you better check the rest of my body because there may be a few areas of concern," I smiled coyly.

Marcus's mouth popped open. He looked like he was going to be sick.

"It was a joke! You better check my body . . . "

He stared blankly at me.

I rolled my eyes. How could he not think that was funny? "Sorry," I muttered. Clearly he didn't get my sense of humor.

He shook his head disapprovingly at me. "That. Was *not* funny." The corners of his mouth protested, curling on their own accord. I smiled back at him.

He took in a deep breath, and taking my hand in his, he got down on one knee. He placed something cold in the palm of my hand and closed my fingers around it before I could see what it was.

I stared at my closed hand for a moment before I looked up into his hopeful eyes. He smiled at me.

The butterflies in my stomach were flapping wildly with anticipation. I opened my fingers slowly to find a breathtaking square shaped diamond surrounded by little rubies. I couldn't speak. I couldn't breathe. I was frozen.

"I thought we should make it official. I made a quick trip to London while you were in the shower to have it sized."

My mouth gaped open as I marveled at the ring before me. It had to have cost a small fortune.

"Do you like it?" he asked. I still hadn't said anything.

"It's beautiful. But it's too much," I protested.

"I haven't even begun to spoil you." He took the ring and slipped it onto my finger. It was a perfect fit. Set in white gold, it sparkled like a thousand prisms when the light hit it. I'd never seen anything like it

"Phoebe Rose, will you do me the honor of becoming my wife, and allowing me to love you until the end of time?"

I stared into his soft brown eyes. I couldn't help but smile. He adored me so . . . It was an easy promise to make. "Until the end of time," I repeated.

His mouth took mine, heating my blood with the intensity of his kiss. I could feel him smiling. He leaned back, and my heart cried out at the sudden distance between us. He was beaming. He held my hand in his—admiring the exquisitely beautiful ring he'd just placed on my finger for life.

I was still in awe. I stared down at my hand in his. Watching the light reflect off the diamond, I took in its size for the first time. I suddenly felt anxious.

"Marcus. How big is this? I don't mean to be rude, but—" I had to ask, it looked massive on my hand.

"The diamond itself is eight and a half carats. With the rubies . . ."

"Never mind." I put my hand up stopping him. That was more than enough information to let me know that I would need my own security detail on any outings I may take.

"It was my grandmothers," he continued with a smile. "Then my mothers."

"Marcus, it's beautiful, but I'd be afraid to wear this every day. I'd be mugged in a minute just walking down the street. Werewolves would be the least of my worries," I half-laughed.

"No one would dare touch you!" The very idea made Marcus's eyes turn black.

I placed my hand on his cheek. "I'll take good care of it. I promise." I leaned in and kissed him.

He lifted me off the chair into his arms and whirled me around. "I feel like flying!"

"What? No!" I choked.

"You're feeling better now, right?" He studied me, searching for any lingering signs of illness.

Unfortunately, I was feeling better. I'd have given anything for a hot flash so I could truthfully tell him I was still sick.

"You are such a scaredy cat," he laughed. "You know I would never drop you."

I winced in his arms as I mulled it over. He could see the conflict in my eyes.

"Just a quick one. The moon is lovely tonight, and the air is surprisingly warm. There is a pond I want to show you. It's absolutely beautiful by moonlight." He added this as an extra enticement.

I sighed in defeat. "You promise you won't let go?"

"I won't loosen my grip for a moment." He carried me through the French doors that led out onto my balcony, then jumped onto the railing without a moment of hesitation.

I looked over the edge—instant mistake. I buried my face in his chest.

Marcus laughed. "Don't make me laugh, I might drop you."

"WHAT?" I shrieked.

He leapt off the edge and rolled like a fighter jet through the air.

"Never do that again!" I screamed, gripping him tighter, molding my body with his

"Sorry darling." He continued to laugh. "I was just showing off a bit."

I couldn't even look. I was terrified.

"Phoebe, look here . . . look!" he urged.

I peeked beyond the safety of his shirt to see a large pond not too far from the horse stables. It sparkled in the moonlight like a million diamonds. I gasped. "Oh yes, it is beautiful!" I looked around, a little more at ease now. The castle was huge, especially from the sky.

"Marcus, is all this yours?" I asked, pointing to the forest that surrounded the castle.

"Yes, and that as well . . . all the way to the ocean." He motioned with his chin. "Shall I show you?"

Before I could answer, we were soaring over the treetops, heading for the coastline. The air was a little crisper as he set me gingerly down atop a cliff overlooking the bluff. The moon's light was brighter here, no cloud cover darkening our view.

Marcus's arms snaked around me from behind. He bent down, nuzzling my neck with a kiss.

"You've made me the happiest man in the world," he whispered into my ear. "I wanted to show you this place in person because—"

"It's where you and I first kissed," I interrupted without thinking. I stiffened. It was the place from my dream. It's where he and the other Phoebe first kissed. I turned my head to meet his stare.

A mixture of emotion hung in his eyes: disbelief, amazement, love, and gratitude. He was thankful I was remembering our life together. So was I.

A cold wind enveloped us. I shivered violently. He took off his jacket and put it on me. I savored the sweet smell as I put the fabric to my nose. I inhaled deeply and Marcus laughed.

I glanced his way, blushing at having been caught. "You smell good," I admitted shyly.

He tilted his head to the side, his eyes watching mine. "Your eyes are yellow tonight."

"What?" I gasped. My heart nearly came to a stop.

"Your eyes. I'd noticed it before, but tonight, they're brilliant. Beautiful."

"What do you mean you noticed it before? Am I turning into—?"

"No, no." He held my face in his hands, trying to calm me. "The last full moon when I took you flying . . . I noticed it then."

My mouth popped open. "I have werewolf eyes?" I squeaked.

"Phoebe, I'm sorry I mentioned it. Truly, it's nothing to worry about." I studied his face. He'd meant it.

"You think they're beautiful?" I asked in a small voice.

"Yes." He grinned.

"But what if someone else notices?" I was panicked again.

"Unless someone has you out in the night, on a full moon . . . which I will never allow," he assured, "they'll never know."

I nodded, shivering as another gust of wind whipped past.

"I should get you home now. Too much night air probably isn't good for you."

We landed lightly on the balcony a few minutes later. I was still snuggling against Marcus when he carried me into my room. He let me down slowly; making sure my legs would hold me before he let go.

There was a soft knock at the door.

Marcus rushed over to let Sarah in. She had a large tray with two covered plates, a small loaf of bread, a dish of butter, and a plate full of raspberry tarts.

"Enjoy!" She winked at me then dashed out of the room quickly with her eyes lowered when she saw that Marcus had seen.

"What was that about?" Marcus asked, still staring after Sarah.

"Nothing. Girl stuff." I tried to play it off.

"Why would she wink at you like that?" he asked, ignoring my brush off.

"It's nothing. Really. It's—" I stopped. Richard didn't want Marcus to know about him and Sarah. I'd have to word this carefully. But he'd want to know why Sarah would care if Richard had taken an interest in me anyway. There was only way out of this:

"Let's eat!" I sat down and lifted the lid off my plate to reveal steak, baked potato, and fried greens. "I'll have to remember to thank Charlotte for going to all this trouble . . . may I?" I took up my knife and fork.

Marcus gave me a defeated look, realizing I wasn't going to explain Sarah's behavior. "Of course darling. I'll just fix the fire a bit."

I took a bite of the steak. It was amazing. Although, I wasn't a bit surprised, Charlotte was a spectacular cook.

There were two bottles on the table. They looked like some sort of wine. I opened one up and poured it into a beautiful crystal glass. It was a brilliant shade of red. I swirled the wine around before I took a whiff of the bouquet.

"Curious. I don't think I can place the scent. It's not a grape . . . does this have some kind of berry in it?" I put the glass to my lips, tilting the liquid back.

"NO!" Marcus flew at me, knocking the glass from my mouth. My chair crashed backward onto the floor. I landed hard, hitting the back of my head into the wood frame of the footboard.

I grabbed my head and held it tightly as I curled into a ball. I could feel the blood on my fingertips.

"What's the matter with you?" I cried, holding my head protectively.

"Phoebe, I . . . " he stepped toward me. His eyes were wild, frightening. I found myself recoiling from him.

"Stay away!" I put my hand out, stopping him as I tried to get up. I staggered sideways, falling back to the floor. I'd hit my head so hard; I was surprised I wasn't knocked out.

He moved toward me again.

"No! Just stay away from me!" I didn't understand why he'd attack me like that.

"I couldn't let you drink that," he snapped.

"What? Why not?" I got up slower this time, still holding my head while I swayed back and forth, keeping a distance between us.

"Did you get any in your mouth?" he asked frantically.

"What?"

"Did you drink any?" he shouted.

"No! I don't know. I don't think so." I was so confused. "How could you hurt me like that?" I was still crying as I studied my bloodied hands then looked back to Marcus

He looked just as shaken as I felt. "That bottle is filled with blood," he said through gritted teeth.

"WHAT?" I gagged. I slapped my hand over my mouth and ran to the bathroom, locking the door behind me. I threw open the toilet seat and vomited. I was physically ill now. I tried brushing my teeth over and over, just in case there was any blood in my mouth, the thought made me sick all over again.

I stayed in the bathroom for hours before Marcus finally knocked on the door.

"Phoebe, are you alright?"

"No!"

There was a brief moment of silence. "I had Charlotte warm your food up for you. It's ready when you are."

Like I can eat now, I thought to myself. I held my head as I pried myself off the floor and opened the door. Marcus was standing there, worried looking.

"Why on earth would you have a bottle of blood on the dinner table?" I asked flatly.

"I thought . . . since we're going to be married . . . I should get used to drinking around you. That it might help with the urge . . . apparently that was a mistake." His eyes dropped to the floor in shame.

Now *I* felt bad. "Marcus, I'm sorry. I want you to feel comfortable around me." I frowned. "You should have told me. What would have happened to me if I'd drank that?" I cringed, holding back the impulse to vomit again.

"Being infected as you are . . . werewolves crave blood as well. Not for food, like vampires, though. For them, it's the victory of the kill. Once they've tasted it . . . they'll do anything to get it again."

"I guess I'll just have to watch what I drink around here." I said dryly. His eyes looked sad, hurt. "I'm sorry I pushed you away. My head was bleeding . . . I didn't want you to get too close. You scared me," I admitted at last. The words harder to say then I thought.

"I'm sorry." He turned to leave.

"Oh no you don't!" I hiked up my dress, ran and leaped onto his back. "You don't give me a ring like this, ask me to marry you, and run out on me." I held onto him and ruffled the back of his hair playfully. Marcus had scared me. He'd hurt me. But the pain of him leaving me would have hurt worse. The very idea of being separated from him scared me more.

"You're . . . not afraid to be alone with me?" His voice was still sad.

"I'm not afraid. I know now you were trying to protect me. I'll never doubt you again. Never." I craned my head around and kissed his lips. "I love you Marcus Ashworth. I'll love you until the end of time."

He smiled and kissed me back.

"Now, how about that dinner?" I teased.

"Anything you wish my love."

I grazed his ear gently with my lip, nibbling on it playfully. "Anything?" I whispered.

He shot me a disapproving glance that immediately softened into a smile.

"I'll just settle for dinner then." I winked.

Chapter 23: Surprise!

I woke the next morning with a killer headache. I could already feel the bump on my head: Just another monumental moment to add to my summer of agony.

Marcus had slept next to me last night—with some persuasion. He'd felt so guilty for what had happened before dinner that he had his "wine" alone on the balcony. He decided not to drink around me for the time being. Considering the thought of blood now made me ill, I didn't object.

I looked out my window into the morning. The weather looked crisp. The sky was overcast, and dark, foreboding clouds hung low.

I was feeling a little keyed up this morning. I hadn't been for a run since I'd left home several days ago. All signs of my "illness" had left me. I was more than ready to leave the confines of my room.

I went to the closet and put on the sweat pants and shirt I had on last night before I decided to change into an outfit that would compliment Marcus's tuxedo. I added a sweatshirt and headed downstairs.

"Going out Miss?" Sarah caught me at the door.

"Good Morning, Sarah. Yes. I thought I'd go for a run before breakfast. Have you seen Mr. Marcus?"

"He had a few phone calls to make this morning. I suspect he's still in the library," she added cheerfully.

"You seem rather happy this morning . . . does Mr. Richard have anything to do with that?" I asked playfully. "Uh huh." I winked at Sarah's blushing face before I shut the door behind me.

I ran softly across the immaculate lawn. The grass was thick; I felt as though I were running on pillows, each step sinking into the next.

I decided to run to the little pond I saw last night while we were flying. I knew it wasn't that far past the horse stables. I found the trailhead directly behind them and started down it. I checked my watch. I'd been running about ten minutes . . . I had to be getting close.

The sun flashed through the unfamiliar trees ahead, casting shadows on the ground. I looked around nervously. I remembered the last time I'd been running through the forest—Brian attacked me. I shook away the memory. This is different. Brian is more than an ocean away. There was no danger of him finding me here.

I stopped suddenly. My mouth hung open in awe. The pond was more like a small lake. Flowering lily pads were everywhere. Toads were croaking their song, while birds chirped in the trees overhead. A small rowboat rested on the bank, waiting for someone to climb aboard. This was a place from a storybook, a place to whisper.

I noticed a large flat rock resting near the pond's edge. I walked over to it and sat. Taking in my new world, I pulled my knees up to my chest and wrapped my arms around them. I took in a deep breath—a hint of musk traveled on the breeze. My eyes popped wide open!

"You look absolutely beautiful my dear." A voice spoke from behind me.

I swallowed deeply. A pair of hands now rested on my shoulders. My back stiffened. I didn't look behind me. I knew whom the hands belonged to. I recognized his scent. "Damen."

"Hello Phoebe. How are you enjoying your trip to England?" he asked casually.

"Well, it isn't without its bumps," I said dryly.

"I see. That is quite a nasty bump you have."

"It's not that big!" I snapped, shrugging away from him. "What do you want Damen?"

"I was just wondering if you were ready to end this charade with Marcus." He was walking around me now, circling me like a hawk, ready to swoop down on its prey.

"Exactly what charade is that?" I made no effort to conceal my annoyance.

"You must realize by now that the two of you can never be together. I expect that's why you're here alone instead of with him now.

"*That* is none of your business," I stood up and faced him squarely with my hands on my hips. I was going to stand my ground.

"Easy!" he laughed. "It's just an observation . . . although, you can't deny that I seemed to have hit a nerve."

I glowered at him. "Is there any point to this little meeting, other than to thoroughly annoy me?" I grumped.

"Yes, although, that is a bonus. You really are a delight," he mused, ignoring the lethal expression affixed to my face—he leaned in closer. His warm breath blew across my ear. "You always were."

I jerked away from him. He laughed, circling me once again.

"As I said, I've come to see if you were ready for me to take you now?"

"I'm not going anywhere with you." I looked at him in disbelief.

"It's beautiful." He reached out and took my hand in his. "It's just what you should have." His voice was low, almost melancholy.

"Damen I . . . I don't understand you." I looked at him curiously. "You seem to care for me in one breath, and in the next . . . you insult me. Scare me. You even tried to have me killed!" I took my hand back.

He looked confused. "If I tried, you'd be dead."

I rolled my eyes at him. "The other night, a pack of werewolves chased me on horseback. They attacked Marcus in the yard!"

"Yet . . . Marcus lives." His voice was condescending.

"Yes, Marcus lives. Thank God!"

"Humph. God had nothing to do with it. Neither did I."

"Like I'd believe you. Just . . . go."

His eyes flickered to my hands. He was watching me nervously twist my ring back and forth. I could see the anger rising in his face. His eyes looked more yellow than blue now. I stepped back a little.

"No! Not this time," he growled coldly. He grabbed me around the waist and pulled my body to him. My breath caught on impact.

I could feel his heart pounding against my chest. I turned my head slightly, trying to put some distance between his face and mine. I could feel his warm breath on my cheek. His arm was firm around the small of my back.

"He's a vampire, you're a . . . it will *never* work!" he thundered.

"We work just fine," I struggled, pushing against his chest—I wasn't going anywhere.

He yanked my wrist abruptly, bringing it to his face. His yellow eyes staring right into mine. "What happened to your hand?" he snarled.

"Me!" I breathed heavily. "Apparently I can't pick up a sword correctly." I glowered at him, yanking it away.

He grabbed my jaw, holding it firmly, demanding my attention.

"Damen you're hurting me." I tried to pry his fingers away.

"Do you realize that he could kill you?"

"You could as well," I reminded him sharply.

"I can control myself," he spoke through gritted teeth, still squeezing my face with his hand.

"Yeah? You're doing a real good job of it now," I winced, still unable to break free.

His eyes narrowed. He released my face, only to grip my neck between his hands. The action so fast, I couldn't have prevented it. He brushed his thumb across my lips—I trembled.

"I could kiss you without having the urge to bite you." He pressed his face against my cheek, inhaling deeply. I was frozen where I stood, afraid to move. His heart was beating louder than mine, drowning out all other sounds around us.

"I can hold you close, without hesitation." His jaw tightened against mine.

My breathing became erratic. I felt as though I were going to pass out. Beads of sweat were forming all over my body.

"I could make love to you . . ."

Despite my protests, his mouth took mine. He held me to him, kissing me passionately. His soft lips moved over mine eagerly. They didn't require any participation on my part. Under other circumstances, in another life perhaps . . . it would have knocked my socks off. As it was . . .

I pushed at him again and again. He finally released my lips, but not his hold.

"Damen, you can't do that." I gasped, trying to catch my breath. "I don't love you."

"That wasn't always the case," he implied, a dark tone to his voice.

"What does that mean?"

He smiled flatly. "It means that I have a problem to remove. One that will free you."

My heart stopped. "Damen, if you hurt Marcus in any way, I'll kill you myself!"

His smile frightened me. "That's my girl." His mouth claimed mine again. His kiss was heady, wanton, and taking me completely by surprise. I almost forgot who was kissing me for a moment—almost

I pushed off his body as hard as I could, trying to free myself. He released his hold on me, sending me tumbling backward into the freezing pond with a loud splash.

"YOU JERK!" I screamed, as soon as I surfaced. "It's bad enough you keep forcing yourself on me, do you have to throw me in a f-freezing, cold, p-pond as well?" I stammered while smashing the water with my fists.

"Let me help you," Damen laughed, his smile touching his eyes. He extended his hand.

"Are you kidding me? Get away from me!" I splashed the water in his direction, missing him completely.

"Phoebe, be reasonable, you know it was an accident," he chuckled.

I looked at him loathingly. If I could spit fire I would have.

"Phoebe please, come out of the water, you'll catch your death." His laughter was subsiding.

"I mean it Damen. Stay away from me." With considerable effort, I got out of the pond by myself and stormed past him—water dripping from my clothes. My running shoes were water logged now, squeaking with every step. "I just bought these shoes!" I whined.

"I'll replace them. And anything else you need. Marcus isn't the only one with money," he smirked.

"I'm not with him because of his money," I growled, stomping off in a rage.

"Phoebe . . ." he called after me. "Phoebe wait!" His voice was sharp. He caught me by the elbow and spun me around.

"Enough of this! I'm not leaving here without you."

I glared at him defiantly.

"Knowing he's in your bed at night, that he could kill you at any moment . . . It should be me with you. Not him!"

I kicked his shin, causing a loud cracking sound.

"Ow!" He cried, grabbing his leg and releasing my arm.

I turned and ran as fast as I could. I didn't look back. I was freezing, soaked from head to toe, and being pursued like some animal. I could feel Damen close behind me. I forced myself to run faster.

"Phoebe!"

I couldn't look. My heart was pounding in my throat. If I could only make it through the trees . . .

"Phoebe wait!" Damen growled.

I came rushing onto the lawn, running uncontrollably toward the castle. My legs burned beneath me. I panted loudly, wheezing as I took in each breath.

"Marcus!"

I pushed myself to run harder.

"MARCUS!"

Marcus came bursting out the doors and across the lawn at a tremendous speed. I could see the look of fear in his eyes as I came crashing into his body—a soaking wet sponge of pond water.

"He's here!" I cried into his shirt.

He held my face in between his hands. His eyes looked wildly into mine. "Who?"

"Damen . . ." I gasped, trying to catch my breath. "He's right behind me. He threw me in the pond!"

It took Marcus an instant to process what I'd said. He scooped me up in his arms, his eyes darting back and forth, surveying the forest before he rushed me inside.

I wrapped my arms around his neck, bringing him closer. I inhaled deeply, feeling safer with each passing moment.

"It's alright my love. You're safe now." With what sounded like considerable effort, he kept his voice calm and even. His face was tight, a muscle ticked below his jaw.

"Let's get you into a warm bath. It isn't good for you to get so chilled, especially after being so sick." He set me down on a chair, went over to the tub, and turned the water on. "It should be ready in a few minutes," he said, kneeling down beside me. His hand held my cheek for a moment. His eyes, still so worried were growing darker.

"Would you like to explain why you were out there in the first place?" His tone was a little crisper than before. He'd seen that I was all right. Now he wanted answers.

"I went for a jog," I explained, trying to brush it off like it was no big deal.

"A jog." His face tightened. "You went for a jog through the forest . . . a forest where werewolves had chased you not two days ago . . . a day after you'd had a fever that nearly killed you?" He was shouting now.

I leaned back in my chair, trying to put some distance between us.

"Well?" he demanded.

"I felt better."

"You—" Marcus was so mad he couldn't even form the words.

"I'm sorry. I didn't think." I took my shoes off and chucked them onto the floor. "I just wanted to get out for a bit. I didn't think Damen would be there—waiting." I kept my eyes downcast.

I felt Marcus's fingers on my chin, lifting it up. My eyes met his. He looked beyond mad, but he also looked thankful . . . thankful we were still together. I felt the same way.

"I've got you all wet." I reached out and touched his drenched shirt.

"It's only water." He smiled flatly—his expression was unreadable.

I grabbed a towel off the counter and started wiping my face and lips vigorously.

"He . . . kissed you?" I could hear Marcus gritting his teeth. How had he known?

I peeked out from behind the towel. "It was awful. He wanted me to leave with him. He kept saying he loved me, and he was in control now. That I didn't have to worry about him hurting me—unlike you." I rolled my eyes through the tears. I threw the towel across the room. "Why must I always be attacked every time I go for a run?"

I added some bubbles to the water, removed my wet clothing, and stepped in. I relaxed the moment my body hit the warm water. The smell of rose water filled the air. I leaned back and closed my eyes for a moment, letting the tub fill around me. I could feel the bubbles climbing up my shoulder to the base of my neck. I reached out to turn the water off—Marcus beat me to it.

"Thanks," I sunk back into the water.

"You're beautiful," he said as he rested his chin on the side of the tub. His face was still tense.

"Sure." I pulled a weed out of my hair.

"You know, if the rest of my life is going to be fraught with disaster like this, you may want to reconsider!" I held up my left hand and wiggled my ring finger.

He put his fingers in the water and began swirling the bubbles around them. An odd expression overtook his face.

"I wouldn't trade you for anything." His tone was melancholy.

"Marcus?"

"I can't have the grounds unsafe for you." His eyes were blacker than any night I could have imagined. I could see the wheels turning in his head now. I had my hands on the edge of the tub ready to jump up.

"If you could have heard yourself screaming . . ." He closed his eyes, as if reliving the memory.

"Marcus. Don't do this," I begged. I knew his mind.

"I swore to protect you." A low growl came from within him.

"Marcus, I'm fine. He didn't really hurt me. He just scared me; that's all."

"That's not true, now is it?" He held my chin, tilting it a little to the side. His fingers gently pressing into where Damen's had when he'd held my face. I winced, feeling the bruises I'd have . . . or apparently did have.

"I will kill him for that." His tone was calm, which made it more deadly.

He leaned over and kissed the top of my head. "I love nothing more in this world than you." He moved quicker than I'd ever seen. He was out my balcony doors before I could even get up.

"Marcus!" I screamed after him, tears already streaming down my face. I jumped out of the tub, grabbed my robe, and ran out of my room dripping water as I went.

"Richard!" I ran down the main stairs and out the front doors. "Richard!"

Richard came running up behind me.

"Miss Rose." He looked alarmed at the sight of me.

"You have to help him. He's gone after Damen!" I pointed toward the forest.

"Damen is here?" Richard jumped into action, shielding me from view.

"Please Richard, hurry."

“Come, Miss.” He pulled me back toward the house.

“No, he needs help!” I tried to wiggle out of his grasp.

“You need to get back inside Miss. Mr. Marcus would kill me personally if I left you exposed like this . . . *especially* like this,” he muttered under his breath as he pulled me back indoors. He ushered me to my room in record time, looking over his shoulder as we went. He was probably hoping Sarah wouldn’t come around a corner and find him with me less than half dressed.

“Aren’t you going to help him?” I yelled in disbelief. I couldn’t believe we were even arguing about this. Richard should be out there, helping Marcus. Not held up in the castle babysitting me.

“I am helping him Miss. I’m supposed to protect you when he’s not at home. If I leave the castle to help him, and you’re harmed . . . *I’ll* be the one needing protection.

I scoffed.

“Try not to worry Miss. I’m sure he’ll be fine.” He smiled sympathetically before he shut my door, leaving me alone with my imagination to torture me.

I stood there, looking around the room. I couldn’t just wait here, doing nothing. If Richard wasn’t going to help Marcus, I was.

I got dressed quickly and started for the door. I reached for the handle and stopped. I debated for half a second, ran to the fireplace, and grabbed my sword off the wall—I wasn’t going unarmed.

Chapter 24: Raymose

I made it down to the stables unseen. I peeked my head inside to make sure I was alone, but only Rain neighed loudly at the sight of me.

"Hi, boy, I'm happy to see you too." I gave him a quick rub along his neck. "I need you again. I have to find Marcus, and you're the only one who can help me."

I stepped into his stall and saddled him up. Holding onto the reins, I led him to the stable door. I peeked out—there wasn't a soul in sight.

"Ok, boy, let's go." I led him around to the back of the stable and climbed on. We started trotting down the path that led to the pond. It was as good a place to start looking for Marcus as any. Once there, I looked around. There was no sign of Marcus, or Damen for that matter.

"Now what?" I thought aloud.

Rain took off around the pond, heading north. He was galloping at a good pace, so I just let him go, hoping he was leading me to Marcus.

"You know boy, you'll probably be going home alone. Marcus is going to kill me for sure when he finds me out here." I patted his neck lightly.

Rain's speed quickened. I could feel his body tense up beneath me. He neighed loudly.

"What is it, boy?" I asked nervously, looking to the trees. I swear that I saw something brown moving amongst the shadows. I watched closer, squinting my eyes, straining them to see better. It moved along with us, keeping the same speed. It was a werewolf! I watched as it moved in and out of the shadows, veering toward us. I looked to my right—a slightly larger grey wolf was baring its teeth as it joined the chase. We were being herded down the path. Suddenly I remembered: there should be a ravine up ahead . . .

I held onto the reins with one hand, keeping my sword tight in the other. My palms began to sweat. The wolves were gaining on us. I could hear Rain panting loudly and the grunts and snarls of the wolves as they tirelessly kept at my heels. They'd come close to snipping the end of Rain's tail several times now, but he held strong, always remaining just out of reach of snapping jaws.

And then something clicked inside my head. A plan formed. The old Phoebe had somehow taken over, and I was glad for it.

Rain needed to be free of me if he was going to make the jump unscathed. I'd have to time this right. We were almost there. I looked at the path ahead and then back to the shaggy wolf on my heel—it lunged at my leg just as I jumped off. I drew my sword up high and brought it down . . . right across the back of its neck.

I sailed through the air, landing violently on the ground. I could hear Rain neighing loudly. I pulled myself up quick, extending my sword. I stared at the wolf on the ground. Aside from its brown fur blowing in the breeze, it wasn't moving. I couldn't tell if it was dead or just knocked out.

A twig snapping on the ground behind me caused me to spin around. The grey wolf! I looked for it frantically. It slowly crept out from the trees. It was massive; at least three times my size. Its fur, matted and thick, added to its bulk. It didn't exactly look like a wolf . . . though, you couldn't deny the resemblance. It had a much longer body . . . like a man's. Its eyes were not as kind as Damen's. There would be no mercy here.

I swallowed loudly. I could hear my heart pounding as it drew nearer, studying me as it stalked forward.

A deep growl came from behind its teeth.

"Come on then!" The words came from me, but they were much braver than my own. I gripped my sword tightly, lifting it high.

A twig snapped from behind—the injured wolf was now on its feet.

I couldn't defend myself against two. I'd have to choose. The one behind me was closer. He'd attack first. I'd have to kill him and then if I had time—the injured wolf was in the air. I swung my body around, stabbing it straight through the gut. It fell to the ground using me to break its fall.

I heaved, trying to push its massive body off me. I rocked it back and forth, gasping under its weight, all the while searching for the grey wolf.

A loud snarl reverberated around me. My heart stopped. He was standing directly overhead, teeth bared. I was an easy kill.

The sound of approaching hooves caused a distraction. A man on horseback was approaching fast. His sword was drawn, and I was directly in his path. I ducked my head just as his horse cleared the dead carcass that rendered me helpless. He swung his sword at the grey wolf, bringing him down with one swipe. He circled its carcass for a moment before stopping several feet away from me.

"Thank you," I groaned, as I once again heaved, freeing myself at last. I picked my sword off the ground and stood tall, staring back into the eyes of the man that had just saved my life.

He walked his horse closer. His eyes grew wide. "It's impossible!"

"Many things are impossible Sir. We're roaming the countryside carrying swords and killing werewolves." I motioned to the dead wolf at my feet.

"That is what I do, *Lady Phoebe*." He bowed his head.

I looked at the man closely. "Raymose!"

He pulled back a little on his horse—startled by my excitement.

"I'm sorry. I didn't mean to scare you. I know this must seem strange . . . it's taken me awhile to get used to it too. Seeing people from my past I mean." I smiled brightly at him.

Raymose dismounted his horse. He was tall like Marcus, broad across the chest and extremely handsome. His hair was jet black, short and combed neatly. His features were soft, boyish. His dark brown eyes stared at me in wonderment.

He touched the back of his cold hand to my cheek. I hadn't even seen him reach for me. A flood of memories hit me at once.

I didn't know if they were Damen's or somehow my own. I instinctively closed my eyes and smiled as I breathed in his familiar scent—unafraid that he'd hurt me.

I opened my eyes again to find his lips touching mine. It was not the first time he'd kissed me. That much I knew.

"How?" He held me close to him, his eyes dancing with excitement.

"Raymose, I'm not the same Phoebe."

He looked confused.

"I mean, I am Phoebe . . . but I'm not the one you remember." I blushed. I could still feel his kiss on my lips.

"You are!" He held my face in his massive hands, kissing me once again. His lips were soft and next to mine felt almost warm. He pulled away, leaving me breathless.

"Raymose." I put my hands on his shoulders, steadying myself. I had been kissed by more people in one day than I had in my whole life.

He had my wrist in his hand before I could blink. His nose pressed against the bandages. He inhaled deeply—his eyes flashing red.

"You bleed . . ."

I flinched, trying to break free from his grasp.

"What has happened to you!" he hissed, releasing his hold.

I jumped back—extending my sword between us. I had no idea how I was going to fight Raymose.

Realization crossed his face. "No! Don't fear me!" He grabbed hold of me without hesitation. Ignoring the sword pointed at his middle—I didn't even have time to react. He took me up in his arms once again.

"Damen bit me!" I blurted out. I didn't know why I'd told him, other than the fact that Raymose had once taken care of me during my darkest time. He'd been the one to save me—literally.

I could feel the muscles in his arms tense up. He pulled away from me slowly; his eyes were black as coal—frightening.

"Not deep enough to turn me . . . but I have changed. A little." I admitted softly.

"Damen is here?"

"Yes." I winced at the expression on his face.

"Where?" he hissed.

"By the pond, this morning. He . . . grabbed me. "

A look of confusion over took him. "He had you and didn't kill you?"

"Killing me isn't exactly on his mind," I admitted sheepishly. "He sort of thinks he still loves me. He . . . kissed me. A lot."

"He…kissed you!" Raymose looked madder than Marcus had.

"Yes."

"I will kill him, I swear it," he thundered. "I've waited over seven hundred years to avenge your death, and even longer to avenge your honor."

"My honor?"

"You . . . don't remember?" he looked almost thankful.

"No, not all of it anyway."

"I wish I could forget." He closed his eyes, as if trying to shake away the memory.

"I'll never forget the day I found you in the woods. You'd never been so vulnerable, so scared . . . you were completely undone."

"You saved me." My voice cracked a little.

"I found you, yes. But I didn't save you." His eyes smoldered, as they looked long into mine. "Marcus did that."

"You did, I remember what you did for me," I insisted.

"I did what was necessary to keep you alive. You and I were inseparable after that, until I . . . well, it was a long time ago. I was young, and very foolish," he said with a forced smile.

He reached out and touched my cheek softly. His fingers lingered as if he needed the contact. "You're no longer immortal. I hear your heart. It beats faster now." He stepped closer. His body was nearly touching mine. Only a small sliver of air separated us.

I blushed. I could hear my heart pounding. Raymose was beyond handsome, and the way he was looking at me . . .

"No." I admitted as if that were something to be ashamed of. "I am not immortal."

"Come."

"Raymose, I can't ask you to risk your life for me." My heart sank a little. There were so many who would risk their life for me; it was overwhelming. Despite what I'd thought, chivalry wasn't dead—not amongst these men anyway. Honor and Justice reigned supreme.

"You can't go alone. You were lucky with that one." He motioned to the dead wolf beside me. "You've forgotten how to use that properly." He said, now pointing to my sword. "Fear not. I will teach you—again!" he half-laughed.

"Hey, I did pretty good," I said defensively, putting my hands on my hips.

He grinned. "As I said—luck! Rain!"

"You know Rain?"

"You might say we're old friends." He smiled coyly.

Rain was quickly beside me, nuzzling me in with his nose.

"May I help you up?" Raymose lifted me up into his arms before I had a chance to respond. He froze. His eyes were black again.

Rain neighed loudly

"Raymose?" My heart rate had increased. Something was wrong.

His arms gripped me tighter. "Phoebe. I need you to ride as fast as you can," he whispered under his breath. "I'll come for you."

"What? Why?"

"Just do as I say," he hissed. "There are too many of them." His eyes darted from tree to tree.

My breath caught. "No. I won't leave you by yourself."

"You were always so stubborn!" he snapped.

"It's called being moral. I won't leave you." I lifted my chin up defiantly. I wasn't going anywhere.

"Fine," he growled. "But stay behind me. And if I throw you on that horse, you'd better ride or I'll kill you myself!" I half believed him.

"Well this is a surprise."

We looked as Damen emerged from behind a tree.

"Damen," Raymose hissed like he'd just said something vile.

"Good afternoon Raymose. I see you're still looking after Lady Phoebe—Luther's loyal soldier to the end." His eyes narrowed.

"I've always looked after her. Luther never made me." Raymose's grip tightened around me.

Damen laughed. "I'm sure Marcus won't mind you holding his bride to be like that." He jeered.

I threw my head back, as if bored by the conversation. "Like you care."

"Careful Raymose, there's blood flowing through her veins now." Damen mused—he was enjoying himself far too much.

"I'm aware of her humanity," Raymose spat. He set me down swiftly, positioning himself between Damen and I.

"You don't think you can protect her?" Several more wolves emerged from the trees. Raymose had one hand behind him, pushing me back, and his sword drawn out in front of him with the other. "I've fought more," he hissed.

"Yes, but you haven't had to defend a damsel in distress at the same time. One that bleeds . . . it could be very distracting." Damen's words were taunting.

"I'm not in distress!" I moved myself beside Raymose. "I'm not going with you, Damen. I'd throw myself in that ravine before I let you take me.

Damen laughed heartedly. "He wouldn't let you do that. Raymose has loved you far longer than I have." His laughter echoed all around us.

I looked over at Raymose to see him looking at me out the corner of his eye—he wasn't denying it.

This had to be a bad dream. A *really* bad dream.

"You shouldn't have done that," Damen growled as he looked at the two dead wolves behind us.

"I didn't have a choice; he was trying to kill me!" I shouted.

"You?" Damen looked at me in disbelief.

"Yes. Me."

"And the other?" he asked.

"That would be my privilege beast. Although, I wouldn't have had the opportunity if he hadn't been trying to kill Phoebe as well," Raymose spat.

"They wouldn't harm her. I've instructed the pack to watch out for her." Damen glanced at the wolves beside him—they were cowering slightly.

"Well, I think I'll pass on your *protection*. As you can see, I don't need it." I raised my sword.

"You'd kill me?" There was pain in his voice.

"You're not giving me any other option." I answered softly. I gripped my sword tighter.

He nodded his head. "There is still hope. I felt it when we kissed."

"You kissed!" I corrected sharply, as I did my best to ignore the look of outrage on Raymose's face

"Same, predictable Damen. Luther warned you not to harbor feeling for his daughter. He'll be interested to know you haven't changed."

"You fool. You can't take her to Luther. She'll be killed! She's part wolf now, or can't you tell!" he snarled.

Raymose turned his head slightly, glancing my way.

"I told you I'm not the same," my eyes dropped.

"It doesn't matter." He spoke to me. His voice was soft.

"You think you have a chance with her?" Damen scoffed, taking a step forward. "Get in line."

"Stop it! Stop it!" I could feel tears starting to build. "I'm not a prize to be won! I'm not your Phoebe!" I grabbed onto Rain and started to run.

"Phoebe!" Damen shouted after me.

With great effort, I pulled myself up and dug my heels in. Rain moved like we were on fire. I didn't know where we were going, and I didn't care. I cried hard into his fur. I couldn't believe I ran away like that. I literally threw Raymose to the wolves—Raymose, who was also in love with Phoebe. How many men could possibly be in love with the same woman?

Damen was insane, and Marcus was going to kill me for sure—or was he already dead? God, don't let him be dead.

"Faster boy!"

It hadn't taken Raymose long before he caught up with me.

"Phoebe, stop!"

"No! Raymose, just forget you saw me." I cried, not looking back at him. "I don't want to hurt you."

He reached over and pulled back on the reins. Rain halted abruptly throwing me off him.

"Phoebe!" Raymose jumped off his horse and rushed over to me.

I tried to roll over, desperately gasping for air.

"Phoebe I'm sorry. I didn't mean to hurt you; I forgot you couldn't ride well."

I knew he was trying to comfort me, but I couldn't help but shoot him an irritated look. Was there anything I *could* do right, aside from seducing every eligible hunk around?

"Accident," I gasped.

"Just try to breathe slowly."

"Raymose?" A voice called from behind him. I recognized it immediately.

I looked fearfully into Raymose's eyes. I couldn't speak yet; I still couldn't breathe right. I was sucking in large gasps of air that my lungs seemed to reject. How was I going to explain to Marcus why I was here? My breathing worsened as I panicked.

"I'll stay with you and explain," Raymose whispered as he smoothed my hair off my forehead. His face looked suddenly sad. "I know you love him."

Raymose tilted his body so that Marcus could see that it was I he was hovering over.

“No!” Marcus hissed. He flew off his horse with Richard close behind him.

“Phoebe,” He put his arms around me, his eyes searching every inch of me. He cradled my head on his lap, trying to calm me. I was still trying to breathe and wasn’t going to be a big participant in this conversation

Marcus turned to Raymose with black eyes. “What have you done to her?” he growled.

“No!” I gasped, as I reached up and pulled at Marcus shirt. “Not . . . his . . . fault!”

“Well that’s not exactly true,” Raymose admitted casually.

Marcus's face was tense. I could see the muscles in his jaw tighten as he glowered at Raymose.

“You see,” Raymose began “Phoebe was in a particularly hairy predicament. When I found her. She was in the middle of a . . . how shall I put this, you know I don’t like to exaggerate . . . fight to the death with a pair of werewolves.”

I sucked in so much air that I started choking uncontrollably. What the hell was Raymose doing?

“What!” Marcus thundered, ignoring my pleas for air.

“She actually managed to kill one. If its dead body hadn’t been lying across hers, she may have had a sporting chance with the other.”

Marcus looked murderous.

“Naturally,” Raymose boasted. “I had perfect timing and was able to kill the mongrel with little effort.”

I tried to make myself smaller, hoping I would disappear into a speck of dust and blow away.

Raymose laughed lightly to himself. A broad smile had taken residence on his face. “We mustn’t forget our delusional friend Damen—he’s the comic figure in all of this.”

“Raymose,” I begged, my breath returning to me. “He’s going to kill me as it is.”

“Nonsense Phoebe, Marcus is really very understanding.” He winked at me.

I tried to sit up but Marcus held me firm—I wasn't going anywhere.

"Where was I . . .?" Raymose asked playfully, ignoring the tension that loomed over us. "Oh yes. After I realized that it was Phoebe here whom I had just saved—Phoebe, who you neglected to tell me was alive." Raymose shot Marcus an eerie look. "I planned to escort her to safety, when Damen, being the gentlemen that he is, decided to persuade her to come with him—under the protection of his faithful pack who had just attacked her.

"Where is Damen now?" Marcus hissed through gritted teeth.

"I don't know," Raymose admitted, all joking removed from his face. "After Phoebe fled, his wolves attacked me. I only had time to kill one. Damen was already chasing after her. I got to Phoebe as quickly as I could."

"How are you responsible for this?" Marcus was still gritting his teeth. He hadn't looked at me since Raymose had begun talking.

"I tried to stop her horse and she fell off. I'd forgotten what a bad rider she is," Raymose teased.

Marcus turned his attention to me. "What were you thinking?" he hissed angrily. His arms thankfully released me.

I squirmed out from under him. His eyes were dark, deadly, and they were fixed on me.

"You could have been killed!" he shouted.

I instinctively jumped behind Raymose and hid myself. I was such a coward.

"Easy Marcus." Raymose's tone was firm as he protectively asserted himself in front of me.

"Step aside Raymose. She isn't going to weasel out of this. She nearly got herself killed—again! This isn't a game!"

I gripped onto the back of Raymose's shirt tightly. I knew he'd protect me, even from Marcus.

"Stop scaring her!" Raymose growled angrily. "She wouldn't have risked her life if she wasn't worried about you in the first place. History is repeating itself—yet again." Raymose's tone was sharp.

A cricket chirping broke the silence.

"I'm sorry I made you worry." My small voice squeaked out from behind Raymose. "I couldn't stand the thought of you out here by yourself. Damen said he was going to kill you. I couldn't let him take you away from me."

"There. You see: it was all in the name of love." Raymose's tone lightened to the point of condescending.

I peered out from behind him. Marcus had his back to us. His arms were tightly folded across his chest—obviously considering what to do with me.

Raymose looked back at me, winking his eye.

I mouthed "Thank you." I could feel the tears leaking out the corners of my eyes. I couldn't explain it, but somehow I remembered Raymose. His never failing kindness.

His compassion for others—a strange quality for a vampire, I'd always thought. His endless devotion to my well-being. He did still love me. Damen had been right about that.

I grabbed onto Rain and pulled myself up.

"Where do you think you're going?" Marcus asked without turning to look at me. His tone was cold.

"I'm removing myself from this equation," I said flatly.

He turned around. His eyes were dark. Unforgiving. "Get off *that* horse!"

"No!" I blurted out. My face hardened. I stared bravely into his black eyes. I could feel my pulse quicken. I gripped onto the reins tighter for strength. He looked terrifying.

"I explained why I had to come. I won't keep putting you in the position of having to protect me. I'll deal with Damen myself. It's me he wants anyway."

I could see the vein in Marcus's neck pulsating. He was furious beyond words.

"Phoebe, you can't go alone; it's too dangerous." Raymose's eyes were pleading. I knew he'd come with me if I asked him to—he'd follow me to the ends of the earth if that were what I wanted. Part of me wanted him to come with me. I felt suddenly alone and afraid. I couldn't do that to him, or to Marcus—I wouldn't!

"I'm sorry," I whispered. The words had a double meaning. I could tell by the look in Raymose's eyes that he understood both.

"If you're going to fight, it won't be because of me." I reluctantly met Marcus's stare. "But you can't expect me to sit back and watch you die."

I held my hand out to him, my fist clenched tight. He looked at it cautiously for a moment before he reached out. I could feel a lump forming in my throat. His mouth dropped open as he caught my ring in his hand.

I turned Rain sharply, digging my heels in hard. I didn't look back.

Chapter 25: Reckless Behavior

I knew I'd scared him. I knew he loved me beyond reason. But I also knew he wouldn't forget the pain and worry I'd caused him.

I cried hard as Rain carried me through the forest. This would be the last time I'd ride him, and my heart ached at the thought.

The sun was well overhead now. The forest was quiet, aside from us tearing through it at a rapid speed. I looked behind me. Marcus wasn't following. I didn't really expect him to, but I had hoped . . .

I loved him. I needed him like the air I breathed. He had become the center of my universe; I couldn't imagine my life without him in it. I didn't want to. There would be no color left in my world without him. He had my heart.

I cried harder as I pushed Rain to run faster. The farther away I left Marcus, the more my heart ached for him. I wanted to turn back. I wanted to tell him that I loved him. That I'd do anything he asked of me. But I knew he had to let me go—and I also knew he wasn't strong enough to do it. I couldn't exist in his world, not the way I was: a fragile, breakable human. Someone he'd have to watch over every minute of every day. I knew Damen would never leave me alone. He'd find me wherever I ran. I'd have to face him sooner or later. Maybe he was right—we were connected now, and our futures would be forever intertwined.

Rain started to slow a little. His ears were tilting like they were listening for something.

"What is it boy?" I whispered nervously. I gripped onto the reins tighter. "Damn!" I realized I didn't have my sword with me . . . I must have lost it when I fell.

I looked from side to side. I couldn't see anything at first, and then something caught my eye. There, lurking in the shadows, two golden eyes flickered back at me. I wasn't alone.

Rain's speed quickened. I scanned the trees as we brushed past them, my heart in my throat. I couldn't see it. Had I imagined it? I leaned out, strained to see through the tears that still clouded my eyes. Rain suddenly jumped—I fell off, rolling down an embankment.

I lay there for a moment face down in the dirt. Moaning. I rolled onto my back, spitting dirt from my lips. "This is just . . . great!" I pounded my fists on the ground. "I lost my boyfriend, my sword, and now my horse!"

I stood up, dusted myself off, and surveyed the path above me. "Wonderful . . . climbing," I grumped aloud.

I reached for a tree root to pull myself up when a deep growl from behind made me freeze.

I swallowed loudly, shaking as I turned slowly around.

I could feel its hot breath against my face. Its yellow eyes stared right into mine. It was close enough to touch if I would have been brave enough to reach out.

I held my breath, frozen where I stood. My heart pounded loudly, drowning out all other noise . . . except for it's breathing. Its lips slowly pulled back, baring its teeth.

"Marcus . . .help me, " I begged under my breath.

Something flashed past me, knocking the wolf aside. I tried to scurry up the hill backward, slipping back down the soft dirt.

Marcus was rolling around the ground with the wolf. It snarled as Marcus lifted it off him, thrusting it into a nearby tree. It staggered for a moment, regained its senses and lunged in my direction. I didn't have time to react. Marcus had dove in front of me, hissing wildly as he held onto its head, prying its jaw open and twisted until a loud crack like a tree splitting echoed through the forest. I covered my ears, cringing as I saw the wolf fall dead to the ground.

Marcus turned to me, his chest heaving in and out as he breathed in heavily.

I could see his shining teeth, his blackened eyes, and the murderous expression on his face. For the first time, he looked like a vampire. My God, Marcus truly was a Vampire!

He moved toward me. My heart hadn't stopped pounding. My eyes darted back and forth from the wolf to Marcus. I was terrified beyond words. I hadn't seen anything so horrific in my life. I never expected to see that side of Marcus—I didn't know it even existed. The wolf nearly killed me, and Marcus looked as though he were going to finish where the wolf left off.

"Phoebe, are you hurt?" his voice was strained. "Did it hurt you?"

Tears hung in my eyes. I couldn't speak. I was in shock. I wanted *my* Marcus—not the man standing before me.

"It's alright." He spoke softer now, his face resembling more of his own. "You're safe, it can't hurt you."

I staggered a few steps back. He stopped, realizing it was not the wolf I feared.

"Darling, I'm not going to hurt you. I swear it." He extended his hand out to me.

I looked at his hand skeptically, then staring into his black eyes. I was torn. My mind was telling me to run for my life; although, I had very little faith that my legs would cooperate. My heart reminded me that I swore never to doubt him again. I closed my eyes, deliberated with my mental tug-a-war, and took a deep breath. It took all my courage and strength to reach out to him. My body trembled as I slowly extended my hand.

"I won't hurt you my love." His voice was smooth like velvet. All signs of aggression were gone.

Our fingers touched lightly—I gasped as he pulled me to him, holding me tight. I could feel the tension in his arms as they wrapped around me. The sweet smell of rainwater filled my senses. All the fear, all the pain from the day came crashing down on me all at once. I clung onto him desperately, sobbed hysterically as I fell to my knees.

"Shhh, it's alright darling. I've got you." He kissed my face over and over. "You're safe now."

"You came for me," I cried, my lips breaking free from his momentarily.

"I could never let you go," he kissed my lips again and again. "Don't you know by now there isn't anything I wouldn't do for you?" He took my face in his hands, holding it firmly. "I would die for you!"

His mouth took mine aggressively. I didn't protest. I was in Marcus's arms, safe, and no matter how hard I tried, I knew I wasn't strong without him. I needed him more than I'd realized. More than I'd wanted to admit. I needed him as much as he needed me.

He pulled back from me, his thumbs desperately trying to wipe away the tears that were still falling. "Never risk your life for me, do you understand?" He touched his forehead to mine. "I can't live without you again, I can't! You *are* my life. You are the only reason for my existence!" His mouth crushed mine. I could feel how badly he wanted me, how badly he needed me.

My arms found their way around his neck, pulling him closer to me, my body meshing up against his. His kiss heated with an intensity that rivaled any other kiss. I didn't want it to end, and neither did he, but one of us had to breathe . . . eventually . . .

His lips reluctantly broke free from mine. The both of us panting as he pulled my left hand up to his mouth and kissed the ring that had somehow found its way back on my finger. "This belongs here; never doubt that."

Tears were falling from my eyes once again. "I don't want to leave you Marcus, but Damen—"

"Will never touch you," he interrupted.

"I know I scared you," I began. His face hardened a little. "I put myself in indescribably danger—I'd do it again!" I glance away from him for a moment, trying to maintain my courage. "I couldn't breathe thinking you were all alone out here. I had to come!"

He turned my face to his. He stared long into my eyes.

"Marcus, please say you understand, that you forgive me."

He shook his head. His lips protested, curling up into a slight smile. "I . . . forgive you," he said in defeat.

I threw my arms around him again, hugging him to me.

"I was so scared when I couldn't find you . . . and when I saw you lying on the ground with Raymose crouched over you, I thought he'd . . ."

"You thought he'd killed me?" I asked incredulously.

"Yes!" he hissed.

"But surely you know Raymose is in . . . he cares for me deeply. He'd never hurt me. I know it."

"I'm aware of his feelings for you. He's never hidden it." Marcus's voice rose a little. "In fact, he has just made it quite clear that should anything happen to me . . ." Marcus didn't need to finish.

I half laughed, blushing at the thought.

"You are human, and wolf now—his reaction to you was completely unknown. He could have just as easily killed you." Marcus stressed.

"He was so happy to see me, he—" I noticed the uneasy look on Marcus's face as he watched me. I could feel my cheeks blushing again. "He was really happy to see me." I repeated quickly, turning my head a little to the side, avoiding his stare.

"I told him I'm not the same Phoebe, although he insists that I am." My face still burned from the memory.

"He . . . kissed you." Marcus's voice was shaky.

"Marcus." I wasn't sure what I should tell him. "He was so excited I was alive . . . he just . . . reacted."

Marcus looked as though he were turning green. I reached out and gently grazed his lips with my thumb. "You must know by now that yours are the only lips I want to kiss." I stood on my tiptoes and gently brushed my lips against his. "You are the only man I want to love." I fisted his shirt in my hands. "The only man I need."

He grabbed my waist and lifted me up against a tree, pressing his body to mine. I wrapped my legs around him, hugging him tightly. He couldn't hold me close enough.

"I've waited my whole life for you," I breathed. "Don't make me wait any longer.

His mouth took mine, our lips seamlessly moving together. I moaned feeling lost in his kiss, his touch. He pressed me harder into the tree. I didn't care. The world could have stopped moving, and I wouldn't have known it. I gripped his shoulders. My head fell back, exposing my throat. His lips glided along my jaw and down my neck. He inhaled deeply, sending a shiver through my body.

I looked up into the trees, watching them sway overhead. His sweet scent engulfing me—I felt deliciously intoxicated.

"Marcus, I'm going to faint," I panted. My vision blurred a little.

"I'll catch you," he breathed into my neck. His mouth found mine again, kissing my lips over and over, drawing me deeper into his spell. "I want to spend the rest of time loving you Phoebe." His eyes were smoldering.

As if I wanted to, or could, say no. Marcus had rendered me incapable of sorting out the simplest of thoughts. I wanted him desperately. I could feel my body going limp in his arms. I kissed his lower lip, biting it a little. He groaned as if he was in pain—the look in his eyes suggested it was pure pleasure.

"I. Want. You. Now!" He could barely say the words.

I suddenly felt myself being carried through the air. We were flying. His mouth never left mine. I hadn't realized where he'd taken me until I felt the familiar surroundings of my bed beneath me. He leaned over my body, still panting from our kiss, his eyes, red with lust.

"You're sure I'm the one you want? You seem to have quite a line forming of eligible men," he asked in a husky voice.

Oh yes. I was sure. My hands moved down his chest. I watched his eyes as they stared into mine, awaiting my answer. I lifted his shirt up, and he let me take it over his head. I grinned. "You are the only one I want." I removed my shirt in one swift motion.

He stared wantonly at me, wetting his lips slightly with the tip of his tongue. I pulled him down on me. His skin on mine felt silky, soft and cool.

I ran my fingers along his pant waist. He smiled knowingly. He allowed me to unbutton them. I drew my legs up and managed to push them off with my feet.

"You're sure you want me?" I asked reluctantly. My hands roamed freely over his God-like body. "There must be some vampire girl out there who would be less trouble than I am?"

My pants were suddenly torn from my body. I breathed heavily. I still wasn't used to his animal like responses. I glanced at my pants. I wouldn't be wearing those again.

He regarded my lingerie. "Red—"

"You don't like red?" My eyebrows rose a little.

"No, red's fine." He continued to gaze.

"What is it then?" Curiosity had caught me.

"Please remember, I am over seven hundred years old. I've never actually seen . . . you never wore anything like this," he explained.

"Marcus, you're blushing!" I laughed. I could swear his cheeks were flushed.

"I probably never wore anything like this because they didn't have anything like this," I laughed lightly.

His mouth was suddenly on my stomach, moving slowly across it. I could feel my pulse quicken. He lifted his head back. His eyes had changed to deep amber.

"You're sure? There's no going back." It took all his strength to ask me again, but I knew, that if I had said no, he'd find it in him to pull away from me. God I loved this man.

My foot had worked its way up his hips, and with subtle assistance from my hands; I'd managed to push away the last of his clothing.

"I only, want, you." I brought him back to me, my lips taking his again and again.

"I hope you weren't attached to these," he yanked my bottoms off. I could feel his lips smiling against mine.

"Well, they were part of a set." I spoke with false concern.

"Hmm," he mused. "There's no point in splitting up the set."

Snap! I saw a flash of red fly over his shoulder—my mouth gaped open. "How do you do that?"

His face grew serious. "You're really quite lovely you know." He wasn't teasing any longer. "You're more beautiful than I remembered."

He rested his cheek over my heart, listening to its beat. I breathed heavily at the intimacy of it.

"What are you thinking?" I ran my fingers slowly through his hair, combing it back gently.

"I was just thinking of another time: A time when we loved each other so freely. When I didn't have to worry about harming you."

"You won't hurt me. You'd never hurt me." I pulled his face up to mine, my eyes locking with his, "I trust you." He could hear the resolve in my voice. "I trust you."

He sighed heavily, and although his eyes were full of worry, he put his arm under my waist and pulled my body to his.

I hadn't expected the overwhelming emotions that filled me. Our bodies moved seamlessly together. It was as if we'd never been apart—we knew each other that well.

His hands roamed freely over my body. His touch heated my skin, causing my heart to pump faster than I'd thought possible. I gasped, as I gripped him tighter to me. My legs squeezed his body to mine, as if the action might hold him forever.

By the look on Marcus's face, he was wishing the very same—he grinned, taking my lips once again and claiming a kiss reserved only for him.

I was lost in the time that passed. The moans of pleasure, the soft whispers of love he proclaimed to me, and the countless visions of Marcus and I making love flooded my mind and heated the passion I felt for him. My heart was complete in a way I hadn't dreamed possible. I felt love beyond imagination, and peace engulfed me. Marcus was my soul mate: my love for all time.

I could feel the tension in his body as he cried out in complete abandon, his hands gripping my shoulders tightly. I was torn between the pain in my arms and the overwhelming pleasure that moved through me. He pressed his mouth hard against my neck, making an almost inaudible hiss.

My eyes opened wide. The pain was unbearable. "Marcus. You're hurting me." I tried to push him off—he didn't budge.

"Phoebe." His voice was gruff, not his own.

I was afraid to move. Understanding claimed me. He wanted my blood. "Marcus, please!"

With what looked to be great effort, he lifted his head up. His eyes were deep red—a shade that put the ruby that was still around my neck, to shame.

"Please. Don't do this." My voice was barely a whisper.

"Phoebe I . . ." his eyes dropped, to the death grip he had on my arms. He released me immediately. I could feel the blood rushing back through my veins.

I breathed heavily, a tear leaking out the corner of my eye. "I'm fine!" My voice cracked. I was saying it for his benefit as much as my own.

I could see the devastation on his face. He turned his head away from me. "I'm sorry."

I subtly began rubbing the life back into my arms. I knew he hadn't meant to hurt me. Marcus and I physically were a dangerous combination—I understood that now. It took every fiber of his being not to bite me. In the height of his pleasure, he denied himself the one thing he wanted . . . blood.

Our hearts desired each other's love, while our instincts tore us apart. I couldn't let him torture himself. He did after all maintain control. I could be dead now.

"Not all of it was painful," I said playfully as I tickled my fingers down his chest and stomach, earning me a small smile.

His eyes were still smoldering. I knew he still wanted my blood, but the guilt he felt outweighed the desire that was slowly subsiding.

"Are you . . . all right . . . otherwise?" he asked nervously, his eyes still drifting to my arms. I hugged myself, trying to conceal the subtle shivering that ran through me.

"I'm wonderful! I had no idea how passionate vampires were, how gentle they could be. Had I only known . . ." I teased, than quickly hid my face in his chest; I knew the disapproving look that would be coming my way.

He put his arms around me. Despite the fear I'd felt moments ago, I felt safe with him. I wanted him to hold me forever.

"Are *you* alright? I mean, are you happy?" I snuck a peek at him. He looked at me like I'd just asked the most insane question imaginable.

"Well I don't know," I said defensively. "Maybe it's different for vampires. Maybe I'm not—" he put his hand over my mouth silencing me.

"You're perfect."

"Are you sure?" I wrinkled my nose a little.

"You're all I've ever needed." He half laughed.

"What's so funny?" I asked nervously.

"You're a bit more than I remember," he mused, tussling my hair playfully.

I smiled to myself, basking in the after-glow. I had Marcus in every way now. He loved me, and more importantly he'd forgiven me. Life couldn't be more perfect. I lay there on his chest savoring the moment . . .

"Phoebe, I don't wish to spoil the mood, but I must ask . . . "

I looked up into his glorious face. "Anything." I smiled brightly.

"Well, it's just that in our haste, we . . ." his eyes were downcast. "Of course things are different now. I've never been with any other woman, and we never . . .

"You haven't made love to anyone in over seven hundred years?" I nearly shot out of the bed.

"That's not the point of this conversation," Marcus grumbled. He truly was embarrassed.

"I'm sorry," I muttered, putting my hand over my mouth. I forced a look of concentration back on my face—trying to suppress a smile that would soon break free.

"No one! Not once?" I blurted out in disbelief.

"NO! I died with you."

"Yeah, but I thought vampires flew into unsuspecting women's rooms, made love to them, and then—"

"I've never taken a woman against her will!" He looked appalled at the suggestion.

"Sorry! I didn't mean to insult you, I was just teasing . . . sort of," I admitted honestly. The truth was, all those old monster movies I'd watched growing up now suddenly seemed to be documentaries. I truly did expect to see Frankenstein before summer's end.

His eyes caught mine—there was no play in them. "There has never been another for me."

"Or for me," I grinned. My lips took his by surprise. I twined my fingers through the back of his hair. I could feel my heart beating faster and faster against his chest. He groaned, almost sounding frustrated.

"This is reckless," he moved his hand up my thigh and hooked my leg around him. Pulling my body back to his.

"Everything about today has been reckless," I breathed, my body moving with his again.

"Phoebe I . . ."

"Shhh!" I stopped his mouth with a kiss.

I was in absolute heaven. He was much more aware this time, being extra careful not to hold me too tightly. Not to let his lips linger too long against my throat. I held him as long as I could, never wanting him to let go. Never wanting him to stop.

The sun that had once lit my room, now cast a soft orange glow across the balcony; it was late afternoon.

We lay in each other's arms, completely at peace. That is until my stomach growled.

"Sorry," I blushed. "I haven't had anything to eat today. I think I'll head down to the kitchen and see if Charlotte has anything." He caught my hand as I moved to get up. A strange look of embarrassment once again overtook him. "Marcus, what is it? Are you all right? Did I do something wrong?" He took my hands and held them together, placing them on his chest.

"No, my love, you haven't done anything wrong, and I am very well." He smiled peacefully.

"What is it then?" I stared at him, confused as ever.

He scrubbed a hand down his face. "I know you haven't been with another man, but have you by any chance considered . . .?" He looked up at the ceiling.

"Marcus, is it that bad that you can't just come out and say it?" I was beyond frustrated and starting to feel self-conscious.

"It's completely improper for me to ask. We never worried about it in our time."

"Worried about what?"

"When people made love, they accepted the life that might come from it." His eyes met mine; they were full of hope.

I stared at him incredulously. "What are you—" I stopped. I could feel all color draining from my face. My mouth popped open. I jumped out of the bed, taking the top blanket with me.

"You have to be kidding me! You said you had to be half human!" I nearly shouted.

"I said you had to be half human . . . and *you* are."

"No, no . . . " I tried to do the math. One hundred percent human Phoebe- bit by werewolf equals . . . I'm not werewolf . . . at least not completely . . . I don't know what it equals actually. A quarter? I let out a frustrated groan.

He watched me pace back and forth as I went over the obvious once again.

"I'm guessing by your reaction, you haven't planned for this?"

"No! Why would I? I thought the werewolf bite would have thrown off my ratio."

He nodded. "It will be alright. We'll just have to be careful if that's something we wish to avoid at this time—if we can avoid it now?" he added under his breath. The look on his face wasn't promising.

"I can't believe this. Why didn't you say something before?" I stared at him in disbelief. I felt a small flame light within me—I envisioned myself physically injuring him in several appropriate ways. All of which would have failed. The odds of me successfully harming Marcus were zero at best. Still . . . the thought was appealing.

He closed his eyes, avoiding my death like stare. “I’m not certain, but the likelihood you’re more human than werewolf appears to be high. The probability you could conceive . . . ” he didn’t finish. He didn’t have to.

I growled mentally as I walked over to the window and looked out at the orange sky. I couldn’t deny that I’d been a more than willing participant—twice! I’d taken health classes. I was a big girl! The blame was just as much mine as it was his. Like he said, this wasn’t anything we would have worried about in the past. Why would he worry about it now?

“Phoebe I’m sorry.” Marcus stood behind me now, his arms wrapping around me. “If it makes you feel any better, Phoebe and I were together nine years before she apparently conceived.”

I nodded. Nine years . . . that did make me feel better. My life was so unsettled, and the thought of having a child now . . . was too much.

“Marcus, I want to learn how to sword fight again.” He froze, his arms stiffening around me.

“Absolutely not.”

“What? Why?” I demanded, spinning around to look at him. “You can’t expect me to live here and not be able to protect myself!”

“I won’t have you running around slaying werewolves. It’s too dangerous.”

“I won’t! But wouldn’t you rather I could defend myself if I had to? Or would you prefer I’m ripped to shreds like before?”

He grimaced.

“Besides, Richard and Raymose have already offered to teach me. With the both of them, I should be pretty good, maybe even useful.”

Marcus looked murderous. “They went behind my back!” he spat, enunciating each word with as much venom as the next.

"No! I sort of . . . cornered Richard," I admitted quietly. "Raymose offered to train me after he witnessed my skills today . . . or lack of." I frowned.

"No," Marcus said as if the conversation was officially over.

"Marcus. This isn't your decision. I'd like you to support me, but I don't need your permission." I spoke defiantly.

"Yes you do." His words were absolute. "This is a different world Phoebe, a world you're not used to." He reached out and took my bandaged hand and held it up for affect. "This is sword's play compared to what can happen during battle."

"I'm not going to battle. I just want to be able to defend myself!"

"*I'll* protect you," he said fiercely.

"Every minute of every day?" I protested. "No. Either you agree, or I'm leaving.

Tonight." I shrugged away from him.

His expression was hard. He was not going to bend on this.

"Fine." I stomped off toward the bathroom, not giving him a second look. "Will you please tell Richard I need a ride to the airport?"

Marcus caught me from behind. He had his arms around my waist, and despite my attempts to struggle out of his grasp, he held me, gently, until I stilled. "I can't let you go." He sighed. I could hear the defeat in his voice. His hand moved across my stomach and paused. "Please be careful."

I turned and hugged him excitedly.

"I mean it Phoebe. You're human this time. If you get cut . . . Raymose—"

"Will take good care of me," I interrupted. "You don't have to worry about a thing."

"Right." His voice was condescending. Asking Marcus to not worry about me was like asking the sun not to rise the next day.

"I do need to see a doctor though," I admitted.

"Why?" Marcus looked uneasy again.

“Because I want some form of birth control. I’m not going to worry about this every time we decide to be *hasty*.” I couldn’t help but blush.

“I’ll have someone here before dinner.” He smiled slightly, his mind obviously in sync with mine.

“A house call? I am impressed.”

He gave me a wry smile. “I’ll leave you to your shower.”

Chapter 26: Sword Play

Richard was waiting for me on the balcony when I stepped out of the bathroom.

"Richard?"

"I believe you should have warned me, Miss, that you told Lord Ashworth I'd offered to assist you with your lessons." He looked livid.

"Richard, I'm sorry. Marcus wanted me to stay, and I wouldn't unless he agreed to let me learn how to protect myself. It just sort of slipped out that you offered to help."

"Well, it's put me in a rather awkward spot I must say." He looked away, trying to keep up the façade of being angry.

"Please don't be mad at me," I nudged him gently on the arm.

His mouth curled up on one side a little. "Very well Miss, we shall start first thing in the morning."

"Thank you Richard."

"Mr. Raymose is in the garden waiting to speak with you as well. It would seem you've put both of us in a rather awkward position."

I had to look as confused as I was.

"If you should fail, Miss, Lord Ashworth will blame it on bad training." He bowed his head slightly.

I couldn't help but laugh. "Well, at least I know whose neck you're looking out for."

"Forgive me Miss, I almost forgot. Dr. Andersen will be here this evening around seven." Richard shifted uneasily. "I do hope you're well Miss." He moved past me quickly. "If there won't be anything else . . ."

"Richard!" I called after him like he was a child that had just done something naughty.

"Yes Miss?"

I stared at him in disbelief. "He told you, didn't he?" I was completely embarrassed. Now Richard knew we had unprotected sex.

"I am supposed to look after you Miss. It is important that I know any pertinent information that would jeopardize your safety."

I stormed past him in a huff, yanked the newly polished sword off the wall, and started for the bedroom door.

"Miss Rose, where are you going?"

"To deal with a certain vampire," I growled.

I stomped down the stairs and headed for the Library. Marcus was sitting in a chair, reading the paper when I threw open the doors.

"Phoebe, love?" he looked over the top of the paper. He placed it down quickly at the sight of me blazing in armed with a murderous look in my eyes, and a sword in my hand.

I swung it at a vase of flowers—cutting the tops off with one swipe.

His eyes were wide as he rose from his chair.

I walked right up to him and pointed the sword right in the middle of his chest.

"Darling? What are you doing?" He spoke calmly like he was trying to talk down a suicide jumper. "Phoebe, that sword is very sharp; you don't want to hurt yourself again. Put it down, slowly."

"You . . . told . . . Richard!" I thundered.

Marcus sighed as if he'd worried needlessly. "I only told him to keep an eye on you since he'll be training you. I don't want you getting hurt," he said defensively.

"Marcus, do you realize how crazy that is. There is no reason for you to tell anyone anything! The odds of my being pregnant are . . ." I stopped talking as I puzzled for a moment. "Well I don't exactly know what the odds are, but they aren't high!" I yelled, hoping I hadn't lost my upper hand.

"I only want to make sure that you're taken care of. I didn't mean to upset you. I acted out of love."

"And the others?" I glared at him, trying my best to ignore the sheepish look on his face.

"I've said nothing to anyone else, and I've instructed Richard to do the same."

I pursed my lips. "Fine, I can't do anything about Richard knowing now, but that's all!"

"As you wish, my love." Marcus smiled triumphantly, while ignoring the sword that was still pointed at his middle. He sat back in his chair and resumed reading his paper.

"By the way," I lowered my sword just a little. "Raymose will be training me, not Richard." I spoke defiantly.

"NO!"

"Yes! I'm going to learn without any restrictions." I leaned in close, resting my hands on the arms of his chair. I stared bravely into his black eyes. His jaw tightened.

"I mean it Marcus. I won't be unprotected again." I turned and stormed out of the room.

I was shaking all over. I took several deep breaths, trying to calm myself as I walked out the main doors and into the garden to find Raymose. I cleared my mind, put on a happy face, and ran up to him excitedly. He smiled brightly, catching me in his arms.

"I'm so happy you're back with us." He hugged me tightly.

"Thank you," I smiled.

He forced a look of outrage on his face. "You shouldn't have gone off alone; you could have been killed." His face grew serious. "You know I would have gone with you."

"You know why I couldn't ask you to do that." I spoke softly, nearly singing the words.

He shook his head in understanding. "Well, you really should learn to use that thing again," he pointed to the sword in my hand.

"Oh. Um. That's why I'm here actually. Raymose, I need you to teach me how to defend myself."

"Why me? Why not Marcus?"

"Because Marcus won't be objective." Understatement I thought.

"You really want to learn how to sword fight?"

"Please. I can't live like this, not being able to protect myself. Damen's chasing me constantly, and now his pack seems to want me dead. I don't have a choice anymore."

Raymose rubbed the back of his neck, deliberating quietly. "I can teach you. That's not a problem—is Marcus ok with this?" he asked suddenly.

Although I had a feeling his reservations had little to do with Marcus's approval.

"He knows I'm speaking with you about it." I chose my words carefully. "Raymose, you taught me before. I can't think of anyone better." I smiled hopefully at him. "Please . . ."

He stared at me apprehensively. "It won't be as easy as before," he warned. He still looked uneasy. "Your body isn't as durable."

I put my hands on my hips and frowned.

"Alright. But we'll have to be extremely careful. We can't afford the slightest error. I don't want to cut you. Or worse."

"What could be worse than getting cut?" I half laughed.

"The feeding frenzy after your blood is spilt." There was no play in his words. "I'm not as disciplined as Marcus."

My mouth dropped open. Than closed. Then fell open again.

"You ready for your first lesson?" He was pointing to the sword in my hand, distracting me from the many horrific visions that now swam in my head.

He smiled as he pulled his sword from a pocket that had been sewn in his coat. He swung it at me abruptly—I blocked it.

"Good!" he said as he came at me with more force this time. Once, twice, he was strong, and he put his weight behind his sword.

Clank, clank. I blocked both blows . . . although I was a little out of breath. "This is going to be a workout," I breathed loudly.

"You have no idea." He grinned and flew at me.

Clank, clank, clank. I was stepping backward now as I blocked each of his blows.

Two up high and one low, he came at my back, narrowly missing it. I managed to twist and block it with as much grace as an Ostrich on roller skates—I fell.

"Phoebe! Are you alright?"

"Yes, I'm fine," I assured as he helped me off the ground.

He shook his head back and forth, smiling. "Not bad for a human—or a *girl* for that matter!" He punched my shoulder laughing heartedly.

"OW!" I yelped, falling back to the ground.

"Sorry, I forgot you break easily." He hefted me up and planted me firmly on my feet. "My apologies, *Lady Phoebe.*

I grinned and swung at him—he blocked it effortlessly.

"So, it's going to be like that is it?" He came at me from every angle. In front, over head, and down low. He swung toward my back again. This time I managed to block it successfully, while stumbling backward right into a stone bench. I toppled over, landing on my back—laughing. I couldn't remember when I'd had this much fun.

Raymose had his sword pointed right at my middle, his brilliant smile reflecting back at me like the sunset off the sword.

"You never would have missed that before." He extended his hand and helped me up.

"I'm going to have to learn to block that without landing on my back." I subtly rubbed my backside.

"You're going to have to learn more than that!" He laughed, tucking his sword back in his coat.

"Hey!"

"Don't worry my dear, you're teachable." He laughed again, and messed my hair playfully with his hand. "Let's try it on horseback tomorrow, shall we?" He gave me one last flash of his brilliant smile before he disappeared toward the castle.

I was better than I thought. Raymose was going easy on me to be sure; I knew he didn't want to hurt me. But still, he seemed genuinely pleased. Maybe this wouldn't be so hard after all.

I walked back toward the house, up the steps, and into the entry hall. I could smell the baked chicken as soon as I opened the door. I looked at my watch. Six o'clock. I had time for a quick bite before the doctor was supposed to arrive.

I walked into the Kitchen to find Charlotte fixing the dinner plates.

"Charlotte, it smells wonderful."

"Thank you dear," she set a plate down in front of me—baked chicken with mashed potatoes and carrots.

I began eating at once.

"You're looking a little flushed. Aren't you feeling well dear?"

"I sort of missed breakfast . . . and lunch." I shoved in another bite, not bothering to chew it completely before I swallowed and stuffed in another. I was hungrier than I thought.

"Now there's no excuse for you to be missing meals," she scolded.

"I know. I got distracted, and then Raymose began teaching me how to sword fight. I guess I just lost track of time."

"Your pants look like they'd had a run in with the ground." She laughed lightly.

"Make sure you get those to me quick, I've got just the thing to clean them up. They'll be good as new!"

"Sorry Charlotte, I should have gone upstairs and changed."

"Nonsense. I'm glad you're enjoying yourself. Can I assume by the ring on your finger you've agreed to marry Mr. Marcus?" She smiled brightly.

I blushed, looking down at my ring.

"So when's the big day?" She asked without waiting for my answer.

"I don't know exactly, soon I hope."

"You've certainly created quite a buzz around the castle, Miss." Sarah said as she burst into the kitchen.

"What do you mean?" I asked.

"Now I don't make a habit of listening to other people's conversations," she shot Charlotte a stern look, "but I was passing the library just now and heard Mr. Marcus arguing with Mr. Raymose."

My fork fell out of my hand and landed with a clatter on my plate. "Sorry."

"It's alright dear. Arguing? That doesn't sound like the two of them?" Charlotte continued. She spoke like she was talking about two little boys, not two grown men—vampires at that! She poured a cup of tea and sat down beside me, eager for any bit of gossip to break up the monotony.

"Well," Sarah began. "Earlier, I was in the entry dusting the drapes like I do . . . when I heard a loud crash in the library. Naturally, I rushed in to see what broke when I saw Mr. Marcus standing over some broken glass."

"Broken glass?" Charlotte gasped.

"Yes, that reminds me, I need to call a window repair man. Apparently Mr. Marcus was shutting the window, and it fell right off the hinges!" "Lord, he's lucky he wasn't hurt." Charlotte put her hand over her heart in relief.

"What were they arguing about?" I asked subtly, trying to move the conversation along.

"You, Miss." Sarah smiled angelically.

"Me?"

"Apparently, Mr. Marcus had been watching the two of you through the window, before the window broke." Sarah's eyebrows rose slightly, possibly not buying Marcus's "window story."

"He accused Mr. Raymose of training too roughly with you. Mr. Raymose said you're doing just fine, and something about you being able too handle it before?" Sarah was extremely animated when she told a story. Thankfully, she didn't linger too long on any one thing; it might pose more questions than answers for her. Her eyes were wide and full of concern as she repeated her version of the argument.

"Then, Mr. Marcus . . . sort of . . . hissed?" A look of confusion swept across her face.

"Hissed?" Charlotte was hanging on every word.

"It sounded like a hiss? I only heard it through the door, but it was very strange. He said Miss. Phoebe is not the same as she once was, and that he better not find her bleeding in the garden." Sarah raised her eyebrows again. This was just the type of juicy conversation she could sink her teeth into.

"Mr. Raymose said he'd never hurt her, and that Mr. Marcus knows that . . ." She added the last bit under her breath. Her mind was clearly elsewhere now, her wheels turning in an entirely different direction than before.

"Ah Sarah, men are always arguing about what they think is safe for a woman to do . . .especially when they're both in love with her." Charlotte shot me a sideways glance.

My mouth gaped open a little.

"They don't understand that we're strong, and independent!" She continued, raising her fist in the air. "Especially when we've been on our own for so long." She glanced my way again giving me an understanding smile. "It's plain to see that Mr. Raymose wouldn't put up such an argument if he wasn't smitten."

I could feel my face blushing. "Thank you for dinner. Charlotte, Sarah, if you'll excuse me . . ."

I literally ran into Raymose at the stairs in my attempt to escape the questioning faces in the kitchen.

"Where you off to in a hurry?" he said with a laugh.

"Sorry, to my room. I have to call a few people back home before it gets too late. I've been neglecting my business responsibilities far too long." Truth.

"Tomorrow then," he winked, brushing my chin with his finger before he turned and walked out the door.

I ran up to my room, grabbed my cell phone, and dialed Leah's number first.

"Leah—" was all I could say for quite awhile. She had disguised her worry with anger and wasn't going to let me off the hook easily for neglecting to call her.

"I'm sorry, time just slipped by," I explained.

Apparently, Kim didn't have any new pieces to deliver, and the stores were running low.

"Leah, calm down. There's a box in my office that has enough pieces for you to distribute." I could just see her snapping a pencil in half. That was valuable need to know information I should have shared with her.

"Yes, I'm going to be here a while longer. Just box up my supplies and send them. I'll have some new pieces for you in a few weeks. "

I paused and took a breath. "He's asked me to marry him." I was all a glow. "I know it seems sudden . . ." I tried to interject before she started in on me—I was too late.

"Yes I'm sure. Leah, he's wonderful. I've been waiting for him all my life." I admitted freely. "Of course I'm going to keep designing."

After what seemed like forever, Leah congratulated me. Then she ordered me to phone Kim with the good news, and text my address so she could send the aforementioned supplies.

Kim was excited. She said she still had a few pieces and Leah was just freaking out because she hadn't heard from me for nearly two weeks.

Had it been that long? Time really did go quickly in this place.

I took a deep breath and sighed. I closed my phone and fell back on the bed.

There was a soft knock on the door.

"Come in," I said, not bothering to get up. It had been a *long* day.

"The doctor is downstairs. Shall I send him up?" Marcus asked as he entered the room. He took one look at me relaxed on the bed and jumped to the wrong conclusion.

"You're hurt!"

"What? No! I'm just resting, or was. Oh!" I jumped off the bed quickly, checking the quilt to make sure I hadn't gotten it dirty. "Sorry, I forgot I was so filthy. I think the bed's fine." I checked it over once again, swiping my hand over the fabric, feeling for any dirt that may have rubbed off.

"I don't care about the bed," he nearly growled.

"Marcus it's nothing." I waved him off. "I dove to block Raymose's sword, and he missed me completely!"

I went over to my closet and took out a clean pair of jeans. I started to change when I noticed my thigh. I could see Marcus staring at it out the corner of my eye. He looked livid, but said nothing. I pulled my jeans on quick.

"I better not keep the doctor waiting," I urged.

He left the room without another word.

Dr. Andersen was a pleasant man. He looked to be in his forties, had dark hair that was starting to grey, and was average in height. He didn't have any particularly striking features, but his smile was warm, and I felt comfortable with him at once.

I didn't take up much of the doctor's time. I got straight to the point, and with Marcus being whom he was, Dr. Anderson was willing to fill my request discreetly, without too many prying questions, or having to examine me—a formality I was hoping to avoid. I didn't want the doctor to witness the changes in my body due to Damen's bite.

He hadn't left my room for more than two minutes before Marcus was back to check on me.

"Is everything alright?" he looked extremely anxious.

"Everything is fine. He'll deliver what I need sometime tomorrow." I said cheerfully.

"Wonderful, now all I have to worry about is you playing swords with Raymose."

"I'm not playing! And you might want to stop breaking windows unless you want the entire household getting suspicious of your *superhuman* strength."

He sat down on the bed. The anger that once occupied his face was replaced with worry. "I have to leave tomorrow. We need to prepare our army." Marcus's eyes met mine. He reached out and took my hand, pulling me down beside him.

"I'll be fine." I smiled, trying to sound as convincing as possible. "How long do you think you'll be gone?"

He squeezed my hand. I could feel the tension in his body shifting to mine. "I'm not sure when I'll be back . . . maybe a few weeks?"

"I understand. I'll just have to keep myself busy." I tried to sound upbeat.

"Raymose will be here to check on you daily. He still plans to assist you with your training," he scoffed.

I felt a surge of excitement. That would help the time pass, and with Leah sending my supplies, I could work while Marcus was away.

"Well, try not to be gone too long. I'll miss you terribly."

He pulled my face to his. I could feel the tension in his lips as they meshed with mine. He couldn't pull me close enough. His body shifted over mine, pushing me toward the bed. "I can't bear to be away from you," he breathed. His eyes, darkening to a deep red, met mine.

I suddenly realized what he was telling me. Why he looked so worried. He was leaving to plan an attack on the werewolves—they were going to war. There would be hundreds of them—werewolves and vampires both—killing each other. Marcus would be fighting. He may not come back. A reality he'd faced. But I hadn't.

I gripped his shoulders, my fingers digging in, my lips recklessly crashing into his. I pulled his body against mine.

"Careful love, you might get bit." He tried to pull back.

I held him firmly to me, kissing him as if it were the last time, as if it were my last breath. I wrapped my legs around his waist, squeezing him tightly to me.

"Phoebe . . ." he tried to speak past my lips, attempting to untwine my legs—I wouldn't let him.

"Phoebe!" He broke free, breathing heavily. His eyes stared wearily into mine.

I yanked his shirt open, only sparing a quick glance at his insanely perfect body before I pulled him back to me.

"Are you sure you want this?" he asked in a throaty voice. His hand moved up my side slowly, sending a violent shiver straight through me. His face still didn't look convinced that this was a good idea.

"I need you." I breathed. "We may never have another chance." My lips took his again and again.

I don't know how it happened, but I suddenly felt myself naked against his skin. His mouth moved over mine carefully despite my urgency. He pulled my body to his.

This was different. Our bodies moved with a sense of urgency. We held each other tightly, desperately. Time was a luxury we didn't have, and I didn't want to waste a minute with 'should we or shouldn't we'. I couldn't get close enough no matter how tightly he held me. I kissed his lips as often as I could, breathing in his scent, tasting it over and over in my mouth, trying to burn the memory into my mind for safe keeping. I had the strangest sensation that I was floating in the air . . .

He moaned softly, working his lips slowly down my neck to the hollow of my throat. My head fell back—we were floating!

"Marcus!" I wrapped myself around his body, holding on for dear life.

He laughed, rolling himself under me.

"Marcus, the bed!" I panicked, holding on tighter still.

"I won't let you fall," he promised.

I didn't relax until I felt the bed beneath me again. The soft blankets around my body, and Marcus holding me, loving me, was all the comfort I needed. I held him as long as I could. The realization of him leaving had sunk in. I could feel the tears burning in my eyes.

"Have I hurt you?" Marcus was watching me.

"No. I . . . I just don't want you to go." The tears spilled over. "I'm afraid for you."

"You're afraid for me?" he joked.

"Of course I am," I said offensively. I didn't think this was a laughing matter.

"I'll only be gone a few weeks. You'll have plenty to occupy yourself with." He smiled, but it did not touch his eyes.

"I'll be worried every minute you're away," I sniffed.

"You think I won't be worried about you?" He tried to wipe the falling tears from my cheek.

"Well, you don't have to worry about me going in the woods while you're gone, that's for sure."

His face grew serious. "Phoebe, I don't want you anywhere near the woods."

"Don't worry. If I don't see another werewolf again, it will be too soon, I certainly won't go looking for one—with the exception of Richard of course." I couldn't help but chuckle at that.

"You realize we just increased the odds." He gave me a long look.

"I know," I admitted calmly. "I didn't want you to go without holding me again."

"I'm coming back." He held my face gently between his hands, commanding my full attention. "I'm coming back."

"You have to," my voice cracked. "I can't breathe without you."

"In that case, I'll be all the quicker. I don't wish to cause you any discomfort." He leaned over and kissed me so passionately; I thought my heart was going to stop. He released me—limp, and breathless.

"Will you hold me, all night?" I sounded so needy.

His soft brown eyes stared lovingly back at mine. "I won't let go for a moment," he whispered across my lips.

I snuggled in close to him. His soft, silk-like skin felt cool against my flushed body. I breathed in deeply. The sweet smell of him engulfed me, bringing about a calm and content feeling I'd grown to need. I smiled to myself, closed my eyes, and drifted off to sleep in the safety of his arms.

Chapter 27: Questions

I could feel the morning sun stretching across the bed. I thought about opening up my eyes but decided against it. Marcus's arms were still around me. He had stayed with me, all night as promised. I grinned.

"I know you're awake," Marcus sang in my ear.

"No I'm not . . . my eyes are still closed," I sang back, pulling his arm tighter around me.

"Phoebe, just because your eyes are closed, doesn't mean the morning will never come," he firmly pointed out.

"All right, but if I open my eyes, that means you'll be leaving, and I don't want you to go," I pouted. "So I'll be keeping them closed today."

"I'll miss you too, darling. I'll try to get back as soon as I can." He kissed my cheek and sat up.

"Sure I can't persuade you to stay?" I smiled coyly.

He lay back down beside me and pulled my body next to his. "You could but would it be wise?" I could just see little flakes of red swirling through his dark brown eyes—he was hungry this morning. I swallowed a lump in my throat.

He let out a laugh and reluctantly got out of bed.

I thought for half a second, smiled deviously, flipped the covers off my naked body and tried to look as seductive as possible. I knew it was dangerous; I knew I was only prolonging the inevitable, but still . . . I had to try.

"Marcus?" My voice was even, innocent.

"Yes my love?" he looked up from buttoning his shirt. His lips parted.

"You don't have to leave this very moment . . . do you?"

He looked my body over in the amount of time it takes someone to blink. He yanked his shirt off and had me wrapped in his arms so fast; I couldn't help but giggle at how quickly he was persuaded.

We spent the next several hours in each other's arms. I never wanted him to let me go.

"You know I would stay here for eternity with you if I could." His mouth moved up my neck slowly. "Eventually, Luther will send someone to find me."

I frowned. Luther. I'd almost forgotten about him. "You'd better go then," I said in a soft voice.

His eyes met mine. I could see the fear in them. He was just as scared as I was. I had to be brave for him. I had to give him the strength to go. I held his face between my hands and smiled. "Come back to me soon." The words came out softer than a whisper. "I love you."

"I love you too," he whispered back. His lips kissed mine, lingering longer than he should have. I laughed, pushing him playfully out of bed.

I pulled the sheets around me, snuggling into them, as I watched him dress. The sun moved across his body, shining brightly against his pale skin. When I looked at Marcus like this, it was hard to imagine he was a vampire. He was striking to look at. Flawless. He reminded me of a painting I'd seen once of an angel—soft and beautiful. His eyes were brown like his hair. His lips—perfect for kissing—were a light shade of pink. His well-defined body from head to toe only added to the illusion that he wasn't human.

I could feel an involuntary smile sweep across my face.

"What are you looking so pleased about?" he asked as he caught me gawking.

"Lots of things, actually." I admitted truthfully, blushing a little.

He came back over to the bed—a potentially dangerous move, and flopped down next to me.

"For example . . . " he prompted.

"Alright. How is it that you are so absolutely perfect? Your body, that is," I clarified quickly.

He smiled at me like the Cheshire cat. "You think I'm perfect?"

I frowned. "Can you honestly tell me that you didn't know that God bestowed every gift upon you?"

"Fair enough," he grinned. "But God did not bestow this on me. When you become a vampire, certain things about your physical appearance are enhanced, as are your senses and your strength. I don't know why it happens, other than it makes us more appealing to our prey."

He moved closer to me, his lips nearly touching mine. I could feel my heart beating faster and faster as I fell under his spell. "You should run . . ." his cool breath blew across my lips; I could almost taste his skin. "Your mind is telling you to run, but your eyes betray you . . . you're only as safe as I allow you to be." He kissed my lips abruptly and smiled.

I tried to focus.

"Anything else?" he asked, still sporting a smug smile.

I smacked him on the shoulder playfully and frowned before I looked away from him.

"Ask me?" he prompted.

I took a deep breath. "Is it hard . . . *not* to bite people?" My eyes evaded his.

"No. I've been accustomed to drinking another way now for so long that I don't even think of people as food so much anymore." He spoke casually. "As for losing control in the heat of the moment though, that's another story entirely," he smiled crookedly. "Biting while love making is common." His mouth grazed my neck, further heating my blood.

"What about Raymose?" I breathed. "Does he get his food like you do?" I felt a little embarrassed, like I was asking something private.

"Yes, although he hasn't been at it as long as I have. He finds it harder to resist when he's tempted." His eyes narrowed as he saw me avoiding his stare. "There's something else isn't there?"

"It's not a necessary question." I brushed it off.

"Ask me."

"All right, but don't get mad . . ." I began.

Marcus shot me an uneasy look. History proved, that when a woman told a man "don't get mad," it usually meant he was going to get mad. He shifted his weight and gave me an uneasy look. This would be no different.

"If I were bit again . . ." I started slowly, watching Marcus grow more anxious by the second, " . . . by either a vampire or a werewolf, would that harm . . . if I were pregnant, that is . . ." I shrugged, trying to sound blasé about the question, " . . . a baby?"

Marcus's face grew serious, considering the question before he answered. "I do not know what a werewolf bite would do if you've already conceived. Your heart would somehow continue to beat, although you become immortal. Blood would still pump through your veins. A child *could* still live—perhaps."

I sighed. Happy to hear that if for some reason Damen decided to take another bite, all might not be lost.

"As for being bit by a vampire," he continued. "It most likely would kill the child. Your heart stops and your body ceases to work in the normal fashion." His eyes were fixed on me.

"But my heart could still beat, right? I'm partially werewolf already! I couldn't be turned completely. You don't know that my heart would stop beating."

His eyes narrowed. "Why would you ask me this?"

"No reason in particular." I smiled. "I just wanted to know, that's all."

Marcus held my arm firmly as I moved to get up. I hated how he saw right through me . . . I couldn't keep anything from him. His eyes were piercing.

"We've been less than cautious wouldn't you say?" I admitted in defeat.

He didn't answer. The silence was maddening. I could feel his eyes boring holes through my back. I couldn't stand it any longer.

"I'm getting dressed. Raymose will be here in awhile, and I want to eat before we start." I pulled away from him and went to the closet for my clothes. I glanced his way once again before I retreated to the bathroom—he hadn't moved a muscle.

***

When I stepped out of the bathroom, I found Marcus in nearly the same position as I left him. His face looked tense. He was obviously preoccupied, and my questions, I was willing to bet, were the core root for this behavior.

"What time do you have to leave?" I asked, hoping to distract him from resuming our last conversation.

"Soon." His voice was even, careful . . . too careful.

"Well, I'd better get downstairs," I suggested half-heartedly.

"Phoebe, I was thinking. Perhaps you *should* go home. I mean you must have work to do. I'm sure your friends would like to see you again."

"What?" He wanted me to go home? "Leah is mailing me my supplies as we speak. I'd planned on working on that while you're away."

His expression was completely unreadable. "There really isn't anything here for you. I think it would be best . . ." his voice trailed off in my head. I could see his lips moving, but the words were silent. His tone had been as unfriendly as his eyes . . . they were dark and cold. There really isn't anything here for me? I stared at him in disbelief. What about him?

"Phoebe, are you listening to me?"

"You want me to leave?" It wasn't really a question, but I couldn't believe I'd heard right.

"Yes."

"But Why?" I didn't understand.

"I think it would be best if you spent your time away from here; away from me. Away from all of this."

Something snapped inside me. It was as if he'd slapped me across the face. I sucked my cheeks in and took a deep breath. "Fine!"

"Really? You're not going to argue with me about it?" he sounded almost excited. Bastard!

"There's no need to argue; I understand perfectly." I smiled like I was going to eat him alive, and that's exactly what I planned to do.

There was a knock at my door.

"Come in." I said cheerfully.

"Good morning, Miss, and to you, Sir." Richard seemed disgustingly happy.

"I'm not sure it is a good morning, Richard," Marcus noted. He was trying to decipher my reaction to his suggestion.

"Mr. Raymose is here, Miss Rose. He asked me to bring your horse around to the back for you. He's waiting in the library to speak with you, Sir, before you leave." He was addressing Marcus now.

"Thank you, Richard. A ride sounds perfect."

"Very good, Miss. Charlotte asked me to bring you this. She thought you might be hungry." He sat a tray of food down on the table.

I grabbed a muffin and took such a violent chomp out of it, that most of it didn't even enter my mouth. My eyes narrowed at Marcus as I chewed, enjoying his discomfort.

"Phoebe . . ." he warned.

I walked over to the fireplace, grabbed the sword off the wall, and said rather surly, "Have a nice trip!" I stormed out of the room, taking the muffin with me.

I was furious. I couldn't believe he wanted me to leave. After I'd given myself to him! "I think it would be best if you spend your time away from here." I repeated aloud in an exaggerated, snotty tone.

I growled out in frustration as I stormed out of the back doors.

I saw Rain tied to the railing, waiting for me. I climbed up onto his back and was just about settled in my saddle when Marcus grabbed onto the reins. "Hey!"

"You're not riding," he growled.

"Don't worry, I won't hurt the horse," I scoffed, trying to free the rains from his grasp.

"I'm not worried about the horse," he hissed. "I don't want you taking chances. You're not that good a rider." His tone was sharp, and the expression on his face would have frightened anyone including me—but not today. I rolled my eyes at him.

"You can't tell me what to do," I snapped defiantly. "Besides, Rain takes good care of me. Don't you, boy?" I patted Rain's neck softly. "Unlike *some* people!"

"As you said," he stepped closer; the fierceness in his tone was unmistakable. "We've been less than cautious. I'd think it is a safe assumption . . ."

"It's too soon to worry about that. Besides, it's a moot point anyway. Werewolves can't conceive. You said so yourself. So the way I see it . . .you're in the clear. You don't have to concern yourself about it any longer." I smiled victoriously. I didn't know why I hadn't thought about that sooner. I'd worried for nothing!

"What?" he looked at me incredulously. "I never—"

"What's going on?" Raymose came walking down the stairs and right into the middle of World War III. "Didn't Richard tell you I was waiting?" He seemed put out.

"Relax, Marcus." I yanked the reins from his hand. "Raymose will look after me. He always has." I smirked.

"Raymose doesn't understand," Marcus growled under his breath.

"Hey, is everything alright here?" Raymose moved beside me. He looked from me to Marcus.

"No." I answered for Marcus. I turned my head to Raymose and smiled brightly. "Marcus asked me to leave. I'll be going home as soon as I can arrange a flight." I kept my tone as pleasant as my smile.

"Are you crazy?" Raymose yelled at Marcus. "That's the first place Damen will look for her when he realizes she's no longer here."

"You *didn't* allow me to explain," Marcus snapped, although his stare was on me.

"You don't need to explain. I've become a burden. You've had your fun, and now you'd rather I leave than have to worry about me. " I spoke knowingly.

"What?" I could almost feel the heat radiating off of Marcus—he was furious.

"You're not going alone," Raymose promised, his eyes meeting mine.

Marcus turned to Raymose. His expression was one of betrayal. "You do not want to get in the middle of this."

"I am in the middle of this," Raymose hissed. "I won't let her go unprotected. Not again. Never again."

"I'm not sending her unprotected—Richard will be with her. Just until the danger is over." Marcus looked like he was going to explode.

"I don't need Richard to go with me, and I don't need any of your false concern. Like you said, it would be best if I spend my time away from here, away from you!" I threw his words back at him.

"Is that what you got out of our conversation?" he snapped.

I shot him a haughty look and turned away, giving Rain a hard kick. A moment later, Raymose was beside me, his horse keeping in step with Rain.

"You feel like dancing?" He smiled at me as he rode ahead quickly.

Dancing? Ah . . . that's what Raymose used to call swordplay I thought to myself, smiling at the memory. Raymose had an infectious way about him. He was just what I needed right now—a distraction. I gave Rain another kick, urging him faster. I never looked back . . .

Raymose bolted across the lawn as fast as his horse would move. It didn't take Rain long to catch up. He was exceptionally fast. We slowed down to a soft lope as Raymose looked around.

"This looks like a good spot," he said as he brought his horse to a stop.

"Good spot for what?"

He held out his sword. "We have a date. Remember?"

"Thanks." My smile was forced.

He reached out and put his arm around my shoulders. "How can I help?" he asked softly.

I shrugged and slid off my horse. Raymose followed close behind and sat down beside me under a tree. I leaned up against the trunk and looked up into the leafy foliage. It was thick and green still. There was no sign of autumn approaching. I stared at the leaves as they flickered in the light breeze. They looked almost florescent green in the sunlight.

"English Oak!" he said as he tapped the tree with his fist. "Do you want to talk about it?" he motioned to the house with a nod.

"There's no point. He doesn't want me." I shrugged. It hurt to say it out loud. The "there's nothing for you here" comment still smarted.

"No. Not Marcus. He'd never push you away . . . anymore than I would. There's more to it."

"It doesn't matter. Maybe it's better this way." I lifted my chin up. "Being a human in your world is dangerous!" I got up and twirled my sword around.

Raymose lay back on the grass with his hands behind his head, watching me.

"You know you can tell me anything," his voice sounded like a soft song I'd heard long ago.

"What did Damen mean when he said you've loved me longer than he has?"

Raymose stared quietly at me. I'd taken him by surprise but he wasn't uncomfortable.

"It isn't polite to kiss and tell, Lady Phoebe," he smirked, bowing his head slightly.

"You addressed me like that before? Why?"

"Your father is looked upon as royalty. He's our king, our creator. It is out of the deepest respect I address you by your title."

I lowered my eyes a little. I could feel my cheeks burning. "You loved me?"

Raymose's mouth curled up into a smile. "Before you'd met Marcus, a lifetime ago, several lifetimes ago. You and I were . . . once very close. Yes. I loved you."

I continued to play with the sword. I wasn't sure I wanted to know any more; it might make things uncomfortable between us. I didn't want to lose Raymose—ever!

"I used to confide in you?" I asked after a few minutes.

"You knew I'd always be straight with you, help you when you needed it, and even when you didn't." He smirked.

I laughed a little to myself. Raymose was my partner in crime, I'd figured that much out. No wonder Marcus didn't want us 'playing' together.

"Did my father know you . . . cared for me?" I chose my word carefully, evading his stare. I could feel him smiling.

"If you're asking if he approved—yes."

"Did he approve of Marcus?" I asked nonchalantly, still twirling my sword into the light.

His smile broadened. "Yes."

I nodded sharply.

"Now," he began. "Why would Marcus send you home?" he questioned, starting me straight in the face. "Why would he think you're safer there?"

"I don't know, maybe you should ask him. He told me there wasn't anything for me here." I tried to sound uncaring.

"He's already left," Raymose said, his eyes still on me.

"I should get back then. I have a lot of packing to do." If I was going to cry, I didn't want Raymose to see it.

Raymose got to Rain before me. "I thought we'd come to practice," he said playfully.

"You still want to?"

"I promised I'd help you, and you need all the help you can get," he joked. But then his face grew serious. His hand reached out and gently pushed aside a piece of hair that had fallen out of place. I saw the look in his eyes as he stared into mine.

"Raymose . . ." My voice was shaky. I felt like I was losing control of my senses.

"Shhh." He leaned in slowly, I didn't move. I closed my eyes as his lips gently met mine. It was just as I remembered. A peaceful feeling came over me. I smiled, keeping my eyes shut. I could feel him watching me.

"You're blushing," he mused.

"Raymose—"

"Shhh," He put his finger to my lips. "I just wanted to see if you were still in there. If you're truly the same Phoebe." He sighed contently.

"Raymose I'm not." I could feel the heat rising in my face as I lied. "I'm sorry, I can't!" My heart started pounding erratically. All the memories of Raymose and I continued to flood my mind, and I knew, these couldn't be Damen's memories—these were hers—the memories of a Phoebe long ago.

Without warning, he pulled me to him. His arms encircled me as he held me tightly, lifting me off the ground, his lips forcefully taking mine. I didn't push him away like I thought I would—I pulled him closer—wrapping my arms around his neck. I was caught up in the memories and the moment of his embrace. I kissed him desperately, heady. He moaned in delight as our kiss intensified.

"Raymose!" My lips broke free, my senses taking hold of me. He released me, and I staggered back a little, gasping for air.

"I still love you," he admitted just as breathless. His eyes were smoldering. "You remember me, don't you?"

"Yes," I gasped. It was the truth. I remembered him, all of him. Raymose had once been my world. A piece of me still mourned the loss of him.

"That *won't* happen again," he breathed. "Not unless you're free to love me back. I won't take you from Marcus."

I stared at him in disbelief. "Raymose I'm sorry. I can't love you the way you want me to." I could feel my stomach turn. I suddenly felt empty, sad as I watched Raymose smile understandingly—I'd hurt him.

"I know where your heart is. I'll be content being your friend, if you'll still have me?" he looked hopeful.

I reached out and held his cheek with my hand. He closed his eyes for a moment and smiled, leaning into my touch.

"You will always be my friend. Thank you." I put my arms around him and gave him a hug.

"For what?" He hugged me back.

"For loving me, and protecting me." I could feel the tears swelling in my eyes. "You can always count on me for that." He reached up and messed my hair playfully. "Now, defend yourself!"

I screamed playfully as Raymose chased me across the lawn with his sword, laughing wildly.

I spent the rest of the afternoon with Raymose. It was just like it used to be. We laughed and talked, not about anything in particular, mostly about my lack of skills—the topic of preference for him. Secretly I think he was trying to rile me up in the hopes that I'd improve. This would undoubtedly take time—*lots* of time!

We'd finished around four o'clock, and I was exhausted. Raymose was relentless. He didn't take "I'm tired" for an excuse. We practiced each move until I blocked Raymose's sword successfully. I'd learn from him, or die. There was no other option.

I put Rain in his stall and walked slowly back to the castle. Raymose had gone to meet Marcus. He promised to return the next afternoon, and I'd better be here or he threatened to come get me and drag me kicking and screaming back across the ocean. He also informed me that we wouldn't be traveling by plane! I believed him. It was easy to agree to stay another day—I didn't have my plane tickets yet, and since Marcus wasn't here, I was in no immediate rush.

"Miss Rose," Richard yelled out when I came in. "How were your lessons?" he asked a little out of breath.

"Fine."

"This came for you by messenger." Richard handed me a box that was from Dr. Andersen's office.

"Like I need this," I muttered under my breath.

Richard looked as though he were going to be sick. It was the first time I could recall him being fidgety. “Lord Ashworth has asked me to inform you that the jet is ready when you are. However, if you should feel the need to stay . . .”

I closed my eyes and repeated over and over in my head: don’t shoot the messenger Phoebe. Don’t. Shoot. The messenger. I forced a smile. I could feel my blood boiling.

“Thank you, Richard, but I wouldn’t dream of using his jet!” My voice rose with each word until I was shouting.

Richard took a step back. My sudden outburst was unexpected to say the least.

I took a deep breath. “I’m sorry Richard; you’re not the unfeeling jerk.”

“Thank you, Miss. Shall I have Charlotte fix you something to eat?” Richard was always so polite. It almost took my thunder away.

“No, thank you, I’m not that hungry. I’m going up to my room to make flight arrangements. I shouldn’t impose on you for more than a few days.”

“We don’t want you to leave, Miss, and neither does Mr. Marcus.” His eyes were full of concern. “He’s worried for your safety here. That’s all. He doesn’t want to lose you again.”

“Right. If only that was true, Richard.” I smiled flatly as I turned towards the stairs. “I’ll be in my room.”

Chapter 28: Welcome Home

Time is a funny thing, I thought. When you're watching, it seems to slowly tick by, each minute blending into the next. But, when you look away from it, time slips through your fingers like sand through a sieve.

I'd been at Ashworth Castle now for nearly two months. Raymose had made sure to guilt me into staying day after day under the guise of—he'd never broken a promise to me. If I left now, he'd never be able to teach me to sword fight—again, which, according to him, I was in desperate need of learning.

Although Marcus had made himself clear he wanted me to leave, I kept coming up with excuses for myself why I couldn't. It all came down to this being the only place I felt close to him. I wasn't as willing to let go as he was.

I was working half-heartedly on a necklace at the table in my room, something I'd grown accustomed to over the weeks. I looked up at the empty chair across from me.

I hadn't seen Marcus for over six weeks.

I pushed myself away from the table and went out on the balcony. I closed my eyes as a soft breeze kissed my face. I tried to remember his scent, what his lips felt like on mine. I wrapped my arms around myself, trying to hold on to the memory . . .

My phone ringing in the bedroom startled me. I ran to it.

"Hi, Kim!" I was so thankful to hear Kim's voice. "Did you get the box?"

Kim gushed over my new designs. She said Leah was so excited; she couldn't wait to distribute them.

"I'm glad. I've got a few more pieces to send," I added quickly.

Kim prattled on and on about things back home. My little house was just fine. She'd been watering my plants and collecting the mail for me. Leah had picked up my car and had it brought home a few weeks ago. God I missed them. It was time to go.

"Kim, I think I'll be home in the next few days. I miss my little house, and all of you."

Kim picked up right away that something was wrong. I tried to down play it.

"Nothing's wrong. Marcus has been away on business, and I'm just lonely, that's all." It was the truth.

She accepted it and asked me to hurry home.

Being without Marcus for so long had helped me to snap back into the real world. The real world for me was back in Trinidad. I called the airlines and made a reservation for tomorrow. I knew Raymose would be upset, but he'd just have to deal with it. After all, he'd had six weeks with me, and I'd done tremendously well—considering I was a girl. It was time for him to let go, too.

I met Raymose for practice that afternoon in the garden. He was eager to start, as usual. He looked forward to my lessons more than I did. Raymose was a skilled swordsman, and he enjoyed any opportunity to show off his talent. Secretly, I suspected his greatest achievement with me had been training me well enough to block his advances without shedding any blood. Not an easy feat.

"I thought we'd work a little on foot, then end on horseback today," he said as he readied himself with his sword.

I raised my sword. "Raymose, I'm leaving tomorrow."

Clank, clank.

"Why?" he demanded as he attacked me again, with more vigor this time.

Clank, clank, clank.

"Marcus doesn't want me. There's no reason for me to stay here any longer. I miss my friends, my house," I explained as I blocked the barrage of advances he made.

Clank, clank.

"I'm going with you." He swung his sword at my back. Then, like out of some sort of ninja movie, I jumped on a bench and flipped backward to miss the blow.

"Ow!" I yelped.

Raymose dropped his sword and caught me before I hit the ground.

I laughed a little between the stabbing sensations.

"Did I get you?" He looked paler than normal. "I don't smell any blood."

"No, I think I pulled something in my side with that flip." It hurt to laugh. "Ow! I guess I'm getting too old," I teased.

"*You're* too old?" he laughed lightly.

"We'd better call it a day," he said as he started carrying me up the castle steps.

Richard looked as pale as Raymose did when he saw him carrying me through the door. "Miss Phoebe!"

"She's pulled a muscle Richard. You wouldn't have a heating pack around would you? I hear they help strains." Raymose looked the picture of cool.

"I'll ask Charlotte right away." Richard rushed off toward the kitchen, giving me an anxious second glance.

"I can walk Raymose, really. It's feeling better already," I assured.

He set me down carefully.

"Thanks, I'll see you tomorrow before I go?" I gave him a hopeful smile.

"I'll be here and ready to go with you." He brought my hand to his lips and kissed the top of it softly.

"No, Raymose, Luther will come looking for you. I don't want you to get into trouble over me. I'll be fine."

"Now you let me worry about that, my Lady." He smiled convincingly and moved out the door before I could protest any further.

I looked around me. I was alone. I took a deep breath, grabbed my side, and with all the strength I could muster, I slunk back to my room in pain.

I went straight for the bathroom. I needed a hot shower, and Tylenol. What was I thinking flipping like that? How *did* I flip like that? On the other hand, I couldn't have avoided it. If I hadn't, I would be on my way to the emergency room right now .

. . or dead on the ground having caused Raymose to revert back to drinking from a human. I shivered at the thought.

I started the shower and took my clothes off. I went to the medicine cabinet, opened the door, and paused. My eyes landed on the little box Dr. Andersen had given me months ago.

I stared at it, mesmerized for a moment. Suddenly, a sinking feeling had formed in the pit of my stomach—too much time had passed. I started to think when my last period was. One, two, three . . . I counted in my head. Six weeks ago? No. That can't be right! I counted again. It was right! My cycles hadn't been irregular since my last trip to London—courtesy of Damen I now knew. But still . . . I should have had *one* by now. Shouldn't I?

I grabbed the box, tearing it open frantically. I'd asked Dr. Andersen for a pregnancy test—discreetly of course—just in case. It seemed simple enough to use—one step and wait—I took the test.

I got in the shower to relax. I was not going to needlessly upset myself. I took the longest shower I could until the water started to go cold. I tried to justify being late due to the stress I'd been under, the exercising, and the lack of sleep I'd had since Marcus had left. If I threw in the fact that I was partially werewolf and they *couldn't* conceive—therefore, *I* couldn't conceive, the absence of my period was completely normal. So why did I have a sickened feeling in the pit of my stomach?

I got out of the shower and wrapped myself in a towel. I dried completely off before I went over to the counter to look.

Nooo! This had to be wrong. I took another test from the box and repeated the process, making sure I followed the instructions to the letter. I waited anxiously, rubbing my arms with vigor as a large plus sign appeared—again!

I slumped to the floor in a heap. I couldn't be pregnant. Marcus said I was half human, but I was also partly werewolf now . . . that had to counter any probability of me being able to have children. Besides, Marcus was gone, and I was alone. He didn't want me!

"I can't have a baby." I said firmly as I stood up and looked at myself in the mirror. I didn't look pregnant. I didn't feel pregnant. Not that I knew what that felt like. But I did know I didn't feel any different than usual. Well, aside from my acrobatic injury . . . and being tired . . . and slightly hungrier. But that was because I'd been training so hard. Wasn't it?

"What am I going to do?" I mumbled under my breath. My mind spun wildly, trying to form a plan. I needed to go home, before Marcus decided to come back. I couldn't let him find out. If he came for me, I wanted it to be for me. Not because he felt some sort of obligation to me.

I got dressed quickly, despite the screams of pain from my body. I began collecting my things around the room. I had just finished my packing when Richard knocked on the door.

"Excuse me Miss, but there is a cab outside?" He paused. His eyes wandered over to my suitcase answering his question.

"Are you alright Miss? You look a little flushed." He looked me over carefully.

"I'm fine, Richard. The shower was a little too warm, that's all."

"If you need to be escorted, Miss, I would be glad to take you anywhere you need to go."

"Thank you Richard, but I've got a ride."

"Tonight?" He glanced at his watch, a troubled look hung in his eyes. "There's a full moon expected tonight Miss."

I froze. Then grew a backbone. "I'll be fine. Please give my apologies to Raymose."

"Very well, Miss. If you'll excuse me." Richard ducked out of the room quickly, not even bothering to say goodbye . . .

"He's probably ready to get rid of me too," I grumped, fighting back the lump in my throat.

I stood at the door, taking one last look around the room. I couldn't afford to let my eyes linger too long. I had to leave. This part of my life was over. I shut the door and made my way downstairs to the waiting cab.

"Where to, Miss?" the driver asked when I entered the cab.

"The airport." I spoke with authority, not bothering to take one last look behind me as we drove back up the long driveway lined with trees.

"Would you like me to turn on any music, Miss?"

I looked up into the rearview mirror, meeting his stare. His eyes were those of an older man, his mid-sixties perhaps. His hair had already gone completely gray from what I could see in the limited light.

The sun had gone down for the night, not even a hint of it lingered in the sky. Another bleak hour of driving to look forward to before we reached the slightest bit of civilization.

"If you'd like." I finally answered.

I caught him glancing at me periodically through the mirror. Perhaps checking to see if I was still there. I was absorbed in my own thoughts, deliberating whether or not I was making the right decision. Part of me felt guilty for not at least leaving a note, or saying goodbye to Marcus. But he'd asked me to leave. I sat up straight, my heart hardening. I was definitely doing the right thing.

The car swerved violently, screeching the tires. Profanities flew from the driver's mouth at a rapid pace. Something heavy hit the top of the car, denting the hood in slightly. I held onto the seat in front of me, trying to steady myself as the car resumed its normal path.

I could see beads of sweat across the driver's forehead through the mirror. His hands, white across the steering wheel, were clenched tight.

"My apologies Miss. Some bloody animal just ran right at the car." I could see from the mirror he was still quite shaken.

"What sort of animal?" My voice was guarded.

"I couldn't tell for sure, a dog maybe? No, it was bigger than a dog. I really only saw its eyes."

My heart fell. "Its eyes?"

"Yellow as gold. It must be dead now. Look at the size of that dent."

My eyes drifted up. I swallowed loudly. I looked toward the window. It was keeping pace with the car. Just barely out of sight to the human eye, carefully staying hidden from the moonlight—I wouldn't be going to the airport tonight.

"What's your name, Sir?"

"Arthur, Miss." He met my eyes in the mirror. He looked suddenly taken aback. He shook his head. "Some trick the light is playing tonight. Must be the nerves." He laughed nervously; his eyes periodically glanced back to the mirror.

I suddenly felt self-conscious. Marcus had commented once that they were yellow. But that was only in the dark. No one else besides him had seen that.

I knew my eyes must look strange to Arthur. I wondered if they even scared him.

I glanced out the window again. I realized Arthur's chance of survival lay solely on me.

"Perhaps you should pull over, Arthur."

"Oh no Miss. This is a long stretch of road. People are said to go missing from time to time along this very stretch. I wouldn't be human if I let you out here."

The gold band on his finger caught my eye.

"I'm assuming you want to remain that way?" My words came out darker than I'd intended.

There was a long pause of silence. I could see Arthur gripping the steering wheel so tightly; if he had the strength, he would have snapped it in two.

"Miss?" his voice cracked.

I tossed some cash onto the front seat. "Thank you, Arthur. This will be fine."

The car slowed to a stop. I gripped my bag tightly and opened the door.

"Miss?" I could hear the fear in his voice.

"I'll be fine, Arthur. But unless you leave now, you won't be." I shut the door and stepped off the road. I watched the red tail lights fade into the blackness. I took in a deep breath, my eyes searching for any sign of movement.

"I know you're out there, Damen," I called out into the darkness.

His yellow eyes opened, not five feet from me—I jumped, clutching my heart!

A low growl came from behind his teeth.

"I was leaving." I answered him, surprised. He was talking to me. I understood every word.

"Marcus asked me to go. It's just like you said, he doesn't want me anymore." I tried to make my voice hard and unfeeling, but I faltered. My heart was breaking inside with the harsh words that came from my mouth. The pain was almost unbearable.

I stared into Damen's yellow eyes. They seemed softer now. The thick fur on his face blew lightly in the breeze. It was still hard to see him with much detail. If only the moon was a little brighter . . .

"No. I won't come with you." I answered his question. "Damen, you need to let me go."

He turned his body as if to leave. A strong gust of wind hit me from behind, sending a shiver right through me.

He spun around . . . his lips peeled back exposing his teeth, his nose eagerly sniffing the air.

"Damen?" I took a step back.

He crouched, snarling viciously.

"What are you—" I was hit from behind. My body flipped through the air like a gymnast. Marcus set me down gently a good thirty feet away. He already closed the gap between Damen and me.

I watched in horror as their shadows collided in the darkness. Vicious snarling and hissing pierced the silence of the night. I covered my ears, trying to drown out the noise. And then I did what I never thought I'd do—I ran.

I made my way to the road, stumbling several times along the way. I cried. I could still hear them fighting behind me. The distance and my frantic breathing had become so loud now; it nearly drowned them out.

I ran down the hard road frantically, my legs moving faster than my body could go. I couldn't see anything in front of me. A thick fog had appeared almost instantaneously, shrouding my vision. It lingered low, concealing my feet and the path ahead. I tripped over the pavement, the road taking my skin as I moved across it—sliding like I was stealing home base.

***

I lay on the road, unable to move. The pain in my side was back with a vengeance, rendering me breathless.

"Phoebe!" Marcus shouted as he ran toward me. "Are you alright?"

"Marcus?" I couldn't believe it. It felt like it had been forever since I'd seen him. He put his arms under me and lifted me up. "What have you done to yourself now?" His voice was calm. Not what I'd expected.

"Where's Damen?"

"He's gone. For now." I could still feel Marcus's chest heaving in and out.

"Did he hurt you?"

"Hardly," Marcus scoffed.

I leaned my head against him, taking in his sweet smell. "How did you know where to find me?" I asked sleepily, closing my eyes for a moment as I tried to ignore my new wounds.

"Richard said you were hurt, and that you'd gone."

"So that's why he ran out of my room." Traitor!

"What happened?" Marcus asked flatly, his voice a little harder now. He began walking back up the road with me.

I decided to evade his question. "Damen attacked the cab. I asked the driver to pull over and let me out . . . I didn't want him to get hurt."

Marcus stopped mid-step. Even in the dark I could see the look of disbelief on his face. He closed his eyes for a moment, my guess, trying to compose himself.

“That’s not what I meant,” his tone was a little sharper now as he walked on. “What happened this afternoon?”

Of course that’s what he was referring to. I knew that. I just didn’t want to discuss it. No doubt Richard had him already worked up into a frenzy. He hadn’t wanted me to sword fight for this very reason. “It’s nothing. I avoided Raymose’s sword by doing an unexpected back flip.” I winced as another stabbing sensation moved through me. I still couldn’t believe I’d done that.

I could feel the tension in Marcus's arms. He said nothing. He carried me through the night, taking the fastest and least bumpy path—we flew! I was back in my room lying comfortably on my bed before I knew it.

“You’re sure you’re alright?” he asked after a few minutes.

“Yes, it’s just a few scrapes.” I lied, trying to keep my voice as even as I could.

“Your arms tell a different story.”

I looked at my arms and hands, turning them slightly. I must have left half my skin on the road. They were scraped and full of rocks. “I’ll clean them later.” I looked away from him. I felt a crying spree about to begin. Being in our room together brought back the harsh words we’d said before he’d left. I couldn’t look at him.

“So, why did you come home?” I asked.

“I told you. Richard said you were hurt, and that you were leaving.”

“And?” I prompted, my tone bordering surly.

“And what?”

“And why would that make you want to return. You knew I was going to leave. Why come back now?” I was irritated, and I didn’t bother hiding it.

“Phoebe I’ve missed you.”

I snorted. “You never said goodbye. You never even called me. Not once! How can you say you missed me?”

He said nothing.

I turned toward him. My eyes were blurred from the tears that pooled in them. "You shouldn't have come back Marcus. You should have just let me leave." I sat up, forcing myself to stand.

"Phoebe, please lay down." His voice was anxious.

"I have to go. My plane leaves in the morning. I'll stay in a hotel tonight."

"Phoebe it's not safe!"

"Damen wasn't going to hurt me." I growled. "He was going to let me go. I know it." If he hadn't smelled Marcus behind me, I'd be on my way to the airport right now.

"Shit! Where's my suitcase?" I looked around the floor.

"I'll have Richard retrieve it in the morning—and you're mistaken if you think Damen would have let you go."

"All the more reason for me to leave. I—" I looked at myself. My pants were torn. "I don't have any clean clothes." I wasn't going anywhere.

Marcus took my hand, claiming my attention. "I don't want you to go. I never did," he admitted earnestly. "I just thought if you were far away from here, from me, you wouldn't get hurt. I stayed away, hoping you'd leave. It tore a hole in me to think you wouldn't be here. The only comfort I had was, knowing you'd be safe. I love you!"

He loved me? He was just trying to keep me safe? I closed my eyes and sighed. God I was such an idiot.

"Marcus I . . ." I don't know what I would have said. He crushed his lips against mine, and all thought slipped away . . .

His hands were on my waist, maneuvering me toward the bed. I felt the back of my knees hit the mattress. He fell with me, his body landing on top of mine, my breath catching under his weight.

"Darling I've missed you." His lips kissed mine, again and again while his fingers busily unbuttoned my shirt.

I gripped his face, holding him closer to me. Tears leaked out my eyes. I'd almost left this man. I should have known he'd never stop loving me. I would have left without telling him—I froze.

"Phoebe what is it?" Marcus was leaning over me, his face full of concern. "You're crying."

"I . . ." I pulled my shirt closed and pushed myself up to sit. My eyes wandered the room. I was scared to tell him. I wasn't sure how he was going to react.

"Phoebe?" His hand reached out and held my chin. "What is it? You're shaking."

I bit my lip, wondering where to begin. I'd have to come clean. There was no way around it. This was not my secret to keep. I was wrong to run away. As mad as he'd made me, I couldn't keep this from him—like the other Phoebe did.

"Phoebe!"

"Maybe you should stand over there." I pointed to the furthest corner in the room.

Marcus looked to where I'd pointed and then back to me. He looked as if he'd thought I was crazy.

"Ok, you stay here, and I'll go way over there," I said, getting to my feet in the hopes of making a quick get-away if need be.

"What have you done?" His tone was disapproving.

I sunk back down on the bed. "Well it wasn't intentional . . . and it's not entirely my fault!" I added sharply.

Marcus frowned. I could see that his patience was wearing thin.

"Marcus. You came back because you love me right? You love *me*, and you want to be with me . . . forever?" I needed him to say it.

"Yes." He looked bewildered.

"And you'll always love me?"

"Of course. Phoebe you're scaring me. What is it?" His eyes, soft and brown, looked wearily into mine.

"Well, the day you left, remember when you said you didn't want me riding because . . ." I took a deep breath, " . . . you were worried I might . . ."

"You fell off the horse, didn't you?" He rose from the bed. "That's how you got hurt, isn't it? Phoebe, please don't take offense, but you're a terrible rider."

My mouth popped open. "I am not!" I protested. "Raymose say's I'm much better now, *and* for your information, I'm doing quite well with a sword too." I folded my arms in a pout.

Marcus threw his arms into the air as he shot me an exasperated look. "Alright. Refresh my memory. Why didn't I want you riding then? I can only imagine what your mind concocted. You blew that whole conversation out of proportion. I simply was afraid that if you were—" He stopped. A look of confusion, then shock, and then wonder took hold of him. His eyes looking me up and down.

"Phoebe?" He sat down beside me. He reached out as if to touch me, then paused. He swallowed loudly. "Darling. Are you . . ." he froze. The words stuck in his throat.

I gave him a small smile and nodded.

"Are you sure?"

"Uh hum." I nodded again.

"How long have you known?" His face was still full of wonder. This was as much of a shock to him as it was for me.

I cringed a little. "Since tonight."

"But you were leaving . . ." He looked at me in disbelief, and then realization took over. "You were going to leave without telling me!" He accused. His tone grew angrier by the second.

"You weren't home! And it's not like we've been speaking!" I pointed out defensively.

"You should have phoned me. Phoebe, don't you realize how dangerous that was for you to leave on your own? Damen could have hurt you."

I pursed my lips. "You told me I should leave. I didn't think you wanted me anymore." My voice cracked, losing its momentum of anger. Saying that aloud tore at my heart. "If you came for me, I wanted it to be because you love me. Not because you feel some obligation to me."

"Obligation! You're my wife. You're having my child! I *have* an obligation to you." He reached out and took my face in his hands. His eyes were full of concern. "Phoebe I love you. You! Nothing is more important to me than you. Tell me you know that!"

I didn't have to search his eyes long for the truth. "I know it," I admitted.

His mouth claimed mine, his kiss, branding me forever. Wiping away all doubt I had about him not wanting me anymore.

"I love you," he breathed. His arms wrapped around me now, lifting me up onto his lap.

"You realize your sword fighting days are over." His words were absolute—adorable. As if that would ever really stop me.

"Don't worry." I played with a lock of his hair, twining it around my finger. "I'll wait until I feel better before I—"

"You will not have a need to practice," he interrupted. "I'm not leaving you again."

"Marcus you can't stay with me. Luther needs you. I'll go home; I'm ok with it now. I know you love me."

"I do love you," he said, giving me another reason to smile. "But you need me too. You're going to stay right here where I can look after you. I won't leave you, ever again."

Stubborn man. "Marcus, be reasonable. You know that's a promise you can't keep."

"I'll find a way."

I took a deep breath. There was no arguing with him—now anyway.

"I think we should take care of these scrapes," he reminded me gently. I had all but forgotten about them.

"They don't hurt so much anymore . . . well, except for this one." I turned my arm, examining my elbow. It was the worst.

Marcus retrieved the first aid kit from the bathroom and gingerly cleaned my arms. I examined his handy work. He was getting pretty good at patching me up. He didn't even grimace anymore. I took that as a good sign, especially for a vampire.

"What are you thinking?" His eyes flickered to mine.

"My blood . . . it doesn't seem to bother you anymore."

He laughed. "Let's just say I've grown used to the sight of it." He placed a Band-aid on my elbow.

"So the temptation is gone?" I smiled excitedly.

"Only if I hold my breath." His laughter subsided. His face grew serious again. "As long as you bleed . . . you will never be entirely safe with me. Phoebe, you must never forget that. You must never forget what I am."

I nodded my head. I knew he spoke the truth, although I couldn't imagine myself safer with anyone else.

I snuggled into him, our bodies falling back onto the mattress. I inhaled deeply, taking him in. For the first time in weeks, I felt like I could breathe.

"Marcus?" I hesitated. "Everything will be alright, won't it?"

I looked up into his golden eyes. He smiled back at me. "Yes my love. Everything will be alright." His lips touched mine.

I rested my head on his chest, my arm holding onto him. "I missed you."

"I missed you too my love." He reached over and clicked off the light. "Now, sleep."

Chapter 29: A Narrow Escape

I woke the next morning feeling much better. With the rate my body healed, I thankfully didn't have to endure pain for too long. I smiled to myself. Marcus was home, and everything was good between us.

I looked around the room for him, my eye noting that the balcony door was slightly ajar. The sound of soft voices coming from outside told me I was not alone.

I got out of bed and peeked through the door crack. Raymose and Marcus were in the middle of what looked to be an intense conversation—both their foreheads were creased.

"Luther said they're moving this way." Raymose spoke gruffly.

Marcus sighed. "They should be here in three days time."

"You know they outnumber us."

"We've been outnumbered before . . . we'll be fine." Marcus forced a smile for his friend.

"Are you going to ask her to come with us?" Raymose jerked his head in the direction of my room. I ducked back, hoping he hadn't seen me.

"No!" Marcus hissed.

"Marcus, she's good. She could help us. She's almost as good as she used to be. I've never seen anything like it. It's as if she remembered how to fight. She's almost the same except—"

"Except for her not being immortal!" Marcus interrupted angrily. "She'd be killed! She was very nearly killed last night. Had I been a second slower . . ." Marcus turned his head away, hanging it. I could feel the anger emanating from his body.

"Damen has always been a coward," Raymose mocked. "It wouldn't surprise me if while the rest of us are fighting, he's back here trying to lure her away."

"He will not have the opportunity," Marcus hissed under his breath.

"Yet . . . he seems to continue to slip through your defenses." Raymose's tone had become condescending.

"What are you saying? That I'm not able to protect her?"

"I'm saying you were very lucky last night. You cannot command Luther's army and offer the level of protection she needs. You're stretched too thin."

"What would you have me do?" Marcus growled.

"Maybe it's time to tell Luther—"

"No!"

"Marcus. He can offer the level of protection she needs."

"No! She'll be at their mercy. I won't have her anywhere near another vampire."

Raymose shook his head. "Well you can't leave her here. What if you don't come back?"

I clutched my heart, trying to slow its beat. Yes. What if he doesn't come back?

"Richard will be with her. I've instructed him to take her home." Marcus looked uneasy. "The further away she is from the fighting, the better."

They were silent for a moment.

"Raymose. If I do not come back . . ." he paused. They looked at one another; it was as if they had a private understanding, an understanding that didn't need words.

"You know I will." Raymose put his hand on Marcus's shoulder.

"She will need you Raymose. You won't have the luxury of roaming free. She can't be alone now, not ever!"

"She won't be." Raymose gave Marcus's shoulder another pat. "I'd prefer not to look after her under those circumstances my friend. You'd better survive. It will kill her to lose you."

I couldn't listen to another word. I quickly composed myself and bounded out the doors happily.

"Raymose!" I squealed, flashing him the biggest smile I could muster. He picked me up in his arms and twirled me around.

“Morning sleepyhead!” He laughed. “Oh, sorry, how’s the back?” His smile was as bright as ever. If I hadn’t just been eavesdropping, I wouldn’t have guessed that he’d just pledged to take care of me in Marcus's stead.

“Pretty good actually. I feel great!”

I looked over at Marcus. He looked as though he were going to be sick.

“I’m sorry. Did I interrupt? I saw you both out here . . .” I rushed over to him and hugged him tightly. I buried my face in his chest, trying to compose myself once again.

“No, Raymose and I were just talking. Did we wake you?” His tone was edgy.

“No. I just . . . felt hungry. I was going to go down to the kitchen and fix something to eat.”

“I’ll have Charlotte send something up. You should rest,” he urged. His expression was one of worry. “You still look a little pale to me.”

“I look pale?” I laughed, grinning at the two of them. “Would anyone care to join me? I was thinking of having breakfast on the patio.”

“Now that *would* be interesting,” Raymose joked.

I shot him a disapproving look that didn’t stay on my face long. I couldn’t help but laugh. “I’ll see you later then?” I asked, looking to Marcus.

“We’ll be down shortly,” Marcus promised as I kissed him briskly on the cheek and left them to their conversation.

Sarah brought my breakfast to the patio. I munched on scones and fruit while I waited for Marcus and Raymose. I pondered over the conversation I’d just overheard. Marcus and Raymose were both extremely anxious. Was the war with the werewolves only a few days away? I shivered.

Whatever it was, Raymose thought I could help. He said I was as good as I used to be—or almost as good. Did he want me to fight with them? That would never happen. No way Marcus would allow that, especially now. I had to admit, I was less than confident in my abilities myself. But if I could help them somehow . . .

I finished my breakfast and decided to walk down to the horse stables. Rain always made me feel better. He neighed loudly when he saw me come in.

"I don't think we're going to practice today boy." I rubbed his neck affectionately.

He started bucking his hind legs. I jumped out of his way as a hoof broke one of the boards on his stall door.

"Calm down Rain! Shit. You'd think a werewolf was out—" I stopped. My eyes grew wide. The last time he'd acted like this, a werewolf was outside. My heart was already in my throat. I looked toward the stable door. With the ruckus the other horses were making, I couldn't hear a thing outside. I reached for the latch just as Rain kicked the door out. I covered my head—protecting it from the debris that flew at me.

Rain neighed loudly as he reared up on his hind legs. I didn't think about it this time. I leapt on his back, holding onto the harness I'd forgotten to remove yesterday. We burst through the stable door and were at a full run when I looked behind me—he was huge, bigger than any of the others—faster too.

Rain shot across the lawn and down the path toward the pond like a bolt of lightning. I held on as tightly as I could, trying to stay as close to his body as possible.

I glanced over my right shoulder. I screamed as the giant wolf lunged for me, knocking me clear off my horse.

We flew through the air together, a ball of flesh and fur, landing in the pond like a boulder from the sky. I could feel my body sinking under its weight. I kicked and pulled through the water until my head broke through the surface.

I roared out in pain, holding onto the back of my shoulder. I could feel the deep gashes left from its claws. I looked around frantically, searching from side to side. I couldn't see it anywhere.

I started making my way back to the bank when a low growl from behind stopped me cold. Everything was in slow motion. I could feel every blink my eye made. Every breath I took echoed as I exhaled. The water slowly rippled past my body as the wolf moved closer. And then . . . my heart stopped.

I was too scared to move. I was chest deep in water. I couldn't get away if I wanted to. I cringed, turning my head to the side. I didn't want to look. I closed my eyes tight, waiting for it to attack. Something soft and smooth touched the side of my neck from behind. It wasn't fur . . . it was flesh.

I gasped. His scent was stronger than ever. I sighed in relief; thanking God it was only Damen.

"You're trembling." He spoke softly in my ear. I could feel the heat of his breath on the side of my face. He pressed his body up against my back. The muscles that made up his chest gave the sensation of leaning against a rock.

"You didn't think I'd forgotten you?" he mused, grazing my ear with his lips.

I turned my head just enough to see Damen standing behind me. His hands moved up my arms. He pushed my hair aside and gently kissed the back of my neck—I cringed.

"You're not afraid of me are you?" His question was taunting.

"A little," I admitted. "I've never seen you as a wolf before—I mean in the daylight." My voice cracked.

He slowly turned me around so we were facing each other. He didn't allow much air between us.

"Sorry about that," he said looking to my shoulder. "That must hurt." His eyes lingered on it for a moment. "You bleed far too easily."

"It's fine!" I lied. I wasn't about to let him know how badly he'd hurt me. I tried to ignore the blood that ran down my arm.

"I see that's not your only injury." He took my hands, holding my arms out between us.

"I tripped," I admitted, feeling foolish.

He laughed heartedly. "I really should have turned you completely. It wasn't fair of me to leave you so . . . blunderingly human."

I frowned. "It was dark; I fell!"

"Don't worry my love. It's a problem that's easily remedied."

I shifted uneasily.

"I can't stay long my dear. I had to see you again before I leave."

My breath caught. "Where are you going?"

He smiled wickedly. "Don't tell me you'll miss me?"

I closed my eyes and took in a deep breath. I was starting to feel a little dizzy. "So why did you want to see me?" I asked flatly. "Aside from wanting to throw me in this pond—yet again!"

That got me a small smile. "To ask you to leave. To ask you to go home, like you'd planned." His face grew serious now.

"Why should you care if I go back home?"

"In a day's time, an army of werewolves will come through Northern England. We'll take the island and then work our way across the mainland, exterminating them as we go."

"Them." Meaning vampires. My mouth popped open. "Why would you tell me this? You must know I'll tell Marcus."

"Because you're one of us. I don't want you killed . . . and despite what I think of Marcus, I know he'd put your safety first. When you tell him, he'll insist you leave."

I thought back to the conversation Raymose and Marcus were having on the balcony. Marcus had said that Richard would be taking me home, but Raymose wanted me to stay and fight—this was the impending battle they spoke about.

"Why would you care if I survived or not?" I spoke up, my voice sounding a little braver.

He inched closer, his eyes once again falling to my shoulder. I shivered. "You know how I feel about you. I know you can feel the connection between us." His eyes were piercing, blue and beautiful. He moved closer still. The water, not bothering to notice his body moving through it, remained glass-like. He took my hand, placing it on his heart. I could feel the heat of his skin before I even touched it, and when I did, his heartbeat quickened.

His chest was that of an avid body builder, not unlike Marcus's. Only Damen's skin looked as if he'd spent his days playing in the sun.

"You're immortal . . . how does your heart still beat?" I stared at my hand on his chest.

"The same way yours does." His answer was completely enigmatical.

"Apparently not for long."

"You're not going to die!" He looked taken aback.

"Of course I am. You're going to kill everyone."

"Not you. Just the blood sucking vampires," he grinned. "They're hardly worth shedding a tear over."

I sucked in my cheeks. I felt as though I'd been personally insulted. "They are not blood suckers."

"Oh, you've met some refined ones." He grinned. "Shall I take you home? Your beloved dark father could show you some eating habits that would stand your hair on end."

I grimaced. I couldn't allow the thought to linger. My tolerance for blood was spent the night I'd almost taken a mouthful, mistaking it for wine. I suddenly felt sick. I tried not to remember that my arm was ripped open.

"Are you feeling alright my dear? You look a little green." I could detect a small hint of enjoyment in his voice.

"Yes, it's just that blood . . . the thought of drinking blood . . ." I slapped my hand over my mouth, hoping to resist the urge to vomit.

He laughed uncontrollably. "I don't believe it. Lady Phoebe is repulsed by blood? Does Marcus know?" He was enjoying himself to the fullest.

"Can we not talk about this; honestly, it's disgusting." Damen's laughter turned into a howl. Apparently, this was by far the most comical turn of events he could have imagined . . . and he relished it.

Annoyed, I started to move out of the water. My body was beyond cold—probably the only thing keeping my arm from falling off, I thought.

"You know, it doesn't have to be this way," I yelled over my shoulder. "You could get along with them again. You don't have to fight."

"We will not serve the vampires any longer," he growled. He'd snuck up behind me without me even noticing. His hand gripped my arm spinning me around. I winced at the pain of it. "We will not be free until Luther is dead!"

"Well, I'm not one of you." I tried to break free from his grasp. "I'm not a werewolf. Don't expect me to support your cause."

He smiled crookedly. "You were lucky. I have the ability to control my bite, and more importantly, I can control the amount of venom I give. Yours was an accident. I had no intension in biting you. I didn't even know you existed. We simply . . . collided. Imagine, the odds of me literally running into you, after all this time." He stared at me, mesmerized by the very idea.

"The other werewolves, they're not like you, are they?"

"No. They will bite or kill whoever gets in their path." His tone was dark.

"Except me, right? You said they weren't supposed to hurt me." My words were broken and weak sounding. He knew I was scared.

"That is unfortunately not the case any longer." His eyes softened a little. "Luther is the oldest of the living vampires—the creator. He has managed to keep the werewolves enslaved for thousands of years. He must be killed if we are to ever truly be free."

I stared at him, confused. What did that have to do with me?

"You are his daughter," he went on, answering my unspoken question. "But you are no longer a vampire. You're a werewolf! You belong to my world now." There was a sense of malice in his tone. I found myself cringing away from him.

"Luther will not fight his own daughter, even if you are one of the retched beasts he detests."

I gasped at the insult, his words cutting deep.

"He will forfeit his life in order to save yours. Victory will be ours." I could see a triumphant look in his eyes; it was as if he'd already won the battle.

"Damen, I'm not Luther's daughter. He doesn't even know I'm here. I'm not that Phoebe!" I could feel the tears running down my cheeks now. "He wouldn't sacrifice himself for me—why would he have to?" I dreaded the answer before I'd heard it.

Damen grabbed the back of my neck and pulled my head to his. His lips trembled against my ear. "But . . . you are . . . my dear. You. Are!"

My body was shaking. Fear, the chill of the water, and considerable blood loss I'd suffered was consuming me.

"Aidric will offer you in exchange for Luther's cooperation. If he refuses . . . "

"You'd let them kill me?" I looked at him in disbelief.

His expression hardened. "I will not have a choice!" he growled through his teeth.

"No! You'd never let them hurt me if you truly loved me. You're lying . . . Why?"

"To lose you again would be more than Luther could bear. Even he has a heart when it comes to you. Aidric is counting on that . . . so am I."

"Why are you doing this to me?"

"It's normal to want what you can't have. And to fight for what others said you wouldn't." His eyes narrowed. "Luther felt it necessary to constantly remind me I'd never have your love . . . not as long as he lives anyway," he muttered the last part under his breath, but the message came out loud and clear.

"Aidric has offered you as a gift to me for my continued support in this endeavor. He was very pleased to find that you still lived."

"What!" I thundered, completely insulted that someone I didn't even know had the nerve to "offer" me as a gift. "So that's how you justify sacrificing me to Aidric? You really think that's going to earn you points with Luther?" I threw the last bit in for good measure. Knowing it would push a button.

"I don't have to prove anything to Luther!" he spat. "I spent decades serving you, fighting for you, loving you in silence. I proved my love and loyalty to you time and time again!" he thundered. "I took beatings for you! I've *earned* your love!"

I gasped. My whole world seemed to still for a moment as I realized what Damen had said.

His expression gave him away—he'd said too much.

"Damen?" My voice was barely a whisper over the loud pounding in my chest.

"Did someone hurt you . . . because of *me*?" I found myself reaching out to him. My hand trembled against his chest.

He took my hand and brought it to his lips. He kissed it gently before holding it to his heart.

"I am sorry. You are not to concern yourself with that. Forgive me." He bowed his head. He truly looked repentant.

It took a moment before I realized my mouth was still open. My mind was reeling. What was he hiding from me? What wasn't I supposed to know? Who would have hurt him . . . because of me?

"Phoebe I know I could make you happy, if you'd just give me a chance." His eyes were hopeful. I stared at him in disbelief. He'd never looked more human than he did at this very moment, and a small part of me now ached for him.

"You're a werewolf. Why would you have loved me . . . a vampire?" I suddenly found myself wanting to learn the mystery behind Damen's love for Phoebe.

"Because you never saw me as anyone but Damen. I was never a monster in your eyes. Even now, you still don't see me as a werewolf. I'm just a man. It doesn't matter what we are. It never has."

"But you taunt Marcus for loving me. A vampire and a . . . well . . . I'm different than he is."

"Marcus has always been cut and dry. He would never fall in love with a werewolf. We're beneath him."

"That's not true. He treats Richard like gold, and he loves me, just as I am."

"He loves a memory." He shook his head. "It won't last. He won't be able to truly love you—not now. Not the way you are." His words were cutting, and for a brief moment, he looked as if he regretted saying them.

"I don't believe you." I pulled my hand from his. "He loves me, I know he does." I sounded desperate.

"I can't leave you human Phoebe; it's not safe. You'll never survive what's to come if I leave you as you are."

My heart stopped. "Damen, you can't!"

"Shhh!" He took my face in his hands.

"Please . . ." Tears were running down my face again as I pleaded with him, begged him. His deep blue eyes stared longingly into mine. His mouth took mine again and again before he slowly moved his lips down my neck to my shoulder where I felt him pause. I could feel his warm breath on my skin. I shivered. His teeth pressed down on it ever so slightly.

"Damen!" My fingers dug into his arms.

He lifted his head up to look at me, his eyes full of sorrow. "I have no choice. You're different from them, the other werewolves. They spot your weakness. They won't stop hunting you until you're dead." I could hear the anguish in his voice. "I can't protect you like this."

"Damen, no!" I tried to push him away. He gripped me tighter, his hand inadvertently squeezing into my raw wound. I cried out in pain.

"Phoebe, I can make that go away. Let me turn you. You'll heal all the faster."

"No!" I shrieked.

He shook his head. "I'll make this as painless as possible." He moved his mouth to my wounded shoulder, his lips brushing the blood that coated it. He groaned. "You taste delicious . . ."

"Damen I'm pregnant!"

He slowly pulled away from me, his eyes tight with fury. "For now," he snarled.

Instant dread fell over me. He'd known. Somehow . . . he'd known.

"How could he have been so foolish to create a child with you? It's an abomination!"

"I'm not a werewolf!" I screamed out, pushing away from him at last. "And how can you say that? You just said it didn't matter what we were?"

"You cannot create a new species!" he thundered. He was seething with rage.

I tried to put as much distance between us as I could. I jumped backward, splashing my way along, as the water got shallower and shallower.

"Stay away from me," I warned, putting my hands out—as if that would stop him.

"You know I can't do that." His voice was even, unfeeling. His eyes still fixed on me. He moved slowly through the water, closing in on me with each step.

"Damen, I'll go home! No one will know you let me go. They won't find me there," I cried, stumbling backward. "Damen don't do this to me again!"

He stopped at the edge of the bank, water dripping from his body. My mind went blank. My eyes were in absolute shock. I was sure of only one thing . . .

"You're naked!" My eyes were wide, unable to look away. He was absolutely beautiful, and yet the longer I stared the harder he was to see. He gave off his own light, like the sun. I could feel the heat moving across my face—it had to be glowing crimson by now.

"What did you expect?" He grinned, all sense of malice gone.

My mouth dropped. With great effort I forced my eyes to meet his.

"*You're* naked!" I repeated.

"Yes."

"*Why* are you naked?" I felt like a deer in the headlights. I knew I should look away but—

"The only way to catch your horse was if I turned," he explained, completely unabashed.

"Of course." I closed my eyes and shook my head. This wasn't happening. This was *not* happening. I was seeing things. I'd finally cracked. That had to be it. There was no way he was just standing there—in the middle of the woods—naked. No way!

I opened my eyes. He hadn't moved. And he was still naked.

"I don't believe I've ever seen that color on your face before," he teased.

"Will you quit standing there like that?" I snapped. My eyes did their best to evade him.

"How would you like me to stand then?" He tilted his body a little, as if to pose.

"P…put some clothes on!" I turned my back to him. It didn't help. The image of Damen standing naked, water dripping down his god-like body was forever burned into my mind.

"You act like you've never seen me naked before?" His words blew across the back of my neck. I cringed. He was right behind me.

"I've never . . ." I couldn't even say it.

"I'm sorry if I've embarrassed you. I usually return home before I transform back into my human form."

"What does that have to do with you being naked?" My voice was unusually high.

I could hear him smiling. "Phoebe, our clothes are pretty much destroyed when we change."

I thought about that for a minute—it made sense. "Oh."

He laughed. "Are you going to keep your back to me for the rest of our conversation, or should I change into a wolf to ease your comfort?"

"No!" I spun around. My eyes involuntarily wandered. Every inch of his body was solid muscle, and was dangerously close to mine. He looked delighted with himself.

"And not because I want to see you . . . Uhh . . ." I couldn't think; his eyes were dazzling.

"Naked?" he finished my thought.

"Yes."

"You want me," he breathed seductively into the side of my neck. I hadn't even seen him move toward me. His scent was overwhelming, drawing me in.

"Yes. I mean no! No. I *do not* want you." I stared at his lips, so close they were nearly touching mine.

His fingers ran down the side of my face, flustering me further. "It couldn't be because you're afraid of me, in my other form?" The corners of his mouth turned up.

I shifted uneasily.

"That's it isn't it? You're afraid of me as a wolf."

I stood straighter, lifting my chin defiantly. "And I've never seen you naked before," I blurted out firmly.

He laughed heartedly. "You've seen me naked many times; you just don't remember."

"That was *not* me," I clarified sharply. I'm sure I would have remembered Damen naked.

"A technicality," he grinned. "Let me ease your comfort." He moved closer, our bodies were nearly touching.

"How is this easing my comfort?" I swallowed loudly. "You're still naked."

"Yes, but it's harder to see when I'm this close to you, and so much easier for me to finish where I'd left off—" Said the Big Bad Wolf. All humor was gone. "There is no other way. I am sorry. One day you will see that I was right." His voice was softer than before. A heavy look hung in his eyes. I knew he was torn by his love for me, and his duty. I couldn't let him turn me. Not before I had a chance to warn Marcus.

I knew what he wanted from me, and I hated myself for giving in. Out of fear and sheer desperation, I lunged at him, wrapping my arms around his neck; I pulled him to me, meshing my body against his. I kissed him with as much passion as I could muster.

It took only a moment for his lips to catch up. His hands gripped my waist, holding my body against him. His lips were soft, and despite the fact that we'd been in a freezing cold pond, his body was flushed with passion. He wanted me.

I released him minutes later, breathless. We stared at one another. All time seemed to stop. Only the wind rustling the leaves in the trees overhead reminded us that the world was still spinning. And then another vision of Phoebe came to me. I'd kissed Damen like this before.

His chest heaved in and out as he panted. His eyes pinning me with their wild stare made his desire all the more clear. "My love for you hasn't changed," he said in a husky voice. "After all this time, I still love you. The way I always have. You must know that." And I did.

"You have to leave here Phoebe. I won't be able to protect you."

He wiped the tears off my face, no doubt believing they were for him. Truthfully, some of them were. I felt like such a traitor. I'd betrayed Marcus, and now—Damen's heart.

"Phoebe, if they find you, they will kill you. Your child can't live." he spoke earnestly. "You can't ask me again to spare its life; we're even now." His words were chilling, and without question, I understood their meaning. He hadn't spared Phoebe's baby—but he had spared mine—a favor that would not be repeated.

"Thank you." I threw my arms around him, hugging him.

I felt his arms around me once again, holding me close to him. He breathed in deeply, finding the strength to pull away from me. "Go!"

I stared at him, burning his face into my memory. I couldn't move. I felt an overwhelming sadness as I looked into his eyes. He was letting me go? He loved me enough to let me go. This was not the Damen I knew, the Damen I feared. This was the Damen that Phoebe trusted once upon a time . . . the friend she'd loved—and yes, she had loved him. I was sure of that.

I reached out and held his cheek in my hand. I was afraid to leave him. Afraid what might happen to him.

"It's alright Phoebe, go . . ." He looked behind him. His face was suddenly panicked. A loud howling echoed not far away. "Quickly!" He urged once again. He jumped back from me.

"Phoebe run!" His body exploded into a huge, growling beast. He headed off in the direction of his pack.

I ran. I couldn't move fast enough. I was soaked to the bone. My body ached from being knocked off the horse, and the pain in my shoulder was unbearable. I reached up to hold it. I could feel the wet blood on my fingers. My hands were already stained from it. I couldn't let myself think about that now. I had to find Marcus.

I kept seeing Damen's eyes in my mind. How terrified they looked all of a sudden. The realization of what had nearly happened was sinking in. Damen was going to turn me completely. He knew without question I was pregnant. I held my stomach as I ran. We weren't safe here any longer—I'd have to leave.

I felt like I would never get out of the forest. The path kept stretching out further and further in front of me, and then I could hear my name being screamed—It sounded so far away.

I pushed myself to run faster. I could see Marcus running toward me now. His face looked as terrified as I felt. I staggered into his arms and collapsed.

"Phoebe!" He pulled my limp body close to his.

"Hurry, we have to get out of here." I winced, trying to pull myself up. I held onto his shoulders, staining his shirt with the blood from my hand.

"You're bleeding!" Marcus hissed.

A loud howling pierced the forest.

"Werewolves!" I cried. "They're coming!"

He scooped me up in his arms and jumped into the trees like a cat. We traveled to the safety of his castle under a canopy of leaves.

Chapter 30: Honesty

Marcus didn't bother with discretion, such as walking me through the front doors like any other normal person would have. He tried to keep to the trees as much as possible, but when it came right down to it, his worry for me outweighed his need to remain cautious. He flew right out in the open and through my balcony doors—luckily they were still open.

He sat me down as gently as he could, then grabbed a blanket and wrapped it around me, careful not to let it touch my wounded shoulder. I was convulsing uncontrollably. A look of sheer murder hung in his eyes

"D-Damen chased me out of the stables," I shivered involuntarily. "Only I d-didn't know it was him. He was a wolf!" I blurted.

"Damen did this to you?" Marcus snarled, exploding with rage. "He can't have gone far!"

"You can't leave me!" I lunged for him, grabbing his hand with the last ounce of strength I had left. "Please Marcus! I'm begging you!"

I could see the anger consuming him. His black eyes seethed with fury. "Phoebe. This ends now."

"Marcus, he let me go! He could have killed me, but he let me come back to you."

"Not before he ripped you to shreds!" he growled.

"Rain, where's Rain?" My god, I'd forgotten about him.

"He's fine. He came back on his own." Marcus pulled the blanket back around me. His desire to chase after Damen was abandoned for the moment. He held my face.

"I shouldn't have left you alone so long." His eyes were full of regret.

"It's not your fault. I don't expect you to watch over me all the time." The look on Marcus's face suggested that that was exactly what he should be doing.

"I need to take care of that," he motioned to my shoulder, his eyes noting my hesitation. "I'll be right back. I promise. I'm just going into the bathroom."

Hoping I'd have the strength to jump up and grab him if he made the slightest move toward the door, I released him.

He went into the bathroom and returned promptly with a first aid kit. I braced myself. He tore the back of my shirt away, exposing the full horror of Damen's claws—he gasped.

I tried hard to ignore the pain. My skin felt as though it had been literally shredded. "Can it be stitched?"

"There is nothing to stitch it to," he replied softly.

I cried into my blankets while he diligently began cleaning my wounds. I was biting my lip, trying to keep up a brave front so Marcus wouldn't fly out the door after Damen. My brave front collapsed when he applied the antiseptic—I screamed out in pain as I grabbed onto the sheets, trying to channel the pain from my body.

Marcus made all sorts of anguished noises. I knew it killed him to see me like this. He secured the wrapping then crouched down beside the bed. His hand gently smoothed the hair off my forehead. "I wish I could take the pain for you." I knew he meant it. His eyes looked long into mine. "I swear to you: there is no place in this world he can hide. I *will* find him."

I swallowed loudly. I didn't doubt Marcus would track Damen to the ends of the earth to pay back the favor.

"Why *did* he let you return?" he asked a moment later, as if the question had just occurring to him.

I closed my eyes for a moment and tried to remember all that Damen had said.

I explained to Marcus how Damen wanted me to go back home, that I wasn't safe here with either of them. How the werewolves would be here in a day's time working their way across England, and then through Europe . . . eliminating all vampires along the way. Marcus stiffened at the news. "Only a day?" Clearly he'd expected he'd have more time.

I went on with their intention of killing Luther. How Aidric planned on using Luther's love for *me* to force him to surrender and declare freedom to the werewolves. How I was to be Aidric's trump card; he would use me as a bargaining tool. Aidric was confident that Luther would never fight his own daughter, even though I was a werewolf now.

"How would Aidric use you for leverage?" Marcus looked confused. He hadn't connected the dots yet. "And, why would he say you're a werewolf now? Surely he knows you haven't been turned."

"He said that I'm only partly infected, he needed to change me completely—"

"He was going to bite you again?" Marcus raged, jumping to his feet.

"Yes, but I . . ." I was afraid to tell Marcus what I'd done.

"You what?" His guard was up, eyeing me carefully.

"I sort of . . . blurted out that I was . . . pregnant." I winced, seeing the expression of horror that now claimed his face.

"You what?" he thundered. "Do you have any idea the danger you've put yourself in now . . . not to mention our child!"

"He already knew! I don't know how, but he knew!"

Marcus looked like he was going to come unstuck. He ran his hands back and forth through his hair with such vigor, I wondered if he were going to rub his hair right off.

"I panicked, alright! He was biting my shoulder. Look!" I yanked my shirtsleeve up to show the impressions I could still feel in my skin.

He roared. Then grabbing the vase of flowers by the bedside, he launched it across the room at the door—smashing it to bits.

Raymose burst in, his hair, for the first time looking a little disheveled. "You found her!" He stared at the shattered vase on the floor. "Thank you for letting me know." He was clearly annoyed. He held up his cell phone and tilted it back and forth in his hand. "You could have called."

I covered my mouth quickly, trying to suppress a giggle—it didn't work. I had taken one look at Marcus and Raymose's confused expressions and burst into a state of uncontrollable laughter.

"What's so funny?" Raymose barked, sounding more than a little put out.

"Vampires . . . cell phones." I laughed hysterically. I was finally cracking up.

"Phoebe?" Raymose's voice was gruff. I looked up at him, still unable to stop laughing. His eyes were red. He sniffed the air. "You're bleeding . . . a lot."

Marcus had already positioned himself in front of me, his eyes watching Raymose carefully.

"I know." My laughter had turned to tears. "Damen disfigured my back."

"He what?" Raymose spat, all signs of blood lust gone for the moment.

"He disfigured my back," I repeated a little louder through the tears. "I was just chased by a werewolf, knocked off a horse, nearly drowned, physically assaulted, and informed that I will be the downfall of the vampire civilization. I only escaped because I threw myself on his mercy and kissed him." I buried my face in the quilt. Aside from my sobbing, the room was silent.

I cried and cried. I'd been so scared to tell Marcus all the details of my close encounter with Damen. But somehow, I'd managed to blurt them out in almost one breath. By the sound of silence in the room, they were still trying to process it all.

I felt a hand on the small of my back. "You . . . *kissed* him?" Marcus had trouble saying the word.

I didn't have the courage to look at him. I felt like such a traitor. "It was the only thing I could think of to distract him from biting me," I admitted truthfully, my words mumbled into the quilt.

Marcus said nothing.

"He let you go?" Raymose asked a few moments later, breaking the silence. "Why?"

I lifted my head and met Raymose's stare His eyes still held a trace of crimson in them. "He said he can't protect me from the pack any longer. Not even if I became a full werewolf myself. They'd sense . . ." I bit my lip—stopping myself from saying too much. I could feel Marcus's body tense up beside me. I knew his mind. I knew it took all his control not to hunt Damen down and kill him like the dog Marcus thought he was. "It was not without a price," he growled.

"Marcus . . ." Raymose's tone was untrusting.

Marcus's eyes flickered to mine, and for the first time ever he looked afraid for himself. Then his face turned solemn as he turned toward his friend. "Phoebe's going to have a baby."

Raymose stared at Marcus with a look of disbelief before he turned to me, glancing at my middle. "She has werewolf blood in her . . . they cannot conceive. It's not possible!"

"There's never been another like her," Marcus insisted. "We don't know her limitations . . . and it's more than possible. She's still partly human."

"How *careless* could you be?" Raymose demanded. His eyes moved from Marcus to me.

I started to cry again. Never had I been the target of Raymose's anger.

Marcus put his arms around me, cradling me against his chest. "She doesn't need to be attacked Raymose, especially by you," he warned. "You have no right. If you must be angry, be angry with me."

"Oh, I am," he promised, stalking forward. "When I think of the danger she was in every time I left her alone . . . the danger she's still in! How could you do this to her?" Raymose raged.

"I didn't want her left alone," Marcus snapped. "That's why I asked her to leave. I didn't want her here . . . vulnerable to an assault."

"No. You wanted her half way across the world where Damen could have his way with her," Raymose snapped. "She was safer here with me and you know it. She's always been safer with me."

Marcus rose from the bed, his posture becoming defensive.

"Raymose. Marcus. Don't!" I beseeched them both.

"You had your chance," Marcus hissed. "You turned your back when she wanted you."

Raymose's stare was deadly. "A mistake that will not be repeated," he spat.

I tried to focus. There was more going on here than I understood.

"She'd have a better chance saving herself and our child than she did the last time," Marcus growled.

Raymose froze. "What are you saying?" he asked cautiously.

"When Damen killed Phoebe," Marcus's voice cracked. "He killed my unborn child as well."

"How do you know this?" Raymose eyed me carefully.

"Damen bit her," Marcus explained. "She shares his memories. She has seen it through her own memories. The bastard has admitted it himself."

Raymose scrubbed a hand down his face. He looked beyond his last nerve. "There has never been a blending of the species. Never!" His voice rose in anger. "Luther will not tolerate this. You'll be lucky if he doesn't kill you along *with* her."

I slapped my hand over my mouth.

"I will kill anyone who tries to take them from me," Marcus warned. "Anyone!"

I jumped up and ran for the bathroom. I managed to lock the door behind me and get to the toilet just in time . . .

I felt like I was going to die. After several minutes of heaving my lungs out, I slunk to the floor—exhausted—waiting for death to take me.

"Phoebe? Darling, can you hear me?" Marcus spoke through the door. His voice sounded strained.

"Yes," I moaned.

"Can you unlock the door, love?"

"No."

There was a moment of silence. Then, I could hear whispers.

"Just let me die," I whined as I pulled myself back to the toilet and vomited once again. I collapsed back to the floor, pressing my cheek to the cold stone. My eyes watched the room rock back and forth. I closed them, hoping to still the spinning world.

"Phoebe, you're scaring me. Please open the door." Marcus was jiggling the handle.

"I can't," I whimpered again.

"Why not?" Raymose asked in the same worried tone as Marcus. Apparently they were both hovering outside the door. Well at least they weren't ripping each other's heads off I thought.

"Because I'm sick!" I finally yelled out, annoyed they'd ask the obvious. I was sure they were both able to hear me retching. "I'll be out in awhile. I just need to lie here . . . and die," I added quietly. I closed my eyes, hoping the nausea would pass—soon.

I lay there for a good half hour before I tried to sit up. I felt frozen having been on the cold floor for so long. I crawled over to the bathtub and started the water. I rested my head on the side of the tub while I waited for it to fill.

I poured a little rose water into the bath, hoping the smell would wake my senses. It seemed to be working. The walls weren't shifting around so much anymore. I undressed and slipped into the warm water. I hung my arms over the edge of the tub, taking care not to let the water reach my newly bandaged shoulder.

I closed my eyes . . . my mind drifted back to the forest . . . I could still feel Damen's mouth on my shoulder . . . his teeth sharply pressing into my skin.

My body jerked violently with a start, splashing water from the tub. I sat straight up. My heart pounded in my chest. With a trembling hand, I reached up and felt my shoulder. It was fine. No bite marks.

The sound of water spilling over the tub onto the floor brought me out of my reverie.

I reached over and quickly turned it off. I held my face in my hands, trying to steady myself.

There was a gentle knock at the window. I looked over to see Marcus's head poking in. "May I come in?"

I nodded. “Sorry about that,” I said when I saw him looking around at all the water on the floor.

“Didn’t you notice how high the water was?” Marcus was already grabbing towels to sop up the floor.

“No, I . . . fell asleep . . .”

“Wonderful, now I have to worry about you drowning?” he said, as if he was adding one other item of concern to his list.

“Sorry.” My voice sounded so far away, as if it had come from someone else. “Let me help you clean that up.”

“No, I got it, I’m nearly done anyway,” he insisted as he pushed the towel around the floor.

“Is Raymose still here?”

Marcus looked up. His eyes were a soft brown, almost golden—he’d just eaten. “No, he’s on his way to see Luther.”

“Why?” I choked.

“If the werewolves are going to be here sooner than we’d planned, we need to be prepared.” His tone was business like.

“Werewolves!” I jumped up abruptly, splashing water and bubbles as I reached for my towel.

“What are you doing; I just wiped that up.”

“I’m not just going to sit and soak in a tub when we’re about to be invaded by werewolves . . . We need to do something!”

“Not we,” he warned, launching the towel into a corner. “Phoebe, I’d already decided to have Richard put you on a plane today. I don’t want you anywhere near here,” he said firmly. “The further you are from Aidric and Luther, the better.”

“There is no way I’m leaving you now. Damen said you were outnumbered.” I stepped out of the tub and vigorously dried myself off.

Marcus put his arms around me, holding me from behind. “You’re not coming with me.”

“Marcus you need me, even Raymose said you did. I can help. I’ll be careful, I promise. I already feel lots better.” It was a necessary lie.

He turned me around. His hands rested on my shoulders. I winced at the pressure. "The other wolves will not be so merciful," he warned, running a finger across my bandage.

"I won't need them to be." My resolve was strong. He wasn't going to change my mind. If there was any way I could help them, I was going to do it.

Marcus smiled affectionately at my stubbornness. "The vampires will smell the fresh blood my dear." His eyes narrowed. "I know you think I am strong, but even I won't be able to fight them all off you."

I didn't have a response to that. I'd been so worried about werewolves; I hadn't considered my safety around the other vampires.

"I told you before I'd protect you. But I can't do it if you're taking risks." His lips glided across my face. He pulled my body to his, careful of my new wounds. His mouth took mine aggressively.

I was momentarily lost in his kiss. I pulled back, breathing heavily.

He smiled at me. "Nothing matters more to me in this world than you."

I sighed. I knew exactly how he felt. I reached up and placed the palm of my hand against his cheek—he leaned into it, absorbing my touch.

"Marcus. They're going to kill Luther. I can't let them." I watched the smile slip from his face. "I know this doesn't make sense to you, Luther doesn't even know I exist, but he's the only father I have left."

Marcus's mouth fell open. "You would risk your life . . . our *child's* life . . . to save Luther's?" The very idea sounded inconceivable.

"I can't explain it," I began. "I feel drawn to him. He needs me." I was just as shocked as Marcus was when I realized how I felt about this man I'd never seen in this life.

"Phoebe." Marcus gripped my arms, shaking me slightly. Luther will take *your* life!" His words were sharp. "You're not a vampire anymore," he warned. "You're—" he released my arms abruptly and turned away from me, his body seething with anger.

"A werewolf! Is that what you were going to say?" I shouted angrily. "A werewolf!"

"It's the truth," Marcus hissed over his shoulder. "As far as anyone else will see it. Luther will sense it immediately. I can't let you anywhere near him, not ever. He won't quibble about what percent werewolf you are. He'll simply destroy you."

I tried to let that sink in, but my heart wouldn't let it. My heart told me that Luther needed me. That once he saw me, he'd remember he loved me. Even if he didn't, I couldn't turn my back on him. I couldn't let them murder him.

"Have you forgotten the other heart beating within you?" Marcus interrupted my thoughts.

My mouth popped open. "You can hear the baby's heart beat?" I gasped. "That's how Damen knew isn't it? He must have heard the heartbeat too."

A small hiss escaped from behind Marcus teeth.

"Marcus. What would Luther do to you if he found out you were hiding me from him?"

"My deception would be . . . unforgivable."

"Because you kept his daughter from him? Or because of what I am?" I asked.

"A little of both I expect." He touched my cheek with his hand. "As Raymose said, a mixing of the species is . . . unthinkable." His words were firm.

I knew he accepted the laws of his kind and supported and respected Luther without question. That's why the next thought had me immediately on edge. I dreaded the question before I'd asked it. "And the punishment for such a betrayal?" I held my breath. I suspected I already knew the answer. I cringed, praying I was wrong.

He tilted his head a little as he sighed. The look in his eyes made me feel sick once again.

"I see." I gave him a small smile and stalked to my closet. I began searching through the clothing Richard had retrieved as promised.

"Phoebe, you must understand; it doesn't matter to me how others see you. I don't look at you that way." He sounded desperate.

"I understand." I donned a shirt and pants in record time. I wasn't sure what was coming, but I knew that I couldn't face it naked.

"What exactly do you understand?" He sounded almost patronizing now.

"I understand that because of me, you could be killed." I tied on my shoes.

Marcus took my hands and brought them to his chest. His eyes, sought mine. "I'm not worried about it. I've managed to hide you all this time. Raymose will keep our secret. There is no reason Luther would ever find out about you."

"Aidric! It's only a matter of time before he tells Luther about me." I looked concernedly into Marcus's eyes. "I'm just part of the deception. What would he say if he knew we were going to have a baby?"

Marcus's face fell. I could see real fear in his eyes. It morphed into anger. "I will protect you—both of you." His resolve was stronger than ever.

"At what cost?" I closed my eyes, shaking away the image. This wasn't going to happen. I wouldn't let it. If I were gone, Marcus would be safe. He could deny being with me because technically, we wouldn't be together . . . Luther hadn't seen me . . . he'd just assume Aidric was lying.

I knew deep down Marcus would never let me go without him, especially now. He was so protective of me. I also knew that Luther would question Marcus's absence if he were to suddenly disappear. He would most likely question Raymose as well . . . we'd be putting him in terrible danger. I had to find a way for Luther to accept us. It was the only way to guarantee all of our safeties.

"Don't think on it any longer." Marcus reached out and held my face in his hands, his soft eyes melting me where I stood. "I'll protect you both—or die trying," he added darkly. "Would you believe me capable of anything less?"

I gave him a flat smile. How could I not love this man? "No." I shook my head, answering him at last. "I wouldn't believe you capable of anything less." I kissed his lips.

Chapter 31: Damen's Offer

Marcus had informed me that Charlotte and Sarah were taking a brief holiday to go visit their families. This of course was a ruse he'd concocted to ensure their safety. Not to mention he didn't want to have to explain why we were suddenly being overrun with wolves.

We said our goodbyes after dinner. Charlotte had made a mouth watering roast that had enough leftovers for a week's worth of meals.

Marcus had told her that he would be taking me on a little trip the day after tomorrow, so she needn't worry about us eating.

I left Marcus and Raymose in the library to finalize their plans. I couldn't stand to listen any longer. Despite Marcus's reassurance, Raymose was still uneasy about their numbers—which of course added to my level of tension.

I walked slowly up the staircase and down the long hall. The castle was quiet. No Charlotte clanking about in the kitchen. No Sarah humming along as she did her chores. The house felt dead, and I didn't have any life to add to it.

I found myself standing in the center of my bedroom looking around me. I suddenly felt very alone. The room was filled with so many memories of past and present—I couldn't bear to think of being here without Marcus. I shook the image away; I couldn't afford to dwell on it.

I sat myself down in a chair by the window and looked out across the lawn. The sunlight had all but disappeared. I cracked the window open a little and let the night breeze waft in. I sat back, closed my eyes, and tried to relax.

I breathed in deeply—a familiar scent met my nose. My eyes popped wide open. I jumped up, throwing open the window. I leaned out as far as I could, straining my eyes as I searched the darkness.

"There you are . . .." I whispered as I saw him standing by the garden, not fifty yards away. I considered my safety for a moment. He wouldn't hurt me, would he? He obviously wanted to see me. It was at great personal risk that he came—especially tonight of all nights.

I turned and moved quietly as I snuck downstairs and out the doors. I ran as fast as I could through the darkness. The moon's light was directly overhead and lit my way beautifully. Damen was standing near the roses. He had picked one and was extending it out to me.

I approached him slowly. My hand shook a little as I took it from him. "Thank you." My voice was suddenly hoarse. Perhaps this hadn't been a good idea to meet him alone after all?

"I'm afraid its beauty pales next to yours, my dear," he said as he circled me slowly.

I could feel my heart begin to race. I was uneasy having Damen so close to me. Any other woman would welcome such a handsome, well-spoken man paying her attention. I, on the other hand, found it unnerving. Damen looked at me with such desire, such absolute longing. The tension was unbearable.

"You must want to know why I've come?" He moved closer still.

"Damen, you shouldn't be here. Marcus and Raymose are inside; if they catch you . . ."

"Are you worried for my safety?" He cocked his head to the side, assessing my reaction. "You do care, don't you?"

I gave him a dry look. "What do you want Damen?"

"I wanted to see if you were foolish enough to have stayed." He shook his head, a look of pity hung on his face. "You think you can save him, don't you?"

I didn't answer.

"Do you honestly think you're strong enough to fight alongside him? Would he be such a fool to let you try?"

"I won't let him die!" I yelled, tossing the rose back at him.

His eyes lit up. I'd given him his answer.

"He needs me. He . . . just doesn't know it yet." I'd said this a million times to myself already, but somehow saying it aloud to

Damen made it seem foolish. Who was I trying to convince, really? I shifted uneasily.

"So much time has passed . . . yet nothing has changed." His voice was condescending.

"What are talking about?" I folded my arms across my chest.

"You've walked this path before . . .have you not? And here you are yet again, ready to sacrifice your life, and that of your unborn child's, in the hopes to save his?"

I glowered at him. He cut me to the quick and he knew it. "*You* took that life, not me. And Marcus *was* saved," I reminded him curtly.

"A tragedy that will not be repeated," he snarled. "He cannot be allowed to live when he hunts us so freely!" I could see the hatred in his eyes.

"Well then we have a problem, don't we?" My voice sounded unlike my own. It was strong and confident. "You're not going to touch him."

He laughed wickedly, his eyes gleaming like diamonds in the moonlight. "Are you threatening me?"

I took a short breath, taken aback by the direction the conversation had turned. "Yes."

He sneered, his yellow eyes full of malice. "You think you can stop me?"

"If I had to." The words slipped between my lips. They weren't as strong as I'd hoped—confirmation that I doubted myself. "I feel stronger every day." I held my chin high.

"True. With each full moon your strength grows . . . but not enough for what is to come."

I scoffed.

"Let it begin then." I had no time to react. He grabbed my shoulders and threw me like a rag doll across the ground. I skidded to a stop, landing on my newly bandaged arm.

I cried out in agony.

Damen had already closed the gap between us, yanking me violently to my feet. I winced as his fingers dug deep into my jaw. "You cannot win . . . not as you are," he growled. "Soon, you will beg me to turn you." He tossed my body effortlessly, sending me into one of the garden statues. It toppled over, breaking my fall. "Imagine what Aidric will do to you," he mocked as he stared down at my quivering body.

"You can break every bone I have Damen . . . I won't let you hurt Marcus."

Even in the limited light, I could see his fury wash over his face. His chest heaved in and out as he made his way over to me.

"Marcus's fate has been decided," he snarled. "As has yours."

I'd somehow found the strength to pick myself up off the ground. My body felt like a shell—not even my own. It ached from head to toe. Every inch screamed with pain.

"I won't let you turn me," I stood my ground. "I'd rather die than become a werewolf!"

"And so you shall." His foot connected with my chest a second later, my breath escaping me on impact. He growled as he moved toward me. I lay on the ground several yards away, gasping for air. My vision too blurred to see him clearly.

"I have the power to save you," he sneered, "and your child." He baited the hook. "If I turn you now, your heart will still beat."

"No," I cried. Had it come to this? My life would be spared if I agreed to let Damen turn me completely . . . my soul for immortality? The baby would live . . . a life for a life. There had to be another way.

I stared up at him, my body . . . too sore to move. "You're not the only one who could save us," I choked, spitting blood from my lips.

His laugh was chilling. "You'd rather be a vampire?"

"Is it possible?" My voice edged on desperate.

Damen's expression grew more sinister, as if that were even possible. "You think the vampires are going to welcome you—an abomination like the child that grows within you?" He dropped down beside me, his face pressed hard against my neck, as he inhaled deeply. "Blood doesn't lie," he breathed into my ear. "You. Are. A. Werewolf." He lifted me into his arms then flung me to the side, taking out a small wooden arbor with my body. I cried out in agony. I thought all the bones in my body had broken. By all rights, they should have.

"You said you loved me," I sobbed, trying to rise to my knees—I fell back to the ground, disoriented. "How can you kill me when you love me?"

"I've waited far too long for you Phoebe." His mind was absolute. He looked upon me, expressionless. His patience was spent . . . he was through 'playing.' He wanted me—now!

"You won't come freely but you will concede," he threatened darkly. A low growl came from behind his teeth. "Can I offer immortality to you now?"

"Damen—" He had me by the throat, his fingers cutting into my skin.

"I don't think you want to continue doing that." A voice spoke coldly—I recognized it at once. Thank God!

"Raymose . . . what a surprise." Damen pressed harder against my throat. "You may want to step back old friend; there's an awful lot of blood," Damen said with a grin.

I gasped for air. "Damen . . ." My voice was barely audible.

"Let her go!" Marcus hissed.

"I don't think I can do that," Damen laughed. "Now that you know I'm here, I can hardly leave unscathed . . . and I have so much work ahead of me tomorrow . . . or should I say today!" He added cheerfully, ignoring my gurgled pleas.

"Besides, Poor Phoebe here wouldn't stand a chance against two vampires. It would be cruel of me to let her go. As I said . . . there's an awful lot of blood." There was a twisted pleasure in his tone. He was enjoying their torment at my expense. I struggled beneath him, my fingers desperately trying to pry his hand away from my throat.

"Hasn't centuries of reflection taught you that you can't win her affection by beating her to death," Raymose hissed, he was inching toward us, his black eyes deadly.

"I won't lose her—not again!" Damen threatened. His grip on me tightened, nearly causing me to blackout.

"She's not yours to lose!" Marcus spoke through gritted teeth. He circled us, slowly, waiting for an opportunity to strike. "Let her go—now!"

"Not a chance," Damen snarled. His teeth were too close to me—a fact Marcus was all too aware of.

Marcus's eyes met mine. I could see the pain in them. It almost mirrored my own. "You're killing her!" he screamed.

"Not her, just the child you so foolishly created. I'm prepared to turn her." He tightened his grip around me. "Her body will heal." He pivoted so fast; his forearm now crushed into my throat. I gagged. My fingers desperately tried to pry his arm away.

He began backing up, trying to put some distance between them and us. My feet struggled to keep up. They slipped, causing me to choke myself even further.

"I warned you before not to ask me to spare its life again," he breathed into my ear.

Marcus moved closer. His black eyes fixed on Damen. "*I will kill you.*"

"*You will try.*" Damen let out an unholy roar, his body exploding into a giant wolf, his teeth bared and dripping with saliva.

I fell from his grip—Marcus caught me before I hit the ground. I managed to see Raymose colliding with Damen as Marcus crashed through my bedroom doors seconds later, holding my bloodied body in his arms. He laid me down on the bed, his eyes wide with fear.

I curled up into a ball, not caring if Death came for me. I'd welcome him. "It's ok Marcus, go . . ." I choked on the blood in my mouth.

His crimson eyes wandered over my body—he hadn't realized how bad I was. I could see the torment on his face. The eternal fight that burned within him now—there was too much blood.

He shook his head. "I'm not leaving you." His voice was barely recognizable. He closed his eyes, composing himself. "I won't hurt you." I didn't know if he said it for my benefit or for his—it didn't matter. He knelt down beside me. His hands shook as they reached out to me.

"I'm still alive," I half smiled trying to put up a brave front for him. I couldn't bear to see the pained look on his face. I could endure anything but that—and I had.

Sharp pains were shooting throughout my body. It felt like there was an internal fight going on within me. My bones were trying to heal themselves, and it was just as painful as the attack itself. I cried.

"He nearly killed you," Marcus hissed. He looked absolutely murderous.

I coughed, spitting up more blood onto the pillow. "I hadn't noticed. Maybe if I'd spent less time clear cutting the trees with my body, I would have picked up on that."

"I will kill him," he vowed. "If Raymose hasn't beaten me to it already, I will kill him slowly." There was no mercy in his voice.

"You're going to have to get in line," I groaned. Marcus could never know the reason behind Damen's sudden physical attack on me. I knew Damen was trying to teach me a lesson. A painful lesson—that I was in no way equipped to handle the fight I'd so adamantly decided on against Marcus's wishes. It was his twisted way of showing me how much he cared—and I *would* return the favor—somehow. I wasn't going to let Damen stop me. No one was going to take Marcus away from me, not as long as I had a breath in my body. I'd fight.

"There's something more . . ." Marcus's tone was implying. "Something you're not telling me."

I forced myself to smile. "No."

"You're an awful liar Phoebe."

Marcus jumped up onto the bed abruptly, shielding me protectively, just as Raymose came rushing through my balcony doors.

I clutched my heart, hoping to keep it in my chest. I couldn't handle much more excitement right now.

"Easy Marcus, it's just me," Raymose said as he put his hands out like he was slowing traffic.

"Raymose . . ." Marcus's voice was gruff. "There's a lot of blood . . . perhaps you should leave."

Raymose's eyes lingered over me. I could see the red swirling through them. His nostrils flared as he inhaled deeply. "I won't harm her," he promised. His voice was strained like Marcus's. His blood red eyes met mine. And although I knew it caused him great pain to be this close to my bleeding body, I knew he spoke the truth—he'd never hurt me.

Marcus eased himself slowly off the bed, watching Raymose carefully—his faith was not as strong as mine. "Did you find him?"

"Yes. But he wasn't exactly alone," Raymose said casually as he took a chair beside the bed.

"The army is here already?" I could hear the tension in Marcus's voice. His hands fisted at his side.

"The army is here," Raymose repeated darkly.

Marcus walked over to the window and peered out. "How many of them are there?"

Raymose's eyes met mine again. He forced a smile for me. The anger behind it showed he felt like doing anything but smile. "I'd say around eleven hundred or so . . . a little less than we'd planned," he spoke to Marcus.

He took the corner of my blanket and wiped away the blood from my lips. "I'm sorry you suffered." There was real torment in his face.

I took his hand and squeezed it gently.

"How far away are they?" Marcus continued on with his questions like a soldier mapping out a plan of attack.

"We have two hours at the most." Raymose's eyes moved to Marcus now. "We don't have enough time to move her."

I winced at the thought. I could actually hear my bones popping back into place. The sound was sickening.

Marcus growled under his breath.

"Can you trust Richard to get her through? You know Luther has hunters coming in from the west as well as the south . . . perhaps I should take her myself . . ." Raymose's tone changed to a possessive one. His eyes were fixed on me. "We can't afford either of them running across her scent."

Marcus's eyes grew dark. "She *is not* your responsibility Raymose. She's *mine*!" Marcus was on his last nerve. "I trust Richard with my life."

"Yes, but can you trust him with hers?" Raymose growled back at him. "The window is very narrow. And she will always be my responsibility," he added darkly.

Marcus glowered at his friend, cutting him a look that made me shiver. "I trust him with her life," he clarified, his faith unwavering.

Raymose nodded. "Luther must be informed that the werewolf army is assembling. I must go to him now. I'll return within the hour."

Raymose rose from his chair. His gaze, once again, settled on me. "Stay safe," he whispered as he bent over and kissed my forehead softly.

I gripped his hand. My eyes were full of fear—for him.

"I will," he winked, answering my unspoken words.

"You'd better see that Richard gets her to a doctor Marcus; she's lost a lot of blood." With that, he turned and left the room.

Marcus looked at me uneasily. I knew he agreed with Raymose.

"There isn't time!" I forced myself to sit up straight.

"Phoebe, lie down." His tone was firm.

"I'm fine," I moaned, trying to gingerly get up from the bed.

"But the baby isn't!" he snapped.

I froze—taken aback by his sudden hostility.

"Fear not." His voice softened. "Richard will lead you safely while Raymose and I head them off. The Moon Hunters are already in place, and Luther's army is not far. You will be able to sneak out undetected."

"What about you and Raymose?" I breathed. "How do you expect to fight so many on your own?"

"The important thing is that you get away—"

"No! That's not the important thing. I won't let you do it. It's suicide! After they kill you two, they'll be after us. The four of us together—"

"NO!" It's a miracle Damen didn't kill you. Aidric won't hesitate. You're a marked woman." He motioned to my stomach.

"Then I guess I'll have to kill him first!" I warned.

Marcus's eyes narrowed. "You'll kill him?" His tone was every bit as condescending as Damen's had been."

"Aidric is not just a werewolf. He is massive, at least twice my size. We've never been able to get close to him. Never! How do you think you're going to kill him? You can barely move!"

I pushed myself to my feet, wincing silently at the pain. "You're not going to scare me Marcus. Damen already tried that." I averted my eyes. Marcus had keyed in on my slip of the tongue. "Aidric is threatening my life, my family . . . I won't run away from him! Besides, he'd find me, even if I did."

Marcus smashed his fists down in frustration on a nearby table, bringing it to the floor—I couldn't help but jump.

He had my face between his hands before I'd had time to collect myself. "You will go wherever Richard takes you! DO YOU UNDERSTAND ME?"

I cowered away from him as he shouted the words. Marcus had never fixed such a murderous stare on me. He had reached his maximum limit of indulging my ideas on protecting myself. I could hear my heart beating loudly. It echoed over my breathing that had stopped momentarily. I was too scared to move. He looked as if he would crush my skull between his hands if I so much as whispered an argument. He wasn't Marcus anymore . . . he was a vampire.

"Wherever Richard takes me," I breathed, tears streaming down my face. He released me abruptly. I staggered back, never taking my eyes off him.

I jumped again when the door opened with a knock.

Marcus continued to glare at me. His eyes were cold and unforgiving.

"Forgive me Sir, but Mr. Raymose has asked that you meet him by the stables—Miss Phoebe!" I could see out the corner of my eye Richard's mouth fall open at the sight of me. I turned my head away; I didn't want him to see me this way—broken and afraid.

"I'll be right along Richard. Would you give us a minute?" Marcus spoke coldly. He still hadn't taken his eyes off me.

"Of course, Sir, I'll be waiting outside." Richard bowed and backed out of the room slowly, watching me as he went.

"Phoebe," I shied away from him as he reached out to touch me. He paused and lowered his hands "You're . . . *afraid* of me." He looked devastated. "After all this time . . . I've made you fear me."

My eyes were downcast. It was true. Marcus was no longer just a man to me . . . he was a vampire, a monster, and my heart broke.

"Be well, Lady Phoebe. I hope that one day you will find it in your heart to understand that I only want to protect you." He bowed his head. "I'll have Richard see to it that you have everything you need. You'll want for nothing. You . . . will always have my heart." He turned toward the door.

My breath caught. He was leaving. *Marcus* was leaving. Memories, of a Marcus long ago flooded my mind, memories of him heading off to battle, and Phoebe, unwilling to stop him. She knew his duty. She'd loved him for it. She loved him so much that she hid her pregnancy so he might have a clear head. I knew that now without question.

I gripped my stomach. I knew he loved me. That was never a question. But the truth was, Marcus scared me, more than I'd ever let myself admit.

Say something stupid! My mind was screaming inside my head. YOU'RE LOSING HIM!

"Marcus!" The strength in my voice surprised me.

He paused with his hand on the doorknob. He did not turn around.

I could feel the tears falling from my face. My heart screamed loudly, aching for him. I loved him. Nothing else mattered right now. Not Damen or Aidric. Not Luther or the war outside. I loved Marcus with all of my heart and I couldn't bear to be without him—ever. I wasn't going to let him go without him hearing me say it once more. "I love you."

He turned the knob and slowly opened the door. He moved through the doorway, his hand still holding the knob tightly.

"I'll find you . . ." I called after him, " . . . if not now, in another life. We'll be together again."

He hung his head.

"Marcus . . ."

He turned around. There was sadness and an indescribable fear that hung heavy in his eyes.

I tried to stand taller. With each passing moment, new life breathed into my broken body. "I love you," I repeated.

He appeared in front of me an instant later, taking me up in his arms. I ignored the pain of it. His lips collided with mine, not bothering to take care of the blood that still lingered on them.

I could feel the instant spark that had always connected us. I pulled him closer, not allowing any air between us. I kissed him desperately, as if this would be the very last time our lips would touch, the very last time we might hold each other. He shared my desire and I suspected my fears as well—

Too soon he pulled back; his soft brown eyes looked adoringly into mine. He held my face between his hands, a smile touching his eyes. I breathed in deeply, taking in his scent, burning it into my memory for all time.

He brought my lips to his once more, kissing them one last time before he turned and left the room—taking my heart with him.

Chapter 32: Sacrifices

"Excuse me Miss; I knocked . . ." Richard was standing beside me.

"Hum?" I didn't turn to look at him. I was staring out the window, watching Marcus mount his horse.

"I'm sure he'll be fine Miss. Try not to worry." By now, Richard had become pretty good at assessing my feelings, especially where Marcus was concerned.

"You are a sight Miss. Can I call a doctor for you?"

"There isn't time." My response was almost mechanical. I was so engrossed in watching Marcus; I couldn't afford to pry my attention away from him for even a moment. My eyes drank in every detail. For all I knew, this might be the last time I saw him.

Raymose waved enthusiastically from a top his horse—the fool—he was excited to go. After the 'little tussle' with Damen, he was more eager than ever to get his fangs into him. He bowed dramatically, turned his horse and dug in. He was out of sight in a matter of seconds.

Marcus stared long toward the window, his eyes locking with mine. He looked so solemn. I wanted to reach out to him and hold him, to tell him he didn't have to go, but I knew he'd never shirk his duty. Honestly, I didn't want him to. It was one of the qualities I admired most about him. It always had been, even when I was the other Phoebe. He nodded once, then turned his horse and cantered off.

My heart fell as panic engulfed me. His mind wasn't focused. He was worried . . . about me! I saw it in his eyes.

"He's in trouble Richard." I stared after Marcus, gripping the windowsill, watching breathlessly as he disappeared into the trees.

"Yes, Miss."

"You saw it too?" I turned to Richard. He didn't need to answer; it was written all over his face.

It was just like last time . . . I'd had a feeling he'd needed me . . . only this time, I wasn't going after him. This time I'd promised I'd go wherever Richard took me.

"I don't wish to rush you, Miss, but time is of the essence. I have a change of clothing for you in the armoire." Richard spoke hurriedly as he ushered me across the room. I opened the door and saw an outfit that did not belong to me.

"It's yours, Miss. At least it was once upon a time." He smiled.

"I don't understand?"

"It's made of leather Miss. It should help withstand any teeth that may try to penetrate it."

I gave him a confused look.

"You did promise to go only where I lead you . . . It just so happens we're going in the same direction Mr. Marcus has gone." A wry smile claimed him. "Should we happen to meet up with him . . ."

I threw my arms around Richard and kissed his cheek repeatedly.

"Yes, Miss. Don't thank me yet," Richard warned. "You must understand that I am only one. I can only keep so many off you. You will have to look out for yourself."

"Of course Richard, thank you." I collected myself as best I could, wiping the tears from my face.

"Considering your present condition . . ." Richard began, "I'm not sure it's a wise idea."

"I'm fine Richard!" I forced my body to stand straight. If Richard had the nerve to take me into battle, then I was going to stand tall for him. I'd crumple into a heap and die later. Marcus needed me.

"Yes well, you'll need to clean up as much of the blood as you can. We'll be surrounded by an army of vampires as well, so it won't do us any good to have you bleeding now would it?"

"I'll clean up every drop." I assured.

He frowned at my enthusiasm "There are some boots for you as well. I believe you are the same size?"

I picked the boots up, turning them slightly. They were in impeccable condition. I didn't know how they could have possibly stood the test of time.

"I'll have your sword fastened to your saddle. Rain is waiting at the south entrance as we speak; I'll meet you downstairs shortly." He moved to leave the room.

"Richard," I called out after him.

"Yes, Miss?"

I stared at him for a moment, biting my lip. "Do you think he'll be alright?"

"I truly hope so, Miss." He shut the door quietly behind him.

I went to the bathroom and washed my body off as fast as I could. I bandaged every scrape I had, regardless of its severity.

The outfit Richard had provided for me was the same I'd worn in my dreams. I recognized it now. The pants were made of black leather, fairly snug, like the top—although surprisingly modest looking and light for being made of leather. The boots, a perfect fit, came just below the knee and very stylish, even by today's standards. I looked at myself in a mirror. The old Phoebe smiled back at me. I was glad she was with me now. I'd need her strength tonight. "I can do this," I told the both of us.

I moved down the stairs as quickly as I could. Richard was pacing anxiously in the entry.

"Well, Richard?" I asked as I turned around for him to inspect me.

"You are a vision Miss. I was right; a perfect fit." He smiled, obviously pleased with himself.

"Thank you, Richard, for everything." I hugged him once again. I didn't know if it would be the last opportunity I had, and I wanted to make the most of it.

"The pleasure has been mine, Miss. Shall we?" He motioned to the door.

I took a deep breath and followed him to the horses that were saddled and ready.

I rubbed Rain's neck before I got on. His eyes were red tonight . . .

"Richard, I've always meant to ask Marcus, but Rain's eyes—"

"Red? Yes I know. He's immortal as well." Richard said casually as he got onto his snowy white steed.

"But how?" I knew he was from the first time I'd rode him. He could sense a werewolf from far off. His speed was unlike any other horse I'd seen—he was faster than Marcus even! But to hear it out loud seemed more fanciful than Marcus admitting he was an actual vampire.

"It was an experiment. Luther infected him after Phoebe's death to see what would happen. Rain was such a part of her; he wanted to keep him alive forever. You see Luther had given Rain as a gift to Phoebe when she was very young. Mr. Marcus has kept him ever since her death, forbidding to part with him."

"Then, he's a sort of vampire too?" I asked, not fully comprehending what I was being told.

"In a way. He drinks blood as well as water. He's a fairly normal horse with just a few exceptions," Richard explained.

"The others?" I motioned to the barn.

"They all are. Their speed is a great asset when hunting the wolves."

I climbed onto Rain and adjusted myself in the saddle. I looked over at Richard, a question popping to mind.

"Richard . . . does it bother you that Marcus is a Moon Hunter?"

He regarded me carefully. "Lord Ashworth has served your father his whole existence. It's all he knows. His life has been about revenge against those who stole his family from him. Aidric, Damen, it doesn't matter who it was. Until they're dead, he will know no peace."

"You didn't really answer my question, Richard."

He smiled a crooked smile. "I do not fault him for hunting down those who brutally killed his family, Miss." His expression was sincere. "Now, remember Miss, there will be werewolves as well as vampires. I will do my best to protect you, but you must be ready to fight whoever attacks you. That *may* include your father." He raised his eyebrows slightly.

Luther? I nodded my head in understanding. The thought of having to fight my own father left a sickening feeling in my stomach.

"And who will you be fighting Richard?" I regarded *him* carefully. Just what side would *he* take?

"I will be fighting anything that tries to harm you Miss." He bowed his head.

"Sarah is a lucky girl Richard. I hope she knows that." A rare shade of blush colored his cheeks.

"Now Miss," he cleared his throat. "Mr. Marcus will be furious if he sees you. He'll want to protect you. You must hold your own. He can't afford to let his guard down. There will be too many of them to count."

"I understand Richard; I won't be a burden."

I followed Richard in silence. The air was cool and misty. A low fog had already settled in. It would be another dreary day that approached . . . if we lived to see it. We rode quickly through the woods. This was a trail I'd not been on before. The trees didn't grow so close together here. It was easy for the moon to stretch her light all the way to the forest floor. It had dropped slightly, but it was full none-the-less. The sky was eerie tonight. Some might say it was a perfect night for werewolves . . . I shivered.

Aside from our horses' hooves moving across the ground, all had been quiet—except for now—a low roar rose above the silence.

The horses' ears twitched as they moved swiftly through the trees. They didn't need direction. They led us to a steep embankment where they stopped abruptly, rearing up on their hind legs. They neighed loudly, hot air escaping their nostrils. I held onto the reins as I peered over the edge with caution. I could almost feel the heat from the torches burning below us. Their bright glow lit the horror we were about to intrude upon.

There had to be hundreds and hundreds of them! It looked like a scene from a movie, a medieval battlefield: men on horseback with torches and swords, slaying one another. Only these men were fighting werewolves, and they weren't men themselves—they were vampires.

The once low roar from below that carried lightly through the night was growing louder. The growling and snarling and high pitched yelping echoed around us. "Miss?"

I let out a breath of air I didn't know I was holding. "Richard, my name is Phoebe. If we're going down there . . ." the words caught in my throat, " . . . it's time you called me Phoebe."

"Yes, Miss Phoebe."

I rolled my eyes at him and smiled in spite of myself.

A soft glow was coming from the east. Dawn was approaching. My eyes searched tirelessly for Marcus, desperate for a glimpse of him. I had to see that he was all right.

My eyes settled on an unexpected sight. Luther. I recognized him at once. He looked at me in disbelief—as if his eyes were playing tricks on him. His stare was penetrating, his eyes, the bluest I'd ever beheld. He was extremely handsome sitting tall on his horse. He looked almost regal, like a king. His figure was broad and muscular. His face, that looked so stern when we first locked eyes, was softer now. I couldn't help but smile as I bowed my head instinctively.

His mouth dropped open a little. There was no question now—I was real to him.

I slipped off Rain's back and gave him a little nudge. "Go on boy . . . run." He stood there, staring at me. I could swear he thought I was crazy. "Go on Rain . . . save yourself!" I smacked him hard on the rear. He neighed loudly and bolted back toward the castle. I stared after him, wishing I were riding away with him . . .

"Ready Miss?" Richard gave me one last questioning look before he slid down the embankment. I took a deep breath, closed my eyes, and stepped off—

***

I didn't have time to assess my surroundings. Richard pushed me aside as he collided violently with one of the wolves. I was surrounded in a matter of seconds. I gripped my sword tightly, swinging it at the closest one to me, surprising myself as I struck him down with one blow. I spun around, just as a large brown wolf jumped up and over me, to tear at the throat of another—it was Richard!

He didn't seem as scary looking as the rest of them. His fur looked softer. Not ratty like the others. He was extremely large, more so than the ones he fought. I was glad he was on my side. Marcus was wise to leave me with him. He fought ferociously, protecting me from any threat.

But even Richard had his limitations. He'd been right. We were inundated in a matter of minutes. I kept close behind him, holding my sword at the ready, following him into the chaos. I slashed my way through the wolves, killing as many as I could. They were truly vile. I couldn't imagine I would ever be like them. They were grotesquely huge. Their razor sharp teeth snapping at anything they could grab onto. Their piercing yellow eyes were haunting. I killed them without hesitation.

There he was . . . Marcus! I sighed in relief. He was alive!

A sharp blow to the side knocked me a good twenty feet from where I'd been standing. I shook my head, trying to orient myself. I didn't know how, but somehow I'd managed to hold onto my sword. I looked around; I couldn't see Richard anywhere.

"Who are you?" A voice hissed.

I stood up slowly, my sword extended between me and a vampire. My hand shook under its weight. "What does it matter?" I breathed, "I'm helping you." My eyes narrowed as I watched him step slowly toward me.

He was a little smaller than Marcus. His hair was blonde and cut short above the ears. His eyes were red—darker somehow than Marcus's or Raymose's ever were—and they were fixed on me.

I took a step back from him. I could hear my heart beat over the roars around me. I was terrified, and by the look on his face, he knew it.

"You're human!" he hissed sharply, a sound of disgust coming off his tongue. He closed his eyes and took in a deep breath, his nostrils flaring. "I can smell your blood . . ." His eyes popped open. "It's not possible!" His lips peeled back, baring his teeth.

I jumped back, my sword raised higher now.

His head jerked around like a snake trying to decide where to strike. I gripped my sword tighter. Sweat began to drip from my forehead as he circled around me. I moved with him, joining in on the deadly dance.

"You're a . . . werewolf!" He snarled, the sound almost feral.

"NO!" I shook my head.

"You lie! I can smell you." He looked at me as if I were something dangerous and should to be killed instantly.

"Do not touch her, Javen!"

"Raymose," the vampire spoke with such venom, the words nearly spat from his mouth. "She's human . . . and wolf! She should not be alive!" he hissed.

"She's Luther's daughter and is therefore protected!" Raymose snapped as he asserted himself between us, extending his sword. "You will not touch her."

"She is not Luther's daughter," The vampire hissed. "I watched her die!" His words were cold and unfeeling. Something about them struck me.

"I'm warning you Javen. She is not to be harmed." Raymose's tone was deadly. I shivered at the fierceness of it.

"It's treachery to protect her!" Javen snarled, inching closer to us.

"It's treacherous not to!" Raymose roared. "She is your sister!"

The words echoed through my head. My mouth hung open as I stared at Javen in disbelief. “I have a brother?” I gasped. I hadn’t remembered that . . . why?

“You are *not* my sister,” he snarled. “My sister was no werewolf!”

I didn’t know what to say. I stood there, speechless. I had a brother?

“She is your sister,” Raymose growled. “And you will protect her as such!”

“No! She’s nothing more than a rabid dog,” he spat, staring angrily into my eyes.

Raymose hissed protectively. “You think you can get past me, boy?” Raymose’s words were sharp, yet taunting. Javen’s eyes narrowed, deliberating his next move. By the look on his face, I could tell he’d been waiting for this moment for a very, very, long time. He grinned.

“Raymose.” I reached out and gripped his arm tightly—he held me back behind him. Javen took a step closer, his teeth clenched.

“Please, I’m only trying to help you,” I begged.

Javen ignored my pleas, focusing only on Raymose. His smile was sinister. “Luther will have your head for this . . . and I’ll have hers.”

Raymose pushed me back abruptly, just as Javen lunged for him. I landed several yards from where I’d been standing. I scooted back, cowering on the ground as the two vampires fought viciously over me. Their bodies collided into one another with the force of giant boulders. Raymose, who always managed to keep Javen a safe distance from me, was clearly the better fighter.

I was so focused on their fight, that I didn’t notice Damen until he’d grabbed my arm and yanked me off the ground violently. He had his arms around my waist and had thrown me over his shoulder before I could protest.

“Put me down!” I screamed

"Are you crazy? You'll be killed." He growled under his breath as he ran with great speed through the chaos. "Javen wants your blood more than anyone."

"What do you care?" I shouted over my shoulder. I tried to hit him with the back of the sword, as I kicked my legs, trying to free myself.

"You were foolish to come," he snarled, ignoring my attempts to break free.

"Damen, let me go—and why are you naked again?"

He laughed a loud throaty laugh. "Not a chance." He was running away from the fight with his bounty—I wasn't getting away.

We'd just cleared the edge of the battlefield when a sudden blow hit us in the side, knocking Damen off his feet and into the air. I screamed out in agony as his body crushed mine against a tree.

A loud snarl, more menacing than I could have ever imagined ripped through the night. Marcus had Damen by the throat and had flung him over his shoulder with as much force as a wrecking ball smashing through a cement building—Damen had landed with as much grace, crashing into the ground.

Marcus planted himself in front of me, crouched, ready for an attack.

"Marcus," I breathed.

A deep growl slipped from behind Damen's teeth. His eyes, a sinister shade of yellow, were fixed on Marcus. He roared—

I covered my ears at the sound, shuddering as Damen transformed into a werewolf.

My eyes searched the ground frantically, looking for my sword . . . there it was, just a few feet away . . . I didn't dare move toward it.

Marcus was already in the air before Damen had managed to get a foot off the ground. He collided with Damen again, shoving him back into a large tree trunk, smashing it to bits. The treetop came crashing down around them, trapping them between its large, tangled branches.

I dove for my sword. My fingers just barely touched the handle when Damen broke through the branches—my heart fell. He ran at me. I closed my eyes, bracing for the impact—

I screamed, horrified. Blood was spewing everywhere. I scooted back along the ground. Horrified. A loud yelp pierced my ears. Marcus had Damen by the shoulder, his teeth embedded into his skin, dragging him away from me.

Damen fought like a rabid dog, growling and snarling viciously. He kept trying to maneuver his way back to me. He rammed Marcus in the gut with such tremendous force; I didn't know how he had the strength to get up. It was worse than any street brawl I could have imagined.

I kept jumping out of the way. Marcus managed to thwart Damen's efforts every time he came near me. I cringed and turned away. It was a horrific sight to watch. I held my stomach tightly, hoping not to get sick. I didn't want to see Marcus this way—bloodied and merciless.

Damen roared, ripping himself out from under Marcus's bite. He flew at me again, his teeth coming inches from my throat. I jumped back, falling over my feet.

"Phoebe run!" Marcus yelled as he held Damen tightly around the neck—I could see blood dripping from his mouth. "Run!"

I turned away from them and began running. The fighting was everywhere. There was no escape route. Wolves came at me from every direction. I swung at them, not paying attention if I'd killed them or just wounded them. I kept on moving forward through the death and noise. I must have run around in circles. I could see Marcus running toward me through the smoke—yelling my name. I turned around just in time to see Damen rushing at me, his teeth bared. I swung my sword and caught him with the tip right across the chest—blood splattered across my face.

He screamed out in pain as he fell backward onto the ground.

I ran. I didn't care where I ran, just so it was far away from here. I wasn't strong; I wasn't the Phoebe they thought I was, the Phoebe I wanted to be.

The sky was getting lighter now. I choked on the smoke that hung low in the air. The torches had caught several trees on fire. Flames and smoke filled the valley floor. I'd ran up a small embankment, my fingers digging into the dirt, hoping to get away from all the noise and fighting. I stopped just at the top—my mouth gaping open.

"Aidric!" I whispered aloud. It couldn't be anyone else. He was massive, just like Marcus had said. He looked like a gladiator, a block of muscle and strength, considerably larger than Luther. As for me . . . his leg was bigger than I was.

He had shoulder length brown hair that hung loosely around his face. His face was hard looking, yet . . . beautiful! He didn't look much older than Luther. His features were sharp and enhanced by his yellow eyes.

He hadn't seen me. I squatted down behind a fallen tree, my eyes just peering over the top as I watched him for a moment. He was beating his fist on a boulder. Pieces of the rock were breaking off around it.

I glanced back down at the battlefield. The vampires were pushing the werewolves back. Somehow, they'd gained the advantage.

Luther! He was off his horse, slaying the wolves himself! Fighting alongside his men—he was amazing. The strength and determination on his face left little room for doubt that he'd ask nothing less of his men than he was willing to do himself.

I pried my eyes away, looking back to Aidric. He was growling at the wolves around him. They cowered as he ranted.

"No," I breathed out loud. I put my hand up to my mouth, not trusting myself to remain quiet. I crouched lower to the ground. I understood him! This had all been a trap to lure Luther out into the open, away from the safety of the coven where Aidric could kill him. He didn't need me like Damen thought. I'd have simply been a pawn, icing on the cake as Aidric enjoyed the torment Luther would have endured at his daughter's death—no doubt slowly with great pain before his eyes.

The wolves hadn't been able to find me, but it was of no consequence now. I'd have been the backup plan, which was no longer needed since Luther had so gallantly joined his comrades in arms. He was prime for the taking—and who better to secure that victory than Aidric. I could see the lust in his eyes as he glowered at Luther with untold hatred.

I looked back to my father, watching him for a moment. He moved so lithely, effortless slaying the vicious beasts that attacked him. I couldn't let him die! If I could get to him before Aidric and warn him . . . I'm sure he'd forgive Marcus for keeping me from him . . . for loving me the way I am. He had to! If Luther died, there'd be no stopping Aidric from killing the others. Raymose, Richard, Marcus . . . not my Marcus!

I could feel my blood start to boil at the thought of Luther's death. I slid back down the hill, into the smoke, into the fighting. I had to run fast if I was going to get to Luther before Aidric did. All wounds I'd incurred—forgotten as I pushed my body to run hard. My heartbeat sounded like thunder, like a drum hammering, readying the troops for battle. It drowned out all other noise.

I ran to Luther as if he and I were the only soldiers on the battlefield. I pushed past the brawls, past the snapping teeth, past the small fires that threatened to spread, with such speed and determination—I felt unstoppable.

My eyes were fixed on Luther. I held my sword tight in my hand as I ran toward him.

Aidric's body flashed by out the corner of my eye—only he wasn't in his human form any longer—he was a massive gray wolf. A shadow of a memory Damen had given me confirmed who he was.

My mouth had gone dry. Aidric's muscles flexed as he covered the ground at a rapid speed. I didn't know how I managed to keep up with him. We moved as if we were in sync. Like a flock of birds, one moving with the other. But unless one of us stopped, Aidric and I were going to collide—Luther being the point of collision. There was no avoiding it, but I couldn't let that happen. I ignored the burn in my legs as I cried out, pushing my body forward.

The rest happened so quickly . . .

I glanced from Aidric to Luther, who looked alarmed as he saw me running at him, sword in hand.

Luther's head snapped to his right, his teeth barred. Aidric was approaching him fast. Luther looked back to me, fear flashing in his eyes. He could see the resolve in mine, and as I lifted my sword higher, he roared. "NO!"

"PHOEBE NO!" Marcus's voice reverberated all around me, making Luther's scream almost a whisper.

I couldn't stop. I dove through the air, managing to get to Aidric before he reached Luther. I could hear the violent roar of pain as my sword cut through his middle. He pulled my body to his—razor sharp claws slicing through me—I screamed out in agony. Our bodies intertwining as we soared through the air, landed in a violent heap amongst the charred ground.

Aidric's body lay lifeless across mine. I cried out as I struggled to push him off me. I pulled myself up, and with great effort, I pulled my sword from his middle, blood dripping from the blade. The world spun around me. I used my sword like a cane and leaned on it heavily—it was the only thing holding me upright.

I looked around me, my eyes settling on Luther. He was standing not far from me, looking too stunned to move. He stared at me with his blood red eyes—I wasn't afraid.

I felt myself smiling—he was alive!

He bowed his head slightly to me.

"Phoebe—"

I turned my head to see Marcus running toward me. His feet slowed as he neared. His expression: horrified.

I smiled widely at him. I took three slow steps toward him, dragging my sword along the ground behind me. I felt the handle slip through my fingertips as I staggered forward another step. I stared into Marcus's crimson eyes as I felt myself falling . . .

"Noooo!" He caught me before my face hit the ground. He flipped my body over, cradling my head in his lap. I could feel his cool hands on my face. "Darling . . . what have you done?"

"Marcus, there's too much blood." I barely recognized Raymose's voice. It sounded so strained. So unlike his own.

I looked long into Marcus's eyes. I could see him forcing a smile for me as he gently pushed back the hair from my forehead.

"It's alright now my love. You're safe." He looked as though his heart had been torn from his chest.

"I saved him . . . I saved Luther . . .you're safe now Marcus." I choked on the blood in my mouth. "You don't . . . have to worry . . . any longer. He'll forgive you . . . for not . . . telling him . . . about me. I know he will."

"Yes darling."

I sputtered, spitting the blood from my mouth. "Marcus," I choked. "I release you . . . from your promise."

His eyes met mine. "Phoebe?" His voice was shaky.

I reached up and touched his angel-like face. "You won't be . . . responsible for me. You don't . . . have to turn me," I breathed. "I'll find you again." My hand fell with a thud from his face.

"NO! Not like this, you're not going to leave me again, do you hear me?" He demanded, shaking me violently.

My eyes struggled to stay open. I could barely focus on his image.

"Phoebe, don't leave me. I won't live this life without you . . . I'm begging you!"

He wailed as he rocked my limp body back and forth against his.

I felt him lift me up into the safety of his arms. He held me tightly to his chest. I could smell the familiar scent of his skin as I inhaled shallow breaths of air. A sudden feeling of peace engulfed me. I was safe.

"Marcus, you have to let her go; there is nothing you can do for her now," Raymose spoke softly.

"Don't touch her!" Marcus hissed, holding me closer still. "I won't let her die!" I could hear the pain in his voice. He was desperate. I didn't have the voice to sooth him.

"She's already dying Sir." Richard spoke now. The devastation in his voice was unmistakable—his heart was breaking too.

"I'll make this right!" Marcus thundered. "Not heaven or hell will keep us apart again."

"Marcus you can't!" Raymose's words were absolute.

Marcus growled. "You forget, Raymose . . . she is not your responsibility. *She's mine!"*

"My son," Luther's voice, although thick with sorrow, was like music to my heart.

"No." Marcus stepped back, shielding me from them. "I will make this right. I won't lose her again."

I could feel Marcus running with me in his arms. Cool air suddenly whipped past my face. We were flying. I wasn't afraid to fly anymore. I wasn't afraid of anything.

"Phoebe, stay with me; you've got to stay with me." Marcus's voice shook with panic. He held me so very close to him. I could feel the moisture from my chest freezing against my skin. I didn't mind. I wasn't cold any longer.

My heartbeat was slowing. My eyelids . . . they'd never felt so heavy.

"Marcus . . ."

"Just a little farther darling, hang on. I'm going to get you to a doctor."

"Marcus . . ." I breathed. I looked up into his beautiful face and smiled. "Can you still hear our hearts?"

He paused for a moment, hugging me tighter. "Yes my love, I can hear them. They beat very softly . . ."

I took a breath. I knew I was taking him in for the last time, letting his essence encircle me. My eyes fell shut. All pain melting away . . .

"NO! PHOEBE!" Marcus's scream sounded like a distant whisper floating across the wind.

I felt my body jerk as a sharp stabbing pain attacked my neck. It lasted only moments and then, nothing . . .

###

Time Line & Characters Information

*War Between Vampires & Werewolves began in 1012

*Marcus Ashworth: Vampire, leader of the Moon Hunters, and Phoebe's husband

1260- year of birth; England

1286- became a vampire

1287- appointed leader of the newly-formed Moon Hunters

1288- married Phoebe.

*Phoebe: Half human, half werewolf, has a past life; current age: 29.

1142- year of birth; Romania

1177- became a vampire

1299- year of death

*Richard: werewolf

1379- year of birth; England

*Raymose: vampire.

1086- year of birth; England

1114- became a vampire

*Damen Balfour: werewolf

1111- year of birth; Scotland

1147- became a werewolf

1152- assigned to protect Phoebe

*Luther: Leader of vampires and Phoebe's father

year of birth estimated around 30 BC

*Aidric: Leader of werewolves

year of birth estimated around 30 BC

A Glimpse into Book 2

Prologue
Marcus

The sun had rose and set three times now. Phoebe remained motionless. Her heart, still and quiet. Her lungs had not taken in any air . . . although, if she were indeed like him now, there would be no need for it.

Marcus had laid her in bed. Not her own, but another, in a more remote wing of the castle, where no one would happen upon her. He sat quietly. Grieving. Praying. He touched her cheeks with the back of his hand. Strange. Her skin felt almost flushed. Not cold like he'd imagined it would be. The wounds that once covered her ravaged body were gone. His bite had mended them. Or perhaps it was indeed her 'super healing powers' as she had referred to them on many occasions that had healed her. He smiled down at her affectionately.

"Aidric will pay for this," he vowed, his teeth grinding together. He'd rip out his throat personally. He'd lost her twice now. His heart ached more with each passing hour.

Richard had come several times, wishing to take her—but Marcus would not let her go. No one would touch her but him. She was his after all: his to love, his to protect. And he *would* protect her, now and always. No one would ever harm her again. The very thought consumed him with such rage. He bit down on the inside of his mouth, drawing blood. The taste, warm and necessary, gave him release.

He laughed to himself. She'd thought him over-protective before. When she awoke, she'd find him more so. He wouldn't care. He'd rather her complaining than this . . . this never-ending slumber.

Marcus smoothed Phoebe's hair from her forehead. She looked so lovely lying there, so peaceful. An angel sent down from the heavens: His angel. She'd ended his centuries of torment and despair. He'd loved her more than anything in the world. So much so, that he'd never given himself to another woman. Not in the seven hundred and ten years he'd thought her dead. There was no replacement for her then . . . there would be no replacement for her now.

They'd only had a short time together. He'd found her in London four months ago, laying on the ground after Damen, a werewolf and the reason for her death so many centuries ago, had bitten her. Marcus had followed her back to the states. He had to know the extent of her infection. He'd resolved that even if Damen *had* turned her completely, he would not leave her. He could not bear to stray from her side. Not now, after finding her again. He would have Phoebe, no matter what she'd become. He would awaken their love. Somehow, she would remember him.

By a miracle of God, yes . . . he believed there was a God now. For only a God could return his beloved Phoebe to him and bless him with her love once more. Despite the horror of finding out that he was a vampire, she'd fallen in love with him. She'd remembered through her dreams that they had shared a life together: An immortal life as husband and wife. She'd accepted that she had once been a vampire herself and that although Damen had bitten her, by the grace of that God, she would not turn into the monster she feared.

He could taste the venom in his mouth. He'd brought her here, into his world to protect her; and he'd failed!

He growled as he recalled her desperately asking that if the time ever came, if she were dying, for him to bite her. He'd protested vigorously. His venom was so lethal to a werewolf . . . and her, still partly human . . . the outcome was unimaginable. She'd pleaded, begged that he would find some way to keep them together; even if that meant turning her into the unimaginable, a half werewolf, half vampire. "An abomination."

He closed his eyes and took in a deep breath. He would not regret what he'd done. Phoebe couldn't stand to be away from him anymore than he could bear to be away from her, and in the end he'd agreed. He could deny her nothing. Yet . . . he'd hesitated . . . he'd waited too long. Damn. She should have awakened by now, he thought.

He placed his ear over her stomach, listening . . . silently begging. There was no heartbeat. The child he'd longed for . . . the child Phoebe had tried to protect . . . Aidric had taken that too.

Revenge would be his . . . but it would not be sweet. No. This kind of revenge was selfish, greedy; hateful. He would most certainly suffer the tortures of Hell for what he brutally planned. Marcus would gladly accept his fate, if only she might be spared. He bit the inside of his cheek again, savoring the taste . . .

"Aidric will be the one to bleed next my love. On my life, I vow this to you." He bowed his head, resting it on the edge of the bed.

"Sir," a quiet voice spoke from behind him.

"What is it Richard?"

"Sir," Richard's voice cracked. "It's been three days now. You must let her go."

Marcus lifted his head and stared at a peaceful looking Phoebe. "Isn't she beautiful, Richard?" There was awe in his words. "I changed her clothes this morning. I think she'll like them when she wakes up."

Richard shifted uneasily. His heart was breaking. He'd grown to love Phoebe too. Not romantically, but as a sister. She'd accepted him so freely, so lovingly into her heart. He would do anything for her—had done anything before her! He'd taken her to the battlefield as she'd wished. He'd protected her as best he could. But in the end, he'd failed her as well. He stared down at her loveliness, tears escaping his eyes. "Yes sir. She is beautiful."

Richard watched as Marcus hugged her middle. He held her so tightly, quietly sobbing . . . although for Marcus there would be no tears . . . vampires could not cry.

Richard swallowed the lump in his throat. "Sir, Mr. Raymose is outside."

Marcus spun around, a hiss escaping his lips. "He will not take her!"

Richard extended his hands, assuring his friend. “He is not here to take her. He only wishes to see her, to bid her well.” This was true. Although, Richard had already said his goodbyes to Phoebe and Raymose wished to do the same.

Richard had phoned Raymose this morning with his concerns for Marcus. Marcus had remained in Phoebe’s room since he’d brought her home, brushing her hair, cleaning her wounds, changing her clothes and bedding. He wanted her body comfortable. Marcus would not accept that she was gone—and this worried Raymose.

“Yes, she would like that,” Marcus agreed. “Perhaps his voice will . . .” He looked at Richard with pleading eyes, seeking comfort Richard could not give.

“Yes sir, perhaps . . .” He turned and left the room. He hated to give his friend false hope.

A few minutes later, Raymose entered. His face fell at the sight before him. Marcus was still holding onto a still Phoebe. Her lovely hair, soft and smooth, cascaded across the pillow as if it had just been brushed.

“My friend,” Raymose reached out and squeezed Marcus’s shoulder. He knelt down beside him, hanging his head. His mouth felt too dry to speak. “Has she stirred?”

“No.” Marcus’s voice was barely a whisper.

“May I?” Raymose looked to Marcus who nodded giving permission he could touch her. He reached out and took Phoebe’s hand, holding it gently in his. “She’s warm!”

“Yes, she’s been that way since her wounds healed.” Marcus did not look up, his eyes drinking in as much of Phoebe as they could. If the time did come where Marcus would have to say goodbye, well, he’d have the vision of her burned into his mind to fuel his revenge.

Raymose held her wrist, feeling for any sign of a pulse. He reached out, placing his fingers on her neck. He gasped! He put his hand below her nose. Yes, small whiffs of air met his skin. “She’s breathing!” Raymose said excitedly.

"What?" Marcus jumped to his feet, his fingers desperately searching her neck for a pulse. It was faint. So much so that he still could not hear a heartbeat. Being partly werewolf, her heart should still beat—in theory anyway. As far as he knew, there were no others like her . . . he could not be sure of anything except that she was indeed alive!

"Thank God!" He pressed his lips to hers, hoping she'd feel his kiss.

"You haven't fed her, have you?" Raymose asked skeptically.

"I've given her a few drops from my glass." Marcus admitted. He avoided Raymose's stare. He knew where this conversation was going.

"That's not what she needs, and you know it," Raymose warned.

"I will not taint her with our blood," Marcus hissed. He took Phoebe's hand and held it to his lips, kissing it softly. Her scent had become a drug to him, deliciously intoxicating. "Wake my love," he whispered softly into her ear.

"You have no choice now!" Raymose stood tall above him, his body seething with anger. "If she lives, she will only just survive and you know it! She will *never* be strong enough without your blood, *both* of your bloods. She has two creators now Marcus. She must drink from both of you if she is to be whole."

Marcus tensed at the thought. "Once she tastes it . . . there will be no going back," he growled over his shoulder. "I will not let her be like him. She didn't want that."

"There was no going back once you bit her," Raymose reminded his friend sharply. "She'll *need* . . . his blood. And yours, if she is to be strong."

"No!" Marcus was on his feet now. His shoulders squared with Raymose's. There was no way he was going to allow Phoebe to drink from him, or Damen. Marcus knew once she tasted her creator's blood, she'd be forever bound to their way of life. It was bad enough she would be forced to drink blood from time to time—something she would detest. But to have to transform into a werewolf—unacceptable! And that is exactly what would happen if she ever tasted Damen's blood. It would be as if Damen had infected her fully with the venom that flows through him. Something the bastard had to know. Marcus would die before he'd ever let that happen. "She doesn't have to be like us . . . not really."

"You're a fool," Raymose spat.

"The 'wine' will sustain her when she needs it," Marcus insisted. "She doesn't need anymore than that. She doesn't *need* his blood to survive! She doesn't *need* to be a monster like him!" He knelt down beside Phoebe, taking her hand in his once more. "Damen will never touch her again." Marcus's resolve was unwavering.

Raymose sighed and threw his hands up into the air. "You will shadow her then? Follow her, every step she makes? Fight off every evil that threatens her?" Raymose asked, mockingly. "It can not be done. History has proven that my friend."

Marcus looked up at Raymose, his eyes seething with anger. "I will protect her with my life . . . she will *never* need his blood. Or mine," he assured darkly as Raymose shook his head in exasperation.

Marcus's eyes narrowed. "And you my friend?" Marcus asked after a few moments. "Will you not vow the same? Can you stand there and deny her your protection?"

Raymose glowered at Marcus. "You know I would lay my life down for hers. I've never kept my feelings for her a secret," he spat.

Marcus nodded his head in understanding.

"But I am no fool Marcus," Raymose continued. "Danger will come looking for her. Make no mistake about that. She'll never be safe here. They'll want her dead, Aidric . . . and perhaps Luther. There cannot be one strong enough to defeat both. Neither will allow it. Sooner or later, they will come for her."

Marcus nodded once again and turned his attention back to Phoebe. “And I will kill them when they do. All of them,” he vowed.

He looked down on his beloved and smiled. She was alive, and *that* is how she’d stay, forever . . .

###

ACKNOWLEDGMENTS

First, I would like to thank my talented husband, Chris, for his endless hours in creating the cover for this book. He's captured my vision of Marcus's castle with this unique watercolor—which was not easy because I tend to be picky, so I'm told.

My sister: Nicia Rotermund, for her vast expertise in Photo Shop, as well as being my personal IT Tech. She has the patience of a saint!

My Lucky Eight: Ashley Grane, Gina Rotermund, Eleanor Rodriguez, Laura Bastain, Caren Coonrod, Kim Talty, Rachel Perry, and Becki Schirmacher. Undoubtedly the best friends in the world. Who else on the planet would have suffered through all those typos and countless revisions, and still raved about the story? I love you all and would not think of publishing a book before you have had the chance to test drive it first!

My friend: Cheri Chesley, for always being there to answer my many formatting and writing questions. I can't imagine our writing group without you.

Maren Petersen: Editor Extraordinaire! This book would have never been completed without you. I will never be able to express how much you have helped me. I plan to put you in my pocket and keep you forever!

BIOGRAPHY

Nicole Grane lives in Tooele, Utah with her husband and their three children. She grew-up in Arcata, California, fifteen minutes away from Trinidad—Phoebe's stomping ground. When she is not writing or reading, Nicole enjoys collecting cool rocks, oil painting, finding unique pieces of jewelry, and playing on the beach with her family—which she is sad to say is not often.

Nicole has always loved mythology, folklore, and researching unique places. Having been privileged to travel, she can't wait to incorporate some of her findings into her stories.

11803270R0025

Made in the USA
Lexington, KY
02 November 2011